ALSO BY NEIL JORDAN

*Night in Tunisia*
*The Past*
*The Dream of a Beast*
*Sunrise with Sea Monster*
*Shade*

# MISTAKEN

# NEIL JORDAN

Soft Skull Press

AN IMPRINT OF COUNTERPOINT BERKELEY

Library of Congress Cataloging-in-Publication Data is available.

ISBN 978-1-59376-433-3

Cover design by Faceout Communications/Charles Brock
Interior design by meganjonesdesign.com
Printed in the United States of America

Soft Skull Press
An imprint of COUNTERPOINT
1919 Fifth Street
Berkeley, CA 94710

www.softskull.com

Distributed by Publishers Group West

10 9 8 7 6 5 4 3 2 1

For Sarah and Anna

# DEANSGRANGE

I HAD BEEN MISTAKEN for him so many times that when he died it was as if part of myself had died too. And so I attended his funeral, to say goodbye to that part of myself that would abide now in the cold clay of Deansgrange, to be wept over by lovers I may or may not have known, by whatever public still remembered him, by an ex-wife, two children and a family dog. It was the dog that caused the trouble in the end.

Out of respect, out of a misplaced sense of drama, out of that perennial urge 'not to cause any trouble,' for whatever reason anyway I wore a hat to the funeral, a college scarf and a pair of those sunglasses beloved of minor celebrities. I took my place among the mourners—and there were a lot of them, I was gratified to see, in that state of hushed numbness appropriate to one who had died, as the obit said, 'in what should have been the prime of life.' I suppose obituary writers must use some kind of phrase book. Fools for instance were never to be suffered gladly, one's appetite for life was nothing less than lust, and one's family had a bosom to return to and ultimately rest within.

Anyway, he had died in his mid-fifties so the atmosphere within that crowd was one of caught breath. There were real tears and none of the calm resignation that would have been appropriate to a body that had had 'a good innings.' No, his innings had been turbulent, dramatic, and cruelly cut short. The tears were raw and the shock was palpable, which was one of the reasons I attended the funeral and not the removal, where close contact with the family would have been unavoidable.

I arrived late at the funeral mass, stood among the crowd at the back of the church and drove well behind the cortège out to the wind-swept suburb of Deansgrange. I was among the last to walk among the old yew trees to the further end of the graveyard where the newly minted marble headstones rose from the wet grass like dragon's teeth. But you ended up right ahead of me, pulling a sad old dog by the lead, and the dog sensed something, as dogs will, and turned and licked my left hand.

The dog smelt something it knew—sweat, the odour of the familiar. I had always looked like him and now I realized I had his musky essence as well. Your hand was pulled by the lead and your head turned and I saw a pair of brown eyes over a mauve scarf and I recognized, through the tears, the slow dawning of recognition in your eyes.

What to do now? I asked myself. Don't get involved, don't engage in conversation whatever you do, your purpose here is to bear witness, nothing more. But it was already too late. The dog was licking my hand, leaving a coat of saliva over my ringless fingers, and as anyone who has seen a romantic comedy knows, only the villainous smoke cigarettes and react harshly to a dog's advances.

So I said, 'There you go, good boy,' or whatever version of that one says to dogs, and you jerked on the leash and said in a halting voice, 'I'm sorry, he can get over-friendly,' and a hesitant conversation began that was hard to stop. Even the intoned prayers of the priest as the coffin was lowered didn't quite quench it because you cried when the leather straps that held the box touched the laths of wood in the wet earth of the grave. 'I'm sorry,' you said, 'it's so final, somehow,' and your head touched my shoulder and it would have been churlish of me not to extend my hand and apply a gentle, comforting pressure to your elbow.

'I know,' I said, 'I know'—the words were coming out of my lips because I did know, I knew too much in fact, and because of that dog I would come to know much more.

There are other beginnings, of course. I could go back to them— mine, his, northside, southside, the minuscule class difference that can mean everything or nothing. But I suppose the real beginning for me was the dawning awareness that somewhere in this city there was somebody like me. Somebody so like me as to cause confusion, recognition, chaos, heartbreak, and ultimately death. And another death besides his.

I was his lost soul, his other, and ultimately, his ghost. The fact that we looked like each other was not entirely relevant since the shapes we present to the world at fourteen, say, and at forty are so different that any of us might be two different people. And at four-teen, when I traveled across to a dance in the southside suburb of Dun Laoghaire and a young girl asked me up during ladies' choice (it was a quaint institution at the time, a small recognition of the fact that ladies did have choices, albeit only romantic ones) and moved her young body in towards me immediately and asked me how I'd been, I told her I'd been well, though I had never met her before. I accepted the closeness of her small breasts, the welcome thrust of her hips in answer to my fingers at the small of her back as my due, though I subsequently found out that the due was his.

'Gerald,' she whispered and, wisely or not, I refrained from setting her right and telling her my name was Kevin. If she wanted me to be Gerald, then Gerald I was, for the evening at least, which ended on the rocks behind the pier with me untangling her brassiere and her whispering into my ear, 'Now why have you never done that before?'

And perhaps the darkness of that evening, the twinkling ball of light over the dance floor, and the low sodium lamps over the pier might have explained why she confused me with him, but over the years I came to understand that even that explanation was inadequate. It wasn't all about looks—our dark eyebrows and what you came to describe as my downy mouth. And I looked nothing like the corpse that was being lowered into the Deansgrange grave that late winter's day. No. I think the key lay in what the dog noticed, as he sniffed and slobbered over my hand: that we were two halves of the same soul, or to be more prosaic about it, we smelt alike.

Odour, perfume, smell, stink, whatever name you give to the olfactory side of things, is far more powerful, carries more suggestiveness than sight alone, and those flashes of recognition that had blessed or bedeviled my existence were often registered by the nose and not the eyes. Because even when his breath was bad, it smelt like mine. A scent in a room or on a street, the tang of sweat, whatever shampoo I used as a fourteen year old, the leathery whiff of that suede waistcoat I was so proud of as a kid, of the gabardine coat he wore as a student, the combined musk they gave rise to was always common to us both.

And that was what the dog responded to as I withdrew my hand from your elbow to allow you to weep at the finality of the sight of your father's coffin touching the base of its muddy grave. Your mother was at the head of it, your brother beside her, and I remember wondering why you weren't within their privileged circle of grief. There was a small mechanical digger to one side; no effort had been made to hide it from the ranks of mourners. There was a rolled-up carpet of artificial grass, its unnaturally bright green muddied in places with the brown stains of gravediggers' boots. There were the long leather straps, held by the gravediggers to lower the coffin, and dumped then, unceremoniously, on the carpet of artificial green. There was the smoking silver orb that the priest swung in a decreasing arc, then the device like a baby's silver rattle from which he shook and sprinkled drops onto the coffin below. There were the words of the rite that he intoned, about perpetual light shining, but I heard them just as a murmur, a kind of muzak acting as a bed to the muffled sound of weeping. Then the time came, as it does at these events, when the small drama is mysteriously over and one by one they all peeled off and walked back over the muddy tracks through the path of yew trees.

I STAYED. I was uninvited after all, and I was curious to see what was considered a decent interval between a funeral's end and the business of starting up the mechanical digger. One of the gravediggers lit a cigarette, the other tinkled with a set of keys. They both stood beneath a poplar tree, taking whatever shelter they could from the soft mist falling. Maybe they were waiting for the rain to end, I was thinking, when I felt the dog's tongue on my left hand again, the soft furry fungus of it, and the saliva like a snail's trail. I looked down and saw its leash dangling in the mud. Way behind him, close to the line of yew trees, were the massed umbrellas of the mourners, retreating, like so many mushrooms come alive in a fairy-tale forest.

'Hey, Argus,' I whispered, or I thought, as I took up the curled end of the leash from the wet ground. Odysseus had been betrayed by just such a dog, by the same animal affection. I heard the mechanical digger cough into life and saw one gravedigger bundle up the laths, the leather straps, and the muddied green carpet as the other guided the machine in a semicircle, lowered the rust-toothed maw, and began pushing the mound of wet earth down towards the coffin below.

The interval seemed almost indecent but the mourners were beyond hearing, a cluster of tiny umbrellas now, moving towards the car park beyond the yew trees. And maybe that's what they were waiting for. So I walked back, following their muddy footsteps, wondering how I would get rid of this damned dog.

But a voice called out from between the yew trees and I looked up to see your brown eyes glistening above the mauve scarf.

'You've found him.'

'It was more a case of him finding me.'

'He seems to know you.'

'Dogs are funny that way.'

'And you knew my father?'

'Yes, you could say that. I knew him on and off.'

I was lying now, but only whitely.

'I probably should remember your name then. I'm sorry, but there's a lot going on, as you can imagine.'

'Ned,' I lied again. 'Ned Gaskett.'

And I shook your hand. It was a small hand, but with a strong, practical core to it, a sense of strength and fragility there at the same time. I had seen him pushing you on a swing in Stephen's Green. I had watched him watch you through the school railings during his worst days, afraid to approach. But I had never held your hand. And as I held it, I wondered where the pseudonym had come from. He had used a pseudonym once, saying it released something in him. I wondered what this one would release in me.

The Ned made sense, but the Gaskett was an absurd choice by any standards. A gasket was something to do with pipes and plumbing—a mechanical seal, I found out later, between two mating surfaces. It was nothing to do with anything. But as I placed the crook of the leash into your small hand I felt the need to conjure up a history for this Ned Gaskett, yet a third history that was neither Kevin's nor Gerry's. An upbringing in the small houses round Kilmainham, looking over the river towards Phoenix Park and the Wellington Monument. Maybe a job in the middle ranks of the civil service. But any questions as to my identity would come later; and anyway, you later forgot the stupid name entirely. You introduced yourself as Emily and turned and walked towards the car park with the dog now leading the way and the implicit assumption that I would follow.

'You're coming back,' you said, and it wasn't a question, it was a statement. 'There's sandwiches and tea and drinks and stuff. She wants everyone to be there. She thinks it's important—so many people lost touch.'

And she was one of them, I thought, but what I said was, 'I don't think I can.' But the dog intruded once again. He went back to licking my hand.

'Toby's quite insistent too,' you said.

'Toby?'

'My dog.'

And so I kind of sighed and twisted the ball of my shoe in the wet ground and asked where it was.

'She moved house.'

'Did she?'

There was one in Rathmines, I remembered, before things got bad.

'Yeah, you know. When everything went . . . pear shaped . . .'

'Will I follow you?'

'Yes, you'd better follow me.'


THERE WERE TWO cars left in the graveyard car park, a small red Mini Cooper and my German thing. I watched you walk towards the red one, saw the dog leap in through the opened door and settle himself familiarly in the backseat, and I had hardly opened my own door before you drove off.

I followed then, turned right behind you down Deansgrange Road, turned another right at Bakers Corner and headed up Kill Avenue towards Foxrock Church. Why had she moved out here, I wondered. They had been creatures of a different Dublin, those comfortable streets that ended at the Grand Canal. But the opulence of the city was moving southwards, towards the foothills of the Dublin mountains, and maybe she had wanted to avoid him.

The car turned right then, on to the dual carriageway, left again on Leopardstown Road, past the racecourse and traced a route I could never have followed myself, through the industrial parks and the new hotels onto a road below the Three Rock Mountain, past a wooden church painted blue, through a pair of gates where an avenue made its way among old beeches to an ivy-covered frontage and a turnaround of more parked cars.

The house from the outside had some grandeur to it. I guessed it would have been built in the twenties, but it had a late Victorian feel, subdued as it was by the old coating of ivy.

'Your mother's house?' I asked, when you emerged from your parked car.

'Yes,' you said. 'Don't you hate it? She bought it when her mother died.'

I was remembering a magnificent house, a castle really, of rose-coloured sandstone.

'I preferred home,' you said. 'Or Granny's place. But we're loaded now, aren't we, and that's all that matters.'

The tow-headed dog followed you and I followed him through the open door. You were greeted by an avalanche of well-wishers and were saved the necessity of dealing with me, for awhile at least. I didn't so much mingle as slide into the gathering, like a joker card into a game of Newmarket. There were trays of sandwiches, held by pretty young women with their hair pinned back; there was a bar with waistcoated barmen and the loud buzz of conversation—nothing hushed about it now, as if the dead hand of grief had been magically lifted.

There was a hushed centre, though, to all of this activity, a large auburn sofa near the French windows where I could see a beautifully cut head of grey hair silhouetted by the window light which I assumed belonged to Dominique, your mother, his ex-wife, and now, it seemed, his official widow. Would she recognize me? I wondered.

If she had met him at all towards the end, she might not, and I don't think she had. But I recognized some literary types, a tall, sandy-haired talk show host, and a small man with a pencil-thin moustache whom I knew to be his first editor.

I made my way to the bar and had asked the barman for a sparkling water when a woman to my left turned, and a familiar refrain sounded.

'Excuse me, don't I know you?'

'Maybe,' I said. 'I've been around awhile.'

She had blonde hair, and a thin, dark pencil line threaded the shape of her lipstick.

'No, I know you. Were you a friend of Gerald's?'

You couldn't go far wrong here with that supposition, I wanted to say, but I managed to be more polite.

'On and off,' I said, 'over the years.'

'And Dominique?'

'Not for some time.'

'Yes,' she said, 'it's that kind of affair. His and hers.'

'His and her what?'

'Friends,' she said. 'After the . . . thing . . .'

'His last years weren't . . .'

'They weren't pleasant, I heard. I hadn't met him for years. But when I heard, I wept.'

Her eyes, though, seemed fine—bright, the eyelids touched with the same dark pencil as the lips.

'It hasn't hit them yet. Do you feel that? Has it really hit them?'

'Well, no. It takes some time, it has to. A year, I've been told, for grief finally to lift.'

'You sound like a counsellor.'

'No, just a friend.'

'Of both?'

'Once upon a time, of both.'

'And we've never met?'

I began to regret my proletarian hauteur then, and had to come right out with it.

'It's a common thing,' I told her. 'A lot of people have felt that.'

'That they know you?'

'Yes. The way they feel they know television presenters, failed actors. I've always been mistaken, and most of all for the deceased.'

'Gerald? My God, of course. Were you related?'

'We looked alike, or so I've been told, in some way that I could never quite fathom.'

'And were you close?'

'As close as two people could be.'

'That sounds alarming.'

'Let me put it this way. If I was mistaken for him, then from time to time he obviously could be mistaken for me. So it became a long waltz of mutual confusion. There was a sick kind of fun to it, which we both shared.'

I had said too much, and her face showed it. As when one replies to the question 'How are you?' with a litany of digestive complaints, my replies were making her uneasy. Which may have been what I wanted, for I could feel her beginning to retreat and the dog was once again rubbing its head on the back of my hand.

'Toby!' I heard and I felt his head jerk. His tongue came clean off the back of my hand and his head turned towards you. Emily.

'Sorry,' you said, 'I've left you all alone.'

'No, you haven't,' I said, and the other was already gone. 'I've been, what do you call it, mooching.'

'Mooch away then,' you said, and looked at me with eyes that were suddenly amused. 'You know no one here, do you?'

'No,' I said. Though I was sure if I mingled among them, many of them would feel they knew me.

'You've met my mother, surely.'

I had, years ago. I had shared a Mary cake with her in Bewley's Oriental Café. I had felt her hand on my belt through the railings in St. Stephen's Green. But she wouldn't have remembered it as me.

'You don't have to introduce us—'

'No. I don't have to do anything, do I? You're right. I suppose grief has given me a special status. I could get maggoty, fall into the arms of any man here. And while I think of it, I really need another drink.'

'Johnno,' you called, and caught the eye of a young man passing. I got a glimpse of the same features, the same dark eyebrows, the same dominating eyes, but blue ones, this time, like your mother's.

'Get me another one, brother,' and he took your glass and looked at you with a serious questioning gaze, as if one more might be too much. I liked him immediately.

'Take it easy,' he said softly. He was immobilized, I could see, by his loss, by the absence of someone he had not known well enough, and he would be, I sensed, for some time. Fathers and sons, the unspoken depths and the love unconsummated.

'My brother,' you said. 'The glue baby. It didn't work, though, did it?'

'The glue?'

'They went their separate ways, anyways.'

'It tore him up a lot.'

'Okay, okay,' you said. 'I don't want to, as they say in *Friends*, go there.'

'What friends?'

'*Friends*, the TV show. I was quoting. Go there. I don't want to.'

Your blue-eyed brother pressed through the crowd of shoulders with a drink, tried to catch your eye with another soulful warning, but you dismissed him with a light clutch of your fingers round his wrist.

'So I suppose you'd better tell me. How long did you know him?'

'Most of his life.'

'Ah, come on. It's not possible. I'd have met you.'

'We have met,' I said. 'You just don't remember.'

'When?'

'You were around five. He was walking you round the park in Fitzwilliam Square. You had another dog then. Called, if I remember it right, Rebel.'

'My God. That's creepy.'

'Not really. He was doing the single father thing. He needed someone to talk to. He was distressed, I suppose.'

'What else?'

'You really want to know?'

'Yes. I really want to know.'

'I talked to him through the railings. I could see you through them, through the trees, flashing past.'

'And?'

'I remember thinking, you looked like you had always been there. A kind of garden spirit.'

'And that's it?'

'No,' I said. 'There was one more time. He had a place where he wrote, in the first-floor flat across the road. I could see you from it, chasing your dog around the tennis court.'

'And where was he?'

'He was upstairs, with me, looking through the window.'

'Sounds like bad parenting.'

'We didn't know that phrase then. But he could see the whole square. There were two girls playing tennis. Dressed in white. Do you remember?'

'Why should I?'

Because, I thought . . . Because I was dressing in his clothes, in the flat upstairs. Because I walked to the window, and he told me everything was fine except the hair. Because I saw you from upstairs, chasing the dog around the tennis court, round the park. I was dressing for a woman he knew and I didn't, across the ocean in Manhattan. 'The hair,' he said. 'She likes what she calls the Room with a View cut—that floppy, over-the-forehead English thing.' Because, I thought, our similarities killed her.

'Because,' I said, 'he was afraid he'd lose you then, forever.'

'He did,' you said. 'But that was later.'

Later. When the years began to pull our flesh in different ways. By the time he died, all we had in common was our odour.

'You've met my mother?'

'Yes,' I said, 'but she wouldn't remember me.'

'You met his mother?'

'Once,' I said, and I didn't lie this time, but it was not the mother she referred to.

'I wish I'd known her better,' you said. 'She died around the time—'

'Of your other dog. Rebel.'

'Weird. I'd forgotten that. I always envied kids with grandmothers, growing up. Who'd feed you batch bread and chip sandwiches.'

You may have one, I thought. In a caravan, behind a fairground in Courtown. Indestructible. Smoking a cigarette as we speak, feeding her llamas. But I wanted to forget all that for the moment. Our mirrored history began to seem indecent here. Grief was more comforting.

'So what do you do?' I asked, changing the subject. The warmth I felt for you was almost overwhelming. Had I had a child of my own, I felt, it might have looked just so and the fact that you were a reflection of a possibility long dead in me made me want to cry. I could feel tears welling up then, real tears.

'You're changing the subject now,' you said. 'Is it because you're upset?'

'Yes,' I said. I preferred this truth business.

'Doesn't matter what I do,' you said. And you suddenly took my hand. That unasked, spontaneous warmth was all his.

'Come here,' you said. 'You need a drink.'

Your hand wrapped itself round mine. It was freckled like my own, and it drew me towards the bar, towards a sea of drinking mourners, parting now before your mother who was rising from the couch, her black mantilla like a small umbrella over her reddened, faraway eyes. She was hesitant on her high heels and sedated in some way, I presumed, since her son, the glue baby, steadied her as she walked. She kissed you on her way, then turned towards me, and if she saw him still in me she didn't give any sign of it, and if I'd asked her did she remember our Mary cake she would have presumed I was muttering some condolence and replied, as she did to all the well-wishers, 'Yes, thank you.' And all the time her daughter's hand kept hold of mine.

# MARINO

I WOKE UP WITH a vampire whispering in my ear. 'You're alone now,' and when the dream dust cleared and the blades of winter sun streaming through the window came into focus, I realized just how alone.

I was in number 14, Marino Crescent and the window looked out on the forlorn flower beds and cherry trees of Fairview Park. I had grown up in this house. My mother managed the flats above, my father ran a bookie's shop on Lower Abbey Street and on various stands at race meetings around the country when the bookie's shop failed. The house next door bore a brass plaque announcing to whoever was interested that Bram Stoker, creator of *Dracula*, had once inhabited it. I had seen my first vampire film in a Scouts hall on the Howth Road, in the lane by the bridge that carried the trains overhead towards Drogheda. The images in black and white, on a sheet pinned to the tongue-and-groove wall, confused me, but I can still hear the sound: the humming of bats' or vampires' wings, like the humming of high-voltage electricity wires—though I don't think vampires had wings, their opera capes just seemed like wings.

That sound stayed with me for years and seemed to resonate from the house I had to pass to get to ours, particularly at night. I would imagine the Count or Mr. Stoker—and of course in my child's mind I got them confused—looking from the first-floor window of the peeling cement frontage, out on to the bare spindles of the trees in the park. That was in winter. In spring, out on to the cherry blossoms drifting round the beds of tulips. I had to wait for the arrival of the Hammer versions, in full colour and with their heaving, theatrically blood-spattered bosoms, to dispel that sound. They came to the Fairview cinema, across the Malahide Road, past Forte's chip shop. But until that time the park was a garden of horror for me. The sound was everywhere, in the mud-soaked basin of the Tolka river, the cement walkway above it, the small metal bridge that crossed it to the East Wall. It moaned round the gantries of the dock cranes beyond, round the swans weaving their circles in whatever water was left in the mud. The land was reclaimed land, my father had told me, Brian Boru had fought the Danes where the gantries now stood and the sound was theirs, too.

Father. The name evokes an absence, the rustle of the fringes of a gabardine coat, the tilt of a bookie's hat, the smell of cigarette smoke, of turf and horse manure. These were his attributes, but of him, then at least, I can't remember much. The imaginary Count in the house next door, his cloak wrapped round him like a shivering actor, was more real to me. I knew he had met my mother while swimming on Bull Wall. I knew that he didn't swim anymore while she still did. I knew he had worries beyond my understanding. I knew he would pore for hours over racing pages and crossword puzzles. I knew his job demanded long absences. I knew the comb of his hair, that the slick of the vaselined bit to cover the growing bald patch was important to him, but beyond that I knew almost nothing.

I would dream of a different father at times, a hand with a signet ring to hold mine, a dark dress coat, and a dark carriage outside drawn by horses; and in the dream the horse would somehow become the father—Father's Friend, Faith of Our Fathers, running at the two-thirty hurdle—and I would wake up with a need for something I had never known, something I hardly knew how to name. I would walk down in the morning to my breakfast and to the absence that was mine.

My mother ran the rooms above us, rented them out to a succession of lodgers, all of whom came and went with a dreary regularity but for the old codger at the top who mended clocks. Tommy the Clock they called him, and he seemed a distant cousin to the Count next door. His was a long atticky room with sloping skylight windows through which the rain dripped when it fell, which was almost always. Grandfather clocks, cuckoo clocks, alarm clocks, watches, clocks on brooches, clocks on pens, clocks on bicycle lamps—whether they were a business or an odd obsession I could never tell, but they ticked and trundled and boomed and cuckooed, their innards spread on oiled newspapers around the dusty floor. He would leave the door half askew and allow me in to watch him at work or at play, whatever it was in that world of his, of time gone slightly mad. He would brown a marshmallow for me on the coal fire, skewered on the rod of some old pendulum.

I would ask him about the house next door.

'Stoker,' he would say to me, and the name terrified me even more than the name Dracula.

'Is it Bram Stoker?'

'Short for Abraham,' he would tell me, 'his father worked in the Castle all his life.'

There was a pot of hardened porridge always on the ring of the gas cooker. There was a radio which relayed the meteorological situation at oh-two-hundred hours. Twenty-three millibars, rising slowly. 'Your mother,' he would tell me, 'is a generous woman,' and there was some relationship there that I could never quite fathom, a second cousin once removed, a reason he stayed so long, since she never seemed to ask for rent. 'A daily communicant,' he would say, referring not to her religious habits, but to her practice of swimming daily, winter and summer, in the sea at the Bull Wall where she and my father first met.

And Mother, what does that name evoke? Keys, first of all, the enormous bundle she kept in her overcoat pocket, keys for the various flats, for the boiler room, the electricity meters, the outhouses, the wooden gate leading to the back lanes of Marino. A kind of exhausted elegance, a tall, auburn-haired, statuesque frailty, long legs and a perfect seam of nylon at the back calf, patent leather shoes often with laces, always with high heels. So, as you will have observed, I obeyed most of the oedipal norms as a child. I could never imagine killing my father, since how do you kill what is hardly there, but I would have locked him in a cupboard and kidnapped my mother. I would have taken her to another world where the seam on her calf would be forever straight and the heels on her boots would be always unbroken and she wouldn't have been worrying a bundle of keys.

I suppose every child has the fancy or the hope that they were dropped by some accident of fate into the family that faces them at breakfast. If I had been thrown arbitrarily into that house, I imagined she had been too. We had both got lost in a tangled wood and she had forgotten her crown and we had fallen down a disused well and found ourselves here. The Crescent, Marino, where a vampire lived next door. And once here, we couldn't find our way back. Maybe Tommy the Clock's random timepieces were all set to some mysterious hour, when all of the bells and gongs would ring and we would be magically released. Maybe among her bundle of keys was one she had never noticed, that would open the basement door I could never find and allow us back to . . . where, I often wondered? I could imagine the thrill of discovery, the thrill of escape, but any thought or hope of arrival to anywhere else left a blank.

She would take me swimming with her until it became embarrassing. I would watch over her clothes, the neatly folded stockings, the cream white girdle with the strange clasp underneath, the dress she wore that day, the overcoat, one pocket bulging with the keys. I would watch her tread down the concrete steps to the water to swim towards the fractured outline of the city, the gantry fingers thrusting towards the sky. I would hold the towel for her when she came out, watch her wrap it round her wet swimsuit as she ascended the steps towards me, marvel at how deftly she slid the wet swimsuit off her body without letting that towel slip. Sometimes I'd rub her blue feet when the cold got too much. 'Warm them, that's the boy,' she would shiver and I would rub the blue skin above her painted toenails until the blood came back.

Sometimes there were other women there and their nakedness disturbed me. Nakedness, full or partial, in my mother seemed my due, but this unfamiliar flesh aroused me in ways I tried to hide from her, in ways I didn't fully understand. In ways I resented it too, for the

flesh on them was often grey and round, unlike her, who didn't seem
to have any flesh at all.

There was a sere, pure eroticism to our times there, under the
curved concrete platform that provided no shelter at all from the
south-westerly winds. I thought it was in every mother's gift, was every boy's due, and only later discovered how odd, how awry we both
were. 'It won't be always like this,' she'd whisper, 'enjoy it while you
can,' meaning the sea, the weather, the purple clouds over the mouth
of the Liffey, but meaning perhaps also the windblown intimacy we
somehow managed to share. 'Come on now,' she'd conclude, 'your
father will be home,' and happily or not, he rarely was.

'Hello, stranger,' she would say to me coming down in the morning, coming home from school, and I would discover much later what
she really meant. Then the time came when I thought I knew, when
my presence on those concrete steps became an embarrassment to me
and to the other female bathers. My appropriate place would have
been at the men's shelter, beyond the rusted railings that traced the
path of the cement steps down to the sea.

So I stopped going and whenever I walked down the old wooden
sleepers of the Bull Wall bridge with a friend my own age, a girl most
often, I would watch the lazy, saline progress of the swimmers and
wonder which one of them was her.

# THE CRESCENT

THERE WAS A doorbell ringing and I went downstairs to answer it and when I saw the silhouette behind the mottled glass in the doorway I remembered I had phoned an auctioneer. I knew I should sell the place—I had an apartment and a business in Berlin—but the thought seemed burdensome and there was something to say for being home, however odd it seemed. The Crescent had been refurbished now with the sole exception of the house I had inherited. Stoker's brass plaque was golden and burnished and number 14 stood out like a rotten tooth against the white-painted stucco all around. I could see the neatly pressed suit even through the mottled glass and could already imagine the conversation about guide prices and period values as I opened the door.

He was there, against the panel of bells with the names of lodgers long since departed, printed in those small metal bands that nobody made now. His suit was blue and his hair cut short, and I invited him into the smell of dust and old sickness inside. I walked him through the different floors and remembered the names of the transient lodgers as I passed each door. Quirk, McCarthy, O'Donnell, Coyle. They came and went; they seemed fixtures for as long as they were there, and their names would hang around my mother's conversation for a time after they had left, the way a skunk leaves its spray.

There was a commercial traveler with a pipe who always wore tweeds, who had a rakish, melancholy style about him and who, I remembered thinking, would make a more passable father than the one I had been dealt. Dundon was his name, I remembered—Jimmy Dundon, from Rosses Point or Strandhill, one of those Sligo seaside towns where he gathered his accent. And I often wondered as I got older did he allow himself to hope? She had her own beauty, my mother; that loss of shape round the middle years never happened with her, and I wondered as I opened the door to his room for the auctioneer, had it ever been opened by her with more than rent on her mind? But the thought seemed unworthy, began to annoy me, and his pin-striped suit began to annoy me even more. Even if it had, I thought, she deserved her own life—and we had reached the top floor and I fumbled with the keys to Tommy's room and we entered the wilderness of clocks.

Maybe it was my feet on the bare floorboards, maybe the ghost of the dead clockman, but some of his timepieces began ticking soon after I entered. I could hear the silver clicking of long dead wristwatches, and a rhythmic scraping as if a cuckoo was straining to come back to life. The sounds increased as the auctioneer walked round the room.

'Have they any value?' he asked.

'I have no idea,' I said and wondered at what point the entire population became transfixed with questions of value. And I felt bad then, because he was an auctioneer after all, and only doing his job. But I already knew the word that was coming next.

'Sentimental, I'm sure.'

Sentimental value. The only kind surely, I thought, as the ticking became a hushed symphony, an exercise in counterpoint; found a kind of rhythm, lost it again, and found a different one, seeking I imagined a magical point at which they would make proper music.

The auctioneer coughed behind me and I knew commerce was about to raise its pretty head. It was always preceded by a hush or a cough, indecency shrouded in a cloak of politeness. He talked of guide prices, of one point four, one point five, and I knew he meant millions of course, of how the northside gets a bad rap, if the same Crescent was in Howth or Malahide the sky would be the limit.

'And the fact that Stoker lived next door?' I asked him. 'Would that be a help or a hindrance?'

'Stoker?'

'Bram Stoker? Who wrote *Dracula*?'

'I hadn't realized,' he said. 'Any literary associations are worth a feature in the property section.'

'And that's good?'

'Worth its weight in gold. Might increase the guide price to—'

And I turned, before he mentioned the next million. I put my hand on his pin-striped shoulder, ushered him gently towards the door.

'I'm not sure I want to think of it just yet.'

'Whenever you do,' he said, and his hand began to fish in his suit pocket.

I told him I already had his card and watched him walk down the sagging staircase, listening to the ticking clocks.

I heard the front door slam and sat on the top step, allowing the transient nature of the house to envelop me once more. I could hear

the cries of children from Fairview Park. I could hear the number 30
bus grinding towards the city centre. Everything changes and nothing
changed at all.

# HAWAII

A N OLD LADY had lived next door, Mrs. Considine, who wore tweed suits and carried a walking stick, and of course to my child's mind she was the vampire's caretaker, looking after the house for him in the daytime when daylight things needed to be done. Cleaning, I supposed, and the business of making sure the curtains kept out the sunlight. I would see her returning home from the corner shop pulling her wheelie bag, and once I was in there buying smarties when she came in and gave the shopkeeper Colly her list. Tea, batch bread, black pudding, and orange juice. What did a vampire need with such comestibles, I wondered. Blood was their sustenance and they foraged for that themselves, always at night. And at night he only manifested himself in the haze that clung to the tulips in the park, in the strange circles the raindrops made around the streetlamps, in the mist that hung around the mudflats of the Tolka river, the sleeping swans appearing and disappearing through it as the mist shifted in the slow breeze that came from the mouth of the Liffey beyond.

It was something like the idea of God, the thought of this vampire: a being who could penetrate your thoughts, who could be everywhere and nowhere, from whom there was no hiding. I managed to forget it for hours, even days sometimes, but then another sound would bring the thought back—the creaking of the old sash from the bedroom window, the ticking of the clocks, but most of all the humming. Sights rarely did the same thing. The morning mist that hung around the park could have been him all right, a manifestation of God or the vampire, but a sight didn't intrude on you, shock you into the remembrance that he was still there. Walking home across the bridge over the Tolka river, a faint hum and there he was, he had suddenly returned or had been there, unknown to you, all the time.

God of course was good and the vampire was not. But sometimes even that thought lost its comfort because God's goodness, his searing, blazing certainty that goodness in the end was all, became itself a source of terror. You yourself could never match the magnificence of the goodness of God, you failed daily in your efforts. At heart, you suspected, you were already one of the fallen and had more in common with the vampire himself, just never the courage to admit it. He at least had accepted his lot, was outside of the blaze of sunlight and goodness, beyond the judgment of nuns and priests. You would have liked to discuss these matters with him if you ever met him face to face and while the thought thrilled you, it terrified you even more.

So there were two circumstances in which you might befriend the vampire. One, in which the pressure to be good became intolerable and you wanted to admit—what he had centuries ago admitted—that you would never get there, and you wanted to learn the rules of living without the light. The other circumstance was the one in which you encountered him on his foraging, walking home from the Scout hall or the chip shop, taking a shortcut across the park, and the satiated form rose from an already drained body lying among the tulips and turned and caught you in its gaze. The eyes would be dark, you knew, silver and black, dead and unknowable, and you would want to befriend him then because the alternative was too terrifying.

So you would make the admission of the first circumstance. That you, like him, could never be good. And what was it like, living without the light? Why did his housekeeper bring him orange juice and tea if he patently didn't need them? And what was the significance of the walking stick? And he would take your hand and in one of those rare connections between the living and the undead walk you among the feathery trees and explain it all, finally.

His realm of course was for the most part the night; nothing but his sound ever penetrated the daylight. But once, coming out of the water by the Bull Wall, with my mother still swimming her lazy circles, I became aware of a figure sitting in the shadow of the cement shelter, his entire body blotted from the sun, a dark coat hanging loosely over his shoulders, a black beret on his head. Did vampires wear berets? I had no idea, but remember thinking that even if they normally didn't, it would make a good disguise.

What I felt most of all were his eyes on my body as I toweled myself dry. My clothes were in there on the cement bench beside him, also hidden in the shadow where the hot sun cut across the shelter. They look at you like that, vampires, directly and without shame. Their desire is for the blood that courses through your body, the blood that was reddening my cheeks now—and of course a young kid like me, just in from the cold ocean, wet togs clinging to his groin, exposed just how much blood was available, exposed all of the points which those sharpened teeth would pierce.

I wanted my clothes, wanted to cover myself but didn't know how to get them. The thought of entering that shelter, letting that shadow course over my hot and cold skin was unthinkable. So I walked back down to the bottom step where the water lapped and my mother was swimming back in. I couldn't ask her to go with me to the men's shelter, I already knew that, neither could I dress with her in the women's, but I knew her presence would provide some solution, a solution I could not as yet imagine, since mothers always do.

'You're shivering, lovey,' she said, coming out of the cold sea. She wasn't. She never felt that cold. And the water cleaved off her skin like a sheet of fine plastic that magically turned into diamond drops.

'Why haven't you changed?'

'Waiting for you.'

'Lazybones. Go on, before you catch your death.'

And she put her arm round my shoulder and turned me towards the shelter and to my inexpressible relief, he was gone.

He was afraid of her, I realized. She brought sunlight with her, sunlight all around her, the way a pipe smoker carries his air of tobacco smoke even if he's not smoking: You can smell it from a few feet off.

We keep secrets from our parents. Mine, at that age, was him. He would return, I knew that instinctively, it was one of the rules of his species. He feared sunlight and mothers, he liked shadows and dark, and he always came back.

I next glimpsed him without his beret, but with the kind of homburg hat that detectives or gamekeepers wear, keeping pace with me behind the dark stripes of the poplar trees in Fairview Park. I was taking a shortcut from East Wall and could see the silhouette in the shadows of the trees, outlined by the bright green of the sun on the grass field behind. The bark of the trees was perfectly dark, the line of his hat and the shadows themselves were dark, and he was safe as long as he stayed there, as I was safe as long as I stayed out here, where the sun hit my face and the boys kicked a football behind me.

I saw him on a bicycle some weeks later and winter must have been coming in, because there was a wind tugging at his dark trenchcoat and a skein of dark clouds behind him. It was that time of evening when the streetlights show up against the gathering night, and I was kicking my heels down the green with three others when I noticed the bicycle keeping pace. I caught my breath and said nothing—what could you say to friends your own age?—and I noticed the black beret had come back. I kept the others between me and him as I walked, but I noticed that he kept pace too, moving the pedals as if in a slow bicycle race, head always turned towards me; and the cement generator was coming near us with the low electric hum, the vampire moan, and I didn't want to hear that, so I said goodbye to them quickly, crossed the Clontarf Road, and caught a passing number 30 bus which had slowed down by the traffic lights.

And there was one last encounter, in the Strand cinema in North Strand, across the road from the ruins of the houses hit by the stray German bombs. Elvis was playing in *Blue Hawaii*, and I was mitching school in the half-empty cinema on a Tuesday afternoon. The sea in Hawaii was blue, the sand was a greeny white, and Elvis was wearing a Hawaiian shirt with a garland of flowers around his neck and girls were shaking coconuts that rattled when the vampire sat beside me. He was wearing the black beret again and black leather gloves, the purpose of which, I supposed, was to hide his long curling nails. It was dark in the cinema of course, a permanent night, and there were no mothers about so I supposed his time had come. I could feel his hot, soft breath on my cheek, heard an odd word that he kind of sighed or whispered. 'Well.' And then he repeated it. 'Well.'

And as Elvis was singing *Rock-a-hula baby, oh how I love to kiss my little hula miss,* the usherette threw the long beam of her flashlight towards him and he slipped away again, leaving my popcorn scattered on the sticky floor. He was afraid of the light all right, but I knew by then there were no such things as vampires. And when I walked home over the Tolka bridge and saw the mists that hung around the mudflats, the swans appearing and disappearing out of them, I knew the mist was nothing to do with vampires: It was what they had told me in school, something to do with the change in temperature between the water and the air.

When I got to the Crescent and saw Mrs. Considine ascending the steps with the help of her stick towards the door with the brass plaque that said BRAM STOKER LIVED HERE I knew I didn't have to worry about why her master needed tea and orange juice. When I got inside and my mother asked me how was school, and after my long silence asked me was everything all right, I told her I always thought Mrs. Considine was a housekeeper for somebody inside, but she said no, she owned the house that the man who wrote *Dracula* once lived in, and she wondered what it was like, all alone in a house with so many stairs, when she needed a walking stick, poor woman, because of her varicose veins.

# DUNNE & CRESCENZA

THERE WAS A note scribbled on a beer mat in the pocket of my funeral coat. It said: *Half past one, Dunne & Crescenza.* I had made an arrangement which I couldn't remember now, at his wake, in the crush round the bar.

Half one meant lunch, I supposed, and it was half twelve now. I began to walk, past the Crescent, across the Malahide Road where I bought a takeaway coffee from an Eastern European waitress in a new café at the corner. I walked then past the carpet store that used to be the Fairview cinema towards the Five Lamps, when I saw a bus halted by the traffic lights at the Tolka bridge and I ran across the lines of stalled cars, the coffee scalding my fingers, and jumped through the concertina doors before they shut.

Forgive me the details, Emily, because sometime soon I will come to realize that this is a letter to you, and the things that had changed since my childhood are important, because they form a map, so to speak, of all the different places in which I was mistaken for him, the father whom you only vaguely knew. The Fairview cinema had been a pit, always, only matched in its decrepitude by the Strand, and soon by the New Electric in Lower Abbey Street, which charged jam jars for admission and allowed the kids to urinate below the screen. You couldn't get a cappuccino in the Dublin of my youth and the buses had an open door with a silver pole that you could swing around and it was in one of them that I was first mistaken. I had jumped on the bus, probably just there around the Tolka bridge, and taken my seat by the back door, when the bus conductor clipped me round the ear and accused me of not paying last time.

I was confused, of course; there had been no last time and I never would have dreamed of not paying, when he went on, 'Thought I wouldn't recognize you without the uniform.'

'I never wear a uniform,' I said.

'Liar,' he said, 'all you cissy Belvedere boys do. You owe me seven pence.'

And so he took the two shillings I gave, giving me only ten pence in change. So I was mistaken for a Belvedere boy, a cissy at that, and I had to cough up his bus fare.

And I wondered what this Belvedere boy was like, tried to imagine his uniform. I had seen them in the city centre, or on the buses, traveling out to Howth or Sutton, longish grey trousers above knock knees and a grey blazer with a fringe of green or blue on it. They looked like imports from an English comic strip or a Billy Bunter illustration, dumped by accident in the squalid city centre streets, and now one of them was so bold as to skip his fare. The Pillar was intact then, Horatio Nelson still preened over the grey city on top of a thousand steps and young girls waited for their dates at the base. I got off the bus in Middle Abbey Street and tried to catch sight of a Belvedere boy's uniform, but there weren't any. School must have finished by then.

I got off a different bus now, forty or so years later, in Marlborough Street and saw the metal spire where the Pillar used to be, vanishing into the haze above. I had made a decision, although I hardly knew it yet. It's often that way with decisions, they're made in some hidden part of us and the awareness secretes itself slowly into that conscious part of us that imagines it decides. I walked up that proudly multicultural street and crossed the river at O'Connell Bridge. I looked down into the water I had stared in so many times when I was younger—brown, somehow ancient, but hardly tainted by any of the other changes. The river changed by the minute, its flow, colour, movement, ripple, wave, and yet the whole of it, the curve, heading back towards the sunlit tip of the Wellington Monument, somehow stayed the same.

I would stay in my father's house, I knew that suddenly, walking over. I would leave that apartment in Schoneberg, Berlin without me for awhile, because it wasn't permanence I was after, it was transience—that strange impermanence I had felt throughout my childhood, the feeling that the walls around me were never mine, were never meant for me, that there was another home I could have lived in, should have lived in. I would explore that thing, the whole of it, and I would write it down. And these thoughts must have taken me up Westmoreland Street, past the façade of Trinity College, up Nassau Street to the chairs outside Dunne & Crescenza's, where you were sitting.

'NED,' YOU SAID, 'I wasn't sure you'd remember.'

'It was written,' I said, 'on a beer mat.'

'Order us coffee, will you?' you asked, your small freckled nose tipped upwards towards me. 'And then sit down, if you don't mind the dog.'

I didn't mind the dog. I liked the way he took me as a familiar, already part of his world. And I ordered coffee through the doorway, wondering how much of it all I should tell, how soon.

'It's not Ned,' I told you.

'No? Could have sworn you said Ned.'

'Maybe I did. I was embarrassed. I lied.'

'How weird. Why did you lie?'

'I felt like an intruder there. Someone else, at someone else's funeral. It's weird, it's strange. Don't ask.'

'And so, you are?'

'Kevin. Kevin Thunder.'

'Kevin Thunder. Ned Gaskett. Explosive names. Do you work in explosives? You must have told me what you do. I forget.'

'I design games.'

'Computer games?'

'Yes. The kind spotty young males play.'

'How strange. I always thought they just turned up online.'

'Graphics. Backgrounds. Cities. The streets that twirl around the crashing cars.'

'Okay.'

'And you?'

'You mean what do I do? Nothing at the moment. I'm in mourning, amn't I? I feel like I should be wearing a black veil. Some kind of habit. So people would know.'

'Know?'

'To back off. Keep away. I don't feel like talking. I feel like street-walking, in silence.'

'Should I back off then?'

'No.'

And you brushed your hand over mine. It felt totally natural, yet brought a blush to my face.

'You're part of it, somehow. The feeling. It's loss, but it's not quite grief. Not yet.'

'Why not grief?'

'Because I never knew him. Not in the way daughters know their fathers.'

The word 'father' was like an old Chinese gong. It reverberated.

'It's like a black cloud of something that I don't want to leave.'

'Have you said this to your mother?'

'Silence, that's what it is. I'm in a cloud of silence. And no, I don't want to talk to her.'

'You're very articulate.'

And your fingers tapped off mine as if they were a table top, and removed themselves.

'I'm talking a lot, amn't I . . . ?'

Amn't I. I hadn't heard that Irishism in awhile.

'. . . For someone in a silent cloud. There was a voice I heard once, years ago. I know I'll never hear it again.'

You ruffled the dog's head, and lit a cigarette.

'But I can talk to you. And it's easy. That's strange, isn't it?'

And the dog was now nuzzling at my elbow.

'It's the way you smell,' you said.

'Smell?'

'That came out wrong. Your odour, scent, whatever the polite word is.'

You brought your small nose towards me and circled my neck like a cat.

'I remember his smell. A kind of earthy musk. It's possibly the only thing I have of him. And what shocked me most by the graveside was that it had gone. He had vanished into an odourless world.'

'Forever,' I said.

'The dead,' you said. 'They don't smell. Nobody told me that.'

I was lost for words. Your face, your pure expressiveness. Your girlishness.

'Tell me when you met him first?'

It was a question, but I couldn't avoid the answer.

'I suppose I knew him before I met him.'

'You're being mysterious here.'

'Well, it was mysterious. I was mistaken for someone.'

'Him?'

'As it turned out.'

# WOOLWORTHS

S O I TOLD you about the bus, the bus fare, and the Belvedere boy I was mistaken for. We had a combined history—neither my life nor his, but a mistaken one—and its next chapter—hardly a chapter, more like an episode and then again hardly an episode, more of an event—happened in Woolworths on Grafton Street on a Wednesday afternoon. I know it was Wednesday because my mother went to town that day and sometimes took me with her, and we were walking through Woolworths, through the displays of goods in their little plastic sections, when something happened with her suspender belt.

'Godfathers,' she said, 'my suspender,' and she bent down and tried to hitch something underneath her skirt. 'My stocking's come loose,' she said, 'it'll be flopping round my ankle. You wait for me here.' And she made her way to the sign that said LADIES, and the arrow pointing down the stairs, walking with her knees pressed together, the way girls in the schoolyard did when they wanted to pee. It was strange, seeing a smaller girl in my mother, stranger knowing that something had happened beneath her dress. And I stood there, looking at the displays of buttons and zips and needles and threads, when I noticed a set of DC comics displayed further up, against the wall.

I walked towards them, thinking how easy it would be to slip one into my pocket.

I was a child alone among adults in that shop and if I stole one, or even two, only God or the vampire would ever know. And I was inching towards them, when I felt a hand on my shoulder, heard the voice of a male shop assistant. 'Don't turn round,' he said. 'I told you, didn't I, never to come in here again.'

'I haven't ever,' I muttered, and the hand tightened. Its grip was anonymous and terrifying.

'I said don't turn round. I'm going to walk you to that door and leave you on that street and if you ever come back here, you poncy little thief, I'll call the police.'

That was the way he said it. Police. As if they were a different race. I gathered later, from his accent, that he must have been Scottish, but I didn't turn round, I let myself be frog-marched to the glass doors and thrust into the chaos of shoppers on the street. I stood there, staring at the jewellers opposite. Had he read my thoughts, I wondered, had he a window to the future, had he known what I was about to do before I even did it? And I remembered the phrase, 'I told you, didn't I?' He had met me before, somehow; he wasn't a soothsayer or a mind reader, he had met me before, told me never to come back there. He thought I was someone else, who had stolen something and been caught in the act. I had been mistaken once more. For the same boy, I wondered, the Belvedere boy? But he hadn't mentioned the uniform, so maybe it was someone else. A thief. A poncy little thief.

I was a poncy little thief now. I skived on bus fares and robbed DC comics from Woolworths and sometimes wore a Billy Bunter

Belvedere school uniform. I felt like I was in that game, *Animal, Vegetable, or Mineral*, who was I? And only when my mother came out, it seemed like hours later, did I discover who I was again. 'Kevin,' she said, 'Kevin, I've been looking everywhere, what are you doing out here?' And she put one arm around me and walked, properly now, her knees no longer stuck together, down the street towards the river.

# FUNLAND

THE WAITRESS ARRIVED again and you ordered a sandwich and stubbed out your cigarette. Whether you were bored or entranced, I couldn't tell and so I asked: 'Was I boring you?'

'Depends, I suppose,' you said smiling, and I realized you had smiled for the first time since we met and it was like the sun coming out, 'on who you are.'

'You're bored then,' I said.

'No,' you said, 'I like the sound of that voice. Tell me more.'

So I told you more. And it was so long ago, I was hardly sure it happened. On the bus again, I said, and I was alone, which was significant, alone and older. I got off at Nelson's Pillar and saw the amusement hall across from it with a flashing neon sign above a smiling face which read, COME IN AND HAVE FUN IN FUNLAND. I had passed it with my mother many times, longing to be the kind of kid who walked in there without a second thought, winklepicker shoes turned up at the toes, hands stuck in the pockets of the bumfreezer jacket, and played the slot machines. I had neither pointed shoes nor bumfreezer jacket but I was on my own that day and so I crossed the street below the Pillar and summoned the courage and walked inside.

The light was low in there, there was a whirr of slot machines, a jingle of falling money, a mechanical hand in a glass case and a pool table under a chinaman's lamp near the back. There was a coffee bar to one side and a kind of televised jukebox: You pushed some money in the slot and when a Ricky Nelson song came on, you saw him on a back-projected panel above the box. So I walked in, heading for the jukebox, reaching for the coins in my pocket, but I was stopped just inside the bar before the daylight turned to neon by a man in a stained dress suit, a thin moustache, and a thinner tie.

'Didn't I tell him,' he said to the woman behind the glass change booth, 'never to show his face in here again?'

'Remind me,' she said, 'who is he?'

'The little fucker that jiggered the horse machine.'

I didn't know what to say, other than that I would have loved to have been the little fucker that jiggered the horse machine. I didn't know what jiggered meant, didn't even know it was a verb, but I could see the horse machine behind him, the small cutout jockeys moving in a kind of jagged unison towards a cardboard finishing post. I would have loved to have been able to jigger them, a process I could only imagine meant manipulating their progress in some way so the jackpot of coins would spill into the brass cup.

'Ask him where his blazer is? There were three of them, in blazers.'

Three jiggers, I thought. Which one of them was I?

'Out the door,' he said and he grabbed me by the jumper as I protested, 'You've got it wrong, it's my first time here.'

'And your last,' he said and I was once again pushed through a set of glass doors, which he held closed with his boot behind them. I saw the silhouettes of the passersby around the Pillar reflected in the glass with the neon lights behind and because I was older, maybe, I felt for the first time the freedom of being someone else.

'FREEDOM?' YOU ASKED, as your sandwich arrived.

'What I mean is,' I said, 'did you never feel you'd been dumped into your life by accident, given a set of circumstances that, whether you deserved them or not, seemed quite arbitrary?'

'That you'd like to be someone else?'

'I suppose.'

'I would like to be in a different city, in a different time. But with somebody else, now? Other than you? No.'

I was stopped for a moment.

'That's quite a compliment,' I said.

'I know,' she said. 'It feels even odd to have said it. Maybe I'd like to know more. About him. About you. I told you that I'd never really known him.'

And so I told you more. How the next encounter with that other happened beneath Nelson's Pillar, when a youngish man in a leather jacket offered me a cigarette from his silver cigarette case while I was waiting there for no one in particular. I was mitching from violin class: My mother loved the idea as much as I hated it and the Pillar was as good a place as any to kick my heels, swing my violin case, and pretend I had been learning scales. He had deep lines around his face, I remember, a mouth too wide, something immaculate about his appearance, about his buttoned-down collar beneath the leather jacket that looked both cosmopolitan and unfamiliar. 'You got the time?' he asked, and I glanced over at Clery's clock as he could well have done and answered, 'Ten past three.'

'I knew that,' he said. 'What I meant was have *you* got the time?' Emphasizing the *you*.

'For what?' I asked.

'Oh, I don't know. For a cigarette. A chat.'

And he flipped open the silver lid and I saw ten or so Sweet Afton held neatly in place by a band of black elastic.

'Flow gently, Sweet Afton,' he said.

'I don't smoke,' I said, though I would have loved to, the way I would have loved to jigger the cardboard horses.

'You did,' he said, selecting one and almost flipping it towards his broad lips, 'the last time.'

'What last time?' I said. 'I've never met you before.'

'I never,' he said as he lit a match, 'forget a face.'

'So you remember mine?' I asked him, and for some reason I felt myself blushing.

'Hair's different,' he said, 'but the face is the same.'

'So,' I asked him, 'what's my name?'

'We didn't get to names,' he said, as if getting to names was an event of great significance. 'But I never forget a face.'

And he held out the case again, with the lid still flipped open.

'You sure?'

And he smiled, and I saw the tip of his tongue protrude from his lips in a flicker of uncertainty, or a hint about a world of adulthood of which I had no idea. I felt the blood rush to my cheeks again and out of embarrassment, out of the urge to be the type of person the situation demanded, I took one.

'Here.'

He pulled open his jacket to ward off an imaginary gust of wind and he lit a match. I had to lean in close to light it.

'Smell the same.'

I blew out as quickly as I drew. I suddenly felt sick.

'What?'

'You're the same kid, I know. The hair's different, but it smells the same. Brylcreem.'

It wasn't Brylcreem, it was hair oil, the same as my father used to slick what remained of his hair over his bald patch. But for some reason I felt complimented.

'We went into Funland for an ice cream. And you're telling me you don't remember.' There was a sense of immense disappointment at universal ingratitude in his voice.

'We played the horses?'

'Yes. I showed you the sequence. Red, yellow, red again, and green. Showed you how to change the sequence, if you angle up the table with your hip. Don't do it too often. They'll throw you out.'

'He did,' I said, and suddenly felt adult and smart.

'Did what?'

'Did it too often.'

And I saw my mother coming out now, swinging through the doors of Clery's, packages in her hand.

'It was someone else,' I said.

'Who else?'

'Someone else. That smokes. Smells of Brylcreem. Jiggers the horses.'

And I threw the half-smoked cigarette on the ground, was about to twist it with my round-toed shoe when he did it for me. He had chisel-toed shoes, I noted, with a small Cuban heel.

# PALMERSTON PARK

YOU HAVE TO understand, I told you, what shoes meant to us then. Not like now, where the choice is endless. In my pathetic early youth your shoes defined you. There were tribes then, Mods and Rockers—not that we belonged to them, but we had heard of them, heard enough to know that it all started with the shoes. Those round-toed brown things I wore were a constant humiliation; in time I would persuade my mother to buy a pair of chisel-toed Cuban heels and later on a parka with a hood and a green suede waistcoat.

'You're losing me now,' you said, and your sandwich was finished, and I could feel our meeting was nearing its end.

'The point is,' I said, 'I wanted his shoes.'

'Whose shoes?'

'His. The one I was mistaken for.'

'There was one? Not several?'

'I was beginning to realize they were the same. And I wondered what his shoes were like.'

'I wanted to talk about my father.'

'I was. And I wanted his shoes.'

'I'm lost.'

So we talked about other things as I waited for the bill.

And I thought that some things in this telling should be written down. To hear them from my lips might seem too unlikely, too embarrassing, too direct. And perhaps they didn't happen, after all. And as you blew the remains of the froth off your dead cappuccino I thought of how I would write it down, the chapter's end, the crux of the matter: The day I saw myself, or thought I saw myself, on a bus.

THE BUS WAS stalled in traffic lights at Westmoreland Street, every window was misted with breath or condensation and the upper floor obscured by cigarette smoke. There was a figure at the top that I recognized—something about the way he sat, the way his upturned collar made his hair stick out at the nape of his neck like a hedgehog. I stopped, waiting for the bus to pass, then realized that I was recognizing, in some obscure manner, myself, me, Kevin—those glimpses you only get from face-to-face mirrors, that angle of the back of your head that everyone sees but you. And he was somehow, indefinably me, the way he rocked back and forwards as if in time to some silent tune he was humming. I saw the glow of a cigarette tip and thought irrationally that I was far too young to be smoking. If I was thirteen, then so would he have been. Then the lights changed with a grinding of gears and a cloud of diesel and he was retreating through the clogged city and I was suddenly panic-stricken that I would never get to see him again, that this moment would be like a dream that I could never define and so I ran, jumped on to the tailboard, grabbed the rail, and climbed up the stairs to the upper deck.

The cigarette smoke was thick, the windows dripping with condensation, and I parked myself on the only seat I could find near the back, when I realized I had no idea what number bus I was on, what destination I was heading towards. And the prospect held a strange frisson for me. Here was another whose actions had been impinging on my own; whose actions, I could even say, in the manner of the new mathematics which we were all studying then, were tangential to mine. If I was a set he was my subset or vice versa. There was another life he was heading towards, a destination unknown on a bus I didn't know, but it all felt frighteningly familiar because of the shape of the nape of his neck and the hair above his turned-up collar.

It was strange, the bald heads and caps and the clouds of tobacco smoke, the unfamiliar streetlamps passing by the windows, and it was familiar in a way I couldn't even now define. There had been the rocking, the rhythmic bowing of his head to the unheard music; but that had stopped now and the only movement of his body was the one forced on it, on all of us, by the bus, as it swung round corners, juddered to a halt, and started off again through the bleached-out streets. There was no uniform that I could see, just the grey-blue coat with the collar turned up, jammed into the tuft of hair at the nape of his neck, the same uncut fringes there that I sported. We let our hair grow to the extent that the Christian Brothers allowed, but he was a Belvedere boy and would have had to answer to priests. There was a whorl of hair curling at the crown like a bathtub emptying into a plughole. I leaned left a little to get a glimpse of the shoes, and to my grim satisfaction, they weren't chisel toed or pointed, they were brown-toed things like my own. It was the cigarette that threw me: pulled at with a certain flamboyance, as if he was proud of his maturity, of the corner-boy ease with which he twisted it dead with his shoe.

The absurd narcissism of my study had proved so beguiling that when the brakes began their long whine and the bus's frame began to judder in preparation for the next stop, I was taken by surprise. He stood up abruptly, ran down the smoke-filled aisle, down the stairs, grabbed the metal pole to steady himself, and almost vaulted off the deck. I saw nothing of his face. I rubbed the condensation from the window and saw his feet hit the pavement below, his coat swinging with the movement, and the bus juddered into action once more and he was gone.

I got off myself at the next stop. I walked back and saw a park bounded by railings, with monkey puzzle trees, and large spacious gardens leading towards fawn brick-fronted houses—mansions would have been a more appropriate word: to me they seemed huge. I seemed to have stumbled out of that bus into a different city.

The daylight was almost gone and the lights from each living room spilled across the park. Two boys in short trousers were playing cricket, and he walked past them with a gait like mine. I had seen cricket bats in English comic books but never seen one for real, like a reinforced hurley, a strange lumpen mass of wood attached to a handle, and when the ball hit it, it echoed with a crack. Someone was playing a piano in one of the houses, a Chopin polonaise. I know this because my mother played it on her turntable. And he was walking towards his front door now, towards a life I could have never imagined. He had his own key.

AND YOU WERE staring at me now, Emily, and there seemed to be tears in your eyes.

'I like it,' you said, 'the way you can sit and say nothing.'

'I'm sorry, I was dreaming.'

'Talking's overrated.'

'Do you remember your grandmother?'

'I remember her house.'

'And?'

'One of those big old ones in Palmerston Park.'

'Sounds rather grand.'

'Maybe. Why do you say that?'

'Because the most important distinctions are the smallest.'

'Meaning?'

'Like the ones between the middle and the upper middle classes.'

'And how would you define them?'

'My father was a bookie, I grew up in Marino.'

'Marino?'

From the way you said it, I knew you didn't know where it was.

'Are they really that different?'

'I would say the gulf between them is fairly absolute.'

'I thought we were classless, in the Ireland I grew up in.'

'We like to think we were.'

'Her house smelt of leather. There were saddles in the hallway.'

You leaned towards me and brought your nose close to my cheekbone.

'The way you smell of him. And I have to go now.'

And you stood, and kissed me on the cheek.

'Can we meet again? When I want to talk about him again?'

'Please.'

You flipped open a mobile phone.

'Open yours.'

I did as you asked.

'Call 087 963 2765.'

I did. And your phone rang. You pressed a button.

'Save me under *Daughter*.'

And you turned and drew your dog back towards Nassau Street.

I WALKED BACK down Nassau Street and could see you dragging your dog through the mess of buskers, bad clowns, and weekend shoppers. When the crowds masked you from view, I suddenly missed you. I missed the quiet way you allowed your grief to inhabit you. I imagined it would dominate you for years and wondered could I help with that. I opened my phone and saw your number there, saved under *Daughter*. Daughter to him of course, but it had a special resonance for me. I wondered which of us would make the call first. It would be made, I had no doubt about that—there was too much to be known, about you, about him. He wasn't a good father, but even in his worst days he held the notion of you close, like an inviolate part of him that could never be sullied.

YOUR GRANDMOTHER'S HOUSE had no number, just a name, Sans Soucis, without worry or care. And the odd thing was that in its garden, in its proximity to parkland, it wasn't too dissimilar to my own. But my park was haunted, had rows of municipal tulips, his had monkey puzzle trees and a piano playing Chopin. Its air of opulence, of peace, was such that it could have been in a different country.

I later came to study architecture and used to argue out the relative merits of the squares of Dublin. The Georgian ones came first, of course, but they were grand and somehow uninhabitable. The mid- to late-Victorian version had something else to recommend it.

Dartmouth, Kenilworth, Palmerston, the squares, Herbert, Leeson, the parks—and I sound like an auctioneer now, I know, Emily, but there was a sedate, tranquil permanence to those places that I wanted as I walked back home on a series of damp pavements. Around that park with its monkey puzzle trees and copper beeches, down those wide, seductive streets, I was happily lost for awhile, without any bearing on the north and south of things. I imagined my mother in another version of her life playing Chopin on the piano, the sound spilling out beyond the gardens, across the railings, into that square. I was somewhere in the picture, in a bedroom upstairs maybe, listening to the creaking of the pedals as they changed.

I was an only child. He couldn't have been. There was something about the impulsiveness of the way he swung around that pole, the way he took the stairs two at a time that implied someone who had no questions about his place in the world, who lacked the isolated sense of things. I passed a cinema then, called the Kenilworth, on a street where an island of sad trees divided the traffic, and wondered had my vampire ever traced him there. The confusion would have been possible, if we looked so much like each other: Those leather gloves and that homburg hat could have traced the passage of his feet round about these southside streets, into the dark of that cinema where a Norman Wisdom film was playing. Could the vampire make his moves, I wondered, without the sound of Elvis singing *oh how I love to kiss my little hula miss?* With the Gump, his hat turned backwards, singing *Don't laugh at me 'cause I'm a fool* and the spilled popcorn and the usherette's flashing light? No, I decided, the vampire needed Elvis and his Hawaiian shirt and his garland of flowers and the coconut maracas. He needed the other side and the cold concrete shelters and the Strand cinema, not the Kenilworth. And Norman Wisdom was not of his world.

And the canal was there then and a swan paddled behind a silver wall of falling water and I passed a succession of bridges to a street where the buses were familiar and I caught one of them going towards the northside.

MY FATHER WAS home when I got back, an unusual event in itself. He was grilling cheese on toast, a dish he called Welsh rarebit, though what was Welsh or rare about it I never understood.

'Where have you been?' he asked.

'Here and there.'

'Where?'

'Palmerston Park.'

'Long way from home. Where the barristers live. What's in Palmerston Park?'

'A friend of mine.'

'You have a friend, way over on the southside? What's his name?'

'How do you know it's a him?'

'You have a girlfriend?'

And he rocked back and forwards on his heels as the cheese sizzled.

'Same as mine. Kevin.'

I chose an odd and symmetrical untruth.

'Two Kevins.'

And it suddenly made him insubstantial, as if he had never existed.

# THE BULL WALL

TWO HOURS AFTER I left you I was sitting among Tommy's barely ticking clocks. The tulips gleamed like wineglasses in the dying light. A swan flapped its way over the poplar trees.

I felt an attack of *heimweh*, but for what I wasn't sure. For my offices in Babelsberg, my apartment in Berlin? Or for this park where homosexuals have been known to be beaten to death. Where unexplained childhood ghosts brushed their wings off my sleeping face. Where the cinema had been turned into a carpet shop. Where the webbed feet of the swans got stuck in the mud of the Tolka river. How can you be sick for what never felt like home? I had had dreams of another home for years that would turn the idea of home itself into a kind of physical longing. And when I followed that other one across the city I found a kind of home for that longing. The feeling had an image to support it, another park, the sound of a piano, two boys playing with a cricket bat.

But I managed to forget the encounter, or at least to bury it in that part of oneself where all the unacknowledged longings reside. I went on with what writers would call my life. Until one day I saw my mother packing her swimming things to head to the Bull Wall and I decided, what the hell, maybe the sea is warm again, maybe I should give her back that pleasure, maybe both of us should go. She managed to hide her delight quite artfully as I packed my togs in a fresh towel, rolled it up with excessive neatness the way we all did back then, like a large Swiss roll. We walked along the seafront, past the afternoon kids playing five-a-side soccer, past the small cement shelters with the fluted pillars down towards the wooden bridge of the Bull Wall.

The tide was full and the stanchions had almost disappeared in the water and I could feel her pleasure like an invisible wave emanating from her perfectly flat stomach. She wore a polka dot dress, I remember, and a pair of flat shoes for once, and the seams must have been banished from stockings by then in the onward march of whatever women wore, because I don't remember any. So we walked and we talked and the old wooden bridge echoed with the sound of cars passing over it, and when we came within sight of the dunes we heard her favourite sound—the whistling of larks, ascending from their nests in the sea grass. When we reached the bathing shelters with their male and female signs hanging above them in rusted metal, the sea looked cold and there was a wind blowing from the river's mouth raising the waves into tiny frigid scallops.

'Go on yourself,' I said. 'Let me build up to it.'

'Promises,' she said, 'promises.' And when I protested she laughed.

'Don't worry. I won't force you.'

So I sat in the mildewed shelter and saw her slim figure in its lime-green swimsuit treading down the steps towards the water. She took one breath and dove straight into the cold water: Once more I wondered how she did it, without catching a breath. I decided to walk then, along the promenade above, which led to the cement plinth of the Virgin Mary and the view of the B&I ferry making its way to the North Wall. I knew she would be twenty minutes or more. My mother, hardy, thin, and indestructible, or so I thought then.

There was a girl cycling slowly on a bike, her elbows leaning on the basket above the handlebars, close cropped hair, her brown eyes peeking above her arms, her chin resting on her wrists. She was hardly cycling at all really, one foot on the pedal, the other pushing along the raised pavement, the bike swaying idly from one side to the other, a kind of free-form movement somewhere between cycling and walking, and I was looking at her, wondering whether the bike would finally topple. As she drew close I looked away, in the way one does to feign lack of interest, but I could feel her eyes catching mine and as she came nearer her head kept angling in my direction until she had passed and I heard the brakes squeak and I heard her say, 'Hey.'

'Hey what?' I asked.

'Just hey.'

'Hay is what horses eat,' I said.

'You trying to be smart?' she said, and she edged the bike backwards until she came straight into my eyeline.

'No,' I said. 'But hey, what?'

'Hey you,' she said. 'You didn't call.'

'Was I meant to?'

'You promised you would.'

And I felt it happening again. I felt my face going red with a desire I couldn't fathom. She had dark hair and dark eyes and a bow mouth like a Chinese acrobat. She wore a fluffy pink cardigan with the sleeves rolled up to the elbow. She kept her face perched like a question mark above the handlebars.

'Well,' I said, and tried to hide my confusion. 'I must have lost your number.'

'I told you I didn't have a phone. You said you'd call the shop.'

And when I fell silent she raised her chin and I could see a tiny dimple there, like a pinprick.

'Tuite's? Vernon Avenue?'

She began to smile and two more pinpricks made their appearance, one in each cheek.

'Yes.' I lied once more. 'I meant to. Something came up.'

'Oh. Yeah. Belvedere boy.'

Of course. I was a Belvedere boy. The horses in Funland. The bus in Middle Abbey Street.

'Next time you play then, call round. Or don't. See if I care.'

Play what? I wondered. Rugby, of course. I was a Belvedere boy.

She inched the bike along the roadside towards the bridge, back the way she had come. I could see my mother swimming towards the cement steps. And for some reason I didn't want her to see me.

'Tomorrow,' I said. 'I'll call round tomorrow.'

'You've got another game?'

'Practice.'

'I'll believe it when I see it.'

She put her pleated skirt in the saddle then and began to cycle home, and I could see the skirt blowing back towards me and wondered what it looked like from the front or the side, from anywhere except where I was standing. And she grew smaller and smaller, heading towards the wooden bridge and the traffic on the Clontarf Road.

My mother was shivering, wrapped in her towel by the time I reached her. I leaned against the metal handrail dividing the women's shelter from the men's and marvelled at the way she kept the towel in place with her chin while doing the little wriggling dance out of her wet swimsuit.

'You didn't feel like it.'

'Not really.'

'Too cold.'

'Maybe.'

'Nothing to do with the girl.'

'What girl?'

'The one in the pink sweater.'

'No. Nothing to do with her.'

# TUITE'S

THE CLOCKS GRADUALLY slowed their ticking to something like silence. But I've never found silence, even in sleep. The walls creaked, something low moaned outside the window, like wind but so barely present as to be barely sound at all. As a child I would have thought it presaged a visit from the being next door, but as an adult I knew it was the constant hum of the new and questionable city growing up where the gantries of the docks used to be, across the water.

My phone was on silent, but I felt its rumble, and saw the screen light up with the word *Daughter*. I didn't answer, since I wasn't sure who I was at this moment, whether my memories were his or his were mine. Maybe my life was a dream of someone else's.

I got up at last and walked out of the house, and followed the path my mother had taken so often, left at the park on to the green sward with its cement shelters and the sea to my right. The cranes of the new city perched against a mauve glow from the old city behind it. After fifteen minutes walking, I could see the old wooden bridge still there, black against the yellow reflected streetlights. I turned left again where the generator still hummed, up Conquer Hill Road and Vernon Avenue. The small bungalow where Tuite's Sweets used to be was still there, but there was no glass counter by the entrance and of course no shop. I stood there, remembering old crimes. I had stolen something from around Tuite's shop, and it wasn't sweets. I had stolen him.

I WALKED THERE the next day after school, and saw no sign of the girl with the dimples, but there was a line of schoolkids queuing on the small lawn before the bungalow. There was the ridiculous sign, TUITE'S SWEETS, above a small eave over the front door with its glass counter. A petite, dark-haired woman was dispensing ice-cream cones and the sweets of those days, choc ices, Flash bars, and Maltesers.

I took my place in the line, fished in my pockets for change, and found I had enough for a cone. The woman was her mother, I could see that immediately, the same Chinese dimples and dark Italian eyes. As she pulled the ice cream, I saw someone move in the darkness inside the bungalow, the flash of a pink cardigan. Her face was dark against a cabinet that was shining with reflections of glass and crockery and I immediately wanted to be inside there, to find out what her home was like. I glimpsed a smile and tried to smile back and her mother looked both ways.

'You're a friend of Jean's?' the mother asked.

'I suppose,' I murmured, and could feel a blush spreading over my ridiculously prominent cheeks.

'What's your name?' the mother asked and the girl from inside piped up.

'Gerry. He goes to Belvedere.'

'Belvedere,' she said, and she took a Cadbury's Flake from the counter and stuck it in the whorl of ice cream, even though I hadn't paid for it. It was a gift, and my name was Gerry.

And the girl whose name was Jean came out then into the sunlight by the counter, and there was something indescribably pleasant
in the resemblance between the two of them.

'You going for a walk, love?'

'I think. He's come all this way.'

She ducked low beneath the glass counter and took my arm, and
we walked past the queue of shifting kids as if some ancient rite demanded it.

We walked then, up Vernon Avenue, Furry Park Road, Sybill
Hill, past St. Paul's College where the other one had met her after a
rugby game. Past boys in a field there, kicking the brown egg-shaped
ball. We walked down the long avenue through the wooded park to
the abandoned mansion and by the end of it all we were, as the rite
had it then, going out.

How this was decided I wasn't quite sure, but I knew it was a fact
when I heard the dull throb of a motorbike behind me. I turned and
saw an older youth on a black Kawasaki keeping pace with us, about
twenty yards behind. I don't know what I was more impressed by, the
fact that he could keep the bike balanced while throbbing forwards so
slowly or the fact that someone not too much older than me could afford a Kawasaki. He had slicked-back hair and a leather jacket which
made him look like a genuine rocker.

'Ignore him,' she said, pressing red-painted nails into my elbow.

'Why is he following us?'

'He thought he was going out with me. But he's not anymore.
You are.'

So that settles it, I remember thinking. But not for him. He
throbbed and putted his motorbike behind us all the way past the

football pitches, back down Vernon Avenue, and when we stopped outside her mother's sweet shop he roared past, leaving a cloud of black exhaust fumes like a wreath around us.

'See you tomorrow,' she said in her sweet voice that implied it was the only arrangement possible.

So a romance of kinds started, the kind that can only happen at the age of thirteen, where you hold hands and share bicycles and arrange to meet after school, where her mother calls you to the top of the queue and sticks a Cadbury's Flake into your ice-cream cone. She went to Holy Faith Convent, by the old gaunt church facing the Clontarf Road and the sea. Their uniform was a hideous grey pleated thing that she had generally managed to change out of by the time I arrived from my fictional school. And our walks around the suburban streets, down the long road through the park to the abandoned mansion, were always accompanied by the dull *putt-putt* of that motorbike, like a malignant chaperon. And for all I knew he could have been her chaperon, her older brother or cousin, charged with the task of keeping an eye out for physical contact. Because anything other than linking arms or holding hands was impossible in front of his black-leathered silhouette.

But for a time I managed to keep up the pretence that I was like the other, a Belvedere boy. St. Joseph's was the school I went to—Joey's we called it, a grey cement building on Fairview Strand run by Christian Brothers, the name being the only Christian thing about them. I remember school there as a series of sounds: the smack of a leather against an outstretched palm, the quick intake of breath, heads banged against wooden desks, the swish of beads and soutanes,

hurleys raising clumps of mud, smacking off other hurleys, cracking against knuckles, heads, and occasionally off the sliotar, a tough,
stitched-leather ball. I wondered what the sounds of Belvedere were
like. I had seen the school elegantly looming over the tenements of
Great Denmark Street. I imagined plainchant for some reason, and
of course a distant piano practising Chopin or Liszt, a refectory bell
ringing, and hushed, Jesuitical conversations.

Belvedere. The word implied ruined gardens, decorative follies,
like the ones we wandered through in St. Anne's Park. It implied an
elegance I knew I didn't have. But then again, neither did the hulk
following on the Kawasaki.

I was walking back through Fairview Park one evening when I
found him there in front of me. His bike parked on the mud path by
the tulips, his leathers sitting on its perch. There was no way round
him, so I kept on walking.

'The thing is,' he said, 'I know you go to Joey's.'

'So?' I asked.

'Told her you went to Belvedere.'

'I didn't. She told me that.'

'What's the difference?'

'I don't know. But there is one.'

'I'm telling her you go to Joey's. If you don't stop hanging round
with her.'

'Go ahead.'

'I'll make you stop.'

And he swung at me, and I saw it coming from a long way off. I
ducked and he stumbled towards me and I was already swinging back.
I caught him, to my surprise and considerable pain, straight between

the mouth and the nose. His feet slid forwards and his leather-clad bum slid backwards and ended up in the sad tulip bed.

'I respect that,' he said, oddly enough.

'I'm sorry.'

'No,' he said. 'You got me fair.'

I stretched out a hand to help him up. He took it, and to my surprise, he didn't hit me back.

'Okay,' he said. 'You can keep pretending.'

AND I PRETENDED well, for a number of weeks, until the time of our first kiss. He kept his word: The Kawasaki never sounded behind us and I took her walking over the dunes in Dollymount Strand. Beyond the golf club, both of our push bikes tangled in each other, the larks filling the air above us. Her mouth was small and delicious and I felt her tongue rub against my teeth. And for some reason afterwards, when she smiled to herself at my embarrassment, I told her I didn't go to Belvedere at all, I went to Joey's in North Strand.

'Why did you say you did?'

'Because you thought I did.'

'Thought you did what?'

'Went to Belvedere.'

'Oh. Maybe. Does any of that matter?'

She put a blade of grass between her teeth and brought it towards mine and we both chewed the grass until our lips met in another greeny kiss.

But it did matter, I found; it mattered a lot. The boy who went to Joey's lacked the imagination, the longing, or maybe the urgency of the boy who went to Belvedere. Or to put it another way—you have to understand I was too young to understand the dynamics then and am too distant from events to be a reliable witness now—once the pretence was gone a certain dream was deflated, like the balloons at the end of a birthday party. We met again, her bow lips held the same attraction, she even led my nervous hand towards her bra strap behind the cottages in Conquer Hill Road, but things had become ordinary somehow and she knew it. Her mother would still stick a free chocolate flake in my ice-cream cone but she was finding others to talk to behind the hedge outside.

# GREAT DENMARK STREET

MOTHERS NOTICE THINGS. My own noticed my presence in the kitchen again after school and asked me about the girl with the pink cardigan on the bike by the Bull Wall, and when I said nothing, asked me would I come swimming again. But I wanted to keep my romance and its ending to myself, and so I took to walking after school to the city centre, past the Five Lamps down Summerhill past the Gloucester Diamond to Great Denmark Street where the Belvedere boys in their grey blazers braved the abuse of the inner city kids who hung around the tenement steps. I would search their faces for one like my own and, when I didn't see one, stand back and observe the general ribaldry until one afternoon a red-haired kid whacked me from behind with a rolled-up copy of the *Beano*.

'Have you got it now?' he asked me.

'Got what?' I asked him.

'You fuckin' know what, two and six or you're dead this time,' and he swung the *Beano* towards my face again and I ducked and kicked my foot out without thinking and caught him hard between the legs. He crumpled, suddenly, and fell onto the dusty pavement.

I was learning things, I realized. First the punch, and now this. And the Belvedere boy was teaching me them, even though he wasn't there.

'Where'd you learn that, you fuckin' cunt you—'

'You hit me,' I said, rather pointlessly.

'And I'll hammer you tomorrow if you don't have it,' he said. 'Where's your uniform?'

He was rising again, getting his breath back, and I imagined the next time I wouldn't be so lucky. So I turned as calmly as I could and walked on towards Parnell Street.

It was happening again, I realized, like a clock that ticks to its own rhythm, and I walked past Walton's music shop and saw the blazers of the Belvedere boys reflected in the window above the gleaming brass of the saxophones and trumpets. And sure enough, two days later somewhere off the side streets round Mountjoy Square, I saw a figure in a grey blazer on the pavement, being given what was colloquially known as the mother and father of a hiding by the same boy with the red hair.

I grabbed the lid from a rubbish bin, came behind, and brought it down as hard as I could. There was a dull sound, almost musical, that echoed round the narrow alleyway. I felt like a boy in the Artane Boys Brass Band who had hit the cymbal just right. I watched him fall to the ground once more, howling for his mother, and as the other boy in the grey blazer looked up I found myself looking at myself once more. Not quite myself though: There was blood on his lips and his hair was a dusty mess and he was wearing, I noticed uselessly, those chisel-toed shoes with the Cuban heels that my mother would never buy me.

'You have to give as good as you get,' I said as the red-haired one stared from me to him and became gradually aware of the blood spouting from his forehead.

'It's not as bad as it looks,' I said, and threw the lid on the cement with a clatter which alarmed him even more. He began to scurry backwards down the alley like a crab, feet and heels propelling him away from us, his bum and trousers scraping on the pavement. And the Belvedere boy stared at me and wiped his bloodied mouth and smiled.

'Why did you do that?' he asked.

His accent was different. Of course it would be.

'He jumped on me the day before yesterday. He thought I was you.'

'Why?'

'Fuck knows,' I said. And I was proud of the way I said it. I was proud, inordinately, of the whole situation. My introduction to myself could not have started better.

'He thought you were me.'

'Yeah. He wanted pocket money. You didn't give it?'

'I was doing that when you . . . did the thing with the dustbin lid.'

I looked around the ground. There were coins scattered here and there, and schoolbooks. I bent to pick them up and felt him looking at me all the time. I stole a glance or two at him as I placed the coins between his fingers and put the books back in the bag. It wasn't as if the resemblance was perfect. He bit his nails and I didn't, his eyes were the same colour, his hair the same colour but a different shape, but he was me, somehow. His mouth was the same, most of all.

'Stop staring, would you,' I said as I drew him to his feet. 'You must have known this was happening.'

'What was happening?'

'Mistakes. You for me and me for you.'

'What mistakes?'

'That kid hit me with a *Beano* because he thought I was you. They threw me out of Funland because you'd been jigging the horses. You met a girl called Jean.'

'Jean.'

'Yeah. You said you'd call her and didn't. She thought I was you.'

'Jean. Over by Dollymount.'

'The Bull Wall. You should call her.'

'Why?'

'Why? I don't know. Because you said you would. After one of your games of rugby.'

'At Raheny? With St. Paul's?'

'Walk down Vernon Avenue to her shop. Tuite's. She'd like that.'

And I was about to tell him about the greeny kiss and the bra strap, but I could tell that he felt it was getting strange enough already. He walked on a bit, then stopped by Walton's musical instrument shop, with the brass trumpets gleaming in the window. And I could tell he never felt safe until he had reached it.

'Thanks,' he said, as if to break the silence. 'But he'll get me again tomorrow.'

'No, he won't,' I told him. 'He'll be afraid.'

'What's your name then?'

'My name's Kevin. I go to Joey's in Marino. You go to—'

'Belvedere.'

'I think I knew that. You take the 47a bus from Middle Abbey Street to Palmerston Park.'

'How did you know that?'

'Because I saw you on it. I followed you there.'

'That's creepy.'

'I know. Something's creepy. It's not my fault if people mistake us all the time. Hasn't it happened to you?'

'Yeah, now that you mention it.'

'Somebody says you've been somewhere you haven't been. Somebody knows you that you've never met.'

'It happens all the time.'

'Well. That's me.'

'I'm not sure I want to know you.'

'And I'm not sure I want to know you.'

But I lied. I wanted to know everything about him.

'Come on,' I said, 'I'll walk you down to the 47a. Just in case.'

'In case what?'

'In case somebody goes for you again. You still have pocket money.'

And so we walked. Down Parnell Street, down O'Connell Street to the steps by the Pillar where I met the man with the lined face who had offered me his silver cigarette case.

'You smoke, don't you?'

'Sometimes.'

'You shouldn't. Bad for you.'

'Fuck that,' he said, and I was suddenly proud of him.

'Where did you get the shoes?'

'Place in Stillorgan. Near the bowling alley.'

I had never been to either. And suddenly I was jealous. I remembered how I had wanted his life.

'What does your da do?'

'He works.'

'At what?'

'Solicitor. What does your da do?'

'How do you know I have a da?'

'You mean he's dead?'

'No.' I relented and told the truth.

'He's a bookie. My ma keeps lodgers.'

We walked in silence for awhile, him throwing glances at me every now and then, and me throwing them back. But every time our eyes met, he looked away. One of us was making the other uneasy. But I would have walked like that for ever, down O'Connell Street, across the river, and all the way to Palmerston Park.

'You have to tell me about cricket. Someday.'

'Why do I have to tell you about cricket?'

'I don't know. Thought you'd know about it.'

'Cricket. Cricket's stupid. And there's my bus.'

There was a nervousness creeping into him that made him turn. I could see he wanted to go, forget about it, and it made me sad.

'You can get another one.'

'Not for hours.'

He turned back to look at me. The streetlights were on now and it was like looking in a mirror.

'You said her name was Jean.'

'Yes. Call her.'

'Maybe I will.'

And he ran and grabbed the rail and swung on to the tail-board, and I could see him ascending the stairs, vanishing, reappearing again as he took his seat and I could see the back of his head once more as he sat down, the tufts of hair sticking out nonchalantly over the collar of his Belvedere blazer, and I felt that if we saw one another again it would be by accident or through someone else's mistake.

# ST. ANNE'S

H E MUST HAVE called her, though. Jean, with the dimples and the pink cardigan. I was coming out of Joey's after school and heard a familiar sound through the squawks of seagulls and the cries of boys playing football. It was a dull throbbing, a *putt-putt-putt*, and I thought, ah, I've got a new sound to follow me now that I've grown up a bit. And I knew who it was without having to turn. A circle of kids had already surrounded his Kawasaki.

'Knew you went to Joey's,' he said.

'Yes,' I answered. 'I knew you knew.'

And I knew something else by now, so I turned round and asked what civility demanded.

'What's your name?'

'Mucky,' he said.

'Mucky,' I replied.

'Yeah. Micky really, but with the engine oil and all, they call me Mucky.'

'And where do you go to school, Mucky?'

'I don't.'

My admiration knew no bounds then.

'Work with my da. Conway Motors. Collins Avenue.'

He gunned his bike alongside me.

'You want a lift?'

The thing was, he told me, as the wind whipped our hair and faces and he opened up the throttle around Fairview Park, that the southside boy had come back into her life. A sly return visit, in his Belvedere uniform, to the line-up outside Tuite's Sweets. And only out of obligation, he thought I should know. 'What kind of obligation?' I asked him, and he shook his head, the wind tossing his greasy hair, as if the answer was obvious. We were friends, weren't we?

'Anyway, he's from the southside, something about him's not right,' he said. 'She was better off with you, one of our own.'

'One of our own?' I echoed.

'Let me show you,' he shouted over the wind, and he twisted the handle and the bike roared off, and I saw the Bull Wall bridge approaching, figures like dark matchsticks walking up and down it, and none of them looked like her. He turned onto the bridge and I could feel the large wooden sleepers bounce underneath the wheels and he roared the bike left and carved tracks in the sand all the way to where the beach ended in a little spit of shelly water, and Portmarnock and Howth were so close across the sea you could almost touch them.

'They might be in the dunes,' he said, 'but I doubt it.'

'Why do you doubt it?'

'Because,' he said, and he grinned a little, 'he's not like you.'

'Not like me?' Meaning, he didn't chew the dune grass with her until his lips reached her mouth. And I missed her suddenly.

'Let's try the park,' he said, and he roared off again, carving parallel tracks in the sand: He was a beast in constant motion and he telescoped the distances with his wheels. And we found them in the park, walking down the long avenue hand in hand towards the ruined mansion. He slowed the bike to something like a walk, and had to use his leather boot every now and then to keep it upright.

I could see his grey Belvedere blazer and she was in her Holy Faith uniform too, matching greys. She turned and saw the bike, and I wondered did she know there were two of us on it. I saw her hand grip his, as he turned to look, and pull his body back around. I imagined him hearing the *putt-putt* of the Kawasaki and I imagined her saying, 'Ignore him. He thought he was going out with me. But he's not.'

'You want to buzz them,' Mucky said, and I said, 'Yes, why not buzz them,' and his wrist twisted towards the floor and the exhaust thundered and we tore off towards them, passing them in a flurry of wind that lifted her pleated skirt and I could see the grey stockings that curled up towards her knee. He was staring back at me staring at him, and I could see the surprise on his face that looked so much like my own. And I felt sad then: I had lost something I could have had, and somebody else had it now.

'You want to buzz them again?' Mucky asked, but I told him to keep going, so he skidded the bike sideways, down by the small river that led to the artificial pond with ducks paddling on the green slime. He parked the bike there, in the ruined Greek pagoda thing that was covered in graffiti and smelt of dogshit.

'What's the story?' he asked. 'Are you cousins?'

'No,' I told him. 'I don't know who he is. Just get mistaken for him.'

'Ah,' he said, as if it happens all the time.

He began throwing stones at the ducks.

'Look at them,' he said. 'They all look the same.'

And the ducks were rising now, trailing ripples in the water, exposing their coloured wings. Soon there was just a pool of green slime, and no ducks left.

'We could sort him out,' he said, 'if you want.'

'No,' I said. 'Leave him to it.'

'Yeah. She'll get rid of him too.'

He drove me back home, and if it seemed for a moment that we had both made a friend, there was something in the configuration of things that decided differently.

The next time I saw him he had her on the back. She was wearing a pair of high white boots and both of her hands curled round the front of his leather jacket. I was walking on the beach at Dollymount Strand while my mother was swimming when they buzzed me, and he waved a hand as the Kawasaki carved its tracks towards the dunes at the other end.

# DREAMLAND

THE VAMPIRE MEETS me in my sleep. When my head hits the pillow he has taken over, a group of them, all lodgers in different rooms and my mother rattling her keys, collecting rent in whatever coin they can pay. Mrs. Considine visits from next door, her cane tap-tapping up the stairs as she brings the comestibles she bought for them in Colly's shop. Orange juice, batch bread, and black pudding. Elvis's voice drifts through the windows from the Fairview cinema, *oh how I love to kiss my little hula miss.* And Bram Stoker follows, dreaming of Henry Irving. They tick and tock, these creatures, they stroke and they hiss. And I have questions for them all.

Why, of all the lodgers that passed through, did Tommy the Clock remain the longest?

Simple, says the caped one—Stoker, or was it Irving? They were second cousins.

Not lovers?

Lovers, of course. One Saturday, when your father took you to Fairyhouse, on the couch downstairs—

A chorus of clocks.

One evening when the gasworks across the river exploded.

He wouldn't remember.

But I do. Three in the morning. The whole seafront on fire.

People, on the streets in their night attire. Leads to—what's the word—concupiscence.

The father was away.

Always away.

Why the clocks?

They are, said Stoker sonorously, something to do with time.

Why the cloak?

Irving wrapped it round himself. A little theatrically, some thought.

And I saw green eyes glistening from a tiny clock face.

You should sell this place.

And the dream had a smell. Crushed cigarettes, old popcorn, and rancid butter.

Why should I sell this place?

Because, he said, you should cover your tracks. That business in Manhattan.

A long time ago, and besides, the wench is dead.

That's a quote, he said. *The Jew of Malta.*

Yes, I said. I designed a set for it once.

And the dream had another smell then. A musty cellar, the sediment of old wine. Blood. A perfume, made of whale oil.

# TICKNOCK

*I*NCOMING, THE VAMPIRE said next morning, and my phone was ringing. He was gone by the time I had fully woken, reached for the button, and heard your voice. He's afraid of you, I remember thinking, they don't like mothers. Mothers, daughters, sunlight. And there was sunlight streaming through the window too.

'Can I talk to you?' you said.

'Of course. I'm here, listening.'

'No,' you said. 'I mean talk, properly.'

'You mean meet.'

'I suppose.'

'I was thinking of going to Deansgrange again.'

So soon? I wondered. I wasn't sure if I could take it. No more grief.

'The doctor gave me a Xanax for the funeral. I don't remember much.'

You remember me, I thought.

'And I think I need to remember.'

'Certainly.'

You should. And I should, too.

'You'll remember the house, then.'

'Your mother's house?'

'Can you pick me up?'

I didn't answer. And you must have heard my hesitation, because after a pause you said:

'Call me when you're close. I'll be at the gate.'

I TOOK THE M50 out to the new developments around Sandyford and got off at some exit that I hoped was near Ticknock. I passed the blue wooden church and remembered I was meant to call. So I punched in *Daughter* and told you I was near and drove around in circles to give you time to walk down the avenue to the iron-wrought gate. I saw you then, a little speck in the distance walking through the beech trees, your arms wrapped round Toby the dog.

'You don't mind him?' you said as I drew alongside and opened the door.

'Hey, Toby,' I said, proud I could remember his name.

You placed him in the rear seat and toyed with the lead from the front.

'Should we get flowers?' I asked.

'You think?'

'People tend graves. I always found it touching. Never knew why.'

'Why you found it touching?'

'Why they did it, too. The dead don't notice.'

'What if they do?'

'Then I'm truly doomed.'

And for some reason you laughed.

'My father's buried with my mother. Out by Howth. I've never been back.'

'I'll go with you if you want.'

'Why would you do that?'

'I don't know. Feel like I could happily visit graves for the rest of my life.'

'Are you depressed?'

'No. I said "happily," didn't I?'

And it was my turn to laugh.

'I'd be a happy mourner. What kind of flowers, do you think?'

And you turned to me, and there couldn't have been a happier mourner just then.

'Lilies. Has to be lilies.'

There was a Texaco garage by the turn-off to Deansgrange. Of course they would sell flowers, I thought, like a hospital newsagents. I pulled in but we found no white lilies, had to make do with a bunch of daffodils and roses.

'He would have liked the roses,' I said.

'Why?'

There was a reason, but I couldn't tell. I remembered walking up the steps of a brownstone in Manhattan, carrying red roses. The rose-coloured sandstone. The pink dawn. The red of it all. The event that only the vampire knew. I blocked the very thought of it. There would be a time to tell, I knew. But not now, not now.

'Just,' I went on. 'Your father. A born romantic.'

'Was he?'

'Didn't you think?'

'I didn't know him that way.'

'Read his books.'

'I never could.'

'Why not?'

'I just couldn't read all that shite. The past, priest-ridden Ireland, nostalgia, bachelors, spinsters. Why couldn't he write about what he knew?'

'Maybe he did know it.'

'His granny knew it.'

And I had to laugh at this.

'No, I mean that. He wrote about a world he imagined his granny knew.'

And you looked upset then and the dog made you stumble, and you took my arm for a moment to steady yourself.

There was another funeral, gathered at another grave. The same gravediggers by the same JCB, smoking while they waited for the end of another spectacle of grief. You didn't seem to notice, absorbed as you were in a critique of your father's oeuvre.

'Summers in Rosses Point, dances in the tennis club, that shite about the war of independence.'

'Was it shite?'

'Didn't you think so?'

'He said to me once, "We have careers now. It used to be Irish writers succeeded or failed. Now we have careers."'

'Anyway I didn't know him. Only read him.'

'So you lied earlier. You said you didn't.'

'Yes, I lied. I took the books up, put them down again. I wanted something to know, to hold on to.'

'You didn't find it?'

'No.'

'So he failed. The judgment he valued most. It never came.'

'Whose judgment was that?'

Yours, perhaps, I thought. But I didn't say it.

'Maybe his own. He said to me near the end that he'd only led half a life.'

And that makes two of us. Again, I only thought it.

'Anyway, where is it?'

We were both lost, had no map to this graveyard. There were lines of yew trees, spreading at right angles, to forests of gravestones. But the dog had a map. The dog knew. He found his way to the newly minted marble slab, where strips of newly laid grass had replaced the Astroturf. The mound of wreaths were already discoloured, petals falling off the flowers.

I was shocked once more at how final it all was. And you stood there, the dog's leash still curled round your left hand and wrist.

Then you whispered something.

'What did you say?'

'I told him I could write a book.'

'I live next door to Bram Stoker.'

This was apropos of nothing. But I had nothing else to say.

'It's a song, silly.'

'What's your book about?'

'I can only tell him.'

'Tell me.'

'Is that the same?'

'No, but—'

Almost, I thought.

'About a daughter. Who never knew her father. And she's pregnant.'

I took a breath. Mothers and daughters. The vampire avoided them both.

'And did he know?'

'How could he?'

'Of course.'

'I hardly knew.'

'And your mother?'

'She has enough to deal with.'

'Does she know the father?'

'He's not worth knowing. The dead can't speak, I know. But don't they communicate?'

Never when you want them to, I wanted to say. But I waited in silence, to see if you would find this out for yourself.

'Why am I telling you this?'

'You have to tell somebody.'

'You're right.'

You knelt down and for a moment I thought you were about to pray, but the dog read your gesture better than I did.

'Maybe Toby knows.'

'But he can't speak. Isn't it all unbearably . . . Irish . . . in some horrible way . . .'

'You mean, like his books.'

'Oh my God. I suppose. Can we walk back now?'

'What about the flowers?'

'The flowers. Daddy, how could I?'

And you laid them down beside the browning wreaths.

'So there,' you said, and rose to your full height from your crouching position. Your legs must be strong. Athletic.

You clipped the leash to the dog's collar and turned, began to walk back. You looped your hand through the crook of my elbow as if you had been my daughter, not his, and I felt all of the comfort he should have felt, all the years of your childhood.

The dog drew us back towards my car, his guiding system intact, his instincts impeccable.

'I'm sorry. I had to tell someone. I thought I was telling him. But you heard and now I've told you. And it's a burden, knowing someone's secret, isn't it?'

'Maybe a privilege.'

'Oh, goody,' you said and your elbow crooked on top of mine. 'So I can share all of my confusions with you . . .'

'Only if you are . . . confused . . .'

'Of course. Isn't that the point of pregnancy? To be confused?'

'I thought the point was to have a child?'

'Or not . . .'

'Oh,' I said. 'I see.' No more deaths, I thought. I've been party to enough of them.

'Have you told the father?'

'I will. But I'll tell him too late to have any influence . . . on what I have decided . . .'

'Is he that awful?'

'He had a nice, hairless chest,' you said.

We were passing the other funeral now and their time of burial had ended and they were crying their way back to their parked cars. I hoped that grief was similar to the other emotions. That it would end, the way happiness did. Or laughter.

'But can I talk to you again?'

'I would like that.'

'"I would like that." How properly said.'

'What's the father's name?'

'He's an auctioneer.'

As if they didn't have names, I thought. Hairless chest. Undeserving father. He would have to be an auctioneer.

'He'll find out. He has offices in Dawson Street.'

You said this as if you meant, because he has offices in Dawson Street, he will find out. Non-Socratic logic.

'How?'

'They find out everything. Who owns what. Who left what to who. What is the way to that old widow's heart who's sitting on the pile out on Vico Road.'

You turned to me, eyes bright.

'I got pregnant there.'

'Vico Road?'

'He was examining the house of someone recently deceased. Someone needed a guide price. He asked me to come with him. We walked through those dead rooms. The sea outside, a silvery swell. There was a couch by a grand window. There was no one to disturb us. Maybe ghosts. I'm not sure I believe. The windows rattled and the sea moaned outside. I used an old lace doily to clean myself.'

I needed none of this information, but you must have needed to tell me.

'Does that make me bad?'

I shook my head.

'Soiled at least? Like the doily?'

'You should tell your mother,' I said, if not to change the conversation, to move to another facet of it.

'I will. When Dr. Lyon changes her prescription. She can't take too much reality at the moment.'

We had reached my car. The other mourners had gone. I opened the front door and the dog bounded in, as if his place in the back seat was now part of his history.

'And neither can I.'

# THE SOUTH PIER

OMETHING WAS DIFFERENT as you walked through the iron-wrought gates and up the avenue of beech trees. The faint smell of salted popcorn and cigarette ash alerted me to a change of mood, if not a presence. A cloud was crossing the sun and large unruly shadows followed you until you turned the corner to the house. Then the sun came out again but the mood persisted. I drove down through Dun Laoghaire to find my way back and parked my car where the old baths used to be. The pier had been transformed with a new smooth surface to cover the old granite blocks. There was an ice-cream van, a burger van, a cappuccino van, and the pencil-like shadows of crowds of people walking to the lighthouse at the end.

I walked with them, as crowds have that effect on me, I want to do what they do, to journey towards some point of revelation, which of course never comes. In this case it was an open space where the sea wall ended, where the seaweed clung to the granite blocks, appearing and disappearing in the ocean's swell. There was an old man playing the tenor banjo in the Neapolitan style, *Come Back to Sorrento* plucked in tremolo with an Irish twang. Across the bay from us were the gantries of the North Wall. The walkers circled round here, uncertain for a moment, like migratory birds, their journey ended, not knowing what to do. Then they regained their momentum and began the walk back.

There were clubs and dance halls dotting the city in my youth, Sound City on Burgh Quay, the Number Five in Harcourt Street, the Blind in Drumcondra, the Go Go in Sackville Place, odd furtive places that mostly played the mod bands of the time, the Animals, Manfred Mann, Booker T. and the MGs. My mother had long relented on the Cuban heels, I had a pair of boots with chisel toes and a suede waistcoat I had bought somewhere and a mohair jacket and had begun to wander from the north-side clubs to the city centre, and one Friday evening took the 45a bus to the Overend on the main street of Dun Laoghaire where my accent might betray me. I got past the bouncer though and made it into the dim, purple-lit hall that would blaze every now and then with strobes. There were couples lurching, youths leaning on the dimly lit walls, girls in discreet groups, and somewhere, down the end of the hall, a DJ with a turntable. He lifted the needle from one record and placed it with an amplified bump on another and *Green Onions* sounded out. And it must have been ladies' choice, because a young girl in black stockings and a purple blouse and very high heels crossed the hall and took my hand and moved her body close to me and asked, 'How've you been?'

'Well,' I said, 'and how have you been?'

She pouted her mouth in answer and moved her body closer, and I could feel her thin hips and her small breasts and I placed my fingers on the satiny fabric that covered her thin ribs. She felt she knew me and it was happening again. And then the slow strobes came on and I tried to catch a glance at the purple lipstick on her mouth and the

Hammond organ of *Green Onions* kept up its relentless skipped beat and she misinterpreted my glance and said, 'Oh go on then, Gerald,' and brushed her mouth on mine. It was a sideways kiss, the corners of our mouths touching for a full bar of the Hammond organ until the beat skipped again and she withdrew, as if that was enough of that, but she moved her body even closer to mine. And I was the other boy again and his name was Gerald and my name for the moment would be Gerald too.

'Say my name,' she whispered, as her thin hips swayed against mine.

'You say it.'

'You've forgotten it already, haven't you?'

And she smiled, as if she expected the same.

'Donna.'

'Okay. Donna.'

'Too hot in here, isn't it, Gerald?'

And Gerald agreed it was too hot and suggested a walk out by the pier.

'Certainly. You like the pier, don't you?'

'No more than you.'

'You remember the pier. Just remember my name next time.'

I agreed I would.

WE GOT OUR coats from the coat check and hers was a bumfreezer like mine, navy blue—with the black stockings and the high heels it was quite a combination. And we walked down by the pier then and it was a forest of tapping masts as the wind was coming up, and I learned that she had left school early, the Holy Child in Sallynoggin, to take up a job in a carpet factory on Wicklow Street and when I expressed surprise she said, 'It's 1964, not 1864, you know.' And I wondered, as I walked with her, how my Gerald compared to his: was mine more authentic, more composed, did his fingers play with hers the way mine did, clasping and unclasping and squeezing and unsqueezing her long purple nails?

We reached the end of the pier, by the lighthouse, where the gantries of the North Wall gleamed yellow across the water and I led her back on the other side of the sea wall where there was a smell of seaweed and the granite blocks sloped at an angle towards the water.

'I wondered, you know, would I ever meet you again.'

'So did I.'

'Liar.'

And she was right, I was a liar. But I kept going.

'I've been studying, you know—'

'I know. You told me. Your father.'

'Yeah.'

'Doesn't approve. Of dance halls and things. I went back twice. Never saw you there . . . So,' she said, and she leaned back against the sloping wall, 'why did they let you out this time?'

'They're away.'

'Oh goody. Can we go there, to that big house you told me about in—'

'Palmerston Park.'

'Yeah. Wherever that is.'

'Not far from here.'

'This is Dun Laoghaire. Everywhere's far from here.'

'Suppose it is.'

I was looking across the water towards the lights of Bray in the distance. A train was trundling towards it. I leant back on the sloping granite wall and suddenly felt no desire for her whatsoever, which is maybe why when she turned her face to me and found my lips again, I slipped my hand underneath her blouse and felt the thin bumps of her spine and followed them up to where the clasp of her bra was. She shifted imperceptibly as I did this and the clasp popped open.

'Now why have you never done that before?' she whispered, with her teeth at my earlobe, and she turned her body towards me so I could open the buttons of her purple blouse.

'There,' she said, when the first three were open and the black lace of her brassiere showed against her pale skin.

'Oh come on,' she said, 'I'll do the rest,' and she unbuttoned the others rapidly, wiggled her body so the bra fell downwards to reveal two thin breasts, nipples dark against them.

'Here,' she said, and she turned her bum towards me, took both of my hands and placed them beneath the lace.

'Work away there,' she said. 'Just don't make me wet.'

'I'm a Belvedere boy,' I said.

'I know,' she said. 'You don't do things like that.'

I put my teeth on her neck and she held her hands over mine and massaged them against her nipples and she said, 'No more than that now, no more than that, Gerald,' but she noticed something wrong then. She felt her neck wet and turned.

'What's wrong?'

She reached a hand out to touch my cheeks.

'You're crying.'

I turned my face away to the granite.

'You a weirdo, Gerald? You a strange one? Why are you crying?'

'I don't know.'

But I did. I was crying because I was Kevin, not Gerald.

'Come on, crybaby. Tell me.'

'I can't. It's just . . . something.'

I turned and walked back towards the light. Down the dark sloping rocks with the smell of seaweed. She must have buttoned herself quickly, because I heard her heels then behind me.

'You going to ask me out then, crybaby?'

And the tears had stopped by then. I wiped both cheeks with my hands.

'Yes. Where?'

'Next Saturday. By the Blackrock Baths.'

HE WAS JOHN the Baptist to my Jesus, he was preparing the way. I thought about her on the bus home and wondered why the tears and wondered, did I cry because I didn't really like her very much? And then I realized, no, the tears came because I felt, I suspected anyway, she didn't really like me. The one she liked was him. How can you mistake someone, yet move your body against him in that way? I didn't know but I knew it happened. The body did its thing, it carried on regardless whether you liked or didn't like.

He was preparing the way. He would prepare the way for many years, map out the roads that I would take. He imagined the ones I took; I read about the ones he took. And there was one last road that he should have taken, which I took in his place. I walked down it with his ghost walking beside me; only the vampire knew where it led.

MY FATHER WAS up when I got back, pouring a drop of whiskey into his freshly brewed tea.

'Are you winning?' I said to him—a phrase I hated, but he used it and I knew it broke the ice.

'At Fairyhouse on Saturday, I'll be on the course. Come and help me with the odds.'

'I can't,' I told him, 'I've got to meet someone.' And I realized, almost to my surprise, that I would meet her again.

'You liked to go once,' he said and sounded almost hurt.

'Is Mam in bed?' I asked, to change the subject maybe, and maybe because I knew an outright refusal would hurt him even more.

'Yes,' he said. 'She likes her sleep. No more than you.'

'And you don't.'

It wasn't a question. I already knew the answer.

'Time enough to sleep when you're dead.'

I moved towards the door, the girl on my mind.

'Goodnight.'

'Take her swimming in the morning, she'd like that.'

I nodded. I knew she would and resolved to do that.

I thought of the girl again in bed, long swathes of her and tiny whorls of ice cream squeezed into miniature cones. We were out for the day in a tiny dream, we were tiny and the pier was tiny and the miniature ice-cream van took my miniature coins and I placed my hand around her back as she licked her miniature cone, but my hand was too large somehow, could hardly fit under her purple blouse which spoiled the dream and I woke up. The house was creaking with the sounds of lodgers shifting in their beds above me, my mother and father among those sounds, I presumed, and all the creaks combined made up a kind of symphony of sleeping.

The sense of that vampire was back, though I long knew by now he was fictitious: It had been some years since I had seen the Technicolor one with Christopher Lee—*Brides of Dracula*, I think it was called. But there was the sense of something still awake in this house of sleeping strangers, something wide-eyed and observant that never slept. And it took some time for me to realize, in the creaking darkness, that this someone was me. There was always a hard core of alertness in me, even when I slept. I would wake up in the morning, eyes open, and aware already as if the night's interregnum had been a deceit, a pretence of sleep, a wafer-thin wall of oblivion that barely interrupted this relentless, bright, never-ending thing. Awakeness. The vampire was me, observing myself when I slept, observing my thoughts as they spooled inside my head, my reactions as I thought my thoughts, and there was nothing in me that was spontaneous, sui generis, unobserved. And I envied him then in the other house. I wondered did he sleep better, was I perhaps a dream he was having and within that dream was I condemned to be always awake? And I must have fallen asleep then because the next thing I remember is my mother singing that song of hers on the way down the stairs. *Pale hands I loved beside the Shalimar . . .*

She was making tea when I got down there and above her, all around her, were the sounds of her disordered souls beginning their day. I knew my father wouldn't wake for another hour at least and remembered my promise to go swimming with her.

'You sound happy,' I said.

'Is that unusual?' she asked. 'That's sad.'

'I didn't mean that.'

'It's summer,' she said, 'the sun's shining. I have you. What more could a woman want?'

'What's the tide like?' I asked.

'It'll be in at ten. Good for the next three hours.'

'Okay then.'

And I knew she knew I would go with her and I thought, maybe that's what's making her happy. I felt sad for a bit; if that was all it took, such a simple thing, why didn't I make her happy all the time? Because the ocean was cold was the answer, because a time comes when you go off with friends, because, because, because. There were so many reasons, but the signs of her pleasure were so obvious, she was like Snow White in the morning with the birds flying through the dwarves' cottage, I wished I had gone swimming with her every freezing winter morning, even when the ice covered the concrete steps.

'I'm thinking of getting a job,' I told her.

'That all sounds good and adult. What kind of job?'

'For the summer. Out in the market gardens round Portrane.'

'A farm?'

'A boy in my class works there.'

Large ears, a red face, bog accent. He traveled in by train each morning.

'So. Everything's different.'

'Must be.'

'Do you want to try somewhere different? For a swim?'

'Where?'

'Sutton. The Hole in the Wall.'

AND I HAVE to get the details right here, Emily. It was the last time I would swim with her. There was a bus we had to take, by the tulip beds at Fairview Park, which took us out to the Sutton House Hotel. There was a beach there, on a round spit of land, which we couldn't access so we had to walk down this small sandy lane by the back lawns of houses which faced the sea. They seemed to have been dropped by some giant aeroplane from Norway or Cape Cod, these houses, made of peeling painted wood, with large verandas. Once more I was in a different world, but now she was there beside me. And the sandy lane did lead to what the name implied, a small broken wall with a hole in it. A beach beyond.

She had her towel rolled neatly round her bathing suit. I had mine draped over my neck and was swinging my togs by the cord like a lasso. It was impossible not to share her happiness, though I had a sense of how fragile it was. If it was dependent on me, my youth, my person, it was very fragile indeed since I wasn't even sure what a person was or whether I would ever fully become one. She was humming that song again that had nothing to do with the summer, everything to do with hands that were pale and a river that was cold. But I had that vampire awareness now where every detail would etch itself on my brain and I let them all soak in. The brown sand through the broken wall and the mound of Ireland's Eye beyond it with the passage of water in between, so shallow it seemed you could walk to it.

'Ireland's Eye is a bird sanctuary,' she told me, when she had finished with her song. Somewhere out of sight to our left was the place we had come from, Dollymount Strand. 'I wonder,' she said, 'will I get my depth,' and then we talked about girls, the one I'd met with the pink cardigan and the bicycle, others I'd met since then, the way they could wrap boys round their little fingers if they wanted to. I mentioned I had met one, all the way over in Dun Laoghaire, called Donna and she said, 'That's a bit of a foreigner.'

'Not really,' I said, 'just a bus ride.'

'Oh we're all grown up now, are we?'

'Maybe,' I said, and wondered how much I could tell her. And I realized, with a kind of ache, that I could tell her none of it. Of the sense I had there was another home out there, the boy like me I'd been confused with twice now, two girls, many kisses, and probably more on the way. That I only appeared to be the one she thought I was, the one who made her sing the song about pale hands and the Shalimar; in fact the reality was quite different and in fact I had no idea what or who the reality was. Was there another mother out there, I wondered, more elegant than her, with less fragility, who found a way of expressing her happiness without singing long dead songs?

We had reached the water's edge now. There was a fishing boat passing the hump of the island and there were no bathing shelters here, so we undressed on the fresh white sand and I wondered could those people in cars see us, but I didn't care at all. There were two ladies down the beach from us, black pear-like shapes with large white thighs beneath and bulging veins. They walked slowly in and did find their depth because they were soon making the same circles in the water that enormous tadpoles would. She walked towards the sea against the dark shoulder of Ireland's Eye in her green swimsuit, a lavender cap covering her ears, and in the curve of her waist, the twine of her legs, from behind she looked like a girl my age. And I walked after her across the warm sand into the cold water and realized that even if there was another mother out there, in a larger house where I would dream better dreams, I wouldn't have wanted her. I would have taken the house, maybe, like a captive castle but would have taken this fairy queen with me.

# BLACKROCK BATHS

I STOOD FOR A long time there, on the newly made pier. The banjo plucker changed his tune from *Come Back to Sorrento* to *She Moved Through the Fair* and somehow managed to make it sound the same. The new ferry was coming in, a Swedish hovercraft thing that raised freak waves and drowned a swimmer every year or so. I looked across at the North Wall and wondered was the old B&I still working, leaving that wake with its undertow.

I walked back then, wondering why structures that gouged into the water always reminded me of the transitory nature of things. Piers, harbours, bulwarks, bridges. There were silhouettes walking towards me, swinging their arms grotesquely, the way the health magazines told them to. But decay was coming, whether they liked it or not. I could see the rusting frame of the Blackrock Baths across from the old North Pier. I had lost my virginity there, and hers. His would be lost much later.

The baths were alive and crowded then, girls my age quivering around the ladder of the high stone diving board as they waited for the boys to plunge in. I had taken the train there and was waiting in the alleyway outside, my towel hanging round my neck, and was still swinging my bathing togs from the string I had wound round my finger like a swivel. I could see the boys jump and dive, take to the air, and then sail downwards, disappearing from sight below the concrete wall, and I had to imagine them splash. I heard a whistle then which I knew only a girl could make and turned and saw her high above the train tracks, walking over the bridge from the station. She was wearing a polka-dotted dress which blew up when the train went underneath but she didn't seem to mind. She had sandals on with heels that clacked and echoed as she came down the iron steps.

'You going swimmin'?' she asked.

'Yeah,' I said. 'You said meet at the baths.'

'Said nothin' about swimmin',' she said. 'I hate the water.'

'Okay,' I said and she came towards me, all dazzling blue and white dots.

'Come on,' she said, 'we'll walk along the tracks. I know a place.'

She slipped her arm through mine and pulled it close to her thin breast.

'You're not gonna cry on me now, are you?'

The strange embarrassment I felt. For a moment I was tempted to tell her the truth. But the truth didn't matter now. I just was whoever she thought I was.

'I like you but I hate crying.'

'No, no crying.'

'Good. Only smiles and . . . ice cream maybe . . .'

'You want one?'

We were heading away from the station, the baths, between the low concrete walls, and the possibility of ice creams would soon be gone.

'Not now,' she said. 'Maybe later.'

'If we were going out together now,' she said, 'not that we are, but if we were, you'd have to meet my brothers.'

'How many do you have?'

'Three. Domo, Tommy, Padraic. They all have jobs in Guinness's.'

'Lucky bastards.'

I said it because I thought it would sound right. But when it came out, it sounded kind of wrong.

'You know Guinness's?'

'I know the pool.'

And I did. It was the envy of the city, north and south, and if you had a friend who had a father who worked there, you could have a swim.

'Are we not going out together?'

'Dunno. Are we? Met you twice in the Overend, two walks along the pier, and now this.'

'You're working, aren't you?'

'Yep. I can buy you an ice cream if you're good.'

'How can I be good?'

'If you promise not to cry again.'

'Stop saying that, please. There was a reason.'

'What was the reason?'

'There was a boy I knew.'

'Friend of yours?'

'Sort of. I took his girlfriend.'

'You took her, like you'd take his bike?'

'Kind of.'

'She must have liked you better.'

'I suppose she did. And it made me kind of sad.'

'No crying now—'

'No. But when I had her, I didn't want her anymore.'

'That's not sad. That's just manky.'

'I know.'

'Is that what you're like?'

'I don't know.'

''Cause if you're like that, I'm not sure I'll go out with you.'

'I'm worse than that.'

'Worse?'

She said it with false alarm and pressed her arm with my arm closer to her breast. The alleyway had given way now to a walkway, with the train tracks to one side and the sand and sea to the other. And the air no longer smelt of dogshit.

'We'll see,' she said, and then, as if to change the subject, 'Man killed himself on those tracks a few months ago.'

'Who?'

'Famous man. Brainbox. Scientist, or something. Across from the bird sanctuary. They were picking up bits of blood and hair for days.'

I could hear the cry of waders now, and saw the low swampy expanse of green, brown, and silver pools dotted among it. A bird with a long beak and delicate legs. A curlew.

'Was he depressed?'

'Mental, more like it. Here. Give us your towel.'

There was a space of green scutch grass, a few mounds of dune, between the concrete walkway and the train tracks. I gave her the towel and she flattened out the space there for us. She did it like a serving maid in the Bible preparing a bed for an apostle. There is one who will prepare the way. She seemed to be following a precise set of instructions, handed down to her by generations of practice. Smooth away the sand here. Lay the towel over the grasses. And then—

'Bob's your uncle,' she said. 'Come on, sit down.'

I stayed standing above her.

'You're blocking the light. Sit down.'

So I sat. I broke off a piece of sea grass and placed it between my teeth.

'I've read about how far girls go.'

'Where?'

'*Mandy*, *Judy*. My brothers told me only go so far.'

'How far?'

I turned to her and moved my head so the end of the sea grass brushed off her lips.

'You've read that stuff too?'

'Some of it.'

I had read. A lot of it.

'That tickles.'

'I know. Grass is good for you. You can eat it.'

The broad bit of the grass end was between her lips. She opened them and gripped it with her teeth. I remembered another greeny kiss by another set of dunes, around Dollymount on the northside, but I was on the southside now and wondered did they do things differently here.

And the long blade drew our lips together and I found things weren't that different after all. I imagined him, that other one who had prepared the way, whispering in my ear, 'Be gentle,' and it was not that I wasn't gentle with her. I had only read about it, never done it, I didn't know how not to be gentle with her. But when I heard the curlew or was it the lark begin his ascending warble over the train tracks I realized I had decided to be conclusive with her. This was to be no awkward fumble on the towel above the sand and grasses, no fingers clutching underneath that bra to find and make pronged that nipple, this would be the real thing, the big thing.

And of course I didn't know what to do but when my knowledge of what to do floundered I thought I would let the imagined him take over. In fact, as I was to discover later, he was far more innocent than I, but that afternoon that didn't matter, I was enlivened by him, allowed myself to be the part of him he didn't dare think of, that I didn't dare think of, the parts of me that caused those wet sheets around my legs in the small of the morning, the parts of me that lived in his shadow, in dreams.

So I pulled the bra down, under her polka-dotted dress, until one breast was exposed, then the other, and she expected this, having read about it in *Mandy* and *Judy*. I applied my tongue to them as my other hand felt for the elastic round her knickers, the lower half of the polka-dotted fabric round her hips now. I brought my mouth downwards and found the white flesh of her thin left hip indented with the scutch grass she was lying on now since my towel was too small for both of us, and I would have done what I had only read about, pulled the knickers down with my teeth and forced her legs open with my chin, used my tongue to open the soft, fish-smelling tuft of hair between them. But that would have been too alarming, was probably not mentioned in *Mandy* or *Judy*, would have caused her to cry out and the sound might have caught the attention of the swimmers on the other side of the concrete wall.

So I brought my lips back to hers, coward that I was, and allowed the large thing to press against her tuft of hair and gradually insert itself. Now, I thought, what will your brothers think; but there were soft sounds coming from her, not language, but sounds of definite compliance coming from somewhere inside her, and the cries gradually became more urgent like cries of pain until my fishy hand clamped over her mouth and stilled even them and it was slowly over in a loud warm rush and I could hear the sounds of children splashing in the water on the other side.

The lark or the curlew had reached its full height, the trills were distant, way above and drifting leftward.

'You pig,' she said.

I know, I thought. I am the pig that fouls another's trough.

But what I said was, 'I'm sorry.'

'Why?' she asked tonelessly. 'We're both pigs. I'm not sorry. I knew I'd do it with you.'

'When?'

'The first time I met you. Or the second.'

'Which was it?'

'It was the second. You'd come back to look for me. That was important.'

She felt between her legs and gave a little sigh, like the lark or the curlew above us, barely a whisper now it was so far away.

'I'm all wet,' she said.

'Let me wipe you.'

'With what?'

'With grass. With the towel.'

'Fuck off,' she said. 'I can dry myself.'

And as she did so, she asked:

'What will you do if I'm pregnant?'

'Vanish.'

'I know where you live. My brothers'd find you. They'd make you do the right thing.'

'Okay.'

'But I'd never marry you.'

'No?'

'No. You don't do it like that with someone you marry.'

'How do you do it with someone you marry?'

'I don't know,' she said and she had straightened herself enough so she got to her feet. 'You don't do it like that.'

But she took my arm anyway, even though she wouldn't marry me, as we walked back through the alleyway that smelt of dogshit, and when we were back out in the station she bought me an ice cream.

I TOOK THE train back in an odd dream. The seats were like cinema seats, wine coloured and dusty, and the seascape flashed by through the windows as if on a bright screen, not quite outside. In the dark arches of the bridges and the shadows the houses cast I saw, or imagined I saw, the outline of a man with a black beret. He was neither happy nor sad, he didn't smile or frown. He just was. Then the city encroached and it was all shadow until we pulled over Butt Bridge and the river snaked away in a ribbon of hot white and it was dark again coming up to Amiens Street Station where I got off and walked down the back streets of East Wall, across the Tolka bridge to Fairview Park where the Crescent sat with a beam of bright sunlight all to itself.

WHEN I GOT inside the kitchen my mother was standing by the table crying.

'What's wrong?' I asked her and heard another sound behind me.

Tommy the Clock was making her a cup of tea.

'Hush,' he said, 'maybe now's not the time—'

'Your father lost the shop,' she said. 'We'll have to take more lodgers.'

'Or get those mangy boggers to pay—'

'Shush, Tommy.'

'I'm a Meath man meself,' he said, apropos of nothing.

'He'll be away a lot,' she went on. 'He'll have to do the courses.'

'If he keeps his licence.'

'He'll keep his licence, Tommy, he paid his debts—'

'You hope—'

'Remember that summer job you told me about?'

'Yes,' I told her. 'Market gardening, out in Donabate.'

'You might have to take it, Kevin.'

'What?' I said.

I didn't recognize my name.

'She said you'll need a job, son,' and he put the steaming tea on the table before her.

It was strange. Everything was changing. Strangest of all was to be called Kevin again. I had so enjoyed being called Gerry I almost told her it all. But that would have overwhelmed her. She had enough to deal with, it seemed, with my father's lassitude. With Tommy the Clockmaker's solicitude. He had his hand on her shoulder as she sipped his tea.

My father came home late, full of whiskey and spilt secrets. He'd taken too many bets on the Cheltenham Gold and what with the margins and the rents the way they were he'd had to let the shop go and he'd be back to course betting, dragging his van and his boards and his chalks from Leopardstown, Fairyhouse, Punchestown to Listowel, Tralee, Galway, and the summer Strand races up and down the coast wherever there was a mile or so of sandy beach. He'd take me with him if he could, and I remembered the holidays I'd gone with him and enjoyed the arcane language, the hieroglyphic fingers of the tic-tac men, the fresh smell of horse sweat in the winners' enclosure, the arcs of spray the ponies' hooves raised in the pools left by the tide.

'But,' he said, 'but—' And I felt there was a further secret here he wasn't telling.

'But there'd be no money for two,' he said. 'Your mother said something about a job in Donabate.'

'I'll find out about it,' I told him. He fell down in the sofa and lit a cigarette.

'And at the end of the summer,' he said, 'we'll see how it goes.'

'What do you mean?' I asked him. The cigarette smoke drifted towards the window as if to hide something.

'Times are hard,' he said. 'Might have to stretch the net. Aintree, Royal Ascot, Cheltenham.'

'We'll be leaving?' I asked him.

'No. Not youse,' he said. 'Could never afford that.'

And he turned to me and, in a rare show of intimacy, tousled my hair.

'He's growing up, eh? My little Kev.'

And maybe I was.

# GRAND CANAL DOCK

I DROVE BACK THEN, Emily, through the new city that was growing up round Grand Canal Dock. I could have been in Potsdammerplatz with all of the cranes that were decorating the skyline. There were new trains, new train stations, and new bridges decorating the brown waters of the Liffey. I had read somewhere that cities retain their traditional functions, no matter what degradations modernity inflicts upon them. Prostitutes still cling to the fringes of the streets that were rebuilt around them. Howth still slumbers to the north of Dublin Bay and Bray to the south, like the giant paws of some age-old sleeping sphinx. And this city will always be split in two, by the very fact of that river that cuts like a knife through its middle.

I thought of circus ladies, an old nun in a room like an army barracks, grey November daylight seeping through the windows, crucifixes on the walls. I was innocent then, and he must have been too, more innocent than me, I'm sure. I was committing his transgressions for him.

My father had a woman somewhere in England, I worked out that in retrospect, though the sleeping part of me probably knew it then. Something to do with blonde hair and pale ale and the pier at Southend and Kempton Park races. I was to take his place, as a breadwinner of kinds, and it freed me for awhile. I could enter the only persona I ever really felt secure in, the one that looked after her.

# DONABATE

S O I TOOK a job a few days after my new girl said she wouldn't marry me. She after all already had one, and I'd told my mother I would. I took a train out to Donabate, feeling all adult and alone among a bunch of schoolgirls going blackberry picking, walked through the market gardening fields and greenhouses of St. Margaret's, up the long lane to the farmhouse where my classmate with the jug-red ears said he worked.

He didn't so much work there as run the place. His father owned the farm, his brother ran the tractors and hay balers, and he ran us, whatever day labourers could stand the work. When a crop reached harvest time he would hire the mental patients from Portrane, arrange them in long rows above the ridged fields, and sit above them on a horse, with a loaded shotgun in the crook of his arm. He would fire it every now and then at the crows that flapped down to pick the barley, and a low moan of panic would pulsate through the asylum pickers, which seemed to please him as much as the crows he hit.

I worked the tractors and the hay balers with Joey, an illegitimate kid from Donabate, and May, his sinewy mother, who was rumoured to be the town prostitute. She sold me condoms in the hay barn, so there may have been some truth to the rumour. My body grew brown and hard, forking the hay bales onto the tractor's

ever-growing pile. We walked back in the evenings to the pub with
the corrugated iron roof, where Joey bought me a new thing, a pint,
saying I could buy him many more when I got my first pay cheque. It
was dark and creamy and tasted of adulthood. Everything tasted of
adulthood now—his mother May, drinking her cider, cadging cigarettes from the local hard chaws, the pack of condoms in my left-
hand pocket, the talk of fights outside the chip shop, of donkey der-
bies, of the farm labourers who went for seasonal work to Scotland,
and of the blacksmith Crinion who'd had seventeen children with
their various wives.

I'd take the train home then with the schoolgirls, their faces and
hands stained with blackberry juice. I'd soak in a bath for an hour,
hear my mother fussing in the kitchen downstairs, then eat whatever
she had cooked, as if my father had never existed. We'd talk about
the lodgers, about Tommy's complaints of them underpaying, about
whatever racecourse my father was on at present, and I could sense
a restlessness in her, a lack of purpose, a sadness even which I did
my best to assuage. Then Tommy would knock on the kitchen door,
a new development, and she'd put her coat on for the pub since a
woman could never venture in there without a man, as she told me,
and a little drink never hurt anyone.

I got paid on Friday, lining up outside a run-down outhouse
where my classmate sat, his jug ears now burnt orange by the sun,
counting out notes and coins from a biscuit tin. I walked back down
the hill towards Donabate with Joey and May while the asylum pickers piled into a bus for their institutional home in Portrane.

'Don't they get paid?' I asked Joey or was it May.

'They have an arrangement with the madhouse,' May answered. 'The doctors think it does them good.'

'What's the word, Ma?' Joey asked.

'Therapy,' said May.

'What's therapy?' Joey asked.

'Therapy,' his mother said, 'is your back bent double for eight hours a day and not getting paid.'

I bought Joey back his pint in the dusty pub.

'You not having one yourself?' he asked.

'I can't,' I said. 'Have to be somewhere.' And for some reason I felt even more adult saying that.

'Got a girl, have we?' said May. 'You gonna use them rubbers?'

'Stop it, Ma,' Joey said, as she did a little dance around the wooden floor. She was wearing a scuffed leather jacket and a pair of jeans held up with twine. A cowboy shirt, incongruously, underneath the jacket. And as she danced she sang:

*I found my thri—ill on Blueberry Hill.*

'Maybe,' I said. 'Maybe I have a girl.'

'A working girl?'

She laughed at her own joke, a laugh that ended in a wheeze of coughing and cigarette phlegm, while Joey beat her on the jacket and told her to shut up.

On the train home the schoolgirls counted the coins they'd earned with their purple-stained fingers and I wondered how much of the money in my pocket should be mine. I knew if I asked my mother, she would say keep it all. She had that way of keeping all her needs hidden. I had no idea what my father sent her, or took from her, in his wanderings round the racecourses of the West of Ireland. So I put the coins in one pocket and the notes in another and counted the notes out slowly, casually, like a gambler in a cowboy movie, on the kitchen table, and pushed half of them towards her.

'Half?' she said. 'I can't take half.'

'Why not?'

'Because you worked for it.'

She didn't push them back, though. And I felt an odd sadness at my own deceit. She was so trusting, I could have given her anything. But deceit has that way with it, once you set it in motion it keeps going.

'He's off at the Galway races,' she told me. 'Be back next Saturday. You need a bath.'

And she poured me one, let me soak my aching limbs in there, while she sat outside.

'How is it?' she asked me.

'Strange,' I told her. I was thinking of other things. And I could tell she was too.

'They hire mental patients from Portrane.'

'And they get paid the same as you?'

'No.'

'Must be one of those new schemes. What do they call it?'

'Therapy.'

'Therapy,' she echoed. 'Whatever happened to making baskets?'

# WICKLOW STREET

I TOOK THE BUS to Dun Laoghaire and danced again to *Green Onions* with the girl who said she wouldn't marry me. Though I felt more adult now, and when the strobe lights began I said, 'Can we get out of here?' And she took my hand and led me all the way past the pier back to the concrete walk between the beach and the train tracks.

Four trains passed us by the time we had reached the silent hulk of Blackrock Baths. I could see the lights flashing on her face as they went by and knew from the way she wouldn't look at me where she was headed. We passed through the smell of dogshit and we found the same place where I had laid down my towel, and the sand around the grass was flattened as if it remembered our bodies. Though of course the marks could have been made by someone else. She was much more awkward than the first time, embarrassed even, and there were long silences between us where we could hear the curlews or whatever birds they were from the bird sanctuary. But I liked the silence with her and I thought to myself, how often can you be comfortable beside someone saying nothing?

And I said that to her. I said, 'I like lying here with you not having to say anything.'

'So do I,' she said. 'And I like the sound of birds. And the trains.'

She moved her head towards me and she wound her legs around mine. And when I took out the pack of condoms, she said, 'What the hell's that?'

'Rubbers,' I said. 'To stop, you know . . .'

'So I won't have to marry you,' she said.

'Yes,' I said. 'We don't want that.'

Though the truth was I wanted everything she could give to me, but was just afraid to say it.

She said she didn't like the rubber feeling, though I didn't quite believe her. 'Gerald,' she said, 'that hurts,' but in a tone of voice that implied it didn't hurt at all.

And afterwards we counted four more trains and the intervals between them were getting longer.

'They tell the time, those trains,' she said.

'So what time is it?'

'Late,' she said. 'Too late.'

So I asked could I meet her tomorrow and she said, 'That would mean we're going out together.'

'If we agree we're not going out together, then, can I meet you tomorrow?'

'I suppose,' she said. 'I don't want my brothers to know.'

'What would they do?'

'They'd batter you.'

'Maybe I'd batter them.'

'No,' she said. 'Not them.'

She stood up to walk back and I was glad she reached out for my hand. And I wondered what else would I have to do to be properly going out with her.

'In town,' she said. 'I get off work at one. The carpet factory, in Wicklow Street.'

THE CARPET FACTORY in Wicklow Street was a red-bricked building with stained-glass windows and no sign on the door to show they made carpets inside. She came out around one, and her hands were all stained, like the girls who picked blackberries on the train home. But hers were stained with many colours, orange, green, and red. She worked with dyes, she told me, and had to find a bathroom to scrub the colours off. But she took my brown hand with her multicoloured one and I found her coloured fingers round mine wonderfully adult and strange.

I brought her fist to my mouth to taste the dyes.

'Are you kissing my hand?' she asked.

'No,' I told her. 'I'm tasting the colours.'

We walked down towards O'Connell Street where the picture houses were.

So we fell into a rhythm, or maybe an understanding, me and this girl who wouldn't go out with me. I'd meet her on Friday in the Overend, on Saturday at the carpet shop where I'd take her red and green and orange fingers in mine. I'd take her down to Dollymount, the Phoenix Park, the zoo, places she'd never been, where her brothers wouldn't see her. The river was a dividing line for them, she told me, they hardly ever crossed north. And in the grass behind the Hollow bandstand, she said it again. 'Gerald, that hurts.'

'Why are you working on a farm,' she'd ask me, 'isn't your family loaded?'

'I'm not my family,' I'd say.

'Oh,' she'd go, 'all dark and mysterious.'

'That hurts, Mr. Dark and Mysterious,' she said on the perimeter of the zoo, behind the wire cage of the baboon compound. 'You think it hurts when they do it?'

She was funny in a way that I wasn't, and I liked her even more for it.

And after a week baling hay in Donabate I graduated to picking tomatoes in the vast greenhouses and it was so hot in there I had to work shirtless with Joey shirtless too and his skinny mother stripped down to her black bra. There was a green, dusty mould that came from the leaves and we'd emerge a dull verdigris, like old brass statues. I'd scrub what I could off myself but since my hands did all the work I could never get them clean. So when I met her on Saturday I had green hands, to match her multicoloured ones.

And we walked across O'Connell Street, my green hands in her red and yellow ones—'like the Irish flag,' she said, and I wished I had thought of it. She was funny in a way that I wasn't, and I wondered if I was as funny, would she have agreed to go out with me, and I wondered how funny her brothers were. We queued outside the Astor for a film in the early afternoon, *I Am Curious Yellow*. She would invite my green hands all over her body in the dark of the cinema and cover mine with her own technicoloured ones. She was happy then, I knew, but she had no idea how easy it is to be sad.

# BRAY

WE VENTURED OUT to Bray one Saturday, which worried her, she said, because her brothers often watched the football matches in the Bray Head Hotel. But as she said to me, 'You can't spend your whole weekend skulking round the northside.'

At the funfair on the promenade, two girls screamed at her from the rollercoaster.

'Keep walking,' she said to me, 'down the promenade.'

'Do you know them?' I asked.

'What do you think?' she answered.

So we walked among the promenaders who came towards us like ghosts, because the sun was behind them. One of them turned as we passed him and all I could see behind the sunshine was a barrel-chested man in a donkey jacket.

'I hate you now, you know that,' she said to me, pulling me on.

'Why?' I asked her.

'Because,' she said, 'you should have left me alone.'

We took the chairlift up Bray Head, which she said was all right, because it was a favourite of old ladies, priests, and men with walking sticks. But knowing that she hated me took the fun out of it. And the silences were not enjoyable, not enjoyable at all.

There was a tearoom up there called the Eagle's Nest and we had tea and sandwiches with the old ladies and the priests.

I asked her why she hated me so suddenly.

'Because,' she said again as if the word was her favourite. 'Because, that was my father down there.'

'So?'

'So,' she said. 'Someone saw us by the Blackrock Baths. You should have left me alone.'

'Who saw us?'

'Doesn't matter who. I lied, said it couldn't have been me. Now he knows.'

She got up from the table and rubbed the sandwich crumbs from her skirt.

'Come for a walk,' she said.

She was wearing a tartan plaid skirt with chunky heels. I followed that skirt up through the pine trees. I remembered the heels she had worn when she had first asked me to dance and I was glad she wasn't wearing them. She wouldn't have been able to walk in them and besides, they would have broken my heart.

There was heather at the top and a view across to Howth. We lay down in that heather, with its small pink flowers the colour of her lipstick.

'What's my name?' I asked and I felt her flat thin hip underneath the plaid skirt.

'Gerry. And what's mine?'

'Donna.'

She leaned back in the heather. The smell was all around her like a dusty perfume.

'You're my secret, Gerry. And I suppose I'm yours. But we're a bit too young, aren't we? To have secrets like this?'

'Why does it have to be secret?' I asked.

'Because,' she said. 'I have brothers. You live in Palmerston Park and I live in St. Begnet's Villas.'

It was the first time she had told me where she lived. St. Begnet's Villas. I could imagine roses, inside a garden fence.

'Don't you love me?' And the word stunned me suddenly with its possibility.

No, she said, she didn't love me at all. The way she said that hurts.

Her head curled in the heather and the white and pink flowers got tangled in her hair.

On the train back, she pointed to a row of small back gardens, all, it seemed, with the same washing lines.

'There you go,' she said. 'St. Begnet's Villas.'

The train was pulling to a halt, and she kissed me at her stop.

'See you on Friday.'


THE WAY IT goes is, something has happened, but you don't know that it has happened yet. You only realize later: That's when it happened. So she left me on the train and I could see her vanishing at the station going towards St. Begnet's Villas and I didn't know then that I wouldn't see her again.

I went home to the Crescent where my father was back from his travels and he shuffled round the kitchen while my mother's feet sounded up and down the stairs, cleaning the lodgers' rooms. I took the train again on Monday morning and stripped to the waist with

Joey in the glasshouses, getting our bodies green again from mould on the leaves of the tomato plants. My green boys, May called us, when we emerged at lunchtime and queued for the doorstep sandwiches outside the small outhouse. I thought I wouldn't bother washing the green off until Friday; I'd wash my hands and face but forgo the bath and the tensile scrub that would have made my body brown again.

So I stayed a green boy as if the plants had taken hold of me, the weeds and grasses of the flat fields around; as if their tendrils had crept up inside my boots and inhabited my skin. I was a person from a comic strip, the green shadow from some story that had not yet been told. And when Friday came I took the train home again and soaked in the bathroom while my mother talked to me from the stairs outside. I was happy then, watching the green stain the suds of soap and listening to her voice because I didn't know it had happened yet. And when all the green was gone from my skin I dried myself and put on a white shirt that I knew would glow in the ultraviolet lights.

I took the train across the city to the southside where I was meant to be from, and walked into the Overend but I could tell immediately she wasn't there. There was an absence in the hall that was only emphasized by the crush of people. They were playing Manfred Mann from the other end, 5–4–3–2–1, and someone smaller than me but older, much older, said, 'Are you Gerry?' and I had to think for a minute. Of course I was Gerry, and he cracked me on the nose suddenly with his forehead and I fell on the dance floor and curled up there as boots came flailing out from behind the legs of the dancers— Cuban-heeled boots, winklepicker boots, round-toed boots—and I knew what had happened then. The strange thing was, it didn't hurt: Perhaps it hurt Gerry but it didn't hurt Kevin, me. And then they were gone just as quickly and the bouncers came and did a bit of kicking of their own and that hurt, because they knew how to do it properly.

I walked back down towards the train station and crossed the bridge to the other side. Every step was painful but the darkness and the cries of the birds from the sanctuary seemed to make it better. I stopped for awhile outside the Blackrock Baths and saw the buttons were all torn from my shirt and looked at my thin ribs which were purple now from the variety of shoes that had kicked me. I was the purple shadow now, not the green shadow any longer. I tried to remember in the darkness where we had lain down together but there were no trains flashing by so I couldn't find it. She had always led me there anyway, she had always known where to go. I was Kevin again, not Gerry any longer. I wondered would it hurt less being Kevin. I wasn't sure. I thought of his house in Palmerston Park and wondered would her brothers wait outside the wrought-iron gates at night and catch him coming home across the green and give him another hiding. I wondered would it hurt me again if they kicked him. I kind of hoped it would.

It was strange, going home to the Crescent and knowing she could never find me there, even if she wanted to. They were all asleep when I let myself in. There was a forsaken, curling quality to the darkness in the kitchen. There were the sounds of voices from Fairview Park. There was the loud snoring of some lodger from upstairs. I curled up in bed and imagined her walking round the railings of the park he lived by, hoping she could see him again. She would catch a glimpse, maybe, of his head as he walked past the monkey puzzle tree and feel everything she had felt for me. But she wouldn't talk to him. No, she wouldn't talk again to him, or to me.

# THE B&I FERRY

AND SO SHE was gone and I went back on the train on Monday to Donabate with the blackberry pickers, walked up from the station to the low fields where I made my way through the ridges with Joey, his mother, and the asylum pickers. I felt it should be raining, that the weather should have suited my desolation, huge black clouds over those endless ridges and our bent backs and the hedges beyond, but the sun stayed out as if to mock the fact that I was in my own black cloud without the girl who wouldn't marry me.

And the sun stayed out until Friday, the day I should have been thinking about the pay cheque and going out to the Overend. It was the kind of thought you want to get out of your mind because it makes you too sad, but then when it's gone from your mind you feel sadder still so you invite it back. If this loss is to be your only companion you better get to like it. And so. And so. And so.

So Joey's mother must have noticed something because she turned, her face close to the dusty rhubarb ridge, and asked me, 'Are you all right, sonny, you look like you could cry.' The collar of the leather jacket was scuffed near her cheek, she wore it turned upwards so long it made a line underneath her cheekbone and I would have cried anyway at her question but the rain came along then and helped me out. It fell slowly at first, doing my work for me, rivulets of water running down my cheeks. Then a wind coursed over the field of barley next to us, an almost biblical wind that pulled the rhubarb from our fingers, sent May's straw hat flying from her head. She stood and the wind seemed to carry her after her hat.

The rain came down in sheets then and we ran towards the only shelter, a metal container that held the sheaves of rhubarb we had picked. We had crowded inside when the thunder began. Forked lightning danced over the sodden ridges and a primitive howl went up from the asylum pickers inside. We could have been slaves in a coffin ship. May bent her sinewy breastless body to the metal floor and began to pray for forgiveness.

'Would you stop it, Ma,' Joey shouted at her, 'you're frightening the dummies.'

'No, you don't understand, son, the moment comes and we never know when it comes because we never know the day nor the hour.' Another roll of thunder happened with a burst of lightning and the asylum pickers roared even louder and there was a loud bang and a flash of blue and the metal trailer shook with the force of it and the air inside there filled with smoke. We crouched down inside as if we had already died. And when the smoke cleared, we saw beneath our feet that each carefully woven skein of rhubarb had been burnt to a cinder.

I walked outside, through the smell of burnt rhubarb. There was a river flowing now over the rhubarb ridges.

There were rumbles of thunder, but the lightning had moved on to Skerries and Portrane and the thunder only echoed now and the lightning was a pale reflection of itself. 'It's okay,' I said to them, Joey, May, and the asylum pickers who seemed to think they were dead already. 'It won't kill you. It didn't kill me.' And the rain wrapped round me like a new cloak and the pain for some reason had gone, like the lightning, somewhere else.

I TOOK MY pay cheque home and shared it again with my mother.

'You're going out?' she asked me.

'Maybe not,' I told her, and she knew something had changed and I knew that she knew.

'He's away this weekend again,' she said. And I knew what she should have known, but again didn't say it. He was away for good.

I took her walking to the Hollow on the Saturday and sat down with her in the grass while the baboons squawked somewhere behind us. There was a new understanding between us, of things unspoken. There were those we wouldn't see again, one for each of us.

'You've got your Leaving next year,' she said. 'It'll be good to have the house quiet.'

'What about the lodgers?' I asked.

'I'm letting them go.'

She was letting everything go. I finished work in September and began the drudge of study as the house above us gradually emptied itself. One by one the lodgers went. Tommy supervised their leaving, cleared out the rooms, tinkled the keys. Letters came, from Ascot, Cheltenham, Aintree, with a postcard always bizarrely inside and never any money.

'They were more trouble than they were worth,' she told me.

She had taken to going to Gaffney's with Tommy of an evening, for, as she put it, the one. I'd sit with books at the kitchen table and hear her knuckles on the door, the door itself slightly ajar and her face turned away in the hallway.

'I'm just going down to Gaffney's with Tommy, love, for the one.'

I would wonder was that what I had to call him from now on, 'Tommy love.' And of course it was never the one. I would hear her walk home later, the front door opening, the giggle half suppressed, then the too steady, elegant shoes on the stairway up. Tommy always waited below, fiddling with the keys, as if he wanted to allow a decent interval between them. She would appear at the kitchen doorway and ask about my progress, and the intoxication was all inside. I could see it in her eyes, hear it in her voice; it wasn't merriment or abandon, it was a kind of stunned despair.

'How are things at school, love?' she would ask me.

'I would have preferred,' I told her, 'to have gone to Belvedere.'

'We did discuss it once,' she said, 'your father and I. Couldn't afford it, really . . . You never liked Joey's, did you?'

It was the kind of question that didn't demand an answer.

'Be all over soon.'

And I would wonder how he was doing, in the perfumed halls that echoed of plainchant, in the house that sang with Chopin. I would wonder had the girl who wouldn't marry me ever tracked him down, taken up where she'd left off, said to him, 'Hurt me, Gerry.'

She had given up her swimming, but one evening in April she said to me, 'They're stretching again.'

'What?' I asked, wondering did she mean her stockings.

'The evenings,' she said. 'I think I'll take a walk, love, down by the Bull Wall.'

'You're going swimming?' I asked.

'One last splash,' she said, 'the sea must be warming now.'

'You want me to come with you?' I asked, and she said, 'No, you've got your exams.'

So I sat there, with my *focloir gaeilge agus bearla*, my wrestling with the *gna caithe* as she went to the cubbyhole where the towels were kept and took out her still girlish swimsuit, wrapped it neatly in a white towel like a Swiss roll. She took off her high heels, put on a pair of sandals, and I said, 'Enjoy yourself.'

'He won't call, will he,' she said, which I thought was odd, since he hadn't called for months.

'If he does,' I said, 'I'll take a message.'

'Tell him I'll be back,' she said, and walked down the stairs to the long hallway. I remember the sound of her footsteps, softer now, without the high heels. The tinkling of the keys, as she took one from the pile. The closing of the front door and the silence then, as if the air had been sucked out of the hallway.

AND I DON'T know what it was, some instinct for disaster, I suppose, but an hour later I followed her down. There was still a pale greenish light in the sky and the B&I ferry was making its way past the stone Virgin at the end of the pier on its way to Liverpool and even from the wooden bridge I could see a crowd gathered round the cement shelter and I began to run.

I could hear the larks singing again as I made my way past the clubhouse and the sound of my pounding feet changing as the wooden boards gave way to slabs of limestone and I made it past one shelter to the other where we used to swim. There was a crowd gathered, a few swimmers among them, the rotund men with their guts protruding above the elastic of their swimsuits, no women. There was a wet figure lying on the stone steps and I recognized the same lime-green girlish swimsuit but the skin that it was designed to conceal was already turning blue. Someone was talking about the wave the ferry had left in its wake, the undertow it created, but I thought it couldn't be that, she had swam all her life here, and I knew she was already dead.

I pushed my way through them and there was a hush, an intake of breath, and then absolute silence from them. She was already quiet though. Her face was upturned slightly, towards me, and the cement was wet and cold beneath her. I remember thinking that the sea hadn't warmed up after all. I walked down the last step and took her wet body in my arms, amazed at how light it was, how I could lift it, and through the silence I could hear a skylark still singing and the sound of a siren and I realized that someone among them had called for an ambulance.

I wanted to be him then, more than ever. I wanted to be anyone else but me.

# HOWTH

I PRESSED *d* ON the find button of my mobile phone and the word *Daughter* came up. You answered and I could tell from the tone of your voice you were surprised to hear from me. I tried to imagine where you were, and saw again that room full of mourners, with your mother's profile under black lace by the front windows and the crowded bar to the right of the stairs. I asked you did you want to continue our tour of gravestones, and you asked, Deansgrange again, and I said no, this one is out by Howth, on a sloping field that faces Ireland's Eye. And you said yes, as if it was the most natural thing in the world to visit graves. 'Whose is it this time?' you asked, and I told you, 'My mother's.'

So I drove out there, towards the mound of Howth which had always seemed like a promise to me, the end of things, the end of the city, I suppose, on its northern side, with the answering hump of Bray the city's end to the south. Howth, where Aideen had died of her legendary sorrow. Anyway, we had buried her there in a graveyard with oddly flat gravestones, no upright ones that could gather moss. He came back of course for her funeral, he had to, from a race meeting somewhere near Glasgow, and he tried vainly to make coherent sentences, began to say things that he could never finish. That had become his mode of speech: a subject, a hesitant predicate, but never an object. His mode of punctuation would have been the dash, the ellipsis, never the full stop.

Such a beautiful day it was, you could hardly think the time had come for the gathering, the reaping, for the earth to take its own. The sun spilled over the Wicklow Hills and hit the water on Dublin Bay, rippled by small winds that refracted it into a million mirrors of light. The hearse picked her up from Marino Church and paused outside the Crescent and paused again by the Bull Wall where the cement bathing huts sat way beyond, in shadow. There were porpoises leaping out by Sutton Strand and the mound of Howth sat beyond it again, obscenely bathed in sunlight. The world presented the kind of face that said, 'This is all I am, this is me at my best, there is nothing hidden beneath me, nothing unseen.' The world, of course, lied.

Every lodger that had ever passed through her house came out to that odd, flattened graveyard. All itinerant bachelors still, the kind she favoured, none of them, even then, seemed to have families of their own.

I PICKED YOU up from the station at Howth. It was still pretty, low eaves overhanging the fawn brickwork, the masts of the new marina visible behind it. You were alone this time, without the dog, and I drove you up to the flattened graveyard, the marble slabs glinting in the sunlight, sitting in their beds of grass. There were families sitting, kneeling, standing, tending plots.

'Your father too,' you said, when you saw her grave, and I said, 'Yes, I have quite run out of parents.' You asked why the graves were flattened and I couldn't give you an answer, except to say that it had a pleasing futuristic aspect to it, a strangely American feeling, Mormon or Seventh Day Adventist, as if this hill was in Minnesota or Utah, some place where the old Irish realities had been long abandoned.

I told you I was thinking of writing it down, as a sort of long letter, all the times our lives had impinged one upon the other.

'Like a book,' you said.

'Yes,' I said. 'I suppose like a book.'

'Why not just tell me?' you asked.

'How much time do you have?' I asked.

'All the time in the world.'

And you sat by my mother's grave and traced her old name with your finger. Some brown earth came off on the skin of your hand.

'There's a reason,' you said, 'isn't there? There's a reason you can't just tell me.'

There are many, I thought, but one in particular. There's a building in Manhattan, with rose-coloured sandstone.

'Why did he leave?' you asked. 'My father. I was never told. As a child, I remember secrets.'

'Maybe I was his secret.'

'You?'

'We took each other,' I said, 'to strange places.'

'You're being mysterious,' you said. 'Do you have to be mysterious?'

'I do,' I said, 'in a way. That's why I have to write it down.'

'I'm not sure I like you,' you said, 'being mysterious. And I so want to like you.'

'You do?'

'Yes, I do. Like you. And I don't want to stop.'

You stood up from the grave then, with that swift movement of yours. You took my arm quite naturally again.

'Was there a woman?' you asked.

'There were,' I told you. 'Several. They would confuse us.'

But there was one in particular, the vampire whispered.

'The way I must do,' you said. 'I remember seeing him outside the gates of my school. And when I got to the road, he was always gone. I suppose it could have been you.'

'No,' I told you, 'it was never me. But he talked to me. About tracing the path a father should have taken. About seeing you, wanting to approach, feeling he couldn't.'

'Drink,' you said.

'Yes,' I said. 'That and more.'

'My mother couldn't stand it.'

'Neither could I.'

'You don't drink?'

'Rarely.'

'Your mother?' you asked, looking back towards the flattened graveyard. 'Did she drink?'

'Towards the end,' I said.

'It was an accident.'

'The B&I ferryboat,' I told you, 'created freak waves every now and then. We used to wait for them to hit the cement wall when we were kids, and dive through them. Or else.'

'There is an or else?' you asked.

'Or else she died of sorrow.'

# THE GREEN LOUNGE

THERE WAS A club in Dublin called the Green Lounge and I took to going there in my funeral suit. I had chosen it carefully, bought it with what was left of what I'd earned that summer—mohair, dark green, so dark as to be almost black, high lapels, four buttons, tapered trousers, the perfect mod fit with the Cuban heels. I had a shirt with a high buttoned collar and a thin dark tie in a Windsor knot. I could imagine myself as the perfect spectacle of grief at that graveside and in the months afterwards kept that suit on—the shirts changed of course, I had to wash them, but the suit stayed the same. Don't approach, he is sanctified by loss, he never smiles, his eyes reveal nothing, his suit is dark and unchangeable, his walk funereal. I acted that part, confined myself to it, there was no other emotion I wanted to colour my days with and my suit stayed dark.

I would go to the Green Lounge when school had finished on a Friday afternoon, from the bright sunlight into the funereal gloom where girls moved slowly in black lipstick while the strobes came on and off and purple hearts and mandies were exchanged across the counter. And I saw him in there. He was unfamiliar in that environment, I could tell immediately, like me, in a happier, more innocent time. But innocence disarms you, leaves you without a guard, embarrassed in an environment made for hardened souls like mine. And I watched him from the bar, in my funeral suit; I watched a girl I knew brush by him and take him for me, begin a conversation and walk off in mid-sentence. And I realized I had never seen him since that episode on the bus; it was odd since he felt so familiar to me, almost part of my skin.

I walked behind him almost as if I was going to ask him to dance. 'Gerry,' I said, and he turned and saw me.

'You,' he said.

'Yes, it's me,' I said. 'I've been mistaken for you several times and the consequences have always been strange. Come to the bar,' I said, and he followed me there.

It was a coffee bar, serving Coca-Cola and soft drinks and Nescafé coffee, very adult and continental or so the denizens of the Green Lounge thought; we were the vanguard in this godforsaken city, listening to Manfred Mann and Alexis Korner inside this black hole in the daylight hours.

'What's your name?' he asked.

'Kevin,' I told him. 'Can you explain it?'

And he said no, that he couldn't, but that he knew it had been happening, he wasn't sure why or how. In Woolworths he had been accused of stealing; there had been a questionable young man in a leather jacket who offered him cigarettes by Nelson's Pillar; there was a girl called Jean he went out with, over on the northside, and a greaser on a motorbike who followed them, accusing him of things.

'I've often wondered,' he said, 'what your life was like.'

'You want to swap?' I asked him, and he said that on certain days he wished he could. He had written a story, he told me, about this other person, more adult, somehow, than him, more able, more mature.

'That would not be me,' I told him.

'No,' he said, 'but the person we're mistaken for is neither you nor me, but maybe a third, with an identity all of his own.'

'So what should we call him?' I asked, and he said, 'Something between Kevin and Gerry, Kerry maybe,' and I said, 'That's a girl's name,' and he laughed, as if I'd said something funny.

It was odd, seeing him laugh, the smile breaking out suddenly showing his white teeth perfect in shape, unlike mine—they had better dentists on the southside, maybe. And I realized I hadn't laughed for months. 'Make me laugh,' I told him, 'the way I made you laugh. I feel the need to laugh.'

'I can't,' he told me, 'I'm not good at jokes.'

'Any joke,' I said, 'like the dyslexic who walked into the bra,' and he laughed again and I said, 'That's not fair, you're laughing again and I'm not,' and I felt anger rising inside me, an irrational anger and I thought I had better leave before I ruined this encounter.

'Your mother,' I asked him, 'what's she like?'

'I have a mother?' he asked, in all innocence, and I suddenly laughed. It was funny, I don't know why—he must have judged her unmotherly; but the question, delivered deadpan like that with a straight face, made me laugh, and keep laughing.

'It wasn't all that funny,' he said.

'Yes it was,' I told him, 'thank you, I needed to laugh again and I better say goodbye before I say the wrong thing,' and I walked out into the grey evening light in my funeral suit and made my way home.

# DOLLYMOUNT

S O I DROVE you then from the flattened graveyard past the wilderness of rhododendrons round Howth Castle back along the Clontarf Road where the dark mass of the green trees of St. Anne's estate filled your window of the car and the pale waters of Dollymount filled mine. I turned left over the old wooden bridge and you said, 'How sweet, the way it bumps,' and I told you it was the old wooden sleepers, which they hadn't changed since before my mother's time.

'She swam from here,' you said.

The walkway stretched out before us to the middle of Dublin Bay, with the horrible stone Virgin at the end and the cement shelters to our right. The day had turned and the winds were blowing the sea into a frenzy.

'Yes,' I said. 'From the shelter there.'

'It looks so cold,' you said.

And it did.

'She didn't seem to mind.'

'Why are you telling me all this?' you asked.

Your face was turned towards me in the breathy interior, the windows all misted up, and I remembered the mauve scarf you had worn at his funeral.

'Because,' I said, 'I feel the need to.'

'Was it a suicide?' you asked.

'No,' I told you. 'The vampire took her.'

'What vampire?' you asked, and there was a hint of disbelieving laughter in your voice.

So I told you, as our breath misted up the windows, about the vampire who I thought had followed me as a child, who turned out to be a pervert of kinds, who removed his black gloves in the Strand cinema as Elvis Presley sang *Rock-a-hula baby*. How I wondered had he followed your father too, since our resemblance was so close, tracked him down to the Kenilworth cinema where Norman Wisdom could have been singing *Don't laugh at me 'cause I'm a fool*.

'Would that explain a lot?' you asked.

'It might,' I said. Though some things are beyond explanation.

I thought of the building in Manhattan and the bridges in Central Park. The pink light and the sounds of squawking from the Central Park Zoo.

'Are you going to tell me more?' you asked.

'Maybe,' I said, 'I could write a book. How does the song go?'

'*About the way you walk and whisper and look.*'

So we sat there and watched the sea go quiet and said nothing for awhile.

'I like it,' you said, 'when we sit and say nothing.'

'You never sat with him like this?' I asked.

'You know I didn't,' you said. 'But this must have been what it would have been like. And that's an awkward sentence, isn't it?'

And you laughed again.

# FAIRVIEW STRAND

**M**Y FATHER STAYED. The house was his now, he took whatever rent he could from Tommy. He began to work the courses again. Soon it was the flat racing season and it was strange how little time they took him now, how a visit to Fairyhouse or Gowran could have him back home by six o'clock. I would sit behind my castles of books on the kitchen table, watch him come in and make tea and begin those sentences that never came to a conclusion, that needed no reply.

'Two months gone and you'd never think it, would you, with the . . .'

A whistle then between his teeth and the sound of his breath blowing the scalding tea.

'Tommy's a great comfort after all, I mean they were butties, weren't they, and that's—'

The sound of Tommy's hobble on the stairs then, and his head would turn sideways like a creaking bird.

'Going down to Gaffney's for the one, son, sure the one never hurt . . .'

Anyone, I wanted to say but didn't.

I would see their two heads through the window, framed by the penumbra the streetlights cast on the damp trees behind them, moving towards the Tolka bridge and Gaffney's. It could have been her with Tommy out there and if he could only put his clocks in reverse it would still be. I would think of the vampire I had imagined years ago and wondered would he help me bring her back. Come on, you undead creature, I would think, somebody has to help her in that cold earth. Cold clay. Mrs. Considine was long gone, buried in Glasnevin as far as I remembered, where the graves were upright and gathered moss. *Oh how I love to kiss my little hula miss.*

THE CHRISTIAN BROTHERS paced the long exam hall in their swishing soutanes, their leathers hanging by their side like enormous sexual organs. But I was long beyond the need for a beating. The only sounds were the scraping of pens, the soft rustle of serge, the almost respectful plodding of feet. I scoured the paper with my nib and wrote my name at the bottom, Kevin Thunder. I wondered did the Jesuits in Belvedere College sound the same. I imagined him signing his own name, *Gerald Spain, AMDG.* That was what you wrote in Jesuit schools, and it meant, *For the greater glory of God.*

The three of us went to Gaffney's the night I finished. Me, the clockmaker, and my turf accountant father.

'If she'd only been here to see it, Tommy, if she'd only—'

'She'd have been proud as, proud as—'

There were two of them at it now. 'Punch,' I said.

'You want punch, is it?'

'No,' I said. 'Guinness will do fine.'

'A pint of plain . . .'

'Your only . . .'

'Man,' I said.

I left for a building site in England the next day.

# KILBURN

THE SKY WAS a pale green, as the B&I ferry pulled out past the stone Virgin at the end of the Bull Wall. I watched the wake from the boat and wondered for the umpteenth time how it could have caught an unsuspecting swimmer, how it could have left an undertow that would have dragged her downwards. Or maybe it was the undertow left by my father's absences that had undone her, a metaphoric undertow that had unhinged her, left her circling in a downward spiral that ended with the last few bubbles escaping from her lips and the brown casts the lugworms left. I didn't think it possible, and still don't. Whatever currents ran between them, they never seemed to include the kind of passion that would have ended in self-harm. No, it was a freak wave, two currents crossing, nothing more, nothing less. And now the vampire had her.

I had an address from Joey, a relative who would give me what was known as 'a start.' I liked the phrase. It seemed adult and arbitrary, meaning nothing and everything. The ship began to roll as we went onwards, the drinkers clogged the bars, and the decks swilled with vomit. I slept in a lifeboat and woke up to find three others sleeping with me.

I got a job on demolition with a Mr. D. Franknum, who gave me a crowbar, placed me in an eighteenth-century room, and told me to have it stripped to the bare brick by lunchtime. There was a rare pleasure in wrecking things, I found, smashing fittings from the floor and ceiling, tearing through the crumbling plasterwork with the metal hook. I broke through a blocked-up window with a sledgehammer and as the dust cleared, saw a cricket match in progress on the green outside.

I saw a girl in diaphanous white kissing Jimi Hendrix on the platform of the Bayswater tube.

I slept in a squat with fifteen others, played poker with our earnings at night.

I bought bell-bottom trousers and an Afghan waistcoat, I let my hair grow long.

I played a Ouija board at a party in Kilburn and the whirling glass spelt out a message for me. It said someone was thinking evil of me. It spelt out the name *Gerry*.

I met a girl, a hairdresser, who introduced me to dope. I preferred amphetamines, I came to realize, to cannabis resin. We would chew pills and model each other's hair in her empty salon after work in Hackney.

I saw Fleetwood Mac in the Roundhouse.

A Jamaican chippie told me Peter Green had had a bad trip in Munich.

I worked on a wall of scaffolding with an affable bank robber. He signed on each Thursday with an entity he called Old Bill. He told me the main problem in his line of work was drivers shitting their pants when the alarms sounded.

I met a white witch on Hampstead Heath.

I took LSD in Southend on the longest pier in Britain.

The same Jamaican hippie told me Peter Green had left Fleetwood Mac.

I drank in Ward's in Piccadilly, where you could buy a twenty-pound note for a fiver.

In September I came back, took the train from Euston Station to the long halls in Liverpool docks, took the B&I ferry back to Dublin, which showed up black and gaunt against a purple sky. Howth Head guarded the northside like a dark giant paw.

I walked back through the gantries of the North Wall, past the Point depot, beneath Goulding's fertilizer plant which smelt of acrid nitrogen. The swans were still paddling in the mudflats of the Tolka. I walked the metal bridge across the river, through Fairview Park to the Crescent where the man who wrote *Dracula* once lived.

It was half past ten and there was nobody home, no lodgers had replaced the ones my mother had let go. I walked left then, past the Marino strip, the Fairview cinema to the lights of Gaffney's pub. They were in there, of course, him and Tommy the Clock, many drinks past 'the one.'

He rose on unsteady feet and embraced me.

'Didn't he do well, Tommy, didn't he do . . .'

'He did,' said Tommy.

# THE MIDDLE THIRD

*I could write a preface on how we met*
*So the world would never forget.*

YOU WERE SINGING now, as if to break the bubble of silence in the car, on the Bull Wall, with the foamy sea in the
windscreen.

'I got six honours, in my leaving cert,' I told you.

'Only six?'

'He got ten.'

'How do you know?' you asked.

'I saw his picture in the *Irish Times*. The first of many.'

'I got five hundred and eighty points.'

'Almost perfect.'

'Yes. That was always me. Almost perfect.'

You shifted in the car seat and your hands were clasped over
your stomach. No one could have told that you were pregnant, and as
a practised liar, I wondered if that was one too. Or a strange, fanciful
hope. I had known several of those.

'Have you told your mother?'

'I was hoping you would do that.'

'You're joking.'

'Yes. Take me home now, so I can tell her.'

And so I drove you up Howth Road, through Killester, through the oddly named Middle Third. I walked you through to the small station, the tiny houses with their winter cherries, and remembered when I took the train from here, from the other side of the tracks, to Donabate.

'Then he went to Trinity.'

'Yes.'

'And you?'

'I went to Bolton Street. A course in technical drawing.'

'Both in the centre city.'

'Yes. But not the same city.'

'You banging on about that class thing again?'

'Different worlds.'

When the train came, it was one of the old ones, as if we were stepping back in time. As you opened the train door, its old leather strap hanging loose beneath the window, you turned and kissed me. A companionable kiss, on the cheek. You sang again as the train took you off.

*And the simple secret of the plot*
*Is just to tell them that I love you, a lot.*

# BOLTON STREET

A T THE TOP of Parnell Street, past the rows of pawn and second-hand musical instrument shops, the furniture repairers and the carpet emporiums, in the land of the Black Church and the Gloucester Diamond, where the early houses opened at half past five for the fruit and vegetable sellers of the Smithfield Market, we formed a group of uneasy lower middle-class youths who had been told the future might, just might, belong to them. Of course I didn't believe it. Trades had been elevated into careers, but not yet professions. I studied technical drawing and enjoyed the precision of angle making and even now can't enter a building without making a mental note of the symmetry of windows, space lost and gained by hallways and the arrangement of the various opes.

There were girls, of course, from Ballyfermot, Artane, Cabra, Donaghmede, and they were knowing, smart, had an ease with sexual jargon that seemed designed to intimidate rather than seduce. It seemed the sexual revolution had passed the boys by. They remained edgily virginal and maybe the girls did too but I wasn't interested in either.

His Trinity College was just across the river and I knew he went there because I saw him during Rag Week with his face painted white hoisting a girl from a blanket on College Green. His hair was shorter than mine now, and thereafter I began to glimpse him occasionally, the magenta and grey scarf dangling off his shoulder, his hair growing all the time, and girls with him who could never have gone to Bolton Street, in Afghan coats and gypsy dresses, thigh-length boots with miniskirts, girls who could never have come from Ballyfermot, Artane, or Donaghmede. I would walk through the grounds occasionally and get a glimpse of another life. Pints of shandy and lager by the white wooden clubhouse with the vaguely colonial feel. Young men drinking them, actually in cricket whites. By their clothes you shall know them. Class had done its job quite effectively. I became used to stares, as if I had come to snatch a handbag or rob the buttery till. It was beautiful, though, a world of cobbled elegance and casual learning and I could only imagine its delights.

ONE EVENING I took a shortcut through from Lincoln Place and I saw a lone figure coming towards me across the cobbles, a shadow just like mine leading his way. Our footsteps fell in sync as we approached each other. His hair, I saw as I glanced up, had reached my length exactly and his eye looked up to see if I was looking and caught mine.

I walked past, but heard him stop.

'It's you, isn't it?' he said.

'Kevin,' I said.

'Are you following me?'

'No,' I lied. Because I always was, in some strange way.

'We met,' he said, 'about a year ago.'

'In the Green Lounge,' I said. 'You made me laugh. It was important.'

'Why was it important?'

'Because my mother had just died.'

'I'm sorry.'

'Don't be. I asked about yours, and you said, "I have a mother?" It was funny.'

'I was funny?'

'Then.'

'You were following me.'

'No,' I said. 'I was mistaken for you.'

I turned then and walked back towards him.

'It happened a lot?'

Past tense.

'Yes,' I said. 'It hasn't happened recently.'

'No?'

'I've been careful.'

I was his height. His hair was my length. His face was mine. He wore a long fawn gabardine coat. I was wearing a short, bumfreezer leather jacket. And I was suddenly glad there was no one about.

'You have to be careful?'

'About being mistaken? Yes.'

'You take a drink?'

'I've no money.'

'I have.'

Of course he had money. And he drank—a lot, I was to find out. He had the kind of personality that changes with it. He took me to the Lincoln Inn and I watched his features, my features really, darken, all of the lines in his face fall towards the floor. And after the third pint, he looked like me no longer.

'There was a girl,' he said, 'you met, she thought you were me.'

'Did she have brothers?'

'Not that I know of.'

'Not the girl who wouldn't marry me.'

'What?'

Not Donna then, I thought.

'Jean.'

'Forgot her name. She lives in—'

'Vernon Avenue. Clontarf.'

'I met you years ago, didn't I, or did I dream it? Told me to call her.'

'And you did.'

'Her mother had a shop. Called . . .'

'Tuite's.'

'She did this thing with a blade of grass.'

'You both chewed it.'

And I could feel her greeny lips approaching mine. Who had the better memory, I wondered.

'This is too strange. You're from the northside.'

'Marino. I grew up in the house beside the man who wrote *Dracula*.'

'And what do you do?'

'Draw.'

'What kind of drawing?'

'All kinds. Architectural, mainly.'

'There's a story I read. Edgar Allan Poe. Story of a student who was driven mad by his double.'

'Must read it.'

'You gonna drive me mad?'

'I don't intend to. And, I'm not your double.'

'What would you call it?'

'We just have this thing. This mistaken thing. You lead a life I could have led.'

'You want to swap?'

I looked at him, his shoulders hunched now, downing half of his Guinness in one go. I shook my head.

'Don't like what you see?'

'It's not that. You're nothing like me. Just, maybe, you could have been me.'

'You mean I could have grown up beside Bram Stoker's house?'

Yes, I thought. With Tommy the Clock. And a drowned mother.

'Would you have liked that?'

'I like Stoker. And you could have grown up in Palmerston Park. Believe me, you would have hated it.'

'Did you?'

'Hate is too sweet a word.'

I could feel the darkness coming from him then, like paint.

'Try a father who's a high court judge. A mother who holidays in Bayreuth.'

He looked at me through heavy-lidded eyes.

'Wagner. She worships Wagner.'

'Not Chopin?'

'Too simple for her. They have expectations, you see. Of yours truly. Maybe you're just the one. To fulfil them. You want to study law? Do the bar?'

'You're studying law?'

'Apparently. What's your name, then, brother?'

'Kevin Thunder.'

'I'm Gerry. Gerald Spain.'

And he finished his pint. Stood up abruptly.

'Forget about me.'

He walked then, unsteadily, towards the door, without looking back.

# HOLLES STREET

YOU CALLED ME this time and when I saw the word *Daughter* pop up on my screen I wondered was it because you felt it was your turn to call or because you felt the need to talk. And when I met you, outside Mulberry's Auctioneers in Dawson Street, I realized it was neither.

You pointed at a figure in a blue suit, with cropped hair, behind a window painted with the auctioneer's lettering.

'That's him,' you said.

'Him?' I asked.

'The father of my child.'

There was a bump showing now on the last two buttons of your lavender-coloured tweed coat. So it was true and you hadn't lied. I felt a strange, honey-filled sense of relief.

'I know him,' I said.

'You what?'

'He came to value my father's house.'

He was sitting by a desk inside the window, all pin-striped business, flicking through a brochure with a woman opposite.

'Him?' you asked.

'Yes, as it happens.'

'What a coincidence.'

And I told you then that coincidence had been the driving force of my life, as in any B movie or dime novel.

'Coincidence,' you said again. Then you looked up at me and grimaced.

'Terrible time to sell,' you said.

'Maybe ghosts,' I told you, 'bring an added value.'

'You have ghosts?'

'One, at least. What are you doing here?'

'I was weighing up whether to tell him. About his—how would he call it? Sprog.'

'He'd use that word?'

'Definitely. But you can't, can you, tell a callow youth who'd use a word like that that you're having his child?'

'Some women could.'

'I'm hardly a woman at all. Still a girl, surely. I've to go for a scan in Holles Street. He should be with me, by rights, don't you think? But I can't bring myself to ask him.'

'Should I go?'

'No.'

You turned away, towards Hodges Figgis bookshop, then turned back, your downy mouth somewhere between a grimace and a smile.

'Would you?'

'You say it's a bad time to sell?'

'Terrible.'

'Okay.'

THERE WAS A pregnant woman in a candlewick nightgown smoking outside the Holles Street entrance. Two expectant fathers, I presumed, next to her.

'My gynaecologist's name is Hannigan. The mummies of South Dublin swear by him.'

'And how are you going to explain me?'

'You're my support,' you said. 'Just a friend.'

There was a Victorian stairway, corridors with more expectant mothers, and a doctor's office at the end of it. So many beings, I thought, waiting to get into this world.

He was tall, Hannigan, silver haired and exactly what you would expect of a gynaecologist. Long-fingered hands with well-trimmed nails.

'Indeed,' he said, 'indeed,' and he looked at me abstractly with eyes that asked no explanation.

'Any change?' he asked you and you shook your head.

'Just this,' you said, and you patted the two lower buttons of your coat.

'Come inside,' he murmured, or purred, opening a door. 'If you don't mind waiting, Mr.—'

'Thunder,' I said.

'Mr. Thunder.'

You both went inside then, and that odd sense of suspension descended, specific to doctors' waiting rooms. And somehow, the vampire made his presence felt. There was dust wheeling in the air behind a framed photograph of a lake in Canada. Elvis singing *Rock-a-hula, rock rock-a-hula*. A shadow sitting there, made out of wheeling dust, and a humming beneath the song from *Blue Hawaii*. Please, I thought, don't let this be your domain.

'I have my place,' the shadow whispered, if dust can whisper. And yes, dust can whisper. 'I am here, whether you like it or not.'

There's another being here, I thought, knocking on the door, whispering, 'My time. My time too.'

The dust wheeled beneath the picture of the lake in Canada and as the sun went in, the dust began to vanish.

'Murderer,' it whispered.

And was that quite right, I wondered. Was I a murderer? There was a death, certainly, but within the language of jurisprudence, the crime was not entirely mine. It belonged to both of us; it could only have emerged from us. He wanted it, I executed it, he suffered the consequences. A shared thing, the crime and punishment, like most things between us.

'Nitpicker,' it whispered, as it vanished.

And in that it was right, I thought. I was without doubt a nitpicker.

And the handle of the other door sounded and I was alone once more.

'Here we are,' said Hannigan, as he ushered you back in. 'Can we show him?'

'It's a boy,' you said, and handed me a photograph.

Tiny, like a curled dream, shades of grey and black in a cloud of unknowing. It was a shadow. And you put your hand in mine as if I were the father. There were tears in your eyes, and I was trying to stop them in mine.

# THE EBLANA

H E HAD TOLD me to forget about him, and I managed, for awhile. Until I walked into the Eblana bookshop one Saturday morning and thumbed through a student magazine and saw my name there. Over a poem, a roughly metred sonnet. I knew it was a sonnet because I remembered them from school. *Abababababcdcdcd*. With this key Shakespeare unlocked his heart. This one was un-rhymed, but a sonnet without doubt, in that it had fourteen lines, was in vague iambics, and expressed desire for an unnamed female. *'Mediochre' by Kevin Thunder*. The pun was clever as were the refer-ences to various shades of red and auburn, the impressionistic, re-fracted image of a girl whom I could picture quite clearly, so the writing must have had some merit. I knew immediately it was by him. The darkness that spread from him like ink from a squid. He had neglected to forget about me.

I was a pseudonym now, and I felt stunned and vaguely favoured. More than that, I suppose, I felt validated somehow, as if my instinct, my obsession, my preoccupation was shared. I had been a thief of his identity three or four times now, without his knowledge, and here he was, returning the theft in full public view. I say full public view but nobody read those broadsheets: magazines clipped together from typed photocopied originals or printed on dull yellow paper with the type running. And I thought no one read those broadsheets until one Saturday I was sitting in the Crescent with my father as he tore the racing sections from the various newspapers and pinned them together into what he called his bible for the day and he muttered, without looking up, 'Oh we're the dark horse, aren't we?'

'You've got a tip?' I asked him.

'I mean the dark horse here, sitting in front of me.'

'Could you be more specific?' I asked. And these were more syllables than we had exchanged in a year.

'The writing,' he said.

'Ah.'

'It was Tommy,' he said, 'drew my attention.' And he opened a copy of *The Irish Press*.

'New Irish Writing,' he read. 'Kevin Thunder. Poems, is it?'

I took the paper from him. It was in five broken stanzas of three or four lines each. An image of a beetle climbing under a rock. Of a crow rising from the guts of a crushed fox on the Dublin–Monaghan Road. Of a woman's feet crossing the cobblestones of the Trinity quadrangle. Of a line of exhaust from an aeroplane in an empty sky.

It was strangely moving, sitting there with my father and his racing cuttings in my mother's kitchen.

'Is there any money in that game?' he asked me.

'It's not me,' I said. 'There's another Kevin Thunder.'

'Reads like you. Has you all over it.'

'Another Kevin Thunder,' I repeated.

But for a moment I felt as if I had written it. It expressed something I had felt. A dislocation, an arbitrariness, a longing for meaning in a world that won't give it. I don't know. Something like that. And the use of my name was a validation no longer, it was a punishment now, a bald statement of my inability to express such things.

HE PUBLISHED A full story then. The story upset me, it lacked the bite, the pithy brevity, and I suppose the sense of strangeness of the poems. But oddly, it seemed more like him. There was a girl in the story whom I thought I could recognize as Jean, involved a football match, a flirtation afterwards, the possibility of a relationship that was never fulfilled. It was set in a small town, like the small towns of all Irish stories, and the match was a Gaelic football match; there was a dance afterwards, with a priest supervising and lemonade and a walk home by a boreen (he did use that word) with the sense of neighbours watching. A furtive kiss and some rubbish after that about another boy who her family felt was more suitable for her affections. Some stuff on a golf course then, and another fumble in the bunker of the eighteenth hole. But if this was expressive of him, I wondered, were those first poems expressive of me?

I decided we would have to meet again and took to taking short-cuts through the quadrangle. They were shortcuts to nowhere really, I walked that way in the hope of meeting him; but if the meeting did happen I had decided to justify them in that way, or if someone thought I was a thief of anything other than his identity—a handbag for instance—I had it in mind to say, I was just taking a shortcut from Merrion Square to Pearse Street and the shortest distance between those two points led through here.

I looked different, I knew, from those languorous students there. I wore a short bomber jacket with cheap flares and boots with a stacked heel. My body was coiled with something that was absent from theirs. Resentment, maybe, rage. I had the physicality that made them edge aside when I came close. And a sense of shame too, that some days made me want to rip a handbag from an untroubled elbow, headbutt one of those elegant noses. But I managed to keep it all in check with something like contempt. And one evening, I saw his feet moving over the cobbles and I followed. Out through College Green, down Dame Street, those small lanes between it and the river, and when he felt someone following and turned away as quickly as if expecting an assault, I said, 'Don't worry, it's only me.'

So we walked, Emily. Down towards the river and Adam and Eve's church towards the Brazen Head Inn which he told me was the oldest pub in Dublin. He apologized immediately for using my name, said he thought of other pseudonyms, Jason Reilly for instance, but what use is a pseudonym, he asked me, if it contains nothing of yourself? My name, Kevin Thunder, had a ring to it and it released something in him. Like a mask, he said, a persona, a lie that revealed a different truth. 'Have you never found,' he asked me, 'as a kid, that to tell a lie effectively it must contain something of the truth? If you use the third person singular, speak of yourself as he, invent a name, a character, a mask, you find yourself speaking with a different voice, revealing parts of yourself that otherwise would lie hidden.'

I was the lie, he told me, that enabled him to speak the truth. I was his objective correlative, the thing that allowed him to voice the voiceless. He had written for years, he said, nothing that had any value, but when he used my name he had an objectivity and a distance from his own thoughts, his own experiences, that released something in him. And, besides, he was shy. He had been sending stuff to that student magazine under his own name, Gerald Spain, but when he sent the sonnet under mine—without an address, mind—a notice appeared on the billboard of the literary department, *Would Kevin Thunder please contact the Icarus office?* And it was then he had realized something new had been released. So could he apologize for using my name, and at the same time, could he make a strange request of me?

I was, as they say, all ears.

He had won a prize, he said, for the short story. The New Irish Writing section of *The Irish Press*, under the editorship of a man called David Marcus, had judged him worthy—or had judged me worthy, he added, judiciously—of inclusion in an anthology of their year's work. There was money involved, of course, which he would share with me if I insisted. But the time had come to declare himself, in a literary sense. He was not Kevin, he was Gerry.

'Be my guest,' I said, and didn't say what I thought. Which was, how odd to have won for weaker stuff.

'The problem is,' he said, 'I cannot bring myself to walk into that office and tell them who I am not. Would you do it for me?'

'You mean,' I asked, 'would I walk in there and tell them I am you, not me?'

'I can't see any other solution,' he said.

'Other than you walking in and telling them you are you, not me?'

'I can't, I can't, I can't.'

He brought his fingers to his temples as he said this, and continued, 'Let's go for a drink.'

In the Brazen Head, among the old oak-panelled walls and the tourists and the students, I saw his face undergo that transformation once more, from something like me into something else.

'My problem is,' he said, 'I suppose, I have an insecure identity. I know who I am but that never seems sufficient when I meet other people. Being you for a time was a release, but I can't bring myself to have the conversation that will explain it. So if you just walk into that office, explain the ludicrous nature of my dilemma, say you used someone else's name, they can publish me as me, and that will be the end of it. For my father,' he said, 'my mother, publishing poetry is outside the ken of their social world; they want a barrister for their son, a doctor, maybe, an academic at the very least, not some itinerant Padraic Colum, and maybe that is why I presumed on you as a pseudonym. But the story, I don't know why, I can explain to them.'

'How?' I asked, and for a moment I felt favoured in the father I had been dealt.

'They'll understand it. Holidays in the West, a boreen, lemonade at a dance. New Irish Writing, *The Irish Press*, it belongs to their world, you know?'

I told him I didn't know.

'It's not embarrassing, okay? No self-revelation. No stuff you can't explain. It belongs to the realm of things you can talk about at dinner.'

Dinner. I didn't understand the concept. What we had in the Crescent we called tea.

# BURGH QUAY

*T*HE IRISH PRESS was on Burgh Quay, one of the phalanxes of Victorian buildings that fronted the south side of the Liffey. I walked there across Butt Bridge, leaving the Georgian pillars of the Customs House behind me, feeling the draught of wind from my left-hand side and the river's mouth. There was the smell of metal inside there, old print, stacks of bound copies of recent editions on stands, people leafing through them, looking for records of births, marriages, and deaths. Actually, I don't know what they were looking for: They were lost souls in long overcoats probably looking for warmth, but they were sliding long rulers down the columns of newsprint and none of them looked happy. An old creaking lift with a metal melodeon door took me up several floors and I was led to an office where a neatly suited man with fine comb lines in his oiled hair introduced himself as Mr. Marcus.

'Mr. Thunder?' he asked, and I nodded and shook his hand.

'Your story was most welcome, shows much promise, and I hope it will be the first of many.'

'I intend it to be,' I said, and then wondered if I had been too forthright. Would Gerry have taken a humbler tone?

'If I may say so, the main flaw I found in it was its too ready use of the dash and ellipsis.'

'Punctuation,' I said. And he nodded and went on.

'Perhaps the sentences could be allowed,' he said, with a wry, self-deprecating smile, as if to imply the whole conversation might well be ridiculous, 'to finish themselves.'

And I had to agree: that annoying use of dashes and dots, the impressionistic half-sentences, like my father, as if memory was defeated by the effort to express itself.

'It is prose, after all, we are engaged with here, not poetry.'

'Too true,' I said.

'And Kevin, if I may call you such—'

'You may not,' I said.

'I may not?' He seemed surprised then at such rudeness. 'Mr. Thunder then—'

'Not that either. It's what I wanted to meet you about, Mr. Marcus. I submitted it under a pseudonym.'

'Oh.' And his mouth flickered for a moment. His tongue came out and he licked his lower lip. 'How odd. Was there a reason?'

'Embarrassment,' I said. 'Shame, maybe. But more than that, I suppose. I felt I could only write it if I invented someone else. If it were to turn out worthless, for example, I would be spared the rejection. I've always felt worthless, undeserving of any notice, and this other person I came up with, Thunder, he was my barrier, I suppose. He could deflect all of the imagined disappointments.'

'And your real name?'

Embarrassment was flooding the room now, like that black squid's ink. I could tell he wanted the meeting to be over. But I kept going, because I had to.

'And this Kevin Thunder, he seemed to live the life I wanted to live. His thoughts flowed freely whereas mine have always been clogged, had no apparent exit, like the pink colourings inside boiled sweets—I'm making no sense now, I know, and if he were here maybe he could, but he isn't, it's just me, and my real name, abjectly and shamefacedly, I must admit, is Gerry. Gerald Spain.'

'Oh. And you would like the anthology, and the announcement of the prize, to reflect that?'

And I had to pause for a moment. If I said no, would Kevin Thunder have a life he otherwise might not have had? But we were already past that point.

'It will have to, I'm afraid.'

'Kevin Thunder had a ring to it . . .'

'But the story still stands, surely?'

'It's good,' he said. 'More than good.'

'Except for the punctuation.'

'The dash, the ellipsis. A little overused.'

'Gerry won't write like that again, I can promise you that.'

He stood there, like a small bird, all of his weight pressed on one foot, the other foot raised slightly, like a dancer, on tiny hand-stitched leather shoes. And for some reason, I suddenly liked him enormously.

'Well, thank you then, Mr. Gerald Spain. I will, as I said, look forward to more.'

# DAWSON STREET

I T WAS ODD, Emily, like most things between us. But nothing was odder than sitting with you in that doctor's waiting room with the ultrasound of that tiny curled foetus in both of our hands. His grandson.

It was odd in that *The Irish Press* and New Irish Writing—it's hardly innovative, but definitely a worthy literary page that became a kind of institution—would form a pivotal part in his future, as a writer and as whatever a writer is when he's not writing. What Yeats called, I suppose, a bundle of accidents. The bundle of accidents that was your father would be provided, later on, with that oddest of things, an alibi. And I suppose the other odd thing is that the real story would have had all of the elements that you find missing: in his fictions, I mean—presuming you, not his granny, have read them. You lied about that, I know. We all lie. Maybe it's genetic. It had Manhattan as a background, instead of those Irish fields and seaside villages. Manhattan was the scene and a better scenic background could not have been found. But maybe this is my part of the story, not his. He needed green fields and drystone walls. I needed that skyline. Was it because it had formed the background to so many bad musical sets that I found something theatrical about it? Something compulsive, demanding of the tragic? It gave rise to rhetorical questions. Was it to complete those mean streets that we left our bloody mark there? Questions like that.

He was shy, your father, I told you, walking down the marble stairs in Holles Street to where the waiting fathers smoked their cigarettes outside. And shyness, I'm convinced, is to blame for more pathologies than the world admits. Adolf Hitler was shy, Charles Manson was shy, and maybe Shakespeare was shy, which might account for his enduring anonymity.

'Wouldn't that be funny,' I said, and you took my arm as we walked back towards Merrion Square, 'if the greatest mystery in the whole of literature was caused by the tendency of the bard to blush.'

'I'm shy,' you said then. 'I blush at the slightest slight—that doesn't sound right, does it?—for the slightest reason.'

I met that kind editor twice afterwards, I told you, once in the National Gallery in front of Rembrandt's tiny oil painting of the Flight to Egypt, once outside Greene's bookshop, flicking through the second-hand piles, and each time I had to keep up the pretence.

'Was it fun,' you asked, 'the pretending?'

'Fun isn't the word,' I told you. 'It was arch, it was deceit, but it was somehow necessary. His shyness was genuine, even pathological, like his need to write, and if I had to be him for a time, so be it.'

'I SHOULD TELL him, shouldn't I?' you said, and you had the small Polaroid-like image in your hand.

'Yes,' I said. 'You should tell everyone.'

'But what,' you asked, 'if I don't love him?'

'I thought you didn't.'

'No,' you said, 'it was a thing, an afternoon thing, but I had liked him for awhile before it happened. And now, something else is happening.'

'You want me to tell him?'

'No,' you said. 'I'll do it myself.'

And we had turned left down Stephen's Green, and we turned right again, down Dawson Street, and I could see, through the plate-glass window, the same auctioneer rising from his desk, ushering a couple towards the door.

'Here goes,' you said.

# KERRY

THERE WERE MORE stories, of course. As I immersed myself in copying Romanesque arches and flying buttresses in Bolton Street, he must have been writing. I did nixers with my father on weekends, driving the van to Fairyhouse or the Curragh, and I'd retrieve his copy of Saturday's *Irish Press*, minus the racing page. I read Gerald Spain's tale of a stillborn calf during the two-thirty at Leopardstown. I read his sad account of a Leitrim nurse's undoing during the steeplechase at Gowran. And on the weekend of the Listowel races I saw a photograph which involved a bronze or golden dog with a barrel round its neck, an award of some kind. He must have overcome his reticence to accept it, so even his shyness had its limits. He stood to one side, in a surprisingly elegant dress suit, Mr. Marcus on the other. Of the two, Mr. Marcus looked the more forlorn and I felt pity for him suddenly, or was it warmth, as before? If I had chosen a father, it would have been one like him, soberly dressed, punctilious in expression, and with that odd sense of melancholy propriety.

There was a girl, studying architecture proper, Darragh, whom I shared a laugh with. She had high cheekbones, hollow cheeks, she liked to smoke dope on the roof at lunchtime, or as she put it herself, skin up. She was from Donaghmede, had a dry, almost anaemic wit:

We shared the same sense of things. Her father was a bus inspector, her mother ran a vegetable stall, and she was, as she put it, their ticket to the middle classes. One hot day up there, with sun coming through the fumes of the midday traffic, she took her top off and lay back as she inhaled. There were pink polka dots on her bra which made a perfect contrast with her skinny ribs and the white skin on her flat stomach. 'Could be worse, Kev,' she said, and looked at me and smiled.

I knew the invitation and put my hand on the spot where her flat stomach met her thin ribs and realized then that any romance in my life thus far had come from him. She raised her lips towards mine and blew inside and I felt the last fumes of the cannabis she had inhaled.

'It's okay,' she said, 'no one comes here but us.'

Her tongue flickered round my teeth and I tasted her saliva but all I could feel was that—tongue, lips, and teeth, nothing of whatever would make it hurt, Gerry.

'And you know what,' she said, as she withdrew. 'If you don't want to, that's okay too.'

'It's not that,' I said, 'it's just—'

'Don't tell me you're a virgin, Kevin Thunder.'

'In a way,' I said.

'No sexual history, Kevin Thunder?'

'Maybe,' I said, 'if you called me Gerry.'

'All right,' she said. 'Gerry it is. Gerry, Gerry, Gerry.'

And she turned towards me again and I could feel her legs separating under her black skirt.

Afterwards her lipstick was smeared all over her cheek. As I wiped it off, she asked, with a mocking smile, 'Can I call you Kev again now? Or should we combine them both, and I call you Kerry?'

So I BECAME Kerry for her; it was a joke between us, I suppose. But more than that too, for who knows what hidden springs govern our lives. She, for example, couldn't stand the smell of air freshener, it made her physically ill, and when I asked her where that came from, she said, something from a car, on a rainy day out by the Portmarnock mudflats. And the sex thing, once dealt with, vanished entirely. We became friends, asexual and inseparable. All of the busmen knew her through her father; they'd waive her offer of fare with a flick of the hand, and mine too. I'd get off at the Malahide Road and wave goodbye to her in the upstairs window, on her way to Donaghmede.

She talked about Malevich, walking past the pawn shops on Capel Street towards the smouldering buses waiting on the Quays; how he'd foreseen abstraction and even Op Art in its totality in his whole career, how he'd painted Bridget Rileys and Mark Rothkos before they were born. She'd design a city, she told me, based on his geometry which turned Euclid on its head and she'd call it white on white. She was exhausting, exhilarating, and far too intelligent for me. Coming up to exams we did an all-nighter. I took her home to one of the empty lodger's rooms—my father was away—and we washed amphetamines down with coffee, raced through the work we had ignored all term. We caught the number 30 bus in early and she took me to an early house in Smithfield Market. 'Hey, Ma,' she said to a woman in a mud-stained apron by the bar, smelling of earth and vegetables, 'today's the day.'

'Shouldn't you be sleeping?' her mother said.

'No,' she said, 'I've been brainstorming all night with my tutor Kerry here.'

'What kind of fella's called Kerry?' she asked.

'It's a nickname, Ma, for fuck's sake. What does Da call you?'

'Sweetpea,' she said and her enormous cheeks blushed.

I SLEPT FOR a full day when the exams were over. I was awoken by the front door banging around mid-afternoon and wrapped a towel round myself and staggered down to find her there, still awake, a not entirely sane gleam in her eye.

'I didn't know,' she said, 'you felt that way.'

'What way?' I asked her, as she walked inside. Straight through to the kitchen, as if she had belonged there all her life.

'Where did you sleep?' I asked her.

'I didn't,' she said. 'Who needs sleep! Anyway,' she said, and sat down by the kitchen table, 'you wrote this for me, right?'

And she pulled a crumpled broadsheet from her bag.

'Didn't even know you wrote.'

She rolled herself a cigarette then and began to read. A series of disconnected phrases, images: a fox sleeping in a hedgerow, a girl with a black skirt, black stockings, a piano playing in a living room, wind over the poplar trees of a suburban garden, the profile of the same girl through a bus window, vanishing through the city centre.

'Like Brian Patten,' she said. 'Only better.'

'Brian Patten?'

'Don't pretend you don't know. The Liverpool poets.'

'It's not you,' I said. I could feel the vampire shifting through the room.

'Not me? Ah, I'm almost disappointed.'

She turned her lovely face towards me, as if waiting for a kiss.

'It's just,' I said, 'generic.'

'A generic girl,' she said.

'Yes,' I said. 'Anyone, and no one.'

It was too complicated, far too complicated, to explain to her who wrote it, and why.

'It made me feel privileged,' she said, 'to be thought of like that.'

'Privileged?'

'Yes,' she said. 'And you'd better kiss me now.'

I brought my mouth towards her smoky lips. Her eyes were alive and mad, deranged by lack of sleep.

'How about the exams?'

'I wrote steadily for four solid hours.'

'You did well then.'

'Brilliant. I am brilliant, amn't I?'

'Yes,' I said. 'You have the brains.'

'We did it once, didn't we? The sex thing.'

'Yes,' I said. 'But we're friends now.'

'Friends don't write like that.'

'No,' I said. 'But I don't know that woman.'

'So she's not me.'

'No.'

'But could she be me?'

I shook my head and turned away.

'I'm out,' she said. 'You got a rollie?'

I told her I hadn't, then watched her reach into the tea caddy, spill some tea leaves into her Rizla paper.

'You're smoking tea?'

'Yeah,' she said. 'It's the coming thing.'

I could feel the vampire shifting, the clouds of dust in the sunlight coming through the windows. And I realized something was seriously wrong.

'You need to sleep,' I told her. 'You've been awake for two days.'

'Yes,' she told me. 'I'm high on life.'

And she was. I took her down to Dollymount to swim and watched her run into the miniature waves in her black knickers and polka dot bra. She pulled her clothes on afterwards without even attempting to dry. She held my arm, walking back over the wooden bridge, the wet from her bra soaking her top.

'Write for me,' she said, 'the next time. Forget about that other one. What did you call her?'

'Generic,' I said.

'Yes,' she said. 'Darragh's a much better name than generic. Make me vanish with your words.'

'You want to vanish?' I asked her.

'Yes,' she said and began to sprint then for a bus approaching on the Clontarf Road.

'I have to find my da and vanish.'


AND SHE DID vanish, for awhile. She vanished from Bolton Street, from our rooftop eyrie where she had rolled her joints, from the north city-centre pubs we used to frequent. She vanished from Bewley's café on Westmoreland Street where I blew on the froth of my coffee as she rolled a joint beneath the table. I went to the early house in Smithfield one morning and met her broad-cheeked mother, smelling as before of earth and vegetables.

'You're looking for Darragh?' she asked me.

'Yes,' I said.

'Well, Kerry,' she said—'is it Kerry?'

'Kevin,' I said.

'After I met you both, she was awake for a week. The examiners called me from Bolton Street. She'd written nothing but her name on the papers. Over and over. Darragh Treacy. I told them we could have taught her to do that at home.'

'Where is she now?' I asked. But I think I already knew.

'She's in the Gorman,' she said. 'You know Grangegorman? The funny farm. Told us she's suffering from hypermania. It's a new type,' she said, 'of mania. Will you visit her, Kerry?'

'And it's Kevin,' I told her. 'Kevin Thunder. Kerry was a nickname.'

'Yes,' she said. 'Kevin. The Kevin who wrote the poems.'

'Poem,' I said.

'She showed me three,' her mother said, and her eyes looked sad and devastated, but entirely without blame.

'The doctor said they weren't helping her—what do they call them?—delusions . . .'

'Tell me if you think it's my fault.'

'No,' she said. 'I could see it coming. Long before she met you. But go and see her, will you? She needs a friend.'

# GRANGEGORMAN

S O I SCOURED the Dublin bookshops for more of my work. Greene's, Hodges Figgis, the Eblana. And eventually in Parson's by Baggot Bridge over the Grand Canal, I found more of Kevin Thunder. In a new edition of the same broadsheet, called *Broadsheet*, coincidentally. Two columns of broken lines, under two new titles. One called 'Filigree,' the other called 'The Dead Racoon.' One about how bronze copper turns to green when it meets the air, the effect the air around the loved one has upon the author—the poet, I suppose I must call him. A metaphor, I thought, until I remembered his words about the objective correlative. The other about a portrait of a dead racoon in some gallery, viewed alone, when, the lines implied, to be truly seen for what it was it should have been viewed together.

On the bus to Grangegorman an old white-haired bus inspector checked my ticket and I wondered if it was her father. He had pale blue eyes like hers and the palms of his hands were red. Were her palms the same, I wondered, and felt ashamed because I didn't know.

I remembered the asylum pickers from Portrane—the dummies, as Joey and his mother had called them—walking up the avenue towards the grey Victorian walls. I asked for Darragh Treacy from the man in a serge uniform at the front desk, and was taken upstairs, down corridors to a long ward where a television gleamed in a far corner, and she lay in a bed near the barred door.

'Kerry,' she said and wound her fingers around mine. And I saw a triangle of red on the soft side of her palm.

'I was mad for awhile, but I'm getting better now.'

'You wouldn't sleep,' I said.

'I know,' she said. 'It's hard to explain. I thought everything was to be celebrated. I thought not a minute of any hour was to be missed. I felt I had to stay awake. And when I read that thing you wrote . . .'

I hadn't the heart to tell her I didn't write it.

'. . . it kind of confirmed that feeling . . .'

'What's it been like in here?' I asked.

'If you live inside your brain, not too bad.'

'Your hands are cold,' I said stupidly, apropos of nothing.

'You wrote two more, my ma brought them. Better than Brian Patten, Kerry. They kind of kept me going. Until the nurses took them from me.'

'Why?' I asked.

'The doctors think they set me off. And they do.'

She looked at me with hungry eyes.

'And I know you said the first one wasn't me. But I could feel myself more in the second.'

'Maybe,' I said. And I was immersed in half truths now, unexplainable realities, necessary lies.

'I've got two weeks more in here,' she said. 'Will you come again? Maybe take me out?'

'I've to go to England,' I told her. And this at least was true. I had another job on the buildings waiting. Tommy the Clock had a cousin who had a brother who worked in demolition.

'For the summer,' I added. 'To earn my fees for next year.'

'How will I contact you?'

'You can write,' I told her.

'The doctor said I should. Write down what's in my head. Said it would be—what's the word . . .'

'Therapeutic?' I hazarded.

'That's it,' she said. 'Where will I write to?'

'The Crescent,' I told her. 'Tommy will send them on.'

'Tommy who?' she asked.

'Tommy the Clock,' I said, absurdly. But it seemed to satisfy her.

# MULBERRY, SWANN & WILSON

'HERE GOES,' YOU said, and you crossed the street and a bus had to jam on its brakes but you didn't even acknowledge it. As the squeal of brakes subsided and the smell of brake fluid filled the air, the bus went on its way again and blocked you from view, then revealed you as the glass doors of the auctioneers closed behind you. I could see you through the lettering, MULBERRY SWANN, and you opened an inner door and he looked up from his desk and saw you. It was strange, the image, like a television with the sound turned off, but the way he stood up wasn't at all abrupt or unkind. He walked towards you, and you said something and he put his arms around you and then walked to the window and closed the blinds.

He should have been here beside me to see this, I remember thinking. And maybe he was. You were a finished thing, as you crossed the street, as you walked towards him before the doors closed, you were finished and undamaged and unafraid. They say crime doesn't pay, but in your case it did. Because you were his prime motivation. I could blame other things, of course. We were to blame, for our similarities, our mutual obsessions, our sharings, our transgressions. Manhattan was to blame, for simply being there, being vast, being anonymous, and so goddamnably suitable for such an event. But you were to blame too. You were what he wanted to preserve. Untouched, inviolable. And he succeeded, in the oddest way. Didn't you, Gerald?

I felt something beside me and I turned, thinking he or the vampire might be there. But there was a Romanian woman with an infant and a McDonald's cup, rattling for change.

I had none.

# HAMMERSMITH

*D*ear Kerry, her first letter went, *I got out on Tuesday. My father came to take me back and home seemed like a small goldfish bowl where everything that moved moved like it would underwater. My mother seemed to leave bubbles behind her when she cleaned the sink. I'm on tablets called Lithium and the doctor said they should have a soporific effect, since my tendency towards what he called elation has to be controlled. I went into town three days later and swore I saw you from a bus window walking down Talbot Street. You looked different, with a coat I had never seen you wearing, and I wondered had you really left for London or was that just a turn of phrase, the kind of thing you say when you don't want to hurt someone but don't want to see them.*

*We were friends, weren't we? I found another broadsheet with a poem of yours in it and in the cold light of day I could see what you meant. The girl could have been anybody, generic, but there is a piece of me there surely, or if not I will pretend there is. I saw you again then in the Dandelion market, without the coat this time but your clothes were still different though the hair was just the same. I called out Kerry, then in case you had forgotten, Kevin, but you didn't turn, you seemed bound for somewhere else and I could have run but I let you go. Maybe then again you never existed, my memories of you are part of my hypermania in its first, elevated phase or maybe then again I am imagining you through the curves and bubbles of this fish bowl that I'm in.*

*Love to clear the matter up so please write . . .*

I read this on a scaffolding in Hammersmith, while the cement buckets rose and fell on their block and tackle. I scribbled a postcard back saying I was indeed in London until the end of August.

*Dear Kerry,* her second letter went, *you don't have to pretend, I know you're in Dublin. This pretence may be to save my feelings, but believe me I have no feelings, which I believe might be the point of the Lithium. The discarded chip bags outside the chipper in Donaghmede seem to move in slow motion, or to put it a different way, when the wind blows them, as it does, there is always a wind when the last bus brings me home and the last bus always brings me home. I walk the city all day, would walk home if I had the courage since it would take longer and the sight of the small council house where I have spent my life with the small nautical hole in the cement of the front porch—and why there should be a maritime theme to a housing estate so far from the sea I have no idea—anyway the sight of home depresses me and I put it off as late as possible, and when the last bus finally brings me home the crowds around the chipper have diminished and the wind is blowing the discarded chip bags but I am cursed with the sensation that I am moving away from them rather than them moving away from me as if I was the insubstantial discarded thing which the wind could blow and they had the place I should have on this street, fixed and only moving when they themselves decided.*

*I walk the city because I have to walk but I punctuate my walking with sightings of you. I search the bookshops for another broadsheet with another poem in the manner of Brian Patten but although you have been walking this city in a route that brings you every now and then into my vision you have not been writing, or if you have been writing, you have not published which is fine. I suppose the three you have already written and the girl depicted there who may or may not be me are already sufficient. Anyway I saw you once crossing the Liffey over Capel Street Bridge, a bridge I crossed once with you discussing Marinetti and the Futurists, their designs which could well have been architectural drawings, blueprints for a city of the future where Lithium would not be a necessity and where all of our walks could have led towards the same route, an avenue where we could have walked together, comfortably and happily without pretending Dublin was actually London, and this avenue I would call the avenue of friends. Because we were friends, weren't we, before this wind came and took my breath away, left me outside of myself, watching myself, walking this grubby ancient city in search of you.*

They always ended in midstream, without a goodbye or by your leave or signature, as if something much more urgent had caught her attention. I always read them on the scaffolding for some reason, picked them up from the letter box, ran to the site, tucked myself beneath the block and tackle around half past ten, for a cigarette and a breather, if anybody asked. The dust and cement matted my hair and when I saw a new hairstyle around King's Road, crew cut on the top, long round the ears, I did it myself and happily endured the taunts of Featherhead.

*Dear Kerry,* her third letter went, *sightings everywhere now. Maybe I know where to look, the streets you take to avoid me, Pembroke Place, Raglan Road, the Municipal Gallery looking at the Turners, bookshops are good I find, and libraries, Pearse Street Library, the National Library, I watch you go in from outside Buswells and two hours later you emerge, there is a reason I know for your deceit so I don't intrude, I relish my status as the ignored one, the ungreeted one, the reluctant shadow. I saw you come out of the Lincoln Inn, swaying—when were you ever drunk, my Kerry? We smoked red leb, Thai stick, liked our uppers when we could find them, but there you were, drunk in the old-fashioned way, you hung on to the bus stop at Lincoln Place and took the 45a going towards the south-side. Are you hiding in the Dublin mountains, Kerry, are you writing haiku up there among the pine trees, a small hut maybe looking over Glencree or in Larch Hill where we used to go camping with the Girl Guides?*

*And I took my heart in my hands and walked back home, passed the Crescent on the way where all the lights were off and up the Malahide Road all the way to Donaghmede where there was no wind outside the chip shop and the empty bags were static for once and I knew things were changing again, there was a new moon over St. Anne's estate and everything was good with the world, there was that crystal clarity again. I walked up to my front door with the nautical hole in the cement porch and heard the tiny sleeping house, into my bedroom where I could hear my father snore and there was the Malevich white on white on the wall beside the poster of Fleetwood Mac and I knew I wouldn't sleep, why sleep when the world has turned again and I have to be alive to every waking moment?*

*Dear Kerry,* her fourth letter went, *in the kitchen I was out of Golden Virginia so I sprinkled tea into my Rizla and Ma and Da were gone to work but everything was still good, perfect I might add and I walked into town past the Crescent where I saw that Abraham Stoker who wrote* Dracula *was born next to you and I walked across a park, over a tiny bridge with swans sitting in the mudflats, down the East Wall Road with the big trucks heading for the ferry to the river, where I walked up to Butt Bridge and there you were again back from your haiku idyll in Larch Hill, crossing Pearse Street with a notebook in your hand. And you ducked through the back entrance into Trinity and I followed the reluctant shadow again and you were crossing the cobblestones and you stopped and turned and said to me, hey.*

*Your voice was different, everything was changed and I repeated, hey, it's all good, I said, it's all good. I know you, don't I, you said, and I said what do you think, Kerry. Kerry, you said, in a voice that had a question in it, yes I said, Kevin and Gerry make Kerry. So I'm Kerry, you said, in a voice so formal it nearly made my heart break and I said come on Kerry please, it's Darragh, don't pretend anymore and you took my hand and said, Okay I'm not pretending. And you led me through the cobbled square to a greeny bit beyond where there were boys in whites playing cricket and I said are you back from London Kerry or did you never go? I never went you said. Why did you lie my Kerry Kerry Kevin Gerry.*

*And you had a blade of grass between your teeth and you placed the other end in mine and you chewed the grass until your lips reached mine and we kissed and your saliva was green, it tasted grassy, and the kiss was long and I was waiting for your hand between my legs but it never came. A girl taught me that, you said, long ago in Dollymount.*

*Does that mean you love me, I asked, and you said out of your green lips, yes Kerry will always love Darragh and I said that's a lifetime's promise and you said if you say so.*

*And I took out my Rizlas and sprinkled in some tea leaves and you said what's that and I said tea, it's the coming thing. I lay back in the grass and you said you're quite mad aren't you, and I said yes my name is mad Darragh and I'm in my manic phase. And I closed my eyes then and waited for another greeny kiss and then you did that thing, you traced your hand up the creamy bit of my leg to where my knickers were tightest. How mad are you? you said and I said mad enough for you and I felt your finger press the fabric round the soft bit and I moved my legs to let it in and your tongue now was licking the green saliva from my lips and I was waiting.*

*I could have lain like that for hours but your hand pulled back then and you weren't you anymore. Don't stop, I said. That madness you said is attractive but I have to go you said, I'll see you later. Where? I asked. Wherever, you said, down at Dollymount round eight. Can we chew the grass again? I asked and you said all the grass we want.*

*And I walked the city until the light began to fade and walked all the way to Dollymount and put a long blade of grass between my teeth and walked up and down the strand. I thought I found you when the dark came down but it wasn't you, there were two of them who weren't you and I walked on up the dune to find you to see what I could see but even if you had been there I couldn't have seen you because they grabbed me by the ankle and pulled me down again, a long scour in the sand. They did their thing by the dunes, in the sand and I had sand in my crotch and they did it again and again until I was raw from the sand and bleeding. And a golfer found me in the morning by the fourteenth hole—he was a kind man with spikes in his shoes and he took me to the clubhouse where an ambulance was waiting that took me to the Gorman where I'm writing this.*

I read this one by the cement mixer with my feathercut hairdo and my face covered with cement dust. There were tears coming down my face and the cement congealed in streaks around them. I felt there would be no more letters and as the weeks passed, no more came.

AROUND THE END of August I received my final pay cheque and took the boat back and saw the purple sky over the Pigeon House tower. I walked back from the North Wall as if I needed to take slow steps back into this half-remembered life. There were municipal workers cutting new flower beds in the Fairview Park and the house in the Crescent was empty but for the sound of shuffling in the upstairs room where Tommy kept his clocks. I tapped on the door and heard him treading among his timepieces and saw the face with the grey workcoat and heard his voice, 'Kevin, Kevin, thought you were due back. Your father's in Tralee.'

'At the races,' I said.

'Yes,' he replied, 'where else?'

'Are there any letters?' I asked him, and 'No,' he said, 'I sent on whatever ones came.'

I took the bus next morning to Grangegorman and when I asked for Darragh Treacy I was told she had been moved to Portrane. So I took the train out through the low vegetable fields past Donabate where I'd worked with Joey and his mother and wondered was she one of the asylum pickers now. The asylum itself was half an hour's walk from the station, high walls surrounding a long driveway up to an old red-bricked collection of buildings, a small city really—Mad City, she might have called it, nothing like the one she would have designed from her friend Malevich—a jumble of stone arches, high slate roofs, and barred windows from a bad Victorian fairy tale. I imagined the asylum pickers heading off from here each morning, *Hi ho, hi ho, it's off to work we go.* There was a round tower across the lawns jutting through the brown wave-flecked sea towards the low clouds above.

I enquired at the desk and was told there were no visitors allowed, only on Saturdays and then only family. 'Are you family?' the wicked witch with the horn-rimmed glasses behind the desk asked, and I had to admit that I was not. And I would have left it at that, but walking back out, I saw a girl sitting in a wheelchair with a nurse by a bench, the round tower behind and the foam-flecked sea, and there was something in the way her hair fell back, though her head was turned oddly to one side. I went up and sat beside the nurse and asked about the round tower, the date of it. 'Ninth century, I believe,' said the nurse and although she was between me and her charge I could see that the hand which she held in her own, and not at all unkindly, was red around the palm.

'Darragh,' I said and I noticed the head behind her turn.

'Are you family?' the nurse asked and I lied this time and said I was.

'Family visits Saturday,' she said. 'But if you want to know how she's doing, she's doing well. Aren't you, love?'

She stood and gripped the wheelchair and turned it, so Dawagh's face circled past mine. Darragh had the same high cheekbones, the same blue eyes, and her eyes crossed mine as the wheelchair turned but they didn't see me. One of us must have changed.

'Fresh air,' said the nurse, 'works wonders.'

She turned the wheelchair towards the mad city and I watched the whey-coloured foam behind the round tower. I imagined long-boats gathering in the waves and monks crouching on the stone stairs inside.

# MANSION HOUSE

I BACKED INSIDE THE railings of the Mansion House, across from the auctioneers, to get away from the diesel fumes of the idling buses. The blinds that closed behind you had stayed drawn. I should have walked home, but I felt some responsibility—towards what, I wasn't sure. Towards whatever you were denied during your childhood, that great theatre of crimes unsolved. And most crimes are like our childhood, never solved, I should have told you that.

We had our own criminal history, your father and I: One left a trail of chaos that the other then took care of, often for reasons of curiosity as much as anything else. What would it be like, under the other's skin? Most people can only imagine another's life. You came out then, and the blinds stayed drawn and you crossed the traffic towards me.

'Are you glad,' I asked you, 'that you did that?'

'Yes, oddly enough.'

'Was he glad?'

You stood there for awhile and watched the buses go by.

'He has a nice hairless chest,' you said, apropos of nothing.

Then you turned, as if to go.

'Can you build a relationship on hope?' you asked.

'Most relationships are built on nothing else.'

'What are you, my father?'

'No.'

But at times like that I wondered should I have answered yes.

'We have to meet, he told me. Talk through it all.'

'That's good, then.'

'It's strange. I'm not used to—feeling things . . .'

'Will you keep me informed?'

'Yes,' you said. 'If you keep me informed.'

'I'm writing a long letter,' I said.

'I thought you said a book.'

'More like a confession.'

'You have sins to confess?'

'Crimes, maybe.'

'Oh goody,' you said. 'A crime novel. A detective book. Don't make it too—what's the word? Literary.'

'You don't like that?'

'Had enough of that. Hate that.'

# THE SOUTH WALL

I MET HIM BY the long pier down from the Pigeon House. Why there, I don't remember now, unless it was to keep something shameful secret. I hit him and it felt like hitting me. He hit me back and I was surprised that it still felt like hitting me.

'If you,' he said, 'if you had things to say and only another name could say them for you, if that name allowed you a mode of speech that no other name would, if the things you said had to be hidden, couldn't be said in your name, would you not—'

The water didn't so much lap as burble and the buoys shifted with the waves like wet seals. I resisted the urge to throw him in the water, after battering his face against the old limestone slabs beneath our feet. Then I wondered would I be able. He had struck me good and hard, and my teeth felt out of joint.

'It's not about that,' I said, 'it's about her.'

'Who's this her?' he asked.

'Darragh,' I said. 'She thought it was me. Anyone would.'

'That mad girl,' he said.

'She's mad now,' I said.

He had a handkerchief out. He was wiping his split lip.

He gave it to me. I wondered would arguments always be like this between us. Short and fast.

'What are you hiding,' I asked him, 'that the guy who writes the stories can't say?'

'I'm in love,' he said, and turned away to face the derricks of the North Wall. There was a large rust-red ship sliding almost silently towards them.

I took a breath. So had I been, I suddenly realized. With Darragh, whose personality blew in wisps around the city now.

'Who is she?' I asked. I hated her already, I wasn't sure why. Because, I supposed, Darragh had wanted to be her. But he wasn't me. And none of it made sense. Yet still, I hated her.

'Dominique,' he said. 'Dominique Barry. She's doing medicine. Her father's a consultant in—'

'Yeah, blah blah blah blah blah blah,' I said. 'Your family knows her family, and let me guess, you saw her walk around that park when you were a kid, you saw her lately all grown up, and she took your breath away.'

'How did you guess?' he asked—sardonically, I felt.

'You mean I'm right?' I was surprised: Cynicism is so rarely accurate.

'Am I such a cliché?'

'Must be.'

And he was laughing at me now:

'The thing about clichés is, they wouldn't exist if they didn't reflect a generalized truth. But the particulars are always different.'

'And the particulars in this case are?'

'I know her, she doesn't know me. Knows of me, maybe, but we haven't met since she was five. I see her with her crowd.'

'Does she see you with yours?'

'I don't have a crowd.'

He walked on in silence for a little.

'Maybe you're my crowd. So I felt those things. I wrote them. I used your name. I'm sorry. But you've been a help.'

'Glad to be of service.'

'I mean it. Thinking the way you do . . . opened up some . . .'

'How do I think?'

'I wouldn't presume to know. But you know about some things.'

'What things?'

'You really trying to pin me down here? Embarrass me?'

'No.'

'Okay. I'm a virgin. I've never, you know . . . and you, I imagine, are not.'

'No, I suppose I'm not.'

'So, that free person, who knew . . . women . . . I could imagine being him, for awhile.'

The rust-coloured ship had reached the derricks. And I could tell he was crying.

'What does she look like?'

'I'll point her out to you one day.'

'Get your hair cut first.'

'What?'

I reached out, felt his damp cheek. Touched his long faux-hippy locks.

'Your hair. So out of date. You've seen the Velvet Underground?'

'Who?'

'You really don't know anything, do you?'

He turned away again. The hair on his shoulders blew with the soft wind coming from the river.

'Is hair important?'

'Hair,' I told him, 'is everything.'

# BEWLEY'S, GRAFTON STREET

DOMINIQUE BARRY. HE pointed her out to me, walking across St. Stephen's Green, with the early morning sunlight spilling through the trees. They were burning autumn leaves, I remember, and the sun made angelic fingers through the smoke. She was wearing expensive leather boots up to her knees and a kind of cape or poncho affair that swung carelessly around those long legs, reddish hair in a pageboy cut, and she walked with a dreamy purpose, as if she had places to go but no particular urgency about getting there. Her clothes suited her name, the French and the Irish, a hint of the Wild Geese about the combination, and I imagined summers in some idyll in rural France and a family that was carelessly bilingual, the kind that knows about wines and pronounces French words correctly.

Anyway, she was perfect for him, I could sense that immediately, or perfect somehow for whatever he hoped he would become. And he left me then and I watched her go, and sat on one of those benches fronting the pond and saw that barely underneath the water, beneath the ripples the picturesque ducks made over its surface, was a bed more like a forest of slime-like green. I didn't take to following her but Dublin was small then, a kind of village really, and once you noticed somebody it was hard not to notice her again.

The next time I saw her was in the large bookshop across from the same Stephen's Green, Hodges Figgis it was called. There was a small poetry section with a stack of broadsheets there, my name hidden somewhere inside them, and I heard the clack of a confident heel on the wooden floor and saw the reflection of the same poncho entering in the window that faced the street and the traffic outside. I could see her reflection move among the reflection of the aisles of books behind me and wondered to myself what was I doing, spying on somebody I didn't even know, when the poncho made a wide movement, as if a wind had coursed through it, and I turned and saw that she was using the billowing cloak to conceal the fact that she was stealing a book.

She moved on then, down the aisle, with the same sense of dreamy purpose and vanished between books to another section, and I walked down to the place she had emptied and found myself opposite the philosophy section, French Existentialism. There was a fat copy of *Being and Nothingness* there, an empty space beside it, and where there was one, I could only presume that a second or so ago there had been two.

I heard the heels then again, towards the front door, and saw her through the plateglass window moving past the traffic on the street outside. And this time I followed, with the same kind of dreamy purpose.

Her reddish pageboy cut bobbed through the crowds and she turned right and left and right again, and crossed the road towards Bewley's Oriental Café.

I sat across from her, at one of those broad tables with multiple chairs.

'Big book,' I said, as she took the volume out from under her cape.

'Excuse me,' she said, in a tone that implied, what right have you to talk to me?

'I said,' deciding to ignore her rather arch tone, 'that's a very big book.'

'Well,' she said, enigmatically, 'maybe it needs to be.'

'A book that needs to be large. Interesting concept. The contents therein demand a lot of pages. How many?'

She said nothing for awhile and I was starting to dislike her. I remembered when he first told me about her on the slurping pier. I remembered Darragh, and the mad city.

'Nine hundred or so,' she said.

'Wow. How much did it cost?'

'I've no idea,' she said. 'I stole it.'

She smiled, in that dreamy way she had of walking, and all of my antipathy suddenly vanished.

'I know you, don't I?'

'You do?'

'Yes,' she said. 'Used to see you as a kid. Across the square. And I see you across the quad now and then, but you never talk.'

'It's an affliction,' I said. 'Shyness.' And I tried to blush, but it wasn't happening.

'Don't seem shy now.'

'I know. It's weird. Some days it just goes. Most days it doesn't. I can't control it.'

'I've read your stories.'

'Yes?'

'*The Irish Press*. I liked the one about the donkey.'

'Thank you.'

'You wrote it as if you were a bogger. But you're not.'

'I know.'

'And I can't decide whether that's a good thing or not.'

'It is,' I said. 'It's a very good thing.'

And she laughed.

'You say that as if someone else had written it.'

'That's the funny thing. About writing. It's as if someone else has.'

She thought about this for a moment, then smiled again.

'I'm going to order coffee and a Mary cake. You want some?'

'I don't know Mary cakes.'

'Mary cakes,' she said, 'have a certain significance.'

'What do you mean?'

'They're to be remembered,' she said. And she laughed then, like a little peal of bells. The laugh was either irritating or charming, I couldn't work out which. And then she smiled after the laugh, and her skin was creamy round her pale lips and I decided it was charming.

'I'd better have one then.'

'Maybe.'

She seemed to know the waitress who was hovering, one of those old Dublin ladies with dyed blonde hair who added 'love' to every question. 'You know what you want, love? You want cream with that, love?' She ordered two Mary cakes and when they arrived I could see why the Mary cake was an object of sentimental value. A brown chocolate cylindrical wall with green icing and a dab of yellow marzipan on top, that seemed to belong to somebody else's past, somebody else's childhood memories.

'Didn't your mother bring you in for these when you were little? What's her name again?'

I bit into the cake to avoid the question. And the sensation of the cake inside stilled me for a moment. I felt the taste of a childhood I had never had. There was a wall of chocolate which collapsed to a creamy fudge, the bitter hint of marzipan, and hard biscuit somewhere beneath it all. The chaos of sensations didn't so much overwhelm me as stop me with wonder for awhile. I wondered what it would have been like to have eaten this as a child, to be remembering it now with someone else who had eaten it as a child, to have this strange doll's house of sensation between us. And I felt suddenly sad and didn't know why.

'Everyone's mother did.'

And I knew why, just as suddenly. My own mother would have loved a ritual like this, the name, Mary cake, the anticipation, the treat.

'Mine did, if I was good.'

'Were you good today?'

'No. I stole. What are you, my confessor?'

'Yes, my child.'

And she laughed again, with the same bell-like peal. I thought he had to hear that laugh, but wondered, would he ever hear it just like that, so unexpectedly? Only if he made her laugh, and I wasn't sure he was funny.

'And I must confess, I have to go now.'

She put the last piece of marzipan between her teeth. There was a thread of chocolate on her lip that I wanted to wipe clean. I decided to be bold, and took a tissue from the table.

'Here. You've got a smudge.'

I leaned forwards and wiped it. Her lip curled downwards, as if in collusion with my fingers.

'Thank you, Gerry. And you promise you won't turn your head away the next time we pass?'

'I wasn't aware I did that.'

'Always.'

She took the tissue from my fingers and I felt her hand ever so briefly on mine.

'See you.'

# CROWE STREET

THE NEXT TIME I saw her, her hair was blonde. And I did turn my head away. There was a bus passing on Lincoln Place, which obscured her eyes just as she tried to catch mine. And he was waiting for me in the vegetarian restaurant on Crowe Street, to which nobody went. So I took the bus's cover, with its hoarding advertising sausages, and kept my head turned and went on towards Temple Bar. The next encounter was to be his.

He had been to a barber's. He had a spiky sailor's cut now, with fringes over the collar, a feathercut like mine and Lou Reed's. If it wasn't for the Trinity scarf, the gabardine coat, and the sense on his face of subdued panic, we could have been twins.

'So, I met her,' I said. 'I talked to her. I was you for an hour or so. I saw her rob a copy of *Being and Nothingness* from Hodges Figgis.'

He said nothing and buried his chin in his scarf.

'She's read your stories,' I told him. 'She particularly liked the one about the donkey.'

He brought a mug of some kind of herbal tea to his lips.

'She likes Mary cakes. She imagines you do too.'

'Mary cakes?'

'Weren't they a treat when you were little?'

He shook his head.

'Small chocolate and marzipan goodies they sell in Bewley's Oriental Café. You'd better try one. She thinks they're something you have in common.'

'How was it, being me?'

'That childhood of yours. I had to imagine it. But since it excludes those Mary cakes, I got it wrong. Or I was imagining someone else. Anyway, she has a nice laugh. Tell her a joke or two, you might hear it.'

My tone was rough and I could see that it unsettled him. But I couldn't care too much. I was done, I was tired of it all.

'We could,' he said, 'construct an elaborate parody of ourselves. You could fall in love with her, graduate, ask her to marry you, have one child, maybe two, I could scribble fictions in my name, which would of course be yours, live one of those lives I've only read about in Dostoevsky or Gogol, hole up in a room in Soho or Tangier, lead a life of quiet desperation, probably die from excess of alcohol, whereupon you could claim writer's block, proceed to the bar, leave those literary conceits behind you, grow old with her, making her laugh . . .'

'But you'd be avoiding a fate,' I said to him, 'that you seem to think is yours.'

'I know it is. I can't explain why. Me, her, a child. I can see it as if it's already happened.'

'That sounds alarming.'

'Yes,' he said. 'I'm an obsessive. Once something takes hold of me, it won't let go. I can't do anything about it, but it won't let go.'

'Okay then. Next time you see her, crossing that cobbled thing in Trinity—'

'The Quad.'

'Okay. The Quad. Don't turn away. Take her for a Mary cake.'

'A Mary cake.'

'Yes,' I said. 'A Mary cake. You'll like them.'

# ST. STEPHEN'S GREEN

H E TOOK HER for a Mary cake. I know this because I saw them both at an early evening's showing of *2001* in the Grafton cinema and I knew the invitation to the pictures would never have happened without the Mary cake. I was a dozen or so rows behind them, and as the Milky Way began to strobe around Keir Dullea's glass-bound face I saw his arm creep over her shoulder and her head bury itself in the nape of his neck. I left the cinema before the lights came up because I didn't want to see more.

He took her for a Mary cake. I know this because I saw them both in Bewley's, eating them. I wondered had his childhood memory returned or had he fabricated one. She broke the corner from hers and placed the broken piece between his lips and as he chewed he closed his eyes. He seemed to be remembering something, or pretending to remember something. I buried my head behind my copy of *In Dublin* and left before the waitress came to ask me what I wanted, love.

Then he stopped taking her for Mary cakes. I know this because my sightings of them ceased. I began to wander the city, looking for them. I knew this obsession was becoming unhealthy, but something inside me wouldn't let me stop. I ate Mary cakes myself in both Bewley's oriental cafés—the one in Grafton Street and the one in Westmoreland Street. There was a subtle class difference between the two. The Grafton Street one was patronized mainly by the wives and teenage children of the professional classes. One would see a well-tended hairdo there and the occasional fur coat. Whereas the clientele of Bewley's Oriental Tea House on Westmoreland Street was more pleasantly diverse: junior civil servants, employees of the Irish Gas Company whose art deco signage could be seen through the front plateglass window, male and female alcoholics having a late breakfast before the day's drinking began, busmen in uniform, secretaries, students like me from across the river.

Of the two, I for some reason preferred the latter. And in the Grafton Street one, I saw her eating a Mary cake alone, with her back to me. And something about her bobbed hairdo and the plaid coat she wore—she had long given up the poncho—seemed immediately and terribly sad. I would have gone to her, had I the courage, to explain to her, and by implication to myself, the strange symbiosis between me and the one she was, as the phrase goes, stepping out with. I would have put my arms around her and told her I was sorry, but the problem was I had no idea what to feel sorry for. For her, in the end, I suppose.

But as it was, some days later, she said sorry to me.

I was walking through Stephen's Green, around dusk, on the grass by the flower beds, with the railings between me and the almost night-lit street outside.

'Gerald,' I heard her voice say, 'I'm sorry.'

The 'Gerald' seemed strange and sent a strange blush of longing through me. I turned and saw her briefly beyond the fringes of privet hedge and the black-painted railings with the traffic going by behind her on the street outside. I met her eyes, then kept on walking, because I had to.

But she followed.

'You have to talk to me,' she said, 'it's not as if—'

'As if what?' I asked, and slowed my walk a little. I knew I could lose her before she rounded the railings, made it to the front entrance, and into the park where I was. But I couldn't lose her, for him.

'As if it's the end of the world. As if I didn't still like you.'

'You do?' I asked, sounding and feeling like a parrot now.

'Yes. And stop walking, will you, this is making me tired.'

So I stopped. I kept my face turned towards the Green, where a man in blue uniform was sounding a bell now, to signify the gate's imminent closure.

'Come here,' she said. And her hand reached through the railings and grabbed the sleeve of my coat.

'I mean here,' she said, and her hands moved upwards through the railings till they reached my face. They turned it towards hers.

'I'm sorry,' she said, 'it's just something I can't explain. My fucked-up family maybe. And I know it hurt you.'

'It did,' I said.

Then her finger touched my lip and her other hand pulled my head towards hers. She kissed me, between the railings, and my heart didn't so much stop as sink into another dimension where there weren't two of us anymore, there was just me and her and no mistaking him for me. Her tongue inched through my lips and began to ripple against my teeth. Then she pulled as suddenly away.

'The sex thing,' she said, 'has always been an issue with me. But can you be patient?'

'Yes,' I said. And I could have waited years.

'Promise?'

'I promise,' I said, and her hand pulled me towards her and she kissed me again. Then the hand slid down my shirt buttons to the belt of my trousers and as she pressed her tongue inside my teeth she unzipped me and took my hardening cock between her fingers. I felt I had to stop this and tried to draw away but she managed to speak with her tongue still in my mouth and what I heard was, 'You promised.'

I had promised. I had no idea what, though. To be patient, then, I remembered; and I was patience itself as she stroked me to hardness and then began to pull repeatedly while on her side of the railings the evening crowds went by. It was strange now, with her tongue exploring the roof of my mouth and her fingers moving over me, pulling the foreskin back and rippling over the tip. Strangely unerotic too, but her fingers moved deftly, forcefully, until eventually I couldn't stop it, and I came.

'See,' she said, 'I'm trying.' She let go of me then and I reached down and zipped my wet trousers closed. Her fingers were wet with semen and she brought them to her mouth and kissed me again. I could taste the salt of something I had never tasted. The bell was still clanging for the closure of the Green.

'So, Gerald, call me.' And she turned suddenly and lost herself among the crowds.

It was dark now. I was the last person in the Green. I ran to the gates where the porter was chaining them, the bell in a small leather satchel by his side.

'You a weirdo?' he asked. 'You want me to lock you in all night? With the other weirdos?'

'I lost something,' I lied, and he let me through. Though maybe I had told the truth. I had lost something, but I wasn't sure what.

# BEWLEY'S,
# WESTMORELAND STREET

I SAT ON THE steps of one of those Trinity halls the next day, the one that afforded me a full view of the cobbled square, the entrance through the small arch onto College Green. He had to call her. My worry was that if he did call her, to apologize for whatever had been the source of their discord, some chaos would ensue. It had been something sexual of course, their difference, and I thought of those virginal, constrained youths who studied with me in Bolton Street, so different seemingly from the languorous types who strolled across these cobbles, but maybe not that different after all.

I was invested in their future now, in a way that surprised me; it needed to be a future, for both of them, but I doubted if it would become a future I would ever want. Their families knew each other, their expectations for their offspring were confident and exact and marriage, perhaps, would have been one of those expectations. Gerry and Dominique, of course. Or Gerald and Dominique, of course. Made for each other. Even look like each other, could have been brother and sister. In the event that that future wasn't theirs, together, some subtle, preordained pact would have been broken. A small house in Ranelagh, what they call a starter home, after the inevitable marriage in University Church on St. Stephen's Green, across from the site of that lascivious event which only I was witness to, which would become, if he was ever made aware of it, a stimulating memory to whatever uxorious bliss awaited them. She was capable, Gerry, of pornographic acts in public, unafraid of them, maybe even needed them.

And I began to wonder, sitting there, waiting for a glimpse of him as the morning sun streaked through the square, were we the same person, the light and shade of the same person? Was I a dream that he dreamt, a darker form of himself, from a subtly different background, was I the part of him he kept at bay, suppressed, that he needed but could never admit to? Or was he a dream I dreamt, was he the dream of the life I wanted, had I conjured him out of the shards of my pathetic background, was his the life I should have had, but hadn't got the courage to grasp? Those poems in my name were mine, the pseudonym was uncalled for, merely a strategy to allow me to say what couldn't be said.

I saw him walking across the cobbles then, with three others, a satchel thrown over his shoulder and his scarf tangled in the strap. He was real, there was no doubt about it, and I whistled sharply, and he somehow knew the whistle was for him and he turned and saw me, and his brow furrowed with something like annoyance and I knew I was real too. We were real and separate and condemned to something, the gist of which might never become completely clear.

'You shadowing me?'

He had excused himself from his three companions and come to sit beside me on the steps.

Yes, I told him, I was becoming his Hyde, his bad self, his other. I knew he liked those terms, the literary ring to them, which to me meant nothing in particular.

'You shouldn't come here, you know.'

'Why not?' I said. 'It's a public thoroughfare.'

'No, you're free to come here, of course. It's just—I've come to like the fact that it's a secret between us. How many people have a secret like this?'

'Maybe everybody.'

'You mean everyone has another version of themselves. Interesting thought. Can I write about that?'

'If you have to.'

'Don't have to. Might want to.'

'Come for a coffee.'

He buried his head in his satchel and took out a single cigarette. He nodded as he lit it, and stood and turned around.

'Bewley's in Westmoreland Street. See you there in five minutes.'

THERE WAS A mid-morning fug there, of tobacco and steam. I took a seat underneath the Harry Clarke stained glass of fairy glades and forests and I knew he had chosen this Bewley's because she never came here. He came in, ten minutes late. His eyes avoided mine and I could tell he had had time to work some things out.

'You met her,' he said, getting right to the point.

'How do you know?'

'Else you wouldn't have searched me out. We had an argument. She . . .' And he stopped and lit another cigarette. 'I don't know how much to tell you.'

There was sweat on his upper lip and there was pain behind his eyes.

'Whatever it was,' I told him, 'she said sorry.'

'How did she say sorry?'

'She saw me through the railings of the Green and she called and followed me, then she pulled me to her.'

'And?' he asked.

'I don't know how much to tell you.'

'Just pretend I'm someone else.'

'Okay. She did something with her hand.'

'Ah,' he said. 'The thing is, I'm no good at things like that. But you, on the other hand, are.'

'How can you tell?'

'It oozes off you, brother.'

And the word was like some admission of guilt. 'Brother.'

'I cut my hair like you. I even walk like you. But I'm no good at being you.'

'You don't want to be me,' I said.

'We spent an afternoon in Herbert Park. There were men in white playing boules beyond the bushes. I wrapped a blanket round her and whatever way I fumbled, I made a mess of it. She sat up then, got upset, walked off, and came back and asked me what I wanted.'

He looked up at me. I could feel the embarrassment seeping from him, but he kept going, and I had to admire him for it.

'Have you read *Ulysses*?'

I shook my head. Like most of the world, I had only heard of it.

'Set on the 16th of June. The day Nora frigged Joyce in a park in Ringsend.'

'Frigged?'

'Don't pretend you don't know what I mean.'

I did, but I had never heard the word. 'Frigged.' It seemed as good a word as any for her fingers on my zip.

'I asked her to do the same. It led to, what are politely called, words between us.'

'She walked off?'

'Yes. And I haven't seen her since.'

And for the first time in all of our acquaintance, I suddenly disliked him. He needed the validation of some book for his erotic exploits. He looked like an enormous spoilt child, curled up across the table from me, rummaging in his satchel for another cigarette. He could have been transposed to the stained-glass window behind him, a bad fairy under a holly tree.

'She loves you,' I said, and tried to keep my voice neutral.

'You think?'

'Anyone who did just that would have to love you. Is there another word for it?'

'Yes,' he said. 'Joyce had a word for it.'

'You should call her,' I said. 'Find some way of thanking her. And arrange to meet her in St. Stephen's Green. Around when the parks are closing.'

He looked at me and his eyes were glowing almost green from the spilled light off the stained glass.

'The porter rings a bell. Tell her you remember the sound.'

I stood up then. It was time to end it.

'And let's avoid each other, in the future.'

'You think we can?' he whispered.

I turned to go, and felt his hand pulling at my own.

'Hey,' he said, as abjectly as a male voice could. 'Thank you.'

# PORTRANE

S O I WENT back to my life and was surprised to realize how lonely it was. Did I need that bad fairy with his strange unrealized desires to keep me company? The house in the Crescent rattled with my father's footsteps late at night. The flat season was ending, the steeplechasing had hardly begun so he was home a lot, a few pints with Tommy in Gaffney's and a naggin to take home. I became obsessed with Piranesi, those drawings of a crumbling, imagined Rome as if ruins could become a template for a degree in architectural draughtsmanship. I signed up for a project on Victorian institutional architecture and found myself the blueprints for Portrane mental hospital, redrew each building in the style of Piranesi, a tottering mental landscape with the round tower always visible, and a wheelchair-bound figure beneath it, whom I recognized gradually as Darragh. I went to the early house in Smithfield and met her apple-cheeked mother and asked how she was. She was coming out next week, she told me, after they had had their way with her. I asked her permission, then, like a Victorian suitor, to be allowed the privilege of collecting her and taking her home. She cried in the bar then and bought me a pint and said, 'Of course, we should be so lucky.'

I walked up Malahide Road again to the Middle Third and Killester train station. The carriage was an old wooden one, with leather straps to pull up the windows, and I saw a horse pulling a rusted plough on the market garden fields I used to work on and it seemed as if I had stepped back to some other time. There was a low winter sun, a Dutch air to the light which glistened off the water in the rutted fields. I was expected this time and she was waiting for me in reception with a lady in white and clothes that no longer fitted her, she had lost that much weight.

'Kev,' she said and it was odd, because she had always called me Kevin, 'you didn't have to come.'

'She's doing much better now,' said the nurse or therapist who held her left arm steady. 'I'm doing much better, Kev,' Darragh repeated, and her face was thin and starved like Joan of Arc in the black-and-white film by Carl Dreyer, more beautiful if possible, and much more beautiful than I remembered. I took her elbow from the nurse as if becoming her replacement and led her through the long cathedral of glass to the doors and up the avenue outside.

'You don't have to look after me, Kev,' she said, 'but it's good you came.'

'What's with the Kev?' I asked her. 'You used to call me Kevin. Kerry. Never Kev.'

'No,' she said, 'you were always Kev.'

'Tell me about Malevich,' I asked her and she said, 'Malevich, yes, I remember Malevich. Who was he now?'

'The painter,' I said, 'you adored.'

'Yes,' she said, 'the painter, Malevich. I just liked the sound of his name. The way I like the sound of yours, Kev.'

'I found God there,' she told me, as we waited for the bus.

'You did?' I asked, and I tried to keep my voice from breaking.

'Yes,' she said. 'He abides.'

'Where does He abide?'

'Inside all of us,' she said. 'And particularly inside Malevich.'

She had a small satchel full of drawings, which she opened on the bus. They were all of a council estate house with a small circular hole in the cement porch.

'That hole,' she said, 'I kept wondering what it meant.'

'It's a nautical hole,' I told her. 'You used to wonder that before, what architect put a nautical hole in a council estate.'

'Maybe,' she said, 'you can see the sea through it.'

'You can't,' I told her. 'That's exactly why you used to wonder about it.'

'Something about this conversation isn't right, is it?'

'No,' I agreed with her.

'But we can put it right, can't we, Kev?'

'Yes,' I told her. 'We can put it right.'

But we couldn't, of course. The bus left us by the chip shop where the discarded chip wrappings used to make her feel weightless and I walked her through the small estate, each porch with its nautical hole, to the one that was her home.

'There's the girl,' her father said, the silver-haired bus inspector, and her mother stood behind, an apron over her stout frame, and I left her there, declined the invitation to come inside. 'Another time,' I said.

'Yes,' said her mother, tears flowing down her cheeks, 'another time.'

# MARINO CRESCENT

THERE WAS A humming in my head and I thought of the power lines on the Clontarf Road and the Count with his opera cape and the shadow with the beret in the cement bathing shelter, and I came half out of sleep and reached for the phone but the vampire whispered, no, it's the door this time. And I woke up then and saw the pale light washing through the window and the doorbell was ringing.

And as I walked downstairs, Emily, there was something about the figure in the mottled glass that I recognized, something about the slim shoulders and the colour of the suit which I could already see through the bubbled glass was blue. And when I opened it, I knew what I should have recognized because there he was, your auctioneer.

'I'm not disturbing you?' he asked.

'No,' I said, 'not at all.'

'We normally wait for a follow-up call, but in this case . . .'

'In this case?'

'The house,' he said. 'Your house. We have had an offer.'

'Did I put it on the market?'

'No,' he said. 'It's a private offer.'

'Aha.'

'A client,' he said, 'who likes the Stoker connection. A good price, if you want it. One point five.'

'You'd better come in,' I said.

Something about his suit and the sweat on his upper lip made me sorry for him. You have a nice hairless chest, I felt like saying. And then, as if disclosing a burden he had been keeping to himself for too long, he came out with it.

'Actually, it's me.'

'You?'

Coincidence, I told you, had been the motor of my life. But as I looked at his discomfited face I thought maybe coincidence has nothing to do with this.

'Yes,' he went on. 'I need a house. I know it's unusual, but not unethical. You can check the price I'm offering with another auctioneers.'

'No,' I said. 'I don't care. I'm not sure I want to sell it.'

'The thing is,' he said, 'I may have a family soon.'

'Oh, congratulations.'

'Thank you,' he said. 'It's not a simple situation but could be a happy one.'

'A permanent one?'

'We live in hope. Mr.—'

'Thunder,' I reminded him.

'Yes, Mr. Thunder.'

I made him tea. I felt I should disclose myself, but a lifetime of dissembling is not so easily broken. Besides, I wanted to hear what he had to say.

'And you think this is the house for you.'

'It's affordable.'

'For your family.'

'I would have preferred the southside, but . . .'

'I grew up here.'

'So. You must have fond memories.'

'I have memories. You're having a child?'

'Yes.'

'Boy or girl?'

'Boy.'

'Won't your wife need to see it?'

'Partner,' he corrected me. 'And, I might, so to speak, surprise her.'

I looked at his brown eyes, his unsettled mouth. I tried to imagine a child of yours, Emily, growing up here. Would I carry the vampire with me, out of here? Does time repeat itself, like one of Tommy's clocks? And I told him yes, I would be happy to sell.

# THE TRINITY BALL

H E TOOK HER for another Mary cake. I know this because he told me, over a Mary cake and coffee in Bewley's, Westmoreland Street. Their Mary cake happened in the Grafton Street Oriental Café, a reconciliation of kinds, as they both chewed the marzipan and he removed the small chocolate whorl at the top and gave it to her. She took it between her lips, he told me, like an invitation and he saw a future for them both once more. He asked her to the Trinity Ball then and I felt sad for a moment, thinking of Darragh in the bedroom of her small council house with the nautical hole in the porch. I imagined a different universe in which I could get my hands on tickets, for her and for me, dress her in something outrageous like a Pierrot costume and join that Trinity world.

The afternoon of the ball, the college was surrounded like a seraglio, with fat, tuxedoed bouncers for all the world like Janissarian eunuchs guarding every entrance. I felt that any event as heavily fortified as that deserved to be breached. I rented a monkey suit in Louis Copeland's on Capel Street and sometime after midnight, after all the Cinderellas should have long gone home, climbed on top of a rubbish truck and scaled the wall by Lincoln Place. I walked along it with my arms spread out, like a tightrope walker or a dancer, and when I felt there was some grass beneath me, I jumped.

I landed in the cricket pitch, close to the pavilion. Why was I here, I wondered, listening to the dull bass thump coming from it, light spilling from the bar and a variety of tuxedoed students in various stages of inebriation spilling in a semicircle round the light. They were wearing masks, Donald Duck masks, Goofy masks, Richard Nixon masks, and the occasional flamboyant ones wore *commedia dell'arte* masks with those ridiculous curved noses, spangled with gold dust. One of them had a Ziggy Stardust mask, with a yellow streak of lightning creasing a version of David Bowie's face. Maskless, I felt almost naked on that cricket pitch strewn with empty plastic glasses, until I found a discarded Zorro mask and put that on.

Masked, it was simple. I wandered. Down towards the Pavilion bar first, where I ordered a tequila and a girl in a white diaphanous dress offered me a joint. She wore a funereal hat with a black lace fringe which functioned as a mask, since all I could see was her mouth—pouty, I think, and slashed with purple lipstick.

'Come on, Zorro,' she said, and 'Yes,' I said, 'where?'

'Deep Purple is playing in the Commons,' she said, and I went with her, saw the rockers in the far distance with their heads bowed over the fanciful guitars.

'Thai stick,' she said, and handed me the burning cylinder of paper again, but the fug of it was getting to me, and besides I saw then what I realized I had come to see all along.

He was dancing with her in the centre of the floor, some kind of feline appurtenance over his eyes, and she was in a spangled dress cut round the knees into strips, with an elaborate fairy thing around her face. They were clinging to each other as if their lives depended on it, as if there was no one who could save them but themselves. It looked lewd and romantic and somehow desperate with longing, a combination that was overwhelming.

'You looking at them?' the girl asked.

'Yes,' I told her. 'I'm not sure I've seen anything so beautiful.'

'That's the stick talking,' she said, and 'Maybe,' I said.

She gripped me close then, turned me to her, and 'Take off the mask, Zorro,' she said, and I said, 'No, this mask is what I am.'

'I hate that,' she said.

'Hate what?' I asked.

'That,' she said. 'I thought I liked you but I hate that.'

'Hate what?' I asked again, and she said, 'Pretension,' and turned abruptly and walked away from me, and I was alone on the floor, and looking for them, but they were nowhere to be seen. So I swayed through the crowd for awhile, right up to the speakers where the huge bass reverberation almost made me sick, and then I pushed my way through outside, to the cobbles and the squares and the students vomiting in the privet hedges.

I took a breath and felt something like sobriety return and walked through the raucous crowd. There were streams of urine flowing over the ancient cobbled stone and I wanted to piss like them but I felt disgusted, so I pushed my way through to the Buttery bar. And I found him there, slumped over the sink in the Buttery toilets, trying vainly to throw up. His hands lost their grip and he fell towards the floor, his chin cracking off the enamel sink. It would have woken a sober person or knocked them unconscious, but with whatever was in his system then, it did neither. I caught him from behind before his head cracked the tiled floor and I lifted him upwards, until he saw my masked face in the mirror.

'Zorro,' he mumbled. His own mask was around his neck, dribbled with vomit. I lifted him outside then, through the crush of staggering students, and the weight collapsed underneath me, dragging us both to the roots beneath one of those privet hedges.

'You're going to leave me here, Zorro,' he said.

'No,' I said, 'I'm taking you home.'

'You're not, you fucker,' he said.

'What have you taken?' I said.

'That'd be telling,' he said.

'You'd better tell me,' I said. I was used to Thai stick and amphetamines, but this was something else.

'Better ask her,' he said. 'Me, I want to sleep.'

I unhoooked his mask from under his chin. And I recognized it now. Felix the Cat.

'Am I Zorro? No, you're Zorro.'

'No,' I told him. 'I'm Felix the Cat.'

'And I'm Zorro.'

'Yes,' I told him. 'And Zorro needs to sleep.'

He pulled the Zorro mask over his face, and his head rolled under the hedge. I could see his neat shoes, the dress suit with the tiny seam of satin.

'Look after her,' he muttered.

'Who?' I asked and he answered, 'Titania.'


I FOUND HER lying on the grass by the cricket pavilion, staring at the stars about her. Her dress was one with mirrored sequins and it sparkled every time her body moved. There was a smouldering joint on the grass beside her, but that wasn't all she had taken, I could tell.

'Hey, Felix,' she murmured, 'where did you go?'

I lay down beside her and stroked the whiskers of her mask. Some kind of elfin thing, with fairylike, slanted eyes.

'To throw up,' I lied.

'Yuk,' she said. 'No need to be so specific.' And she turned her eyes from the heavens to meet mine.

'You said you'd get me through this.'

'I will,' I said, and took her hand.

'It comes in waves,' she said. 'Sometimes I think I'm going to burst inside my head. White lightning.'

I lifted the mask gently from her face to see her eyes. The pupils were huge and seemed to reflect the whole of the Milky Way.

'I saw God,' she said. 'He was dressed in moleskin trousers and a donkey jacket, carrying a pole with one half of a triangle on top of it.'

'A hod.'

'A what?'

'In the eyes of the world He carries a hod.'

'A hod. For God.'

'Who are you again?'

'Titania,' she said. 'How could you forget? You chose, Oberon.'

'I thought I was Felix the Cat.'

'They don't sell Oberon masks. But you're him.'

And yes, I was him. Her huge eyes stared at me and she took my hand and placed it in between her legs. I could feel her thighs move under the sequins.

'Watch it,' she said, as if the gesture had been mine.

I did watch it. I drew my hand away. But I couldn't resist those sequins. Her bare shoulder held a thin stream of them. I touched them instead. It was safer.

'You want to talk about it?' she asked.

'Yes,' I said. I thought she meant the drug, or sequins.

'This tiny thing growing inside.'

And the stars seemed to pulsate for a moment. Did I imagine it, or did one of them streak through the sky? Or was it the Thai stick?

'Do we keep it?'

There was only one answer to that. Yes.

'Yes,' she said.

'You want me to say no?' I asked.

'No,' she said. 'But is that the declaration, Gerald?'

'Yes.'

'Let me hear it,' she said, turning her face to the heavens. 'Loud and clear.'

'Okay. Felix the Cat loves Titania.'

'Does he, Gerald? He is a he, isn't he, Felix? That should make me happy. But it kind of makes me feel . . . lost . . .'

She took my hand and placed it on her sequined stomach. It was flat as a pitch and putt green.

'You took something else, didn't you? After we split that tab . . .'

'Yes,' I said. And I supposed he had.

'Will Titania marry Felix the Cat?'

It was a question for herself. Didn't demand an answer.

'Oberon,' I said. 'Thought I was Oberon.'

'But that's not the question, is it? Will Dominique marry Gerald? And I think I have to go now, Felix.'

'You feel sick?'

'Lost.'

She got to her feet, elegant and unsteady at the same time. I rose with her and held out a hand to steady her. She lay her head on my shoulder and seemed to sleepwalk with me towards the arch, and College Green. I managed to find a taxi, which took us around those Georgian squares, down Baggot Street, and through those mysterious avenues around Ballsbridge where only ambassadors live. She stared at the light through the passing trees and held my hand as if to let it go would break some promise. I stared at the houses passing, stunned at their size, and couldn't quite believe that people lived in them.

'On the right,' she murmured, and tapped the driver's shoulder. He pulled in by a pillared mansion in its own grounds that seemed to belong to the American Deep South. I remembered a word for its architectural style. Antebellum.

'You'd better not come in. My brothers might . . .'

'Your brothers.'

'Yes,' she said. 'The ones who don't like you. They come in late and eat raw eggs from the fridge. They think you don't belong.'

She turned and looked at me, her lipstick smudged beneath the fairy mask. I nodded, mute. She was right, I didn't belong there.

She kissed me then, on the corner of my lip. And I imagined I knew that kiss. It signified an intimacy that would continue for a long time. She turned then and walked unsteadily up the gravelled driveway towards those fawn pillars—though fawn was hardly the right word, they were made of a delicate, almost rose-coloured brick. I made sketches of them in my head. I would have drawn a rural French landscape, or those large spreading oaks of the Mississippi delta, not this suburban south Dublin street.

'Some gaff.'

The taxi driver had spoken. I agreed. It was some gaff.

'Could get lucky there.'

'Yes,' I told him. 'Someone could get lucky.' And I gave him directions back to Trinity.

THE BACCHANAL WAS winding down. Lines of girls in disordered dresses were clinging to each other, waiting vainly for taxis. Young men in what had earlier been impeccable black tie were leaning over rubbish bins, trying to throw up. There was a crush of bodies round the College Green entrance, sitting, leaning, sprawled, nobody standing straight. I made my way through them, through the smell of patchouli oil and hashish, towards the back entrance of the Buttery bar, and saw a pair of patent leather shoes sticking out from under the privet hedge.

I stood there for a long time, listening to the distant bass thump of music, the occasional squeals of pleasure, and hoots of camaraderie, and wondered what I was doing there. I didn't feel desire for her, but a certain protective urge that was even more confusing. She was beautiful, without a doubt, she had looked like a creature from another, more rarefied species, walking up that gravelled driveway towards that house that should have been in some other landscape. She wasn't mine, she was his; she was part of a life I would never have. And there was a spinning unreality to that feeling, as if I was the guardian to a fairy tale that had both of them in it. They were the prince and princess of this story, I was its lowly curator and my only function was to ensure that their story should continue.

So I gripped those patent leather shoes and pulled his body free of the hedge above it and snapped the Zorro mask up and down on his face until he awoke.

'Felix,' he said, and I realized the mask was still clinging to my neck, the cat's eyes somewhere around my chin. 'That was me.'

'Yes,' I said, 'it was.'

He tore his own mask off.

'How did I end up what's his name—'

He held the mask up to the light.

'Zorro.'

'You were out of it.'

'Correction. Am out of it.'

He grabbed a bunch of privet hedge and pulled himself to his feet.

'I'm fucked, amn't I? Where's Titania?'

'I took her home.'

'Oh. Then you're fucked. She worked her magic on you yet?'

'Not quite.'

'She has her spells.'

'And her secrets.'

'So you know?'

'What did you take?' I asked. I wanted to change the subject.

'You mean after or before the acid?'

'After.'

'Bit of silver foil. Brings you down.'

'You should watch that.'

'I know,' he said. 'You have a cigarette?'

'You know I don't.'

He turned to a passing shadow with a glowing tip at its mouth.

'Could I bum one of those from you, man?'

The shadow mumbled, drew out a crushed pack of Carrolls.

'So you know,' he said again. 'We should get married. But Joyce, you know. Did he ever marry Nora?'

'I don't know.'

I was the guardian of a fairy tale that had both of them in it. Only I hoped it was a fairy tale.

'Check it out. Ellmann.'

And he turned and walked towards the emptying gate.

# THE VIEW

S O YOU CALLED and asked to see me, and asked to see my house, and I suspected once more that there was nothing co-incidental about it. I could see you in the bubbled glass of the front door window and I thought of Darragh for some reason, and her Lithium.

'So this is where you live,' you said, by the panel of doorbells. There were flowers like splashes of lipstick on the green behind you.

'No,' I told you. 'Where I lived. I live in Berlin, for many years now.'

'Why Berlin?' you asked.

You walked inside and I took your coat. You were wearing one of those dresses with a high waist underneath it and a curve was beginning to show. Like an elegant S.

'It's anonymous,' I said. 'And it's no longer divided in two.'

'Is Dublin divided in two?'

'For me it always seems that way,' I said. 'There's a pattern that never seems to change.'

'Am I part of it?'

'You're the hidden thread.'

'He called to see you, didn't he?'

'He called to see the house. And why he chose this house, I have no idea. But you can see the pattern there.'

'He doesn't know who you are. But he described it to me, and I knew it was yours.'

And you walked up the old stairs and seemed to enjoy the creaking sounds beneath your high heels.

'Isn't that the point? The pattern finds a way of replicating without the knowledge of the participants. Like a curse. Stoker knew that. Le Fanu. Maturin. All the Protestant ones.'

'Besides,' you said, 'it's a nice house.'

'Don't move here,' I said.

'I like the view,' you said.

We were on the first floor now. And the park outside looked almost inviting.

'There are swans over there in the Tolka river. You just can't see them.'

'Nice,' you said.

'Stoker lived next door,' I said.

'Stoker who?'

'Bram Stoker. Who wrote *Dracula*.'

And you laughed.

'You're trying to put me off.'

'Am I?'

'Why?'

'I was trying to put an end to something. And it seems it's beginning again.'

'What if,' you asked, 'it had nothing to do with you?'

'That'd be nice,' I said.

'Good,' you said. 'And now show me upstairs.'

# THE WELLINGTON MONUMENT

I HAD TO GET away, I knew. I had to leave the city to him, because to me it was rancid in its hopelessness. He had a life beginning there, or the possibility of a life, a family, a home, a career.
I wanted to leave its environs to him—all of those memories, those
Mary cakes, those pubs, those street corners.

I had the Howth Road and the Middle Third, where I'd walk to
the small village of Raheny where all of the houses had that nautical hole in their cement porch. I'd take Darragh for a walk through
the evergreen oaks of St. Anne's estate, through the ruined walls and
gardens of the old Guinness mansion. I'd sketch the ivy clinging to
the crumbling brick, share pencils and drawing pad with her, take
her down the hill to the artificial lake covered in green slime and
the ruined mock Grecian gazebo, where we'd try to ignore the smell
of excrement and draw fantastical versions of the scene in front of
us, the two bare brick columns, the broken plinth above them, and
the rancid pond beyond, with its duckweed and its rusted bicycles.
I would add Triton to the scene, blowing his wreathed horn, in the
phrase I remembered from the anthology at school. She would turn
the whole lake into a puzzle, turn the overhanging moss into hair, the
dark shadows into eyes, sketch a bowed mouth from the ripples in the
water. Always a face, and always similar to her own.

We both had accepted she was never coming back, from whatever territory she had travelled to. She was comfortable there now, as if it was the only place she knew, and any major deviation from her daily habits would lead to a crisis of kinds. She could keep the books for her mother's vegetable stall, she could walk the park with me, but beyond that she liked her room, the white walls scribbled with hieroglyphs that nobody tried to interpret. I would tell her my story, in the third person, of a kid who was mistaken for another kid and how the process of being mistaken came to dominate his life. I wanted her to draw it to a conclusion, to provide some insight such as the mad are rumoured to do, but none ever came.

THERE WAS ANOTHER story of his in *The Irish Press*, called 'Epithalamium,' about a young couple viewing a suburban house. It provided a very precise description of the unfinished garden viewed through the kitchen window. There was a small digger there, a mound of earth and cement, and a view of the 'sand-coloured' sea beyond. The garden was a symbol, I suppose, or what he had called an objective correlative, some message anyway with regard to their future. The woman cried—or was it him? I don't remember which. I read it, felt depressed, then felt strangely happy. They had, I concluded, viewed a house together.

He published another story hot on its heels, called 'The Interregnum.' And here I found a clue to what had happened, that odd dance that had taken place around me: drunken suitors in masks, plangent lovers with secrets inside them. It depicted an affair, though perhaps 'affair' is too complete a word; an interruption in a relationship, a letting go, and a return. And why don't I use his word for it, it's what he was mostly good at: an interregnum. A narrator, male, secure in his affections for another, who, to test them, flirts with a random stranger. Set in the Hollow of the Phoenix Park (I knew that one) with a brass band playing and the distant screech of primates in the background, from the Dublin Zoo.

So there had been a betrayal, I realized, as I read the paper on a Saturday morning over the kitchen table, and this published story was surely an admission of it, to her.

'Can I have the racing page?' my father asked, with unexpected humility. He would be gone soon, to the English circuit. Spreading, as he put it, his wings.

Was she sitting in that antebellum house, the kitchen of which I could not even picture, reading the same story?

On Sunday I walked towards the Phoenix Park, sat by the Wellington Monument, and sketched the steps, the obelisk, and the magazine beyond. And the voice of someone standing behind me quoted from the plaque at the base.

*Now round thy brow the civic oak we twine*
*That every earthly glory may be thine.*

I turned and saw her. Brown hair, jeans, and a leather jacket. Those white boots with the high heels beloved of Dublin girls. And of course, I didn't know what to say.

'Wellington,' she said.

'Yeah?'

'Just because you're born in a stable doesn't mean you're a horse.'

She walked forwards then and squatted beside me.

'That's what he said. When he was accused of being Irish.'

'Kind of rude, isn't it?'

'Maybe not if you were . . .'

She looked up at the plaque again.

'. . . the Iron Duke.'

She observed my sketching for awhile. And somewhere in the distance I could hear a brass band playing.

'You've made it kind of fanciful,' she went on. 'What's wrong with accuracy?'

'Maybe I can't do accuracy.'

'You're good,' she said. 'Of course you could. But you never told me you could draw.'

'There's a reason for that.'

'Yeah? Give it to me.'

'Give it to you? All right.'

I turned and looked at her fully.

'Because we've never met before.'

'You mean fucker!'

'Maybe,' I said. 'But it's true.'

'You have a double then?'

'Must have.'

And she sat there for awhile, drinking me in.

'Jesus,' she said then. 'You're right. The clothes are different. The accent.'

'How would you describe it?'

'Northside.'

'And I have a double on the southside?'

'You must. You remind me of him.'

'How?'

'How? I don't know. You have his quality.'

'What quality is that?'

She took my hand in hers and ran the bones of it along her nose. She inhaled.

'His smell. You have his smell, without a doubt.'

'How would you describe it? His smell?'

'A slight tincture of earthiness overlaid with a nuage of . . . Palmolive.'

And I had to laugh at that.

'Sounds nice,' I said.

'Yes. He was nice. He was walking by the Hollow, listening to the brass band. I was sitting in the grass, on my lunchbreak.'

'Your lunchbreak?'

'I'm doing work experience. Zoology. Primates.'

'Sounds . . . interesting . . .'

'He was interested. He was the kind who was interested in everything.'

I tore the sketch from the pad and was about to crumple it, when her hand touched mine again.

'You going to throw that away?'

'Yes.'

'Can I have it?'

'Maybe,' I said. 'If you tell me more.'


So she told me more. She took me walking past the Hollow, past the brass band playing, to the entrance to the zoo where she used her pass to get us through the turnstile. A busman's holiday, as she called it. It was her day off, but why not? And maybe, after all, she had been walking there hoping they would meet again. He had been the perfect gentleman, not a hint of an advance to her, nothing pervy, as she called it, about his hand on her elbow or the small of her back. She had been wearing a blouse, she told me, a see-through blouse which showed the shape and stretch of her black bra, and she knew what effect this had on guys his age, which was her age. She enjoyed the effect but hated the consequence, the sweaty hand on her midriff, the hot breath in her ear. But there was none of that from him, only a sense of elegant melancholy, and a need to talk.

And the talk, though never specific, communicated a sense of crisis, an imminent decision, something that would define his life, for good or ill, for the foreseeable future. A female, she concluded, using her biological imperative in some manner that seemed to overwhelm him. And as she studied primates, she knew the drill, the shape of such disturbance, always pitied the males, who, despite their appearance of strength and dominance, were putty in the female's presence, at such a time and at such a juncture. And when I asked her to be more specific she stared into the baboon cage and told me that to her it was obvious, that someone somewhere had found themselves pregnant, and he was wondering what to do about it.

'Couldn't that have been a ploy,' I asked her, 'to elicit her sympathy and do exactly what she admired him for not doing, and get his hand beneath that see-through blouse to the clasp of her black bra?' And she laughed and leaned her cheek against the triangular wire and said, 'Maybe. You're funny. What's your name?'

'Kevin,' I told her. 'What was his?'

'Gerry,' she said.

'You were attracted to him then?' I asked her.

'Very,' she said.

'And to me?'

She smiled once more. She took her cheek from the wire fence and it left a grid of triangles on her pale skin.

'Not at all. How odd is that?'

# FAIRYHOUSE

I WAS BECOMING A shadow, a being whose smell belonged to another, who evoked memories evoked by another. I returned to my studies, of opes and beams and stresses and angles, of projections traced on a drawing board of buildings that did not exist. Luck had returned to my father's life, winnings of some obscure kind, and he had bought himself a car, a secondhand Jaguar, talked of reopening the shop on the Malahide Road. One windfall led to another, and I came to realize that fortune doesn't operate on an upward or a downward curve: It comes in bursts, small packages like the quanta I had heard about in quantum physics, is either there or not there at all, like Schrödinger's cat.

My father made a new circle of friends—quixotic, vital men from the North of Ireland, all dressed in pin-striped suits and working in the building trade. He introduced me to one of them, a tall Clark Gable lookalike, drinking with a well-known Dublin folk singer in the lobby of Bloom's Hotel. He again thought he had met me before and before I could set him right embarked upon a long description of an engagement party in a house on Ailesbury Road, fine food and wines and taxis waiting round the block.

'Some money there,' muttered the folk singer into his beard, 'but fine people, the salt of the earth.'

'You write, do you?' asked Clark Gable.

'Not me,' I said. 'I draw.'

'Oh, I could have sworn you wrote.'

'Drew,' said the bearded one, 'like me, Ronnie.'

'What did you ever draw? Only the labour.'

For me, it seemed, the cat was not in the leaded box. I worked towards my finals without the company of Darragh and on the day of the results saw I had passed. I drank a barely celebratory pint with her mother in the Smithfield bar.

'How's Darragh?' I asked Darragh's mother.

'Do me a favour,' she said. 'Forget about Darragh.'

'Do I have to?' I asked.

'Yes,' she said. 'I think all of us have to.'

MY FATHER DROVE me out to Fairyhouse in his new secondhand Jag. He picked up a woman on the way, a carbon copy of my mother but dressed in a tight-fitting black trouser suit with dyed blonde hair.

'This is my beloved son,' he said, 'in whom I am well pleased.'

'And you are?' I asked.

'Belinda,' she said.

I would have preferred a name other than Belinda, but I pretended to be well pleased with her too.

'Life,' said my father, 'has its ups and downs.'

'It does,' said Belinda, 'but more up than down with you, eh?'

There was an inept sexual innuendo there, which sickened me.

'Are you from the southside, Belinda?' I asked.

'I am,' she said. 'Stillorgan, born and bred.'

'I grew up,' I told her, 'under the shadow of a vampire.'

'Ah now, son—'

'There was a Mrs. Considine, the vampire's caretaker. There was Da here, who kept the vampire's books. And upstairs was Tommy the Clock, who kept the vampire's time.'

'And your poor mother,' asked Belinda, 'how did she take all of this?'

'He took her in the end. And at times I think, though I've never shared this with you, Da, that he was her only consolation.'

'Don't listen to him, Bel.'

'You believe in vampires?' she asked, her mouth perched between a grimace and a smirk. Bel. It was getting worse.

'I believe,' I told her, 'that they believe in themselves.'

On the course, he worked his stall and the horses thundered home and his run of luck held firm. He sent me up to the Tote to place a bet for him on the two-thirty. Widow's Peak for a win, each way on Mountain View. And I was in the lineup when a voice I didn't know spoke up behind me.

'Gerry,' the voice said, 'I didn't know you took a flutter.'

I turned and there was a young man there in a pin-striped suit. Reddish brown hair, his tie askew. The word 'flutter' seemed to suit him.

'Occasionally,' I told him.

'Does my sister know that?'

And now that I took time to notice, he had Dominique's eyes.

'No,' I told him, 'it's my dirty secret.'

'What about the two-thirty?'

'Widow's Peak, for a win. Each way on Mountain View.'

'You think?'

'I've got a feeling.'

'Widow's Peak,' he said again, by the glass booth. 'It's seven to one.'

'Take it or leave it,' I said, with the tired air of an insider.

And he took it. He shoved a fistful of notes through to the counter.

'If this comes home, we can forget about the other thing.'

'I've already forgotten,' I said. Though I had no idea what.

'You, maybe. The brothers, no. The brothers, vice versa.'

Of course, the brothers, I thought. Who thought he didn't belong. I didn't want to meet them.

'I like you better on the course, you know that, Gerry?'

'You didn't like me off it?'

'Not me. The other brothers. They're pernickety.'

'Don't tell me. Think she could do better.'

'Well. Some job prospects would be a help.'

'I have plans,' I told him.

'I fuckin' hope you do. Come into the box.'

There were boxes at the racecourse. Of course there were. Behind a glass panel, protected from the Curragh winds. There were platters of smoked salmon sandwiches and buckets of ice with champagne. Three more brothers, with her eyes.

'Ger,' said one.

'Gerard,' said the other.

'No, it's Gerald,' said the third.

'Gerry to you,' I said.

'How are the bukes?' said the first, affecting a Dublin accent.

'He's given me a tip,' said the fourth. 'Widow's Peak. If it wins, he's family.'

I could see my father way down below, through the perfect glass, in the mess of bodies by the track, above his chalk-scratched board, the jockeys behind him lining up the skittish horses. The gates rose and the horses ran. They passed us twice, then three times, and the whole of Fairyhouse rose to cheer and Widow's Peak came from behind, on the outside, to win by half a length. And I understood, probably for the first time, the compulsion that had always driven him.

Her brothers rose with the crowd outside and punched the air and put awkward arms around my shoulder and poured me more champagne. But their elation seemed forced inside here, in their glass box. Was that what wealth and privilege does, I wondered, seal you in a glass bubble? And for a moment I had all the glamour of authenticity, the whip and crackle of the muddy racetrack outside.

'He's the cool one, isn't he?'

'Still waters run deep.'

'So, we can forget about that other thing,' I said.

'What other thing?'

'It's forgotten,' said the fourth.

'She's our sister. You understand. We felt protective. But you're family now.'

So I was family now. I left their warm embrace to collect my father's winnings, and the size of the bundle of notes shocked me a little. He had won on both counts. I made my way back to the course, where he was chalking up odds for the next race.

'There's no need to hate me,' Belinda said.

'I couldn't hate you,' I told her, 'even if I wanted to. Besides, he needs someone. I'm leaving soon.'

'Does he know that?'

'He suspects.'

I placed the crumpled sheaf of his winnings in her hand.

'The thing about luck is,' I told her, 'it comes and goes. But not in a gradual curve. It comes in small bursts and packets. Like quanta.'

'Quantas,' she said. 'You going to Australia?'

# TIMEPIECE

A<small>ND SO</small> I showed you upstairs. Past the doors that only my mother's keys could unlock. The door to Tommy's room, of course, lay open. I could hear the clocks ticking as we approached, as if time itself had just woken up. Or a vampire had walked over them.

'Why all the clocks?' you said, at the door.

'Tommy the Clock,' I said.

'Tommy the who?'

'A lodger. Of my mother's. He worked with clocks.'

'How lovely,' you said.

You walked in. And I noticed for the first time, you were wearing black lace-up boots. The small heels and toes twirled around the clocks in a delicate dance of avoidance.

'Can we keep them?' you asked.

'We?'

'I mean, nothing's certain, you know that. It's all very new.'

'And he has,' I reminded you, 'a hairless chest.'

'Oh don't be silly,' you said. 'I'm over that. He's not that bad.'

You walked further through the clocks. You seemed at home in them.

'I'd just forgotten that I liked him.'

'And you do.'

'Like him?'

You turned and looked at me and smiled. You had that woman's glow now, which is more than the sum of its parts.

'Love, commitment, eternal etcetera,' you said. 'They're silly words, really.'

'What about "like?"'

'Like?' you said. 'Now that's a good word. I like you. And I think I like him.'

The clocks reached some point that almost seemed like music. You turned on your heels, and it seemed almost like a dance. And you half whispered, half sang more of that song you'd been singing. And the clocks almost kept time.

# LADBROKE GROVE

*H*APPINESS. I SAW it in a bookshop window on Charing Cross Road. *A novel by Gerald Spain.*

I stopped of course. I was on my way to Berwick Street, with a portfolio of drawings under my arm, but they would have to wait now.

It was in a plain blue-grey cover, with a photograph that still looked like me on the back, published by Jonathan Cape.

There were wet leaves blowing on the street outside. Black taxis soughed through the skin of recently fallen rain.

*What was that Tolstoy quote*—it began—*was it about all unhappy families being unhappy in the same way, or about all happy families being happy in the same way? Or is it one of those statements about which the opposite is equally true?*

*He tried to remember it one Sunday afternoon, in the living room, the companionable rain falling on the window outside. Because once married he had come to realize he had never had this feeling before, never been in this environment before, never lived through a time where the basic texture of life is good, where wholesomeness seems as natural as breathing.*

*Does that mean all happy families are the same? For him it was the uniqueness of the experience that made it extraordinary. For six solid years the daily stench of misery was banished, each dawn began with the question, what have I done to deserve this?*

'You can read the whole thing here if you like,' a voice said.

I turned and saw the brown-haired assistant, tapping behind the desk into a computer.

'It's all right, I'll buy it,' I said.

'That's another option.'

So I bought it. I got change from a tenner, saw it wrapped in a plastic bag. I walked up Charing Cross Road, turned left at Old Compton, and made my way to Berwick Street. The book seemed strangely heavy in its plastic bag, as if it contained memories, secrets, a weight of association.

I had spent the weekend in a ruined church in Greenwich, sketching elevations and floor plans, arches and architraves. I had a talent, it seemed, albeit a limited one. I could reconstruct the dimensions of a space from the remains of any significant detail. Original plans were a help, but even in the absence of them I could close my eyes and see the skeleton of the original structure. Like a ghost from the past reasserting itself on the present, I could sketch what once was there. It was a fusty, isolated, underpaid occupation—profession would hardly be the word for it—but I could do it and it was mine.

The client in Berwick Street would have razed the whole structure to the ground if he could, but had certain obligations under the Heritage Act before he turned it into a club, wine bar, set of bijou apartments, or whatever his intention was. So he toyed with his ponytail while he flicked through my drawings and considered the future of his investment.

'Fucking hell,' he murmured, 'how much of this do I have to consider?'

'It's a negotiation,' the architect purred. He had long legs encased in tailor-made trousers and never seemed to know what to do with them. Now they crossed and uncrossed like branches in a wet wind, and he gave me a brief, dismissive smile, which I could only presume excused me.

I walked back out to a greasy spoon and placed his novel on the formica table. We hadn't spoken for two years, so the moment was significant. But this book wasn't a conversation, I began to realize, as I flicked through the first pages; it was not the resumption of some dialogue between us, it was something new, somebody new.

THE CENTRAL CHARACTER, a solicitor settled into some form of uxorious bliss in South Dublin, was him, but not him. Just as he was me, but not me. There was a third construct now between us, urbane, witty, happy without a doubt, but the happiness of the title was less the sum of his achievements than another of his felicitous possessions, like the two adoring children (two?), the unimpeachable wife, the various animals that completed their household—among them, two dogs, two cats, and a quite literate parrot.

He suffered from happiness, from an unbroken stream of expectation inherited from his family, from hers, from his college education, friends even, at times, and quite amusingly, from the adoring gaze of the family dog. The larger one that is, the golden retriever, not the small yapping lapdog that his wife favoured. He suffered from happiness as a genetic inheritance, the way some families suffer from asthma, psoriasis, depression. He suffered from happiness, when what he wanted was bliss . . .

*Various animals tumbled down the stairs in advance of her, like the stampede in advance of the forest fire in* Bambi. *Two cats and a very small dog. The parrot squawked, wolf-whistled, and called her name. She sat at the table, unwinding tiny yellow post-its, each scrawled with a child's writing, and said she had to judge the jellybaby lottery.*

Bliss was poetry, ungovernable: It came suddenly, out of nowhere and vanished as suddenly, whence it came. It was unruly, tempestuous, and probably divine. Happiness was prose: It could be bartered with, arranged for, bought. And it was not in the end, as the book inevitably implied, happiness at all. There was tragedy towards the end, as one knew there would be—and what I had to admire was the force with which he built towards it, the way one knew it was coming, yet never knew when, or how. His wife lost a child, come to full-term.

*The dead child lay on a stone catafalque in the middle of the small breeze-block church, behind the wooden shelter that served as a smoking area for the patients at the Coombe Hospital.*

*He thought about several things as he walked in there. He had seen churches in hospitals and airports, with wooden or plastic crosses outside doors that looked as if they housed offices or computer centres, and always wondered why they were there. And now he realized. People die in hospitals, and their bodies lie in wait here, for whatever procedures the funereal bureaucracy has in store. People die in the large building outside and are laid to rest here, which would account for the vague anonymity of the exterior, as if it were hiding its own secret. It could have housed hospital waste, spare trolleys, or gardening equipment, but for the discreet cross above the doorway. And those who walked in this direction from the hospital building always gathered under the wooden shelter with its wooden seat, took out their cigarettes and lit them or cadged a light from those already smoking. Only the profoundly unlucky made the journey past the shelter with its garden of squashed cigarette butts to the rectangle of anonymous breeze block with the cross above the wooden door. Only the unlucky knew it was there, knew it for what it was, a mortuary.*

*The dead child was lying on a raised dais that was draped in laced linen. It could have been wooden, a movable dais or table, but it seemed as if it were fixed to the floor, built for that purpose, so he presumed it was a catafalque, and the word, with its baroque Mediterranean associations, seemed out of place in this matter-of-fact, hushed interior. He thought also of the dead child's name, which he seemed to remember his wife had chosen. Lily. In that cold space, looking at that downturned mouth below that beautiful oriental face that was already turning blue, Lily seemed appropriate. It was eccentric, Victorian, it was a flower that never frees itself from water and an appropriate addition to a church altar. Or a catafalque.*

I didn't cry, but I was moved. The day had darkened round me, the light had turned to neon inside the café, groups of labourers in donkey jackets had come and gone, and I stayed there, ordering a tea every hour or so, reading. The book was short, short enough at least to be read at one long sitting. How many hours since I'd sat down? Five? Six? Whether it was bad or good is of no consequence here—and it was good, incidentally—but what intrigued me was the hidden subject matter.

There was the thinnest of veneers between his life and this fiction. I could see Dominique as if I had lived with her, shared her bed, felt the first erotic year settle into something even more mysterious, enduring, with a tinge of unease around the fringes: the *Happiness* of the title. And there was none of that nonsense about the pram in the hall being the enemy of promise. A child had arrived, to propel the mystery into unknown caverns of delight. He had never thought of children. And now that one was here, there was the terror that this delight would someday depart. It was unrequired, this daughter, he had felt gifted beyond anything he had ever deserved. The hand that gives so much must one day take away. Such happiness could not be without its opposite. Light and shade. I who deserve so little, have been given so much. Some punishment is surely due. And of course, it came.

Had they lost a child, I wondered, or was the dead infant on the catafalque that strange thing he had told me about years ago, an objective correlative? A symbol of the imperfections of this world. I knew little of literature, but I knew my paintings. *The Arcadian Shepherds* by Nicolas Poussin.

I walked home, when the café finally closed. Through the dark, down Piccadilly, by Green Park to the basement flat in Ladbroke Grove. It took an hour or more, the walk, but I needed it, needed to let his tale of what was not happiness after all envelop me. And I fell into the oddest of sensations, the identification with the fictional alter ego of one who was surely my alter ego.

Happiness. I opened the door of my bare basement flat, saw the couch, the television, the rows of illustrated books, the bare fawn carpet. The only light that penetrated here was at night, from the sodium streetlamp outside. The intermittent strokes of headlights across the flower-patterned wallpaper. Happiness didn't belong here. Nor did misery either. I was content enough in my isolated existence, I took a perverse pride in my resistance to company, my ability to endure. But that bountiful, flowing, nurturing thing was what they would have called back home a foreigner.

I made some tea and opened my illustrated catalogue of the 1960 Paris Poussin retrospective, curated by Sir Anthony Blunt. And there was the Arcadian shepherd, bent low over the crumbling, ornamental gravestone, which could, I supposed, at a push, be called a catafalque. Staff in one hand, his other hand pulling aside the ivy that covered the barely visible inscription, which read (after Virgil's *Georgics*, as the footnotes told me) *Et in Arcadia Ego*. I also am in paradise. There was a skull, of course, mandatory in such allegories. The pleasures of these shepherds would be intense but fleeting, they could last for decades or could end in a moment, but end they would and when they ended was in nobody's remit. I remembered my vampire and the smell of burnt popcorn and the *rock rock-a-hula*.

THERE WAS AN abandoned theatre in Southwark, a tiny, Victorian thing that was primed for restoration and I went down there, saw the collapsing stage, the small auditorium hung with meat hooks, the rectangular gallery fitted with a block and tackle grid to swing the carcasses out. It had been used as a meat market for seventy years and now the diminutive, gestural director beside me wanted some drawings that illustrated its former function. He kept talking about space, as if it were a form, an object, something you could touch and hold, and as I began to sketch out some versions for him, he said the inevitable. 'I can tell by your accent,' he said, 'you're Irish,' and yes, I agreed, I was.

'We have an Irish writer coming to the Riverside on Friday. The New Voices season.'

'The Riverside?' I asked.

'Arts centre,' he said. 'Hammersmith. I run it.'

'Spain,' I asked. 'Gerald Spain?'

'Something like that,' he said. 'First novel. *Happiness*.'

# THE RIVERSIDE

THE RIVERSIDE WAS a small, modernist construct that fronted a newly built boardwalk alongside the Thames. It was raining, that Friday, and I spent twenty minutes under an umbrella, watching the mists blow over the brown river, eyeing the desultory crowd that made its way inside. I saw him then, in the inevitable gabardine coat, clutching a rolled-up copybook in one hand and a copy of his book in the other. He looked much the same: hurried, embarrassed, eyes bent to the damp pavement in front of his feet. His hair had grown again.

I walked inside and bought a ticket and took my place behind the crowd. It was quite substantial now, he would not be disappointed, and I felt some relief for him, as if his disappointment was more than I could have taken. There was a girl in front of me, with brown hair wet from the rain, and she kept tossing it with her hand, scattering the drops so they doused my face. I felt an odour like a memory—the smell of long uncut grass by the Wellington Monument, and I remembered that afternoon in the Dublin Zoo with the girl who studied primates. It was her, and even though I couldn't see her clearly, I could sense enough of her to be certain. The clothes were different: The small white, high-heeled boots, and the jeans were gone, she wore a leather coat, belted at the waist, short enough to reveal a kilted skirt with a buckle, and black tights beneath. She had her head bent towards the programme she held and she seemed to be alone.

We shuffled forwards and I resisted the urge to say hello. Something about her bent shoulders and her ritualistically tossing hair brought back the bandstand by the Hollow, the screeching of baboons, and the indentation of the chicken wire fence on her pale cheek. I felt lonely, suddenly, homesick for a Dublin I had never felt at home in. And I realized that if I'd wanted to introduce myself, I couldn't have found the words.

She stood at the back of the hall at the reading, and I found a chair behind a pillar, to the left, and watched her watch him. He was wearing a broad-lapelled, wine-coloured jacket with a thin stripe. The effect was absentmindedly flamboyant, as if he could have communicated the magnetism and allure of some kind of rock star if he had wanted to, but couldn't be bothered. His voice managed the trick of being both captivating and irritating at the same time.

But the hall was entranced. Spellbound, even. *Happiness* had them by the throat. He read six extracts in all. The opening. A lovemaking scene that should have made him blush but didn't. I could recognize Dominique, her hair, her fingers, her rather abstract femininity—her clothes, most of all, as they fell to the bare wooden floor. He read an extended description of her shopping, alone, without him, his isolated effort to picture every one of her movements, her purchases, the way she squeezed a grapefruit to see if it was worth buying, and he managed to make even a supermarket seem erotic. He ended with the description of the dead child. The last word: *catafalque.*

The applause was rapturous. The questions were respectful. And the brown-haired girl who studied primates, still standing at the back, even managed one herself.

'Could you talk about the autobiographical aspects of your work?'

'This person isn't me,' he said.

I sat in the shadow of the pillar. I hoped he couldn't see me.

'All the details might have—what would one call it—a certain remembered authenticity. Some of the events have occurred. But the process of creating a character is the process of letting something emerge that is and isn't you—a mediator between your experience and whatever it is you call yourself. Another. Which is why the naming is important. The name has to bring a certain magic with it, a set of random associations that will grow to have a life of their own. Which is why I let the name come to me, don't search it out. Alan. He had to be Alan.'

And he said a quick thank you, and a queue formed up to have their first editions signed.

THERE WAS A hope, I suppose, that he would come in and have a drink by the Riverside bar. Writers did that after all, they were lonely creatures, needed ersatz friends to help with their isolation—what is that writerly phrase? The company of strangers. Anyway, he didn't and I did and my attire was different enough from his; my hair had acquired a fogeyish quiff to it, in the manner of the new Romantics, I suppose. Adam and the Ants had just put punk to rest. Funny how we could both, if we wanted, trace the changing decades through our hairstyles. Anyway, mine was once more different from his and there was no danger of being mistaken, and I ordered a pale ale and listened to the conversations round me.

She came in then, and took a place beside me at the bar and I got the scent once more, of trodden grass after rain.

'Did you enjoy it?' I asked her.

'Yes,' she said, and tried to gesture to the barman, who was busy down at the other end.

'You got to meet him?' The question seemed natural, if a little out of nowhere.

'Yes,' she said, 'he signed my copy.'

I turned my head to get the barman's attention for her, but she had already realized something, and I could feel her eyes on the nape of my neck.

'You didn't?'

'No,' I said, 'it would have been . . . complicated, I suppose.'

'We've met before,' she said.

'Yes,' I said. 'You mistook me for him.'

She looked at me then, as the barman caught my raised finger, and I had no option but to turn my face to her.

'You want something?'

'Corona,' she said.

'A Corona,' I told the barman, and turned back to her.

'What was the phrase on the Wellington Monument?'

She spoke softly, almost as if affronted:

*Now round thy brow the civic oak we twine*
*That every earthly glory may be thine.*

'You have some memory,' I said.

'Yes,' she said. 'I collect them. Monumental inscriptions.'

'I mistook you for him,' she said.

'I can't help that,' I said.

'Yes,' she said. 'You can, surely. You didn't have to come here.'

'You could consider me,' I said, 'one of his public.'

'I could,' she said. 'But it's more creepy than that.'

'There's nothing creepy. I'm a better version of him,' I said. 'I swear.'

'But a version.'

'I have my own life,' I told her. 'My own flat, my own dreams, and desires. Even, believe it or not, my own profession.'

'And what's that?'

'Architectural restoration.'

'Did you notice,' she asked, 'how he spoke about himself in the third person?'

Enough about me, I thought.

'It's a habit,' I told her, 'a perfectly healthy process. Making oneself an object. The way painters talk about "the work." Not "my work," the. As if someone else made it. Or, as if once made and finished, it had nothing to do with them.'

'So, has it nothing to do with you?' she asked.

'Him,' I said.

'Him, of course,' she said. 'But the objective one, the third person in the book he read from, could as well have been you.'

'Sometimes,' I told her, 'one could feel that.'

'One.'

'Yes. One. We are all of us a first, a second, and a third person, and which one takes precedence at any one time is up to forces we ourselves cannot control. For example, have you never felt that—'

'Yes,' she said, 'I already know what you're going to say. There is another who is living your life and that other is you, and you stand outside yourself and wonder, how did I get to this place, as if someone else has been doing the living for you.'

And for some reason I took the bait once more, I was back in another's skin and allowed all of the coincidences, all of the presumptions to settle round me like a comforting, long lost coat. It provided a warmth and a sense of keenness, a sense of simply being alive that made me catch my breath. The sensation of a frost-sparkled street that greets you in the early morning, your breath displayed in the air in front of you like tobacco smoke, and you are glad, once more, to be living. And that can be my only excuse: that I was glad, once more, to feel that dead weight of this existence lifting and the blissful return of everything that wasn't me.

I bought her drink, moved it close to her on the bar so that our knuckles touched, and talked about his work as if it was mine now, as if I had a proprietorial interest in it, as if that house was mine, that love was mine, the pets bounding down the staircase were mine, like—how did he describe it?—the stampede in advance of the forest fire in *Bambi*.

I am a thief of identity, I thought to myself, I steal his name, his essence, and enjoy the fruits of my theft for as long as decency permits. She let her knuckle graze against mine and I took the opportunity to stroke her forefinger, as I banged on about fiction and the opportunity it gives one to experience lives one could never oneself have lived. 'You have to imagine the release,' I told her, 'that putting yourself in someone else's skin allows you. Another name, another life, a walk across a park with the wind moaning in the overhead wires, one hears the sound and suddenly—'

'One,' she said. She was looking at me quizzically now, and, thankfully, she was smiling.

'Yes,' I said.

'You mean him,' she said. 'He hears . . . whatever sound . . .'

'Yes,' I answered. 'Gerry.'

'And you are . . .'

'I told you. By the Wellington Monument.'

'Let me remember.'

'Kevin.'

'You remember my name?'

'You never told me.'

'I swear I did.'

'Then I've forgotten.'

'Rosemary,' she said. 'Rose, if you want to be intimate.'

'Rose,' I said. The word 'intimate' hung in the air between us, like a dark cloud.

'You still study primates, Rose?'

'I've got a placement in Regent's Park Zoo.'

She brushed her brown hair from her cheek and smiled up at me. Was that the first time I had seen her smile? It must have been, because the effect was like the sun coming out on a windswept field. I didn't remember that.

'Could you do without it,' she asked me, 'this strange state of being him?'

'You mean not being him?'

And she smiled again.

'You're funny,' she said. 'I don't remember him as funny.'

'How do you remember him?'

'Tonight? He was intense, I suppose. Not funny. And before? I remember gentle. Don't remember funny.'

The bar was closing now, so I walked her by the river, towards Hammersmith Bridge, where the taxis came over.

'Come to the zoo,' she said. 'You might enjoy it. You can help me shovel the elephant shit.'

'Don't you study primates?'

'Yeah,' she said. 'But we use a brush for them.'

# DOMINICK STREET

E VERYBODY TIRES OF clocks, I find. You did, after about ten minutes of ticking. You walked back downstairs again and stood at the front door. The sun came out, as if to meet you.

'You were born here?' you asked.

'No,' I said.

'A hospital, like everyone. But this was your childhood home?'

There was no movement in the air, no pregnant moment. The wind stayed quiet on the trees outside. But for some reason I felt the truth could do no harm.

'I thought it was. But I found out, much later, that it wasn't.'

'Where, then?'

'How long have you got?'

'It is Sunday.'

'Come for a walk, then.'

And we walked together. Past the park, past where the cinema used to be. Past the Five Lamps. Down Summerhill, past the Gloucester Diamond to Dominick Street. Where there was a grey institutional building, churchlike in the sunlight. A large rusted cross was studded into one of the eaves.

'You were adopted?'

'Yes.'

'You always knew?'

I shook my head.

'But I did have this fantasy, as a child. That I had been snatched from some magical palace, and dumped in the Crescent.'

'And?'

'Does it look like a palace?'

'No. But,' you said.

And I knew you weren't thinking of me.

'It looks like a dark castle.'

It looked empty. Forlorn. Part of a history that no one remembered.

'Can we get inside?'

'We can try.'

And you knocked on the door. A quick movement, allowing for no hesitations. I was full of admiration.

'And he?'

'You mean Gerald?'

'My father. Him too?'

I nodded. The door opened. An aged nun stood there, as if she knew already the request that was coming.

'He was born here,' you said.

'No one was born here,' she said.

'But he was taken here, as a baby,' you said.

I listened, amazed at the speed of your acceptance of things.

'He would like to see inside.'

'I've already seen inside.'

'Then I would like to see inside,' you said.

The nun hesitated.

'We don't want any bother,' she said. 'We've had trouble enough from journalists.'

'My father,' you said, 'was here as a baby. This dark castle was the first thing he saw.'

The nun looked at me with expressionless eyes, the palest of blue. But the word 'father' had softened her.

'Don't we have the right?'

# LONDON ZOO

I WENT TO THE ZOO. Larger than the Dublin one, but not at all as pretty. The Dublin Zoo was like a long forgotten aunt, wearing a blouse of dowdy elegance whom every now and then you thought to visit and remembered how pretty she was. This was a cement-filled, noisy enclosure surrounded by traffic, sitting by a sunken canal on the Camden Town side. Like an uncle you didn't want to meet again. The primates glowered, the parrots squawked, a cage of restless wolves met you on the way in, and she was in wellington boots, cleaning down the elephant hall with a fire hose.

She recognized me somehow, through the wall of spray.

'Hey,' she said, 'you who are not you, how's she cutting?'

I was definitely not myself. The smell of ordure sickened me. The elephant, as if in response to her fire hose, let loose a river of urine which lapped around the laces of my shoes. She was wearing a yellow oilskin and a sou'wester hat through which her pretty face hardly glimmered. But there was a wiry, busy beauty to her movements, the way she arched her body to steady itself against the thrust of spume through the fire-hose jet. The elephant endured the waves of white water cascading round him with a baleful, withered eye.

'He likes it?' I asked.

'Loves it.'

'How can you tell?'

'Because I wouldn't be here if he didn't,' she said. 'And maybe you should wait outside for a moment, because this hose is coming your way.'

So I waited by the iron fence outside while a flock of school-girls passed, shepherded by their teacher. They seemed as exotic and as worthy of study as the caged animals around. 'Where's Guy the Gorilla, miss?'

She came out then, dressed in trainers and a hooded sweater, looking as if she was going for a run.

'Sorry,' she said, 'for the context. But it's my lunchtime now, and I've got my vouchers, haven't I?'

She had two pale blue slips she handed to the waitress in the caf-eteria. We filled trays from the buffet, among the schoolgirls in their too short skirts.

'I'm surprised,' she said, 'he wasn't jealous.' And I had to con-sider for a moment before I realized who she was talking about.

'The elephant?'

'Sinbad. He can get quite possessive. He's used to me, you see, this tiny thing who sprays him daily. But with men he can get restless.'

'Does that mean he likes me?'

'Tolerates, more like it. And I'm all shy of a sudden. Why would that be?'

'We don't know each other,' I said. 'So can I be shy too?'

'I read the book,' she said, moving right along. 'All of that— what did he call it—uxorious bliss is a little overdone.'

'Do you think?'

'I think I know. Nobody who writes a book called *Happiness* can be happy.'

'So, if he wrote a book called *Sadness*, he wouldn't be sad?'

'You're being reductive. You know what I mean. Tell me you know what I mean.'

'You mean it's an examination of a condition that's foreign to him?'

'I mean it doesn't have the smell of authenticity. It's a fancy. It's a dream. It made me sad, somehow.'

And she turned her face towards me, swallowing a forkful of coleslaw.

'Consider yourself lucky,' she said, between bites, 'that you're not him.'

'Okay.'

'And tell me. About you.'

AND SO I told her. How I worked as an architectural draughtsman, how I had found this niche, doing plans and elevations and graphic restorations of buildings as they used to be. How it suited me. How I had come to accept that I had this peculiarly unmemorable quality, how I could sit and make myself invisible and reconstitute from a ruined wall, a moulding, a long lost architectural design, the thing in itself, as it was, maybe as it wanted to be again. How it paralleled my own life, which had no particular definition: People when they met me remembered the context, the weather on that day, the bench I was sitting on, the park and the play of sunlight behind me, but rarely remembered me. I had no particular texture, no particular taste; even the memories that seemed to be mine were often confused in my mind with someone else's. So I was, in effect, nobody but was pleased, even thrilled, to be sharing coleslaw here in the Regent's Park Zoo with her.

She listened, raised her nose to the autumn sunlight that came through the window, and said—

'Now I remember. You're funny.'

'You mean I make you laugh,' I asked, 'or do you mean I'm peculiar?'

'Both,' she said. 'Can you live with both?'

We walked out, after lunch, among the chattering schoolgirls. She took my elbow, for a moment, by the toucan cage. In the reptile room, while waiting for an alligator to surface, she turned her face towards me and kissed me.

'You have a taste,' she said, curling her lips inward.

'What taste is that?'

'Someone,' she said, 'who doesn't smoke. I don't think I've ever tasted smokeless lips.'

I watched her work for the afternoon, then I walked her along the sunken canal to the place that she called home. It was a canal barge with a wooden gangplank attached to the walkway below Maida Vale.

'I live in a boat,' she said, 'with others. It's not what you would call permanent. And they seem to be out.'

Her room was towards the back, and the barge rocked gently and water moved behind her window.

'You promise,' she asked me, while she cooked spaghetti on the small gas cooker, 'you are quite unmemorable? I don't want to wake someday, needing someone.'

# ST. MARY'S

THERE WERE KEYS attached to a ring, attached to the leather belt of the nun's habit. She pulled the door open and let us in, then locked it again. The sunlight streamed through the high windows and our footsteps echoed on the wooden staircase.

'We don't like to remember those days,' she said.

'I can imagine,' you said.

'Not for the reasons you would think,' she said. 'There was no funny stuff here.'

She led us to the top stairwell, then down a corridor towards a large studded door.

'But if you and your father want to see it—'

You held my hand then, as if to keep the word a quiet, mistaken jest between us. But the word 'father' had its own echo. It reverberated with its own mistakes. I felt two wishes coming, a child for me and a father for you.

'He does,' you said.

Another large key opened the studded door. I thought of my mother. She would always be my mother.

'Who am I to—' said the nun, in that half-stopped way of people of her age. The door opened and I thought of my father. His unfinished sentences. His unfinished state.

The light streamed in from seven Georgian windows on two rows of bare metal beds along each wall. It looked strange, magical, and utterly forlorn.

'You remember this,' you said.

'From about a year ago,' I said. 'I came here then, when I first found out.'

'But from those days?'

'I remember the light. I think.'

'How could you forget it,' you said.

'I know.'

'Two of you.'

'I can only presume. Yes. Two of us.'

'Twins.'

'Can you think,' I asked you, 'of any other explanation?'

# MAIDA VALE

O THERS LIVED IN that canal barge with her. The cast changed regularly, as if under the dictates of some mathematical principle that nobody had bothered to write down. Five would become four, would become three for a period of relative peace, and then would revert to five again. It would swell to six for a period of weeks after which, by some common consent, the new entrant had to go, six being an even number, maybe, divisible by three, or perhaps because of overcrowding, because the sad, diminutive fridge couldn't take the sixth's quotient of bean sprouts, mung soup, and organic yoghurt. Generally two were involved in the arts—dance and the theatre arts preponderant—two in some form of organic horticulture—fronting a stall in Camden Market, say, or selling homegrown weed outside the Roundhouse—and the last in the study of primatology in Regent's Park Zoo. The floating sixth member—and one must remember that numbers four and five could also be floaters—was often either unemployed, homeless—and sometimes both—or the transient partner of numbers one to five.

I was never part of this mathematical design, since I generally came late and left early and early rising was not a pattern of the group. The first night, after the spaghetti Bolognese, we crept into her tiny room where our heads bumped against the wooden ceiling if one of us shifted. 'Your skin is like silk,' she said, and hers was like cream, her legs beautifully thin and muscular as they curled round mine, and her eyelids like hummingbirds against my cheek.

I was woken by a sound later on in the night, a kind of *pitter-patter* with a slithering intent. 'You get used to them,' she said, 'they're just the water rats.'

Rats, I thought, of course, on a canal barge.

I left her sleeping in her bed over the water and took a tube back to Ladbroke Grove where I collected my portfolio and took another tube to Southwark where the tiny theatre director was waiting with impatience written on his small wizened face. I worked all day, with an easel perched between the meat hooks, and returned to Regent's Park just in time to see a small figure flitting by the wire outside the timberwolf enclosure.

'Rose,' I said, and when she turned and saw me I knew that neither of us knew the etiquette of such things. I had turned up too soon: My presence there expressed an urgency that wasn't part of how it went, those days, by that canal, on that barge.

'Hey,' she said, 'you came, I was wondering.'

So I was wrong, I thought.

She had been wondering, all day, she told me, as she did her daily round in the animal enclosures, where this 'thing' would go.

'Is it a thing?' I asked her.

No, she told me, it wasn't a thing yet and she wasn't sure that she wanted it to be, a thing, a part of her life, that awakened needs and memories, that had its patterns, its rituals, that left its residue, which she might not be able to get rid of. The size of the neocortex in a primate's brain correlates directly to the number of individuals it can keep track of socially. If a population exceeds the size outlined by its cognitive limitations, the group can undergo a schism. Her cognitive sphere, she told me, if I didn't mind her referring to herself as an object of study, was almost full. And that my presence on that barge—which would constitute a group in any primate study—would lead to a schism was for the moment unthinkable.

'Does that mean you don't want to see me again?' I asked, in ordinary language.

'No,' she said, 'and there's the problem, I possibly do. Make me laugh again, will you, make me forget this shit.'

'I wish I was that funny,' I said and she, thankfully, laughed.

'That is, you see,' she said, 'funny. Kind of. And I don't know why.'

So she took my arm and we walked along the canal bank, towards the Sea Shell in Lisson Grove, where I bought her a cod and chips and we sat on the large black beam over the darkening water and threw the breaded bits of the cod batter towards the swans, until a circle of white-feathered sinuous necks gleamed in the canal below us.

'You promise that you'll remain unmemorable,' she said.

'I promise,' I told her, 'I'll just be a shadow of him.'

'Of who?' she asked.

The writer, I told her. The one you thought I was. I'll just be a whiff of him, a cheap imitation of whatever perfume he favours. I will have no particular taste, no particular smell, I will be inauthenticity itself. The way I walk will imitate that other's, the way I talk ditto, and any memory she's left with will of necessity be ephemeral, based, as it must be, on the inauthentic me.

AND SO OUR relationship developed into what she called a thing. A sad thing, an ephemeral thing, but a beautiful thing for all that, and some nights I had to remind myself that it was me who held her in that canal barge and not the shadow of someone else. In time she'd forget, I sometimes allowed myself to hope, that the one who met her by the Wellington Monument was not him, she'd forget all of this over-elaboration, but I came to realize it was her protection, it was her guard against any damage to the organ that she shielded with her thin, fragile shoulders: her heart. The thing that was me could damage her, she knew, and she couldn't let it in.

We traversed the villages of London on weekends, haunted the bookshops, came to love the bridges over the brown river. I suppose any real affection that she allowed to exist between us came to be expressed in our affection for that city. I took her to the theatre in Southwark, which was gradually being completed under that director's endlessly fussy eye. He had come to like my sketches, and commissioned a series of set drawings from me for a production of *The Jew of Malta* which attempted to parody Marlowe's already parodic anti-Semitic tract. I was being afforded a gradual introduction to a new world of theatrical design: meetings about avant-garde productions in abandoned warehouses where invariably one loved the space, as if space itself had dimension and substance. I took her on a round of the Hawksmoor churches, St. Alfege's in Greenwich, Christchurch in Spitalfields, St. Anne's, Limehouse. I took her to my flat once, in Ladbroke Grove, but she found it dark, oppressive, too real somehow and, once there, never wanted to visit again. So we returned to her barge where the water rats padded above and the canal lapped and I left with the first light. I was like a ghost, I realized, inhabiting the fringes of her consciousness; she expressed strange affection for me in sleep, but when awake, I was never allowed, or never allowed myself, the full breath of reality.

A YEAR OR more must have passed, because two things happened. She finished it with me and another book of his came out.

The leaving happened gradually. We could both tell it was coming. I had an essence after all, a specific quality; there was a me there which I could tell disappointed her, and who knows, maybe disappointed us both. And there was a her too, a person beneath the thin limbs and the primatology wisecracks, an older crabbed thing, Dublin to its core, that was just passing time in this squat on the canal barge, that was entertaining some play of persons with me, him, whoever she imagined it was. Her voice would harden and increase in pitch, with a cutting comment on the sweaty bedclothes, the pathetic fridge left open, the creaking of my feet, hardly louder than the rats' pitter-patter really, on the barge floor before she woke. She began to nag me, in a word, as if through this nagging she could make me aware of who I was, a person like any other, with habits that could irritate, inflame, drive to a sudden, caustic fury. She came to loathe somebody, in short, and through that loathing gave me more of an identity than I had ever seemed to have. And one morning she pulled on her scuffed tights and said, 'Well, that's it then. I'll see you when I see you.'

I walked out into the dusty London air, with the sounds of jack-hammers thrumming down Maida Vale. A kind of lightness grew inside me, a sense of weightlessness, and I realized that if the person who had loved her was not me, but an imposter of some kind, the person who experienced sorrow, anger, the inevitable ache of longing would not be me either. And I remembered walking while my mother swam in the dunes beyond the Bull Wall. There was a bank of bluebells beyond the sixteenth hole and a lark rose up from them, singing. I stopped and sank into them and the brilliance of those tiny cups of blue took me over. I could see the lark through that veil of blue, and the ascending sound, the dusty smell of pollen, and the blood rushing through my arched-back head gave me an odd sensation beyond all permanence, of being in a bubble somewhere with that lark, seeing the boy sunk in that bank of bluebells, and the shifting sea beyond, through which she moved, gracefully, like a delicate knife.

So I walked through the London dust and the sound of jackhammers, feigning grief, but the person who was me was still sealed in that bubble of sensation, over those bluebells.

# PARNELL STREET

T HE NUN OBSCURED her face from us with the closing door. 'I was about to thank her,' you said.

'Think of it from her perspective,' I said. 'There are lost generations out there, bent on revenge.'

'Are you one of them?'

'No,' I told you. 'I've been lucky.'

And we turned right then, down a street whose name I don't remember, and I could see your face reflected in the plateglass window of Walton's music shop, with the gleaming gold trumpets behind it.

'Is that what this is all about then? Luck?'

'Nobody gets to choose their parents,' I told you. 'And no parents get to choose their child. But mine did. His did. We were the chosen ones.'

'Whatever else may have happened,' you said.

'We were both chosen. My mother lifted me from one of those metal beds.'

'She could as easily have lifted him,' you said.

'Then I would have had his life.'

'Would you have wanted it?'

'When I was a kid, I thought I did.'

'And now?'

'The thoughts get complicated. Even silly. Could I have been your father? Would you have liked that?'

'I would have liked a father,' you said.

And I could see the bowl of a trumpet shimmering behind your cheekbone. You wiped your eye and took my elbow and we walked down Parnell Street.

# LOS ANGELES

I WALKED DOWN MAIDA Vale, over the Harrow Road, across the round of traffic at the Westway towards the Portobello Market. A kind of remembered pain came in waves like a sudden wind buffeting an expanse of water, but I told myself it wasn't mine. The hands that had played down her leotard weren't mine either. I should forget about that person, whoever he was. I had reached the top end of the market when I saw his book, displayed in the window of the Portobello bookshop, in a plain blue-grey cover again. It was tucked into a corner, almost out of sight, and if I hadn't been searching for any distractions from this ache, I wouldn't have noticed it. So the two things happened in concert, his new book, my new isolation.

It was a book of stories. I had read most of them, I'm sure, but I walked into that bookshop with a sense of strange relief. I needed to hear something of home.

There was the tinkle of a bell from the doorway. A few heads turned and the strange combination of indifference and politeness that is English manners greeted me. I looked round the bookshop, the newly published section, but found nothing. I reached in then, over the book display behind the plateglass window, and in my effort to grasp it sent several other volumes of the display tumbled.

'It's all right,' the assistant murmured, 'we can fix them,' and I saw my reflection in the plateglass window and realized there were tears in my eyes.

I wandered through the market looking for a place to sit. There was his photograph on the back flap, and an older version of myself stared up at me. I rarely looked in mirrors, and wondered had I aged that much. People bumped into me as I walked, vegetable hawkers, shoppers, dealers in secondhand clothes and hemp. There was a new aggression in the air. The sixties had ended a long time ago—either that or I had lost my bearings. I found my way to the more threadbare stalls below the motorway, the ones that sold secondhand tapes and boom boxes, objects in that strange no-man's-land between bric-à-brac and junk. I found a piece of cement wall that was free of hawking and, with the traffic echoing round the cement cavern above, I began to read.

Much of it had already been published, in the New Irish Writing column of *The Irish Press*, but there was one new story set in Los Angeles and I realized his horizons had begun to broaden.

*It is difficult to love Los Angeles*—it began—*with its rectangular structures sliced everywhere by the same sunlight, its melancholy surf piling against unresponding boardwalks, but as the aeroplane banked and he saw the grid of its suburbs below, he wondered at the fact that it was not difficult at all to find somebody in Los Angeles to love.*

There was a writer, and of course it would be a writer, on a book tour of Los Angeles whose stay there was prolonged by the purchase of the movie rights of a book of his. There was a hired car, a bare hotel room, breakfasts alone on the sidewalks of Hollywood Boulevard. There was a description of those streets in the rain which brought an ache of nostalgia, since rain seemed as much a foreigner there as he was. There was a drive into a wasteland called the Valley and an encounter with a traffic cop on a boulevard called Van Nuys, the surprising fact of which was that the traffic cop was female. Overweight, with a head of reddish brown curls beneath her helmet, an accent from the Southern states, the white mark of an absent ring on her wedding ring finger, and, as the narrator stated, 'out of such details an obsession could evolve.'

An obsession did evolve. There was a ticket, which he kept like a talisman in his breast pocket. There were more drives down the same boulevard, feigned traffic offences to acquire more tickets, never administered, tragically, by the same cop. An extended riff followed, uncharacteristically humorous, on the sheer difficulty of being arrested in the Valley when one wants to be, and eventually, a spectacular pileup on the same Van Nuys Boulevard which was attended by a phalanx of the Los Angeles County Police Department, among them, thankfully, the same overweight, curly-haired Southern belle.

By the time I raised my head from the pages, the market had gone, as if by some act of sympathetic magic. The streetlights were on, an odourous man was rearranging newspapers for his evening's rest, and the shouts of drug-dealing youths echoed through the underpass.

There was a story there, I knew, behind the story of the L.A. County policewoman in the Valley. And I sensed some kind of havoc coming from it.

# OUR PLACE

'I WANT YOU TO pretend,' you said, 'that you don't know me.' We were in Dunne & Crescenza's again. It seemed to have become our place.

'Because,' you said, 'there's a deceit going on, and I don't know why. But once started, it doesn't stop, does it?'

'No,' I said. 'That's the way with deceits.'

'Yes,' you said. 'They're self-perpetuating organisms. They have their own particular lives.'

'Except,' I told you, 'that they never die.'

'Don't they?'

'Not entirely.'

'Like the things,' you said, 'what's-his-name wrote about.'

'Like vampires.'

'What's his name again?'

'Stoker.'

'Who lived next door.'

'And who are we deceiving this time?' I asked.

'My mother,' you said.

'Why her?' I asked.

'She wants to see the house.'

'So you've told her?'

'About the baby? Oh yes,' you said.

And I was amazed, once more, at how easily life reasserts itself.

'She just needed some time,' you said, 'after the funeral . . . But when you see her, pretend you don't know me.'

'You mean,' I said, 'when she walks through my door.'

'Yes,' you said. 'She'll have that peculiarly uninvolved gaze the Dublin upper middle classes have, when they're viewing houses. She'll notice everything, without seeming to. She's better now, you see.'

'Ah,' I said. 'That explains it.'

'She won't like being there, over in—what's it called again?'

'Marino,' I said.

'Marino. And don't talk about what's-his-name.'

'Stoker,' I said.

'Yes,' you said. 'She wouldn't like that.'

How we all change, I thought. I remembered her poncho, bulky with the stolen copy of *Being and Nothingness*.

'And most of all,' you said, 'don't let on that I know you. The thought of our conversations might . . . upset her . . .'

'Didn't she see me after the funeral?'

'Yes. But she wasn't herself then.'

'Aren't there other houses?' I asked you. 'Half of Dublin must be for sale.'

'We like your Crescent,' you said. 'It has a kind of resonance. The park outside. All those clocks. I can imagine a child growing up there. Like you.'

'I'm not sure I ever did,' I said.

'Did?' you asked.

'Grow up.'

# RUTLAND PLACE

I WENT BACK TO Dublin soon after. The Southwark theatre had been finished, the drawings I had done for the director's *Jew of Malta* had been magicked into sets and he was considering a production during the Dublin Theatre Festival. I took a plane this time and saw the bay from the air, the sea frothing round the edges of it. My father was dapper and ageing; his luck had held out and he ran a new betting shop in Marlborough Street. Tommy had gone to a home so his clocks ticked to themselves in his upstairs room, if they ticked at all. I walked round with my father to Gaffney's, watched him drink himself into a state of mild incoherence, and held his elbow on the walk home.

'You've been finished,' he murmured.

'You mean I'm dead?' I asked him. 'Atrophied.'

'No,' he said, 'your corners have been finished. Smoothed. A woman.'

Yes, I told him, there had been a woman.

'Nice?' he asked.

'Nice,' I said, 'if ephemeral.'

'That's a hard word,' he said, and I agreed, it was.

'Can I meet her?'

'No,' I told him. 'It's over now.'

'Makes two of us,' he said. 'That Belinda turned sour.'

'Nasty?'

'No. Sour.'

And I tried to imagine Belinda turning sour, like a frothy knickerbocker glory in the Stillorgan Bowling Alley, but I couldn't manage it. I realized she'd always seemed sour to me.

'I was always afraid of something in this house,' I told him, as he fumbled with his keys and the old door creaked open.

'Ghosts?' he asked, as he stepped inside. 'There are no ghosts. Only me now.'

'Yes, Da,' I echoed. 'Only you.'


THE HOUSE HAD lost none of its ghosts, though. They whispered, they shuffled, they sang me to sleep.

I dreamt of the vampire, a nightly trawl with him through the youth clubs of Dublin. We were dressed as priests and our white collars disguised whatever ravages the past had done to our necks. We sold raffle tickets, we played guitars, we sang *Kumbaya my Lord* and *Rock-a-hula Baby*. He went for the boys, I went for the girls. Under billiard tables, behind those plastic spheres full of bouncing bingo balls, *clickety-click, sixty-six*, we gouged and we sucked. We retired to a graveyard beside the mudflats of the Tolka river. The swans, for some reason, welcomed our presence.

I awoke the next morning strangely refreshed. My father's voice was echoing through the house: He was singing from the bathroom, down the stairs, through the front hallway. *Low lie the fields of Athenry*. The door closed and the singing passed below me, losing itself in the traffic on the Clontarf Road.

Maybe one turns a corner. Maybe he loved me after all. Maybe Dublin was the place to be.

I walked then, when I'd washed myself and eaten, down towards the Five Lamps past the North Strand flats, over the Royal Canal, up Marlborough Street to where his betting shop was. THUNDER TURF ACCOUNTANTS, the sign read. There was a small arcade next to it, buzzing with one-armed bandits and video games. I wondered idly did he own that too. I could see him through the window, on the telephone, a silent television on behind him, a girl with dyed blonde hair working the counter. I wondered should I go in and have a flutter, then I thought even the phrase didn't suit me, whoever I was.

I walked on then, through the crumbling inner city. I needed an abandoned space for *The Jew of Malta* and it seemed that half the city was abandoned. There was an old Unitarian church on Rutland Place. There was the Teachers' Club in Mountjoy Square. There was the Ierne Ballroom, up from the old Gate Theatre. And that was just a morning's walk on the northside.

Churches seemed to suit me, particularly abandoned ones, so I talked my way past the caretaker of the old Unitarian on Rutland Place and made my way inside, into a huge, dusty, rectangular space, coloured by the sunlight coming through the broken stained-glass windows. There was an abandoned altar, very much like a stage, and a balcony tracing the shape of the floor below, leading to an organ loft with broken pews. I climbed the rickety stairs to those pews and asked the caretaker did he mind if I did some sketches. He uttered something like sketch all you want and I took out my Faber pencils and began to work.

As I drew I daydreamed. I thought I heard the organ playing *Abide with Me*. I saw a Victorian crowd below, singing lustily:

*Where is death's sting? Where, grave, thy victory?*

I IMAGINED ABRAHAM Stoker there with his wife Charlotte and his young son Bram, in this dowdy outpost of the empire upon which the sun will never set. How could this figure who would haunt my childhood come from such stolid, empirical particulars? Their hats were dark and hard, their suits were tweed, their voices tuneless, and their imaginations limited. Even the *Dracula* that he would come to write was an overwritten book, stolid and florid at the same time. And yet the Count existed. He would spread his seed. He would transform, like a Celtic shape-shifter or a manufactured virus, have as many lives as he needed to prolong himself. And no matter how ridiculous it seemed, our conversations would continue.

I NEEDED TO fax the finished drawings, so I walked back down O'Connell Street looking among the burger joints for a photocopy shop. I didn't find one. I thought of Thunder's Turf Accountants and wondered had they embraced the technology yet. I made my way back to the buzzing arcade, walked in the door of the bookie's shop, and asked the girl with the dyed blonde hair was my father in the back. He wasn't, she told me, but they had a fax machine and I was welcome to use it, if I was really his son. Kevin, I said, his one and only, and she lifted the hatch and led me inside while the radio droned on about the Doncaster hurdle.

'Is he at lunch?' I asked her while the fax machine glowed and whined.

'I suppose,' she said.

'Where does he take it?'

'Sherry's,' she said, 'in Middle Abbey Street.'

And I was touched, suddenly. I was almost moved to tears. My mother would stop there, if there was time before the number 30 bus home, for a coffee and a cream cake. 'He takes me here,' she would tell me, 'whenever we're in town.' And I remembered as a child the strange realization, which one never wanted truly to admit, that one's parents had, or once had, a private life. A remembered ritual, a sentimental journey.

I walked round there. I crossed the street through the smouldering Dublin buses, and saw him there, through the old plateglass window. His hair thinning, his shoulders bent, a copy of the *Racing Post* in his left hand, alone at the long café bar.

*I triumph still, if Thou abide with me.*


THERE WAS A ghost there, sitting beside him. With high-heeled lace boots and a short tweed coat and a face full of unrealized dreams, waiting for the number 30 bus.

I walked inside and he saw me in the mirror behind the coffee machine.

'You tracked me down,' he said.

'Like a detective,' I said.

'Used to come in here with her. She liked her sticky buns.'

'You miss her?'

'All the time.'

I sat down, and his eyes caught me in the mirror again. Rheumy eyes.

'You ignore them when they're with you. Then you miss them when they're gone.'

'What about Belinda?'

'Fool's gold.'

'Sounds like the name of a horse.'

He smiled, then his lips settled into a line that was almost noble.

'There is no substitute. You know that.'

'I do.'

He drank his coffee, then grimaced at the bitter taste.

'Won't be long now,' he said.

# THE NATIONAL GALLERY

THERE WAS NO reply to my faxes, but I stayed on. 'Won't be long now,' he had said, and I feared he was waiting to join her. His health seemed fine, he had one of those inner-city, whippet-like constitutions, but the silences between us became almost comforting and I didn't want to leave them yet. I let the flat in London go and wandered round the city, seeking work. I signed on in Gardiner Street, got the odd job drawing renovations, which led to advertising work, and bit by bit I found myself gainfully, if fitfully, employed.

There was a Poussin in the National Gallery called *The Lamentation over Christ*. I was sketching a detail of it one day, trying to copy the Virgin's anguished mouth, when a voice behind me said, 'Have you ever seen such blue?'

I turned and there he was, still wearing his Trinity scarf, his face puffier than before, jowly even, like in the book flap.

'No,' I said, 'and I wouldn't even try to copy it.'

'That mouth is painful.'

'I think he meant it to be.'

'Who?' he asked, and I was surprised he didn't know.

'Poussin.'

'Poussin,' he repeated and sat beside me.

'I was looking for you,' he said softly.

'You were?'

'Yes. It's odd, trying to search out someone when you've no idea where they live.'

'Next to Bram Stoker's house. The Crescent, Marino.'

'Ah,' he said.

'Was there a reason?'

'Yes,' he said. 'I have a story to tell you.'

'About America?'

'How did you know?'

There was a coffee shop in a small outdoor patio, among broken, mock-Grecian remains. I ordered a green tea, while he smoked.

'So how did you know?' he repeated.

'I suppose I read between the lines.'

'Aha. So did she.'

'Who?'

'Dominique.'

'Your wife.'

'The mother of my child.'

'That's . . . complicated.'

'Indeed.'

'And you want to tell me, don't you?'

'I must. Why I wanted to see you.'

And so he told me, and I realized the inadequacy of fiction.

# AMERICA

L ORETTA WAS HER name. She was dark, wafer thin, petite, of South American extraction. He had been flown to Los Angeles by a small balding producer of independent films and asked to try his hand at a script for his novel. They had placed him in a dump called the Magic Castle Hotel, off Hollywood Boulevard, where he had meetings with the producer who kept himself supplied liberally with pharmaceutical cocaine.

It was Halloween night and Santa Monica Boulevard was crowded with men dressed as women, women dressed as men, and fairies dressed as fairies. They met for dinner with an English actor, an ageing group of Hollywood wits, and the dark-haired Loretta. The evening grew confused, he remembered, wine with the meal, trips to the bathroom, and later he found himself in an open-topped car on the boulevard that doubled as a fancy-dress party. She sat on his knee, for no particular reason other than that the front passenger seat could accommodate them both. They ended up in a bungalow in the Chateau Marmont and he had a dim memory of the producer opening the fridge and taking out a plastic bag full of white powder and offering it to him in lieu of an advance. He said no, of course, and felt vaguely sad that he was in the kitchen with the balding producer while the English actor sat in the living room with the dark-haired Loretta on his knee.

He staggered back to his hotel later that night and forgot all about it. But he got a call the next morning. Or the next day, to be specific, since it was after noon when he awoke. 'Loretta,' she said, dispensing with preliminaries entirely. 'I only sat on his knee to make you jealous, but it obviously didn't work.'

'No,' he told her, 'it worked great. I was jealous, I got depressed, and so tootled off to bed.'

'Well,' she said, 'it's a dangerous tactic, you go for something you don't want in the hope that it will throw the thing you want into your lap. You want to have dinner?'

She was direct, Loretta, he found that out later, an alarming kind of directness that managed to be far more evasive than evasiveness itself. She had a slight Brazilian accent to her speech, had been runner-up to Miss Brasilia in a former life. So they had dinner at Spago, it being the hot place then (and the names had an awful kind of romance for me, there in that patio of the National Gallery, Dublin—Spago, Citrus, Santa Monica, Van Nuys—if I ever saw them it would be as a tourist in a rented car, a 'civilian' was the term he used) and he described, rather perfectly (he was a writer after all and had that total recall of inessential details), the slightly orange, deliberately aged paint on the walls, the booths of the windows overlooking Sunset Boulevard, with waiters with those manners he described as European with an edge.

She had that discreet way with wealth, with sophistication: She was already a widow at the age of thirty-two and talked of 'my departed husband' with an air of regret. The maître d' knew her, had her quiet table reserved, and as they perused the menus her high-heeled shoe played with his ankle, then his calf. He spared me details of the rest but described the suit he wore, a silver-flecked silk job—he carried only one suit with him and a variety of shirts—and the next morning, in her bungalow in the Beverly Hills Hotel (pink, he told me, like an endless iced cake) while he was dressing she handed him a can of deodorant and said, 'We tend to use this over here.' And that's when he realized he sweated—he was Irish after all, unused to gyms, odour eaters, and deodorants. 'All right,' he said, 'all right, I get it,' and she said, 'No, you don't get it, it's fine for me, just, in company maybe not so fine.'

'Maybe not so fine'—he loved her slightly damaged English and her way with the world as if she herself was a disembodied thing, an object to be scrutinized and improved upon. She drove him downtown the next night, to what she called the *barrio,* to an old deco building where some Mexican painters were having a group exhibition. He listened to her rapid, unaccented Spanish and intuited a different person again.

And so it began, an affair of kinds, while he waited in Los Angeles to finish a script that few people would read and nobody would make. He only liked the city in the rain, he told me, found a pleasing melancholy in the way the boulevards were ill equipped for water, the way the coursing rivulets would wash the cement clean. He read the daily reports of murders in the newspapers, puzzled at the way the street names held no clue as to their origins—Cahuenga, Bundy, Pico, Orange, Vine. Any romance in the names was belied by the grim reality and after five weeks and an excess of homesickness he began the long journey home.

His book was out by then in an American edition so the journey home became a kind of peregrination. He stopped first at San Francisco for a reading and she followed him there. They visited the strip bars in the Tenderloin district, met a legendary madame, the first of the go-go dancers, aged now, in a sad cowboy outfit. He read his way through the Midwest and ended up in New York, where he found she had an elegant brownstone, on Sixty-fifth and Fifth.

He was tired by now of the wealth and sophistication and told her so, but she managed to delay him like an Upper East Side Circe, each day conspired another dinner out of her acquaintances, another discreet event he found impossible to decline. There was art here, there was wealth he had never imagined, there were rock and roll legends that seemed like casual acquaintances of hers—'Hi, Lou . . . Gerald, have you met Bruce?' He realized the more he wanted to leave the more compelling she would make it, as if his homesickness and her capacity for sexual complexity were in an inverse relationship. Eventually she was called to Florida to deal with her dead husband's estate and he realized that whatever emotional needs she had, money had its own emotionless logic so he made good his escape.

But as the plane came down out of the wet clouds, over the irregular fields and the maze of housing estates, he missed her already, with a pain that was physical. There was a life he could have lived, another person he could have been (always another). Ireland, with its morals, its rain, its sense of literary vocation, he found tiresome. He went back to his life in Ranelagh and found that they, child, wife, and house, had done quite well enough without him. The dog alone seemed to need his affection. 'Whatever happened,' Dominique said, 'don't tell me about it.'

'If I told you nothing?' he asked.

'If you told me nothing it would speak volumes.'

And so he was involved, he realized, in a true affair; the kind you read about in books, by writers who have the kinds of sophisticated lives he had previously only imagined. He retreated to his study at the top of the house, looked out on the brown, wet garden, on his daughter, a doll between her knees swinging idly backwards and forwards, and began the story of the imaginary traffic cop on Van Nuys Boulevard. And whenever the telephone sounded he answered it before it had finished its first ring.

There was a frisson, he realized, in the hand he had dealt himself. A coiled energy that forced him to write. He took to working late in the room upstairs, so late that he often drove his daughter to playschool before he himself had slept. He took to wandering the city with notebooks in his pocket, scribbling in café after café, the place was full of them. He would set himself goals with each cappuccino, one hundred words or so, then finish and find himself another café, for another cappuccino and another hundred words.

His wife was thriving in the law firm; she took to wearing pinstriped suits with padded shoulders and a hobbled skirt. There was an appropriate maleness to her attire, appropriate because her life was increasingly her own, he was becoming the domesticated housecat, no matter how untidy his personal habits were. 'There is a part of you,' she told him, 'that will always be mine.'

'There is,' he agreed and it was something to do with her elegant back in the bed beside him: Whatever hour he clambered in, whatever space in the night was yawning between them, the sculpted white skin below her shoulder blades would always feel like his. But when the telephone rang, a long time past midnight, and he heard the words 'my dear' from another continent, his heart would beat faster. So fast, sometimes, that he feared for his breathing. So fast, that he invented a writerly pretext and paid her a return visit.

'So you're a mess,' I told him, and wondered why it gave me no satisfaction.

'I'm a mess,' he said. 'You can have my life, I don't want it anymore. I took a bread knife in the kitchen to do the business and . . .'

He shivered, then a thought struck him.

'Actually, have you ever tried it? The bones get in the way of the vein. You'd have to cut upwards, not sideways at all—one of those things you only discover when . . . you're desperate, I suppose . . .'

'There are other ways,' I told him.

'You know?'

'I've heard.'

'I have to stop it, but I don't know how.'

And for some strange reason, I knew what was coming.

'Call her up, tell her it's over.'

'I can't. She's pregnant.'

He turned and looked at me.

'She's going to have it. She won't get another chance, she says.'

And he smiled, briefly, maybe at his own appalling fecundity.

'I'm where all of the clichés come true. My biblical house is collapsing.'

'Then let it fall.'

'I can't.'

'Then there's only one solution, isn't there?'

'Yes.'

'I have to hear it from your mouth.'

'You. You're the solution.'

'You want me to—'

'Talk to her. Take her off my back. Give me some space. Some time to think. Some fresh air . . . I have a place I work in Fitzwilliam Square. Just a room. With a telephone. Say the things she wants to hear. Give it time. I don't have any. She deserves it. Someone who'll listen. She deserves it.'

'You want me to pretend to be you.'

'You do it all the time.'

'By accident. Mistakes have happened. I didn't look for them.'

'Call her once then. See how you feel. If you want to stop it, tell me.'

He blinked. His eyes were wet. Me and him. It was divinely or-dained, his eyes seemed to say, it was arranged by some hidden need inside of things for balance, order, symmetry.

# FITZWILLIAM SQUARE

O UR DECEPTIONS, IF that's what they were, had never reached
this level of intimacy before. And he had you with him, when
I saw him the next day through the railings of Fitzwilliam Square.
You ran around the grassy path like some kind of Victorian garden
sprite, with your dog Rebel. It was my first sight of you, Emily, and
when I saw you I knew I had to play his part. You looked so innocent
and happy, the one uncomplicated thing.

And so we walked around the railings while you ran ahead
and he versed me in their conversations. He had me play him and
he played her. Then I played her and he played him. He would
call her 'bitch' when it suited him, in a playful, faux-endearing
manner. When she grew possessive, overbearing as she would, he
promised, he would call her 'mommie dearest,' in a reference to
the Joan Crawford film of the same name. He recited their terms
of endearment until I felt the sickness you feel when you've eaten
too much Baked Alaska. 'Sorry,' he said, and he had the grace to
blush. 'Don't worry about names, mutual acquaintances, I forget
them all anyway. If she mentions a name, just mutter "remind
me." She finds it endearing, the way I forget things, evidence of
talent—genius when she's being effusive; when she's not, of Irish
self-obsession.'

He took me upstairs to his flat while you stayed playing in the park. It was bad parenting maybe, but as I told you already, we didn't know that phrase then. He showed me the room where he worked. Two large Georgian windows overlooking the square with its tennis nets, its beech trees, its tangle of overgrown greens. The small garden sprite that was you, still chasing the dog. It could have been the eighteenth century, but for the parked cars. His room had books piled to the ceiling and a couch that pulled out into a bed. I stepped inside and felt I was entering his soul. I wondered would I let him so easily into mine. There were papers on the desk, a metal typewriter. He gathered the papers and bundled them into his pocket. He wrote down her phone number and seemed desperate to leave.

'Where will you work now,' I asked him, 'for however long this thing goes on?'

'At home,' he said. 'I have a room like this. A typewriter. And it will go on,' he said, 'as long as you can stand it.'

He wrote her number on a yellow pad.

An actor friend told me once that if you force the part you will never find it. But if you let the details take you through, the character will find you.

There was a peeling cigar beside the typewriter.

'You smoke them?'

'She made me promise to try to give up cigarettes.'

'Dominique?'

And the mention of her name seemed indelicate there.

'No. Loretta. She hates tobacco. Regards it as a weakness. Tell her you're trying.'

'But I don't smoke.'

'Even better. You're almost there. Smoke free.'

He was silhouetted by the Georgian window, his shoulders bowed. I would have to gain some weight now, to pass off as him. Slump my shoulders, stain my fingers with tobacco. And the prospect was strangely enticing.

'You'll call her?'

'Yes.'

'I'm going to get you a key cut. I'll wait across the square.'

He turned from the window, walked out, and I heard his footsteps descending the creaking wooden stairs. The front door slammed and it echoed through the house. I saw him emerge then and cross the street and walk around the railings where you were still playing with your dog, inside the park.

I PLAYED WITH the unlit cigar while I dialled the number. I heard the long buzz of a different tone, a very American sound, and imagined the house he had described to me, with its gunmetal spiral staircase and its profusion of paintings on the wall. She answered it after the seventh ring, a very American voice, with nothing yet foreign about it. There was something sad and lonely in the sound and I wondered how much I could find to dislike in her.

'Hello.'

'It's me,' I said, and I could feel, over two thousand miles, the flood of relief in her breathing.

'Dear,' she said, and I had never been called that and I found it unaccountably touching. 'I'm sorry, just let me get rid of Vladimir.'

'Remind me,' I said, and he must have coached me well because she went on without a beat and I began to hear the Brazilian lisp in her syllables, 'You remember that thing in Montauk, that business on the boat. We kept him waiting.'

'Yes,' I said, 'Vladimir. You better get rid of him.'

I could hear footsteps then, echoing on a marble or stone hallway, and I imagined a seam rising from the delicate leather heel over the thin, perfect calf he had described: Seamed stockings had come back into fashion along with other forms of long forgotten elegance and I was thinking of my mother suddenly and I wondered why. I heard muttered talk and a door slam and the *click-clack* of those heels grew louder and it was like the audio track to a film, one of those black-and-white detective ones, these sounds that conjured up another world for me.

'He's gone,' that breathy voice said.

'You sent him packing.'

'Yes,' she said. 'We need never see him again.'

That 'we' took my breath away. It implied a future together that I could only dream of. There was total trust in her voice, somehow, a lifetime's promise.

'So,' she said, 'have you given it any thought?'

'I've thought of nothing else,' I told her. 'Can't work. Not good.'

'You poor darling, I'm so sorry but I kind of had to tell you. I feel weirdly . . . positive today.'

'About what?' I asked her.

'Come on,' she said. 'You know. There's a baby inside me. Maybe four weeks old.'

'Yes,' I said. 'Am I imagining it, or can I hear it in your voice?'

'Don't laugh at me,' she said, and she sounded so sad at that point that I liked her even more.

'There is . . . something different . . .'

And I knew I was on dangerous territory here, so I stopped the thought. I could hear my voice echoing across the distance between us.

'Well, there has to be,' she said. 'Things will be different from now on. I can deal with it myself, if that's what you want.'

'I never said that.'

'But you thought it. Don't feel bad, I've thought of it too.'

'I suppose I've thought of every possible alternative.'

'Yes. So have I. But on one's own, over here, it's just so . . . lonely . . .'

And her voice dropped here. I felt a knot in my stomach.

'I would so love to see you.'

To be so loved. So desired. I hated him then, for a moment. There was a refinement to her voice, she enunciated every syllable with that slightly alien tone.

'I'll see if I can come.'

And there. It was out. I couldn't help it. Was it out of character?

'Oh my dear. You mean that?'

And it was out of character. Did I mean it?

'I mean I'll see. I'll look into it.'

'What about your daughter's birthday?'

'I know. I mean after.'

'And Dominique?'

She knew her name. Felt free to mention it. This was real sophistication.

'Oh God.'

I said what I felt. And it worked.

'You don't need to add to your trouble. If it's possible. Hey? My baby.'

And yes, I thought. I could possibly be that.

HE WAS WAITING by the black ironwrought railings to the park. He had a set of newly cut keys in his hand. There were two willowy girls in white in there now, playing tennis on the uncut grass court. There was a smaller girl, you, sitting by the stump that held the sagging net, watching, a dog in your lap. The setting suggested a crime, somehow, as did his upturned collar, the jangling keys in his hand.

'Well?' he said.

'You're a shit,' I said.

'No,' he said. 'Shit doesn't do me justice. I'm a cad, a mountebank, a charlatan, and a bounder. All the Victorian versions of a shit and more.'

'You are the writer after all.'

'She's good, isn't she?' he said, after a pause.

'How do you mean good?'

'She's a very good . . . actress . . .'

'What if . . .' I began, and then hesitated.

'What if you fall for her?'

I didn't answer. The tennis racquets twanged as the ball crossed back and forth.

'You will,' he said.

# ROOM WITH A VIEW

I MOVED MY DRAWING board and my bits and pieces into the flat. I told my father I'd be away some nights.

'A girl?' he asked.

'Maybe,' I said. 'Just don't wait up for me.'

'Don't worry,' he said. 'It happens.'

It was peaceful there, with the light dying on the square, in that strange twilit world of a transatlantic relationship. Her night was my day, my day her night.

'I'm going to an opening with Ziggy, darling, just in case you felt like calling, and say hello to Ziggy by the way.'

'How's it going, Ziggy?'

'We miss you, man.'

'Yes, yes. I miss you all.'

It was extraordinary what minimal effort had to be made, how into a conversational pause or purr can be read a past history. The truth, I came to realize, the emotional, actual truth of wherever I was, what I was doing, how I felt, was the most effective lie of all. I was tired, I was anxious, I wished the work was going better (all true) and of course, I missed her (questionable, since I hardly knew her). But if an evening passed without her calling, as was inevitable (she had a life to lead), I did miss that voice, that breathy presence, the strange erotic pull of this woman whom I only knew by hearsay. I began to regulate my day by her, keeping mid-Atlantic hours. I would have something between breakfast and lunch around midday and await her call, walk out then, meet whatever clients had commissioned me, come back when the light was dying, and work through till two or three. And one afternoon I couldn't resist, I had to ask her what she was wearing.

'Oh, you . . .'

'Yes. I'm sorry. Me.'

'Hose.'

Not a garden hose, I realized, but nylon stockings.

'With a seam.'

'How did you know?'

'I remembered.'

And that was a lie. Maybe I'd imagined it.

'I'm pulling on a dress now. I'm lying back in bed, got my legs stretched to the ceiling, and I'm wriggling into this Versace thing. I can see my butt in the mirror. You'd still be proud of it.'

'I am.'

'Thirty-five, but still with an ass. And you?'

'Tracksuit. I've been running.'

'Hey, Ger, when did you ever run?'

'There's a square outside. I have a key. Trying to give up smoking, get fit.'

'Darling. I'm proud of you.'

I took to drinking then, late at night. There was a round of clubs in Dublin, after-midnight, bauble-lit places. I'd have a last pint in

Grogan's where the barman answered to a knock on the door, then wander up Leeson Street, to Buck Whaley's, Joy's, the Pink Elephant until the drink took hold and I would realize I was looking for him. I'd see my face in the mirror of a disco bar, fatter now, jowly round the cheekbones, and more often than not his face would appear behind it and I would realize some osmosis was taking place.

She was awaiting his arrival. He had his daughter's birthday to deal with, and a new event. He had been awarded a prize for his stories, the Hennessy Literary Award.

'Prevaricator.'

'No,' he said. 'I'd go if I could.'

There was a subtext here, both of us knew. There was a loved one, with a foetus inside her, growing bigger by the day. And I decided to test him. Told him if he didn't make his mind up, I would do it for him.

'You'd go there?'

'Yes.'

'Why?'

'You can't leave her in that limbo.'

He blew his breath between his teeth and made a whistling sound. 'Passing strange . . .'

'You'd end it?' he went on.

'If that's what you want.'

'I don't know what I want.'

'She knows what she wants.'

'And that is?'

'You.'

'Or you.'

AND SO IT was decided. By whom I don't remember. Me or him. He bought the ticket, came to Fitzwilliam Square to his book-panelled flat with a soft leather travelling case.

'What's that?' I asked him.

'My bag. She bought it for me.'

'I need it?'

'People change their luggage on average twice in a lifetime. I read that somewhere. You'll also need what's inside.'

There was another tennis game going on in the square outside. Spring was turning into early summer, the sagging net was discoloured from the winter rains. The same two girls lobbed balls across it and the sound came a heartbeat later. And a small girl chased her dog around the grassy path, uninterested in the game.

'What's inside?'

'Open it.'

I did. There were several suits there, some shirts, some underwear. A pair of hand-stitched leather shoes. I recognized the silver-flecked one, from his tales. And that's what they seemed like now, just tales. He showed me a photograph of them both in a horse-drawn buggy in Central Park.

'Try it on.'

So I undressed, in front of him. Oddly enough, I felt no shame.

'The underwear?'

'No. Not now. The suit.'

I pulled on the trousers, one of his plain white shirts, and then the jacket.

I looked at the mirror, then at the photograph. We were identical again.

'Your hair.'

'What about it?'

'She likes what she calls the "Room with a View" cut.'

'The what?'

'In the movie. That floppy, over-the-forehead English thing.'

And in the photograph her head was resting on his shoulder, his head tilted forwards, his hair spilling down to his eyebrows in a fogeyish manner.

'I have to get it cut?'

'Please. It would be better.'

'Couldn't you have let it grow?'

'Yes. But for her. She would appreciate the gesture.'

AND HAIR, I realized, was important. It tracked our similarities. We had gone from Marc Bolan to Lou Reed to Adam and the Ants. And now, Room with a View. I had it cut in the basement of the Shelbourne Hotel, where an old-style Dublin barber shaved me first, with a piping hot towel and an open razor, then cut my hair to match the photograph of him in Central Park.

'Happy days,' he said.

'Yes,' I said.

'Funny how you can tell. From a picture.'

'She likes it that way.'

'And who are we to argue?'

He smiled when he saw it. He had already left her, I could see. The restlessness had left him, the panic. He had given all of them to me.

'Call her from the airport,' he said. 'Go to Sixty-fifth, between Sixth and Fifth. Number twenty-two.'

'And then?'

'You'll like her house. One of those old brownstones, her husband left it to her. It's full of paintings. Has a great cellar.'

The concept of a cellar, good or great, was foreign to me. I presumed he meant good wines.

'If she wants you to choose, ask for a forty-seven Bordeaux.'

'A forty-seven Bordeaux.'

'Or one of the better burgundies.'

'You want to make a list?'

'No, stick to the Bordeaux.'

'And then?'

'You try to persuade her. Go to the clinic. Get rid of it.'

'Do I go with her?'

'Of course. Anything else would be unthinkable.'

'Isn't this unthinkable?'

'Besides, she might lie to you.'

'Why would she lie?'

'You'll see.'

'And if she refuses?'

'Well then. All bets are off, I suppose.'

'I could stay with her forever. Bring up the child.'

'In an alternative universe. You could buy one of those American school notebooks, with the mottled hard covers. Scribble in it, write a book.'

'That's what you did.'

'Yes. And look where it got me.'

THERE ARE CERTAIN paths we take, which will change our lives forever, and as the aeroplane was taxiing to its runway in Dublin and
the air hostess exposed her armpits to point to the various exits and
showed us how to pull the red toggle and inflate the life jacket, I began to wonder was this one of them.

I was taking this journey for reasons that were obscure even to
me. There was his dilemma, of course, his distress, his family, his
need to preserve what he thought of as his life. There was the game
of pretence, the allure, the high-wire act of it. There was her voice, on
the other end of the telephone, that 'dear.'

But there was more. There was a dream, of another life. The
dream of the immigrant, perhaps, anonymity in a new continent, but
that paled beside another dream. Of a female, with the thin, taut
body of my mother, an embrace that would last as long as I lived.
Give me your tired, your huddled masses. I was tired, I was huddled,
in my narrow seat in the aircraft—but yet again, there was more than
that.

People lost themselves in America, went through a sea change,
adopted new names, new histories, pretended new pasts. I could
lose Gerald there, lose Kevin, lose even Kerry, through some trick
of events I could not yet foresee, throw myself into that melting pot
and emerge as a beast with new scales. I could leave my droppings on
those streets, my odour on those pavements that I could only imagine,
had never seen, that were, as the songs said, built out of dreams.

And I did, in a way.

# MANHATTAN

THE STRANGE THING about Manhattan was how old it seemed. Even its skyscrapers seemed like a version of the future from the past. From a Flash Gordon comic of 1950s. The bridge that took me from the airport to the island—and it was an island, an island of childlike towers, rising from another brown river—was like another version of another future, from the turn of the century this time. As if H. G. Wells had asked Isambard Kingdom Brunel to construct it in a Glasgow steelworks, tow it across the Atlantic, and fix it here. Great hundred-year-old hawsers and pyramids of green metal rose above the two-lane highway, leading to the diadem of vertical lights beyond.

Once on the island itself I saw a *fin de siècle* elegance that seemed to have vanished from every European capital I had ever seen. Uniformed doormen, at every entrance. An architecture of the 1900s, the twenties, a sense of oddly unbroken continuity from then to now. Malevich would have loved it. His future had become their present, or past. I needed Darragh with me to sort out its significance. But Darragh was mad, and maybe I was mad too.

I DIDN'T CALL her from the airport. Whether it was fear or curiosity, I wanted to see the stage of my deception before the deception itself began. I hired a yellow cab from the airport to Central Park and the cabbie asked me, 'Where in Central Park, you gotta be specific?' so I said, 'Sixty-fifth,' and he seemed to understand.

HE DROPPED ME by a zoo, oddly enough, and I couldn't miss the park beyond so I began to walk in it. There was a mist all round—I would have called it autumnal if it hadn't been late spring—and as I wandered, the afternoon sun dispersed the mist with its fingers of warmth. So I saw delicate curved bridges emerge from the weakening mist, almost Japanese in their uselessness. The architectural draughtsman in me couldn't help but notice that one could traverse this park and never cross a bridge, but they seemed to define the green about them in some mysterious way: dark elegant armpits, and what is a body without an armpit, after all?

I was carrying that damned leather bag of his, or hers—she had bought it for him, I remembered—by means of a strap around my shoulder, so I looked like an itinerant salesman more than a tourist ripe for a mugging, but there seemed no threat of violence in that park, despite the legends I had heard. And I made my way to where the cabbie had left me and realized the bridges were for walking underneath, not over: The word 'tunnel' would have described their function better.

So I found myself on Sixty-fifth—or was it Sixty-sixth, one of the sixties anyway—and the understated elegance of those houses soothed me, made me imagine a life I could have led, the carved stone fences, the steps leading up to the decorated doorways—like the bridges in their own way, quite unnecessary but beautiful. And I found it then, number twenty-two on Sixty-fifth Street, and I understood that a brownstone meant exactly that, old brown sandstone steps leading to a building as beautiful as any I had ever seen. And I was drinking it in when footsteps sounded behind me, the clack of expensive heels on the stone of Sixty-fifth Street and I heard a voice I thought I recognized.

'Gerald, my God—'

I turned and there she was, the keys already in her hand, dark haired with a South American sallowness to her skin. She had an undeniable elegance, a willed kind of beauty. But what shocked me most immediately was, she wasn't beautiful at all.

'Well, maybe it's better. I went out. You hadn't called. I was afraid you missed—'

She leant forward and kissed me.

'—your flight.'

Straight on the lips. She kissed me again. Her lips tasted of cherry and lozenges.

I felt her lips reach mine again, then she withdrew and her forefinger ran over my mouth. It came away smeared with rose-coloured lipstick.

'Me. Coming off on you.'

'I don't mind.'

And for that moment, I didn't.

'Vanity. It gets worse with age. Come on in . . .'

# BROWNSTONE

'I'VE SENT JORGE away for the weekend,' she said, as she closed the front door behind her. It had metal bars with *trompe l'oeil* carvings beneath them.

I was glad. This was the first mention of a Jorge. There was a Maria too, I gathered, Jorge's wife. She was of the kind that needed a family to maintain her.

He hadn't adequately described the house. Or perhaps he didn't understand the interest I had in houses. There was a black-and-white tiled floor and she turned towards me, like a marionette, one high-heeled shoe on a black tile, the other on a white one. The house rose above her like a miniature church of soft pink. There was a curving staircase, in the same brown sandstone as outside, but it seemed to have a more roseate hue. There was a lift, in a cage of latticed metal, and the staircase curved around it. There must have been many more like this on the Upper East Side—the Silk Stocking District, I later learned it was called—but I was stunned by the studied opulence of it all and by the way she belonged within it. Did he fall for her, I wondered, or for this world of ease and plenty of the kind I could only imagine in Vienna or Paris, before this century began to wield its wrecking ball. Me, I fell in love with the house.

'Don't look so stunned, Gerald,' she said.

'I'm sorry. I'd forgotten.'

'What exactly had you forgotten. Me?'

'No. This place.'

'It's yours, if you want it.'

'This could never be mine.'

'Don't let's start that again.'

So, he had felt intimidated too. I was strangely relieved.

She took my arm and led me up the staircase. There was metal to my left and that soft cut stone to my right. I could feel her breast, edging against my elbow.

'*Mein irische Kind.*'

'You speak German?'

'You told me to read it.'

'Yes?'

'You gave me hyacinths a year ago.'

'Oh.'

We had reached the first floor. There was a kind of salon, every square inch of the walls covered by paintings. I recognized Kokoschka, and some that looked like imitation Chagall, but I didn't want to stare.

'Are you tired? Or would you like some tea?'

'Both,' I said.

'I got you some Barry's.'

Barry's tea. Could you buy it in Manhattan?

'Put your things in the room, stretch out on the bed, and I'll make you some.'

My problems then multiplied. Which was their room? But she took my hesitation as exhaustion and drew me by the arm into a room beyond. There was a walk-in closet, a bathroom off, a bed with a satin coverlet. I sat down on the bed.

'Put your head back,' she said, and she kissed me.

Her lips were taut, like those of a small boy. I felt bilious, suddenly. I wanted to blurt out the whole mistaken insanity. But she felt satisfied by the ritual of it, and suddenly withdrew herself. She had a way of moving that was continually surprising, almost like stillness. You hardly noticed it, and then she was moving on. I saw her brown hair swim above me and suddenly realized how tired I was.

'Tea,' she whispered, and I closed my eyes. I saw the plane again, felt the tug of the long Atlantic crossing, saw the waves far below washing off the wooden houses of New Jersey, the huge city in the distance that seemed to demand the sky, not the land. And then I was asleep.

I DREAMED OF him, making love to her. The dream seemed to take its syntax from a Victorian pornographic novel. There were white snowy breasts encased in a bustier, there were stays to be undone, laces to be untied, there were underdresses to lift and flounce, garter belts and black silk stockings that rolled down to expose creamy thighs, there was blonde, peach blossom hair, nothing remotely appropriate to her. Then, somehow, in the way of dreams, there was an air hostess in the same bustier explaining how to pull the red toggle. And then I was landing a plane in Central Park.

When I awoke she was there beside me and an array of clothes were scattered round the bed. Her thin and almost starved but perfect body was curled around mine, and I had no idea of what we had done.

'You were talking in your sleep,' she said.

'Was I?'

'Yes. You talked about air hostesses. Have you an air hostess?'

'What do you mean?'

'In your affections.'

'No. But I've come off a plane.'

'I just don't want another memory of yours . . . to be jealous of . . .'

'There is no air hostess.'

'I have Dominique already. And the child.'

'How can you be jealous of children?'

'I can be jealous of anything. My capacity is endless. I can be jealous of the clothes you want to wear.'

She rubbed her finger on my lower lip.

'But you know that.'

I was beginning to.

'And we better go now. We can join them at the theatre. Or we can have dinner on our own.'

Dinner on our own sounded terrifying. But the theatre sounded exhausting.

'They know you're jet-lagged. If you don't make, they'll understand.'

So between terror and exhaustion I went for terror.

'Dinner,' I said.

'Oo hoo hoo,' she murmured. 'I'm so glad you chose that.'

'Where?'

'Wallse. Where do you think?'

'Oh.'

I was supposed to know it. I smiled in recognition.

'You have to shower.'

I resented the implication, obscurely.

'There's that deodorant in the cabinet.'

I resented that even more.

'Wear the grey suit.'

Her mastery of him was subtle, but seemed all-embracing.

'A tie?'

'You have the paisley.'

'Yes.'

'Goes with the grey.'

Her shower was a gold-spigoted affair with jets of water spouting from the unlikeliest of angles. It was thrilling and delicious. When I came in from it, a towel wrapped around me, she was halfway through her own wardrobe and I experienced the strange assumption of an intimacy with someone I had never known. Her body was half clothed in underwear, there was an array of stockings laid across the bed, gold, plain black, one with a purple sheen, various dresses, and an array of shoes beneath them. It was both fascinating and repellent. Each choice demanded a response from me, some kind of assent, if not outright approval. My function was simple but could have been cut in stone. It was to echo her thoughts, to reinforce choices she had already made, to attest to the glory of the process that would end in the vision of Loretta, fully clothed.

I put on the grey suit she had chosen with a white shirt and the paisley tie she favoured. I saw in the mirror the quite unworthy complement I made to her perfectly wrapped form.

'Help me with the zip, dear,' she said and when I did, she went on, 'Don't even think of it.'

'I'm not,' I said truthfully, though I could see the rose petals on her bra, a fringe of purple lace around her dark breasts.

'I seem to have lost it a little.'

'What?'

'The urge. Must be the baby.'

She kissed me in a way that I can only describe as brotherly.

'Maybe later.' And her fingers traced the buttons of my shirt to my belt and the buttons of my trousers below. His trousers below.

'Maybe—what do you call it—'

As her other hand applied mascara to her eyelids, she began to unbutton me. Him. I was amazed and appalled at her dexterity, and felt a surge of disgust along with a totally unwonted spasm of desire. I moved my hips backwards, beyond her reach. Was this what they did, I wondered.

'Yes,' she said. 'Later.'

She held a tiny cuplike bowl out to my nostrils.

'Smell this. Whale oil.'

What strange hell had he made for himself, I wondered. There was an odd silence between us now as she finished her eyelids in the mirror. I had to fill it.

'Don't we have to talk?'

'About?'

'You know—'

'Yes. The event. We can talk at dinner.'

IN THE YELLOW taxi, we talked. Or rather she talked and I listened. A woman of her age, for whom childbirth had been a possibility always deferred, had to take an event like ours as manna from heaven.

After two abortions in her teens, an arid life with an ageing husband, her womb had to work overtime to retain the tiny zygote it had been blessed with. Into its second month, the little one had its destiny written in her body and mine and part of her life with me, the father, in this city of New York. So divorce was essential: One marriage had failed, another must begin, and his daughter could visit her new home on school holidays—a sad consequence but the upside was she would have two mummies rather than one and love after all was a verb, not a noun.

Every word from her mouth seemed to have come from a self-improvement manual and as the aphorisms flew from her taut, perfectly painted lips with the small black line beneath the lower one, I was hit with the strange suspicion that she, like me, was lying. That we were perfectly matched fantasists both, caught in a web of narrative we needed for our own deeply unhealthy reasons.

'Do you have one of those pictures?'

'Pictures?'

'You know. An ultrasound.'

'The doctor didn't recommend it. I have a fragile ecosystem.'

'You have.'

But in the restaurant my mood softened. She looked beautiful beneath the soft table lights. And this, I realized, was what all that effort had been for: so her hair would highlight the perfectly modelled curve of her cheekbones as the maître d' removed her coat. It was Austrian, Wallse, they knew her, seemed to know me, seemed to know the table we wanted by the window, looking out on the elegant passersby in the streetlights outside.

She was delicacy personified. She ordered for me, as if it was their habit. 'You hate duck, don't you, dear, or have you overcome your aversion?' No, I assured her, duck and me still didn't get on. So she ordered a consommé, a risotto with prawns for me, Dublin Bay ones—'they could have flown them in for you'—a warm duck salad for herself and a wine from Alsace, greenish in texture with what she assured me would be a tangy gooseberry finish.

We didn't talk about the issue and it would have seemed indelicate to bring it up. We discussed a tentative future in which the baby was an unspoken fact. 'You've begun a new book?' she asked, and of course I would have had to, so I began to improvise and amazed myself by how simple it was.

Set in Marrakesh, I told her, about a visit to Morocco by a couple on the verge of separation. It opens with a visit to a tiny square, somewhere in the depths where the gold-beaters work, hammering their squares of gold into long, sun-molten sheets. They have their child with them, a daughter, who wanders off during yet another incessant argument, and by the time they realize she is gone their calling out of her name is drowned by the hammering of a thousand tiny wooden hammers on a thousand tiny sheaves of gold. They roam in a panic round the gold-beaters, asking have they seen a girl, a blonde girl, aged four, wandering on her own, and are met by unresponsive shrugs. A policeman is called, bilingual, to question them and he shrugs his shoulders in turn, tells them there is nothing they could have heard since all of them are deaf. From a lifetime of hammering.

'Terrifying,' she said, 'but it's so nakedly your fear, of losing your daughter. And you know that will not happen.'

'It's a book,' I said. 'I don't care to ask where it comes from.'

Her foot must have slipped out of her angle-poise shoe because I felt her small-boned toes massaging my shinbone.

'Poor you. How does it end?'

'Don't know,' I said, since I was afraid to stop talking. 'He grew up, the husband, in the house in Dublin next door to the house Bram Stoker lived in.'

'Who?'

'The one who wrote *Dracula*. His imagination, I imagine, had always been inflamed. He thinks the old lady with the walking stick who lives there must be Dracula's caretaker. There's some business with a pedophile who he presumes to be a vampire. Some encounter during a showing of *Blue Hawaii* in the local fleapit.'

'*Blue Hawaii?*'

'A film. With Elvis Presley.'

I could see her eyes glazing over, the urge to change the subject expressed by her wiping the corner of her lip with the serviette. I felt all the disappointment of one whose stories did not, could not, enchant. And I realized that, in this, I was no match for him.

'Make it a happy ending, Gerald, will you? I couldn't take more grief.'

'As in?'

'Oh, they find the girl.'

'Where?'

'Oh, in a room full of golden dresses. You Irish, you so love your grief.'

And a change came over her face, almost a cloud, which seemed to me like grief. I felt her fingers touching mine, massaging the second finger of my left hand.

'Where's your ring?'

He had forgotten a significant detail, I realized. I had to meet her eyes then and held them as firmly as I could, trying not to blink.

'It didn't seem right to wear it.'

'You always wore it before.'

'Before, maybe. Not now.'

Her pupils seemed to grow. Her eyes sparkled with hidden light. Then I realized they had filled with tears.

'Do you know how much that means to me, Gerald?'

She wrapped her hand around mine.

'You can imagine? And we should go now, don't you think?'

# THE CELLAR

I N THE TAXI home she wrapped her arms around me, planted a perfectly formed kiss on my cheek, and with a courtesan's hand began to unbutton my shirt.

'I want you,' she said, 'to make the most God-awful hash of my makeup.'

She fluttered her eyelid towards my mouth and I rubbed my tongue over its carefully painted surface.

'Now the other,' she said, and I felt those eyelids like humming-bird's wings.

She raised her face then with what looked like two black eyes.

'All that work,' she said, 'to be ruined in a moment.'

In her brownstone house, we took the lift, not the stairs. She draped one leg over the metal latticework and said, 'Pretend there's a line of people out there, keep them waiting.' And I tried to imagine them, a line of weary office workers, waiting with their folders, their paper cups of coffee, for the lift that never arrived.

It must have worked, for the lift shook and the lattice rattled on the iron cage and she raised the other leg around my hip and my hands found themselves around those laced fringes at the top of her legs where all of her energy seemed to have gathered. I must have pressed her shoulder against the button then because the doors slid open and I could see a mirror fracturing our bodies, the grip and thrust of them, the slide of them against the rose-coloured wall, her dress bunched like unruly petals as we somehow made it through the doorway to her bed.

I imagined I was him then, finally and completely, I imagined Sunset Boulevard and Spago's and Cahuenga and the overweight curly-haired traffic cop on Van Nuys. And we finished up in a kind of rictus on her tangled bedspread, her starved, perfect body shuddering five long times.

'You've changed,' she said, after a long silence.

'Maybe.'

'You've made a mess of me,' she said and disengaged herself, slid off to the bathroom, and I noticed there was blood on the pink satin.

I could see her through the bevelled mirror, multiple images of her, sitting on a bidet.

'You're bleeding,' I said.

'I know,' she said.

'You're not pregnant.'

'And you're not Gerald.'

There was the sound of rushing water and she came back in, her clothes in some semblance of rearrangement.

'Would you get us a drink, so we can discuss it all?'


THE CELLAR HAD the odour of dead matter. There was an old rusting bicycle propped against the wooden cases, there were cobwebbed brick arches, and there was a dim bulb hanging from the bare brick ceiling.

I chose a bottle at random. It was covered in dust so I presumed it was old but I hadn't the energy to search out the vintages he had advised me on and besides, the pretence was over. I blew the dust from the bottle but still couldn't read the name, the label was moulding and curling from the bottle—whatever, it would do, it would do.

I switched off the light and stood in the darkness for a moment or two, considering the situation. I was in unfamiliar territory once more; we seemed to lead each other there, or I seemed to lead myself. The comfort, if comfort was the word, of another person's life had dissipated once more and I felt alone, very much alone. You can deal with this, Gerald, Kevin, whoever we both were now. Though something deep inside, as dramatic as a voice, told me I couldn't.

I walked back upstairs, into the canvas-filled living room. Kokoschka, Arp, Chagall, they all seemed like imitations now. I took two bowl-shaped glasses from the drinks tray, worked the opener on the bottle, and poured the reddish-brown liquid in. It smelt of old decay, like the cellar itself. I drank one glass while I waited. Then another, while I waited some more. She came through eventually, dressed in a kimono nightgown thing now, her pale face quite renewed, and her hair tied back into a widow's bun.

I handed her a glass.

'He would have chosen better,' she murmured. She had some kind of pill in her hand which she swallowed, then she took a long sip.

A funereal air embraced us both.

'I should have you arrested,' she said eventually.

'Is that really necessary?'

'He told me he was an only child.'

'He is.'

'And you?'

'An only child.'

'So can you explain the resemblance?'

'No. I've long since stopped questioning it.'

'You both play games with people?'

'No. Sometimes I think.'

'What, you prick? Make sense of this.'

'We share the same soul.'

'And why are you here?'

'He couldn't cope.'

'Dickhead.'

'You did tell him you were—'

'Pregnant? How do you know I wasn't?'

'You were bleeding.'

'Maybe you fucked it out of me. Maybe I lost it there.'

And I felt sick then.

'Do you need a hospital?'

'You think I'm lying?'

'As a practised liar, I have to admit I do.'

'What's your name?'

'You don't need to know.'

'On the contrary, I believe I do. I'll need your name on the file report. And his. It should do wonders for what's left of his career.'

'You lied first.'

And she hit me across the face. Like Barbara Stanwyck in a film the name of which I can't remember.

'A woman of my age, my predicament, deceived by an Irish hack who pretends to be his own twin?'

She grabbed the bottle and slopped wine into her glass. She swung the bottle then, gesticulating with her hand, and I thought she would hit me with it.

'I have a man, you know, who deals with these things. Wealth brings its own advantages. So don't worry, he'll beat it out of you—'

And as if to show me how, she struck me again and again and began a kind of ballet of slapping, with the palm, the backhand, the fist. I had to step back before the onslaught.

And I pitied your father then, Emily, as it went on, in a fury of emotion, a kind of parody of lovemaking. I was mad at him during the lovemaking itself, but now all I felt was pity, because it couldn't have been the first time. There was a familiarity to her gestures, her hand swinging out to make contact with my face, tearing at my hair, those triangular nails seeking contact with my skin. This had happened before, and maybe it was delicacy on your father's part to spare me the details—delicacy or shame, shame in the end I would say—as I backed down the circular staircase, trying to keep my face intact with my elbows and arms. There was a kind of foreplay to it, like any lovemaking, any bodily contact, where the first moves are just a prelude to the final ones, and I realized that I had known all along what the final move would be.

She threw her face down towards me in a parody of a kiss, but what kissed me was her forehead, drawing a spout of blood from my open lips. And she drew her head back then to do it better this time, and I grabbed her widow's knot of hair in my fist, pulled her face around so she couldn't do it again. She jerked her head back, fiercely this time, and we both would have tumbled down that metal staircase had my other hand not grabbed her black kimono and pulled her back to me. Her breasts stroked my chest and I could feel her winy breath in my face. Then she swung the glass towards me in a long arc and I ducked, missing contact with the glass though not the ejaculation of wine.

My hand swung after hers and the momentum of her misplaced strike turned her body clockwise. I had slammed my fingers round her knuckles and both of our hands continued the movement and slammed the glass into her throat. So you could say we both did it. The glass shattered at the bone of her chin and what remained on the stem sliced a half-moon into the skin below. There was a low gurgle from her, the taste of vintage wine in my mouth, and suddenly an enormous geyser of blood. I wouldn't have thought her starved frame could have contained so much. It sprayed over me in gouts that must have been pumped by her dying heart.

And that would have been it, had she let me go, fallen backwards down that staircase like any prom queen in a dozen slasher movies. But no, she clung to me now as if to force me to share in her last moments. The blood pumped from her open throat on to my lips, it mixed with the wine in a salty, leathery bile. I would have gagged, but managed to hold myself back. I tried to unclaw her from me, but she was having none of it. One hand grabbed my collar, the other my hair. 'Da Silva,' she called out, 'Da Silva,' and I wondered was her Jorge called Da Silva, but as he subsequently told me, it was her dead husband's name.

Anyway, she hung onto me with that extraordinary vigour and I staggered back with her. There would be no escaping her now, I knew I was with her till death did us part. I fell backwards on the metal steps as her blood dripped down onto the floor below. And her hand, though it never relaxed its terrible grip, began to achieve a kind of stasis, fixed itself into an arthritic knot, and after a diminishing series of shivers, went totally still.

She was dead then, Emily, and I had killed her. Killers, they endlessly retrace the steps of the event, don't they, and when I traced back what both of us were doing, at that precise time your father was taking his place with Dominique in the Cabaret Room of the Burlington Hotel by the table reserved for him at the prelude to the Hennessy Awards. A few cameras must have popped because there was his photograph in *The Irish Times*, in a well-fitting monkey suit; he already knew he had won but the quiet smile playing on his face gave nothing away. And Dominique, she looked radiant; she had put on some weight but that added to her allure. Both of them a couple, most of a life still ahead of them. And I was sitting on that metal staircase among those fake Chagalls, Kokoschkas. She was between my knees and she was dead.

I stood up gingerly and tried to disengage myself, and her body slipped down a few more metal steps.

I did what any of us would do, I suppose. I took off my bloodied clothes, my bloodied shoes and thank God he had given me those hand-stitched ones, because I had a spare pair. I turned on the spigots of her elaborate shower and it came into its own then, those jets of seething, boiling water at every possible angle, washing my body clean. I dried myself and dressed again and stuffed my bloodied clothes into one of her plastic toilet bags and repacked the rest of my clothes in that leather suitcase she had bought him. And I took the lift down to the hallway, to avoid that mess we both had left on the circular stairs.

# JFK

I T WASN'T LIGHT yet, in Manhattan. The streets were almost empty, the doormen gone to bed. I walked towards the park and found a seat facing a glimmering pool from where I could hear the nocturnal cries of animals from the zoo. There were no predators around. Only me.

What did I feel, Emily, sitting there, with the strange growls and rustlings from the wire cages near by? Nothing. I was wrapped in a shell of emptiness, as if here at last was my real name. And my real name was zero, zilch, a blank. I not only felt nothing, I became nothing, a human absence that was barely aware of the growing light. My American dream was over before it had begun. I tried to find tears for the loss of that dream, but couldn't. There was no moisture left in me.

And eventually the hoots of the tawny owls and the moans of the silver foxes gave way to more familiar birdsong. I walked on to Fifth Avenue and got myself a cab.

In Kennedy Airport, I found a seat available on the next flight back. 32c. I would like to say it was burned on my consciousness, but it wasn't, I just remember such things. I sat down in one of those plastic chairs and slept for six hours.

I awoke to hear that my flight was boarding, on the public address system. There was a large man in golfing pants beside me, his wife in a pink tracksuit beside him. They were talking about Ballybunion.

I had washed my hands thoroughly in her bathroom, dried them on her linen hand towels, washed them again in the urinals of JFK, dried them in the hot air contraption, but I still felt, passing through security, that my palms would glow red in the X-ray machine. To have blood on one's hands is to arrive at some basic cul-de-sac in the human condition, to realize that it was always there, waiting for you, and that you were the one who just happened to take the turn. Any one of us there, placing our bags through that glowing thing, could have done the same. Yet I alone was the one.

The portly Puerto Rican with the plastic gloves and the gun on her belt who patted me down should have smelt the odour of blood from me, but she didn't. She smiled as if I was a responsible member of the human race and gestured me on. She said, 'You have a nice day, now.'

I felt a glow around me, a dark heat, the penumbra of death, and felt it had to be obvious to all of those anonymous souls heading towards the gates. But the extraordinary thing was that it wasn't. Two extraordinary things, then: I had penetrated the black heart of existence, I had killed another human being, and not only did nobody notice, they were nice to me. 'You have a nice day, now.'

The dog though, the sniffer dog, coming down the line of passengers towards me, the cop guiding him from one pair of ankles to another, surely the dog would smell it? Death must have a smell. But he sniffed my shuffling shoes, nosed around my thighs without reaction, and moved on to the woman in the pink tracksuit behind me.

I boarded the plane, took a copy of *The Irish Times* from the rack in premier class, and made my way down the aircraft. I took a glass of orange juice from the stewardess, picked at the nuts and canapé things, sprawled my bulk over two seats near the back, and felt the Atlantic dark overwhelm me.

I opened the paper and there he was, on page two, already in print. How could this be possible, I wondered, given the events of the previous evening? In a svelte tuxedo, his well-cut hair tumbling over his crown, in what he called the 'Room with a View' cut, some kind of animal sculpture in his hand. Dominique was smiling beside him. It was a dog, I realized, a St. Bernard cast in bronze, the Hennessy Literary Award. He had won, as he knew he would, while his other self was slicing the throat of his girlfriend. His smile was shy but confident, as if the bronze dog in his hand was faintly ridiculous yet to refuse it would have been churlish. Her smile was yogic in its sense of well-being. And nothing, needless to say, in his smile or his demeanour, in those fingers clutching the ridiculous bronze dog, suggested murder. I wondered had he heard yet, then fell asleep.

# THE CRESCENT

I WAS AWOKEN THEN, on a Sunday, by your finger on my doorbell, and maybe it was lucky I hadn't shaved the night before and maybe it was lucky that it was one of those miserable summer mornings where the horizontal rain is blowing and the leaves are already falling. Because I pulled on one of those touk-type hats and opened the door without too much worry about recognition.

There were three of you there, you, her, and him, the auctioneer with the hairless chest. There were the blowing leaves and the wintry summer rain and the park outside couldn't have looked less inviting. And I needn't have worried, because she walked in with that kind of abstract politeness that made me invisible. She was still beautiful, I could see that, softly greying hair, that same great bone structure that gets more pronounced with age. She had spent her whole life in that woolly, comfortable skein of South Dublin—nothing wrong with that, Emily, many people do, and it keeps them young apparently, that much was obvious: the constancy, the common rituals, holidays in France, weddings, funerals.

But she walked inside and my invisibility was perfect, it was accentuated by the house, enhanced even by the house, as if friends of Stoker's vampire had wound a cloak around me; and I realized that to buyers of houses their occupiers must be placed in that zone of invisibility, of no-belonging, since all they were and all of their memories will possibly be replaced. I had spent my whole life as someone's invisible partner, I realized, as I heard you loyally defend the crumbling mouldings on the ceiling against her pithy comments. You liked the wallpaper, she didn't, he liked the curved banisters, the way the first-floor living room had a back stairs to the kitchen.

But she liked the view, I could see, through the mottled glass windows and that pleased me. I had spent so many hours of childhood looking at that view, dreaming of other things maybe, but still looking so that it was etched on my brain, part of my being, even. And when she stood there, looking over Fairview Park, a swan did rise from the muddy bank of the Tolka and flap over the poplar trees. And I took that as a sign, maybe, that it was good that I said nothing, remained unrecognized, and took the three of you up to the room full of clocks.

'So many clocks,' she said and had no idea who had spent time among them.

'We can polish them,' you said, 'and hang them round the walls.'

# TOLKA

THE PLANE WAS coming in over the low fields and there was rain again, rain again, like a children's rhyme that did its best to imitate the remembered sound, the patter of raindrops off a duck pond, a pool in the road, a bedroom window. There were grey clouds over Howth Head which said forget about summer, the red and white windsocks were wet and blowing hard, and grey veils of rain were sheeting down the runway, buffeting the plane door. The passengers walked out with their coats over their heads but I allowed the elements to have their way with me. I was wet going through the terminal, I was drenched waiting for the taxi, and by the time I had made it back to the Crescent, I was coughing hard.

I felt a flu coming on, the intermittent shivering, the pain in the joints, though it could have been a physical reaction to recent events. There wasn't a doctor I could consult on the difference, so I made my way through the empty house and took to my bed. I slept fitfully and woke sweating, and I felt the presence of my childhood friend beside me in the room, there and not there, a smell of must and satin, a humming outside the sash window which could have been the wind. If there was a hell I was confined to now, he would be in it. There were no fires there, though, just an empty iron grate like the one in this room, with the wind whistling through it. A pallid face that seemed to say, I told you so. And then I must have slept again, because I was woken by a gnarled hand on my sweating forehead, another pallid face which I recognized as my father.

'Made a hot toddy for you,' he said. He was mixing a spoon in a whiskey glass. 'Only remedy I know. Cloves and some brown sugar.'

He brought it to my lips, and I tried to drink.

'You've been away?'

I nodded.

'Back to London?'

I nodded again.

'We come and go, the two of us. Off myself tomorrow to the Epsom Derby.'

He brought it to my lips again. I drank it all.

'Strange, isn't it? Going to miss the peace here. Just the two of us.'

He made that whistling sound through his teeth, and I knew he was lost for words.

'Whoever would have thought.'


HE BROUGHT ME breakfast before he went, so it must have been the next morning. A mug of tea, a curling rasher, and a piece of toast. He was a Dublin man.

The other had no accent. He had no smell now, no particular sound, though the wind kept moaning through the gaps in the sash window. Just a presence that let me know he knew we were the same now. There was no need for words.

And after I don't know how many days, of sweating, of sleeping, of dead, timeless communion with this other thing, which may have been sleep, I was woken up by the telephone ringing.

I wrapped a blanket round me, staggered down the stairs. The phone was on the landing, a communal one, with a coin box, and I remembered the lodgers she had kept.

I heard breathing from the other side and the sound of coins falling. I knew it was him, and that he was in a street-side phone box.

Clever, I thought.

'That you?'

'Yes,' I said.

'So you're back,' he said.

'Back,' I said, 'in the land of the living.'

There was a silence then. My cliché had carried too much weight for him. I wondered what words I could say now that were uninfected.

'All right,' he said, apropos of nothing. And those words at least were neutral.

'So,' I said, to fill the silences.

'We better meet then,' he said.

'If you want.'

'I don't want. I feel the need.'

'There's a walkway by the Fairview Park, over the Tolka river.'

I felt like bringing him out of his way.

'Where's the Tolka river?'

'On the northside. By the East Wall.'

I knew I could have been describing Timbuktu.

'Tomorrow night? At eight?'

'There are benches there, just like on the Grand Canal. I'll be sitting on one.'

THERE WAS A soft rain falling, which the swans didn't seem to notice. There were two of them, crammed into the sliver of water the tide had left, surrounded by dark banks of mud. I wondered idly how they kept their wings so clean and white. Then I saw a black umbrella making its way towards me from the Fairview bridge. He must have taken the number 30 bus, I thought, and for some reason the thought made me smile.

'Greetings from Manhattan,' I said. 'Did it strike you the way things are kind of old there? You know that sense of rupture you get in the London architectural skyline—the way the Blitz was a delineating factor between then and now? No sense of that in Manhattan. Their modernism expresses continuity, somehow.'

'Jesus,' he said. 'Jesus.'

'Malevich, now he would have loved it.'

'Shut the fuck up,' he said.

'You mean modernism's not your thing?'

'Jesus,' he said again.

'Sit down.'

And he sat. There was nothing else to do, with the soft rain falling and the swans staring at us in the gleaming bit of water that was all that was left of the Tolka river.

'You heard about it, then?'

'A police officer called. She had my number written somewhere.'

'Your house or your flat?'

'The flat.'

'You shouldn't worry. You weren't there.'

'I was at the Hennessy.'

'I saw your picture in the paper. If I had chosen the moment, I couldn't have done it better.'

'And didn't you? Choose the moment?'

'Nothing like that. You could have told me she was—'

'Unstable.'

'Violent. Though perhaps any of us would have been, considering the circumstances.'

'The circumstances?'

'She guessed. And I guessed. If it's any consolation to you, she wasn't . . . in the family way . . .'

'They think it was the Ecuadorian. The help. What's his name?'

'Jorge.'

'He was illegal. Probably in Ecuador now.'

'It was an accident,' I told him. 'It could have happened to you.'

'It did happen to me.'

'And you did want an end to it.'

'Maybe, but not that. Tell me why.'

'I think you know why. Maybe I should tell you—'

'How.'

And I told him. About my only trip to Manhattan (and I felt a surge of melancholy then, knowing I might never go back there), our meeting in her brownstone, our dinner in Wallse, and the strange segue in the lift, on the bed, and later on the circular staircase. I spared him nothing. If it were a dance, I told him, it would be a tarantella. 'You knew her,' I said to him. 'She was never letting go. Come and have a drink.'

I stood. He stayed sitting.

'Gaffney's,' I said. 'Across the bridge. It's a dinky old place.'

And I wondered where that word had come from. 'Dinky.' Stupid word.

'I can't meet you again. For a long, long time.'

I looked down at him there, on that wooden bench, and wondered how much he had ever known of himself. Wasn't fiction a form of self-knowledge? Then I thought of what I had read of his, and realized it was more a form of avoidance.

'I grew up around here,' I said. 'On the Crescent. Over there.'

'You heard me,' he said, and from his tone I felt that would be the last I heard of him. For a long, long time.

He sat on, in his carapace of silence, and I thought I'd leave him there. I had a drink myself, in Gaffney's. I thought about Bram Stoker and Tommy the Clock and my mother's body on the cement steps of the Bull Wall, and I saw an old man across the bar beneath the television, his head bent over the racing pages, and I wondered was that the figure my father would become. I would have to leave this place, I knew, and whatever late idyll we had enjoyed would have to end. The old man caught my eye with his, blue eyes riddled with red veins.

'Are you winning?' I asked him.

'What's that, sonny?'

And I finished my drink and left. None of us were winning.

# THE NORTHSIDE

THE THREE OF you left then, and I had the strange feeling of having been vaguely violated. It was my house after all, my wallpaper, my clocks, and I didn't have to sell it. I could loathe it, criticize it, subject it and myself to any form of self-examination, but for others to do so seemed—and as I was searching for the word 'impolite,' the doorbell rang again.

'I'm sorry,' you said, 'was that too awful?'

'No,' I lied. 'A bit—what your father would have called—passing strange . . .'

'Did he ever come here?'

How little you really know, I thought.

'Anyway, it gave rise to the most awful row.'

'Your mother didn't approve?'

'She hated it. Couldn't understand the necessity. The northside. The park. The view. Which only made me dig my heels in even more. We shouted a bit.'

'Oh dear.'

'It must have been building. Since I told her about the . . . Anyway, we both let rip.'

'Not good.'

'No. And he must be sweet, because he offered to drive her home.'

'Should I say I'm sorry?'

'No.'

'I am sorry.'

'Take me somewhere, will you? I need a drink.'

# AIDEEN'S GRAVE

W E ARE OUR own punishment, I realized, standing with the lights off in that Fitzwilliam Square flat. I gathered my things and did my best to leave his books and papers untouched. I wondered how he would do without me. I tried to imagine an enquiry, an affable Kerry giant filling the space in here, peaked Garda cap in his hand. That delicate game of insinuation and nuance that was Irish conversation. And you met her, when? All he had to do, I realized, was tell his story, as if I had never existed. And in a while it would be as if I had never existed.

I locked the door behind me, and threw the keys into the canal over Baggot Street bridge. I surprised a swan, and it turned into a giant flapping machine of white, churning up the water towards the Leeson Street lock.

The leaving that was hardest was yet to come. How life surprises, I thought, as I heard my father's unsteady feet ascend the stairs. He had done well at Epsom and had gone to Gaffney's to celebrate his winnings.

'I've got to go, Da,' I said when he had slumped himself in the sofa across from me. I thought, God bless alcohol, the way it dulls all feeling.

'The main produce,' he said, 'of this fucking country is young fellas like you, bred for export. Where are you headed?'

'London,' I said, though I had a suspicion I wouldn't stop there.

'There's something,' he said, 'there's something . . .'

And he couldn't continue, because there were tears in his eyes. There was something, that he wouldn't tell me till many years later.

'You can come over,' I said, 'on your way to Aintree, Doncaster, or wherever.'

'Yes,' he said, 'we can have a flutter. We never spoke that much when you were . . .'

'Younger.' I finished his sentences for him.

'Your mother kept you like a gift-wrapped thing. That she was afraid I would damage.'

'Maybe.'

'We don't deserve our winnings, do we? If that's what they are.'

'Maybe not.'

'Wake me up before you go. Let me drive you to the plane.'

I WOKE UP early and knocked on his door when I had dressed. I remembered crawling into that room to sleep beside my mother's sleeping shape, her hip on one side under the coverlet like Goya's Dreamer. But I had no memory of him ever there. Did I choose my moments, I wondered, and wait until I knew he'd be away? I thought about Freud and the uselessness of childhood memory. This sleeping thing before me now, tangled in the bedspread, malodorous and old and male, was definitely new to me, in this context, this bedroom.

I shook his veined hand until he was fully awake. I could see his eyes trying to work me out and felt like saying, don't worry, Father, I'm already vanishing. But he said my name. 'Kevin.' And I told him I'd make him a cup of tea.

He drove me down the Clontarf Road, past St. Anne's estate, and turned right at Sutton Cross up towards Howth Summit, and I knew he was heading towards her grave. It was a sun-whipped day with the white horses on the Irish Sea brighter than usual and those cotton wool clouds scudding across the sky. I remembered her body on the cement steps, I remembered the vampire hush in the living room with her body laid out, but I had no memory of her grave. I wondered why, but I didn't ask him.

'Aideen,' he murmured, 'she ended up here.'

A lover, I remembered, running from some epic of grief was buried in some megalith on Howth Head.

The graves were the same flat ones we saw, Emily, on the gently sloping hillside. There were flowers scattered round the flat slabs of marble, families tending them, and nothing to break that whipping wind. Hers was a black marble one, untended.

'Dearly beloved,' he said, reading from the gravestone, and I asked how many times he had visited.

'Never,' he said. 'I was never one for what's it called . . .'

'Remembrance,' I said.

'That's the one,' he whispered and he whistled through his teeth and I knew he was searching for the words.

'Have you ever done a bad thing?' he asked me, and I thought, what a question. There was only one answer.

'Of course.'

'Me too,' he said. 'Done several bad things. Forgive us, May,' he said.

What did he know, I wondered. And I asked him.

'Why do you say that now?'

'Put me down here, will you?' he said. 'When the time comes.'

# GAFFNEY'S

THERE WAS A Sunday afternoon crowd, which meant two old men watching racing in the corner. The brown curve of the bar and the fawn tongue-in-groove panels behind gave it an illusory feeling of comfort. You ordered Guinness, which surprised me, and I ordered a Corona and for the umpteenth time I wondered how much I should tell you.

'I asked your father in here once,' I said.

'Did he come?'

'No. He said he never wanted to see me again.'

'Sounds . . . precipitate.'

'Precipitate,' I repeated. 'That's a good word. It was. I had done something that would change his life.'

'What?'

'The instinct to help someone,' I told you, 'must be among the most lethal of all . . .'

'You didn't help?'

'No. On the contrary. It was the beginning of his . . . stuff . . .'

'You're not going to tell me, are you?'

'No,' I said. 'But I've written it down.'

'Oh well,' you said. 'Cheers.'

You lifted your Guinness. Your sense of well-being defied all logic. Lucky child, I thought.

'Cheers,' I said.

# HAMBURG

I BOARDED A PLANE and took to the air, but really I was going to ground. Like a hedgehog, or a bear, entering hibernation. I found a basement flat in Shepherd's Bush and worked on architectural scaled models for the new city that was growing up beyond the Isle of Dogs. My father came over to Kempton Park races one year, to Ascot the next summer, to Cheltenham the next spring, and I wondered when the inevitable decline would begin. There was no sign of it, though; he had the indestructibility of a Guinness barge.

So when I was offered work in Hamburg some years later I took it, devising computer models for submissions to reinvigorate the Hamburg docklands. The laws of gravity were being rewritten, classical presumptions about weight, stress, and tension thrown out of the window. I discovered video games then, began to play with nonexisting cities and realized my history in architectural drawing was just what was needed to delineate those rotating street vistas down which ninja assassins and yakuzas roamed. More years passed and the wireframe models grew three-dimensional, the cities acquired shape, dimension, light and shade like the yakuzas that roamed through them. And I was designing a series of celestial backgrounds to an arcade version of *The Monkey King* when his name popped up on the screen.

An announcement that he would be reading in the British Council on Tuesday of the following week.

His picture on the back flap of the cover came with the announcement. His hair was long and greying and sagging flesh obscured the line of jaw and cheekbone that had been common to both of us once. The title of the book could have been exchanged with any that he had published during the last decade. Was it *Remembrance* or *Bygones*? I forget.

I had read them, of course. And I had been disappointed at how conventional they had become. That strange obsession with past decades, the fifties, the forties, the twenties, that bedevilled Irish fiction. Didn't they ever write about the present? A reinvention of his family, which was odd, given what I later discovered. A grandfather who had been in a flying column in the early twenties, an aunt who had a nervous breakdown in the thirties, an uncle who joined the Oblate Fathers and later left the priesthood—each were given their separate tomes. *Independence. The Closed Ward. Congo.*

I could see my dim reflection on the screen in front of me, superimposed on his face. He drank too much, I could see that already, as if he had spent the intervening years trying to bury that part of himself, myself, whoever it was, under a pad of puffy flesh and broken capillaries. I on the other hand had perfected the thin, starved look of the computer geek. I ran daily round the waterfront. I ate stir-fried greens and goji juice. I had done that trick with the shaven head, so that one didn't know where incipient baldness began and ended. I had starved him out, he had buried me in.

I put the date in my diary, but my light-filled pagodas and heavenly gardens, my endless vistas of waterfalls and celestial clouds, the

levels of hell and heaven for my monkey king absorbed me so much
that I almost forgot the date, and if the computer had not pinged and
had his name not popped up again behind the seventh door of the
seventh level of the first hell, I would have missed his reading entirely.
As it was I had to run through the late evening streets to the public
reading room.

I took a lift up from a neon-lit foyer and found myself in a world
of oak-panelled doorways and William Morris-patterned wallpapers
that could have graced any club off Piccadilly or the Mall. There was
the sound of shuffling chairs and a low Irish voice droning, off. I followed it to a set of barely closed double doors and could glimpse a
figure deep inside, between an aisle of wooden chairs.

I edged one door open. It squeaked, as it would, and it being the
British Council, every head seemed to turn.

His didn't. His modelled, slightly lilting Irish voice rambled on—
about summer in Lahinch, a daughter wheeling her incapacitated
mother past ice-cream stands and young lovers, past men in parked
cars and Micheál O'Hehir's voice commenting on the Sunday GAA
fixture. I was amazed that these odd realities would hold their attention. The way I was amazed that the Irish pub in Feldstrasse was
almost always full. And listening to him, my mind began to wander
through the lineaments of those celestial clouds and blazing pagodas,
level twenty-one of the monkey king's battle with the jade emperor,
all twirling numchucks and arabesquing feet. I wondered which of
them had more substance, the ennui of the daughter in Lahinch or the
wilderness of vistas in my game landscapes.

His weight gave him gravitas but I had the sense that that would
vanish later. There was a sybaritic air about him that I couldn't

quite fix. He was different, and not only in the hair, the weight. We looked nothing like each other now, but the difference was more than that.

He had won a prize, I heard during the questioning, one of the British prizes, hence the reading for the Council. He was endlessly congratulated on it and, to his credit, he seemed weary of the topic. He was asked about his life and he answered with the practised demeanour of someone who was weary of that too.

There was a line of people for a book signing afterwards. I bought a copy from the publisher's pile and joined the queue. It was a dowdy crowd, bookish types of course, mostly women, some with their arms full of multiple volumes. A young girl's backpack nudged my face. She had dark hair, jeans with coins stitched into the tight, perfect rear. Would he flirt with her, I wondered, write a particular dedication that delayed her a bit, ask her to wait for him in the adjoining hall? I would have. And sure enough, his fountain pen seemed to inscribe more than a signature. She said she enjoyed the reading and he asked about her accent: Australian, he guessed, and she said, 'Right first time,' and they both laughed. But he let her move on, and I was next in line.

He hardly looked up as he scribbled, and the one behind me took my place. I moved on past him—there was no hint of recognition— but when I opened the book jacket, I saw what had been written. *Kevin. Don't run.*

I turned back and he lifted his head from the line.

'There's a drinks thing later,' he said.

And he turned his head back to signing books.

'Did he say there's a drinks thing later?'

It was the girl with the backpack and the coins stitched into the
rear of her jeans.

SO I DIDN'T run. I waited outside as the crowd thinned and he came
out alone and said, 'I could feel you through the crowd before I saw
you.' And there were literary types drinking mulled wine and he said,
'Come on, let's lose these people, show me some places,' and I took
him to a bar I knew.

'Do you want my life?' he said. 'No, you don't, do you? Who
would want my life. Why did we do it—to keep my life intact or to
show me what it always was?'

'You wanted your family,' I said.

'And my children,' he said, 'and I've lost them both.'

He was restless, he wanted to move on, and so we did.

'I should write a book,' he said to me, 'about the perfect crime.'

'And place it in the real world,' I said.

'You're cold,' he said. 'Maybe you were always cold.'

'No,' I told him, 'just a shadow. I never had any particular life
and I suppose what I do now suits me.'

'And what's that?'

'I design games,' I told him, 'computer games.'

'And I,' he said, 'have a career as a writer.'

'Isn't that what you always wanted?'

'No,' he said. 'I didn't want a career. I wanted to write. Once
we either wrote well or badly. Succeeded or failed. Now we have
careers.'

There was a figure following, and I recognized the girl with the
backpack.

'You,' he said. 'I knew you'd turn up,' and I realized he'd written on her first edition after all.

She tagged along with us through the round of clubs until it dawned on her what he really wanted. Drugs, any variety of them. He had become adept at reading a room, sourcing out the corner, the glint of piercing or tattooed shoulder or facial hair that implied a hint of what he sought. She moved closer to me after his third exit. The night was winding down, so I was the lesser of her choices. And some things never change, I thought.

She kissed me at our next stop, a waterside dancing place, and the last I saw of him was his shadow behind a plastic curtain in a noodle joint.

'I gather,' she said, 'that place serves more than noodles.'

'I suppose,' I said.

She was swaying in the neon light.

'But not for me,' she said.

She was staying in a small hotel on Herne Strasse.

'How well do you know him?' she asked from the bathroom, after throwing up most of the whiskey she'd ingested.

'As well as I know myself,' I told her.

'And how well is that?' she said, as she came out, naked but for a leopard-skin thong.

'Don't kiss me, I threw up,' she said, and sat on my lap by the small bed. 'And turn off the light, do you mind?'

# BABELSBERG

I MOVED FROM HAMBURG to Berlin, to an office in the old Babelsberg studios where I designed a series of programmes that could make architecturally coherent and rotate even the simplest of thumbnail sketches. And with a group of pale young skateboarders in black T-shirts, I designed imaginary cities of the past, present, and future, complexes of tombs to be raided, alternative histories, undiscovered planets with perspectives unknown to the human eye.

The platform arcade games were beginning their shift to home computers. As in all walks of life the simplest, even silliest idea took off like a rocket. 'What about a character whose name is a pun on the Dark Ages?' somebody asked—Kurt, or Jong, or Helena, it didn't matter which, since we were that most idealistic of constructs, a co-operative. So we devised *Agis Dark*, the game of an orphaned youth who falls into a tomb and finds seven ancient masks, each with a different power. I drew the Middle Ages for them, tiny villages dotted through a Teutonic wilderness of forest, plague-ridden cities, vast cathedrals that were planned but never finished. Dragons, caverns, underwater chambers, mermaids, and unsuspecting knights, whatever it took to construct a level to get beyond.

Berlin suited me. I had a flat in Kreuzberg before the Wall came down. One afternoon I wandered past a video arcade and saw every spotted youth bent over a version of *Agis Dark*. I realized things were about to change forever. They did, and I don't mean by the Wall coming down. When the Wall fell, we were making so much money we hardly noticed. There was a TV manga version in Japan, a movie in Hong Kong, there was the expanding universe of games, which we were riding like a digital surfer. But the wider world must have registered because I devised another game around it and called it, unsurprisingly, *The Wall*.

I no longer needed to live in Kreuzberg, that low-rent punk heaven, but I stayed because I liked it. Then it became tired somehow, as the city around it changed and there were so many cranes in Potsdammerplatz that someone composed a ballet for them and I moved to Schoneberg. I had money coming like water, that I didn't know what to do with. I bought a string of game companies, a low-rent comic-strip publisher to cross-fertilize with them: Vertical integration was the buzzword then and I became vertically integrated and found to my amazement that my comic-strip publisher owned another house that specialized in translations, British and Irish. Among the books they published were his, Gerald Spain's.

I checked on his sales and they were typically abysmal. I checked on his titles. Most had fallen out of print. I had to read them then, and re-entered his world. *Happiness*, and that suburb in Dublin where it seemed to reside. It wasn't happiness at all, of course, I could see that now. It was a blind attempt to keep chaos at bay, a chaos that informed every domestic description, and gave them their power.

The stories then, and the traffic cop on Van Nuys Boulevard. After that began the string of novels where he ploughed his wider family to exhaustion, and though the unintended ironies were multiple there, they didn't inform the prose.

I began to long for even a whiff of the present, some inkling of the world I knew he knew, but he kept it out, almost by an act of will. What was so terrible, I wondered, about the years we had in common that he couldn't write about them? Does nobody Irish write about now? But that summer in Lahinch I had heard him read about, how many years ago was it now, in Hamburg, was the closest he got to the present. Ice creams. A wheelchair. A voice from a Morris Minor radio describing the Sunday match.

From that point on, there was silence. I had severed my thoughts for ten years or so. This return was troubling, exhilarating, infuriating all at once. I had his German translator track him down.

He had stopped writing, I was told, after the birth of his second child. He had separated from his wife and family. There was a history of drug and alcohol abuse. And his address was number 14, Marino Crescent.

There was snow falling outside my office window. The flurries created shadows, like wings. There was a low moan, of a distant wind, stifled by the glass windows. I felt I couldn't breathe, for five full minutes. My vampire had returned, and I wondered could I make a game of him. I would call it *Rock-a-hula Baby*.

I wrote a letter to my home address, as if I was writing to myself. But I addressed it to Gerald Spain.

# EAST WALL

*D*ear kevin, his reply said, *don't expect any literary curlicues from this, I haven't written in a long, long time. I work in East Wall now, in the railway depot as a CIE clerk. I cycle down there every morning, past the Tolka river and the swans, and if I didn't hear you describe them to me, it's as if you did. We last met there, on the bench with the river emptied by the tide, if I remember rightly. Most people wouldn't survive what we went through. I know I didn't, fully, or to put it another way, the person I was then is far, very far, from the person I am now. We met again, I seem to remember, but it didn't feel like meeting, I was already on what is quaintly termed a downward spiral, which ended five years later in the Rutland Clinic on Usher's Island. My habit was large and had an appetite greater than both of us and it left me looking as I do now, nothing like the Gerald you might have remembered, and I hope, nothing like the Kevin you are now.*

*Your father advertised for lodgers, in* The Irish Press, *if I remember rightly, and I was sober then and needed somewhere to live. I don't know what impelled me—curiosity, maybe. And besides, it was cheap. And I came to like the old duffer immensely. He told me I reminded him of you immediately, and I said that's funny, I've always been mistaken for someone over this side of the city and he came out with one of those clichés of his. He missed you terribly at first, and I would take him to Gaffney's and as the drink took over, he would mistake me for you, and the mistaking I have come to relish. We all want a father, I suppose, but the distance fatherhood imposes on sons can be severe and tragic. For me, because he's not my father, I can entertain all of the pleasures and illusions of that relationship without the burdens.*

*As you may have gathered, we are both adopted. My own father admitted as much when my marriage broke up, in the full certitude that one of his flesh and blood would never have taken such a course, would never have written probably. And your dear father—and he is dear, Kevin, your abandonment is painful to him—told me as much, one night on the way home, past Fairview Park—told me as much about you. So I could only surmise that we are twins, as in any fable of separation and confusion, and reconciliation, I can only hope, in the end. Shakespeare wrote one of them, I remember, two matching sets of separated twins, but that was a comedy, and while we have had our moments, I don't imagine either of us would call our mutual experience comic.*

*Your brother, Gerald*

*Dear Kevin,* his second letter said, *I have traced a mother for us both. Her name is Cissy Hassett, she has an address somewhere near the sea in Gorey, Co. Wexford. I imagine she's from the circus family—I remember being taken as a kid to Hassett's Circus at the big top near Booterstown.*

*Clowns always terrified me and the sight of women in fishnet tights swinging from ropes terrified me even more, so I haven't gathered the courage to visit her yet. I did a search of orphanages, though. I visited Artane, where an old Christian Brother showed me photographs of the institution in its heyday, lines of boys in short trousers tending vegetable patches—too old though for us when we were given our respective homes; St. Patrick's out on the Navan Road; Goldenbridge by the river in Kilmainham—the city is dotted with them, haunted houses now, with their old religious caretakers trying to forget the past.*

*I found one in Dominick Street where both of us could have resided. For two months the records say 'Hassett twins,' though the old nun who showed me through it was resolute in her unwillingness to remember 'those days.' There were small metal cots in rows in a large interior with high windows, there was the sound of traffic outside but a strange hush in there; a large crucifix hung from the white triangle of one wall and statues of the Virgin were nailed above each cot.*

*I have no memory of a cot, no memory of a twin brother beside me, and would assume that you don't either. My first memory is of the monkey puzzle tree in Palmerston Park, of a nurse I had called Elizabeth, her long brown hair as she leaned down towards me with a bottle. My adoptive mother's hair was blonde; I remember her smell of face powder, the sound of her playing the piano, but my first inkling of the longing we call love was for Elizabeth's brown hair.*

*Your father's memory is going, he takes me for you, calls me Kevin most days now, and supplies me with remembrances that somedays I wish were my own. Your mother swam, he tells me; they met by the cement bathing shelters on Bull Wall. He wasn't one for the water himself, but you, or I, one of us anyway, took to the water like her, like a duck.*

*Dear Kevin,* his third letter went, *father in Beaumont Hospital, come soon.*

THE PLANE BANKED over Howth and I saw the long spit of beach that was Dollymount Strand. It looked fragile and tiny and the white-caps of the waves seemed about to overwhelm it. Like my childhood, smaller than I had remembered it. The weather socks were stiff in the wind and the airport moaned with it and the taxi driver cursed the weather as he drove me to the Crescent.

I knocked on my childhood door and he answered. How strange could it be, I wondered, but it was about to get stranger. We were different now; age had done its job on us. I had that permanent tan of the upper classes, a diet of line-caught salmon and goji juice and long grain rice had kept me trim. I ran four miles a day, down Unter den Linden, across the artificial lake. He had the grey pallor and the unkempt hair I would have had if I'd stayed, maybe—those hunted, haunted eyes of the recovering addict. He looked unwell. But he was chastened, and he was kind. Or kinder than I had known him.

He told me he found the house unsettling and empty, with my father gone. He would come to Beaumont with me, if I thought it would suit. Or I could go on my own, if I thought it better.

'Have you noticed a ghost in this house?'

No, he said, ghosts didn't interest him.

'Where do you sleep?'

'In the room with the clocks,' he said.

I went up there with him. There was the old camp bed, the clocks on the yellowing newspapers. There were books scattered round, but no desk, no typewriter.

'So you really have stopped writing.'

'How could I write,' he said, 'when there's only one thing to write about? That thing of yours.'

'Of mine?'

'And mine. That thing in Manhattan.'

'Can't you forget it?'

'Should I?'

'Maybe. I think I have.'

'The police came round, you know. A guard from Kerry first. Then a New York detective. All he wanted to do was play golf.'

'What did you tell him?'

'I told him to try the Royal Dublin. Down on Dollymount Strand.'

I smiled. I had forgotten that he could be funny.

'And then he went. I kept waiting for a judgement. But it never came. What upset me most of all was that. How easily it vanished. As if it had never happened.'

'Maybe I made it up.'

'And maybe I made these up.'

He pulled up his sleeves, and showed me the chicken wire fence of track marks on his arm.

'There is accountability,' he said.

'What upset me most was, that I never could go back there.'

'Manhattan?'

'The buildings,' I said. 'They had something to say to me. But I had to leave before I found out what it was.'

'Maybe you should have stayed,' he said.

'Malevich would have loved it.'

'Who's Malevich?' he asked.

# THE HOUSE

S O SHOULD YOU buy the house, Emily? I have no idea. Maybe I'll give it to you. Both of us lived here, at different stages: first me, then him, then both of us, for a time. The child will be born, that little shadow you showed me on the ultrasound, because the vampire will not have its way, I won't let it. It will have two parents and, who knows, maybe they will stay together, stranger things have happened.

So, will another boy stare out of this window on the tulips down below? And there will be tulips there—scattered by muddy footballs, kicked to shreds by the cider-drinking youths, planted again by the municipal workers in their bright yellow PVC jackets, those tulips are perennial. There'll be no cinema past the chip shop, beyond the Five Lamps in North Strand, but there'll be games for him to play, the kinds that I design now, and maybe if he grows to be the bookish type, he'll lie on the sofa here and one day read your father's books, read about an Ireland that never really existed. He invented it, maybe, because the one that did exist pained him too much.

It all seems impossible, implausible even, but then those swans seem impossible. Surely they should have found a home other than the Tolka mudflats, but there they are now, flapping over the trees with those leaves already browning because it will be autumn again soon. Stranger things have happened, as Stoker told us, awkwardly and at intolerable length. But what's important is that if the house is bought, you know the whole story.

# BEAUMONT

THE CAR PARK in Beaumont was run by a private contractor and seemed to have fallen from an aeroplane bound for Frankfurt or Moscow. There was a song by Bob Dylan playing on the radio of the car, *It's not dark yet, but it's getting there*. And it wasn't dark yet, as I parked the car on the bottom level.

I walked through the low cement ceiling and out towards the hospital frontage. It sprawled, like some complex of germs, endlessly multiplying itself into more Portakabins and identikit halls, with breezy, wind-flapped corridors between them. It smelt of, well, hospital, I suppose, when I entered the first corridor, beyond the smoking shed. If I could have wrapped the associations each odour awoke in me, they would have sat together unhappily, each refusing to acknowledge the other. The memory of a school playground in Marino, seagulls pecking at the wet cast-off sandwiches by the concrete urinal; of Gerald's vomit-covered form underneath the privet hedge at the Trinity Ball; and the cloacal pall that descended from the upper part of the house from the lodgers' bathroom.

The pervasiveness of the odours intensified as I went forward until it became almost friendly, melded into its constituent parts, and began to say 'hospital' again. Yes, of course, I was in a hospital, an Irish hospital, Beaumont. Translucent bags of hospital refuse sat on

chairs outside every hospital ward. The large steel doors of the in-
dustrial-sized lift shuddered open and I was inside with three or four
others in pain, the pain of being there or the pain of visiting. He was
asleep, I could see, when I reached his ward; the pale green candlewick blanket rose and fell with his breathing, and he was skin and
bone like one of those plaster saints.

I didn't wake him at first. I sat in the green-tinged light of the
heart monitors and held his hand. The nails had shrivelled to nothing,
the veins seemed separate from his bones, his breath came in long,
slow exhalations. His face turned, as if waking, and then his head
slipped back into something like sleep and it turned again and his
eyes gradually opened. 'You're back,' he said. 'And you only just left.'

I've been gone for years, I thought, but didn't say it.

'It was good,' he said, 'to have you in the house. So much to say.
And we said it, didn't we?'

'Yes, we did,' I said. Though I had no idea what.

'What did you find?' he asked. 'About your mother.'

'I had only one mother,' I told him.

'I know that, son. But you found something.'

'I found a name,' I told him. 'Cissy Hassett. Around Gorey.'

'Hassett,' he said. 'Like the circus. That'd be rich.'

'I'm moving you,' I told him, 'to a hospice.'

'Why,' he asked, 'when I'm comfortable here?'

'There's an MRSA bug here,' I said. 'It'll kill you.'

'I'm dying anyway.'

'And in case you haven't noticed, you're in a ward with three
others. It stinks.'

'I know,' he said. 'What does it smell of?'

'It's got a cloacal nose with a hint of stale food and a finish of urine.'

'When did you get funny?' he asked.

He went quiet again, and closed his eyes. Then his fingers shifted in mine.

'No,' he said. 'The move would kill me.'

# COURTOWN

I DROVE OUT THEN, to meet your grandmother for real in her wintering circus. She wasn't in Gorey. She was in a field outside a dismal funfair in the holiday village of Courtown. A string of circus caravans in the rough grass behind an irregular stretch of chicken wire fencing. I had phoned in advance and been told she mightn't see me. She was upset because some animal had been injured. My car bounced around the fence perimeter until I found a gap.

I walked through, and saw an old lady sitting in one of those metal easy chairs, by an open caravan door.

She was thin, with twisted, sinewy arms, and old skin dried up by decades of greasepaint. Or so I surmised. My mind placed traces of glitter on every line of her face. She was smoking a cigarette and she tapped the ash into a plastic cup, jammed into the arm of the chair. 'Couldn't you have chosen a better day?' she said.

'Is any day likely to be the right one?' I asked.

'No,' she groaned, 'but one of my beasts ran through the fence and got pounded on the Wexford Road. Can you imagine the shock, driving an articulated lorry and finding a young lion on your windscreen?'

I thought she wanted me to laugh, then noticed she was crying.

'Please, mister,' she said, 'I don't have your name, but it's not a good time.'

'Kevin,' I said. 'My name's Kevin.'

'Oh,' she said. 'Thought you were the other one. What's his name?'

'Gerald,' I said.

'Gerald. Where's he?'

'We thought two of us might be too much.'

'Two of yis were too much. Why do you think I gave yis up?'

And she stood, and I was amazed at how agile she was.

'Come with me then.'

And what a wonderful sense of command she had. I followed her, instinctively, as she walked through the wet grass, her shoulders bent with something like sciatica, using a golf stick as a third leg.

'How did you find me?'

'I didn't find you. He did. Through the register of births. They changed the law five years ago.'

'I never bothered with the law.'

And she made her way towards a small shabby tent and pushed the flap open, into the musk inside.

There was a lioness in there, lying in an improvised cage in the trampled grass and sawdust. There was a sense of African grief about the creature, as she bent her head and licked the inert form on the straw beside her.

'Don't come close. She'll go for you.'

She was licking the blood from the dried wound behind the dead one's ear.

'He was small, but he knew how to run.'

The lioness turned a yellow eye towards us and growled softly.

'So tell me, Kevin, who did I give yis away to?'

'Nuns.'

'I know that.'

'Then a family in Marino.'

'Were they good to you?'

'They did their best.'

'Well. You were better off. Your father wouldn't have been . . .'

'Who was he?'

'He was a clown.'

'He was foolish?'

'No. I mean a clown. Romania, Albania, from somewhere like that. You want to track him down too?'

'I'm not sure.'

'Good luck. He left before you were born.'

'Where was home?'

'For me? Here. In the winter. Anywhere we played, when the spring came.'

She walked forwards, tapped the bar of the rickety cage, took a bone from under her smock, and the lioness forgot her dead charge and ambled forwards. It took the bone in its yellowed teeth and dropped its head between its paws, to gnaw.

'You see how quickly she forgets?'

There was movement at the other entrance to the tent and the sunlight poured in. Another woman stood there, held up by another golf stick.

'That's the other half of the Hassett twins.'

'You mean . . .'

'My sister. Marion. This is my son, Marion. One of them anyways. Tracked me down.'

And Marion said nothing, as the sunlight shifted with the blowing flap behind her.

'My name's Cissy. But you'd know that, wouldn't you?'

She turned away from the feeding beast and gripped the rope that was dangling from the apex of the tent. She pulled herself up it, one hand over the other, with an agility that belied her ancient legs. She hung there above me, swinging gently from side to side.

'Still got it, sister, haven't we?'

'We have,' Marion replied.

# THE HOLE IN THE WALL

A S WITH MOST illnesses, there was a false recovery. He was put on a new set of drugs and perked up enough for the doctors to allow us to take him out, for him to crack a pale joke. 'If I was a horse you would have put me down.' So we took him to the Leopardstown races in one of those wheelchair taxis, a refitted Hiace van that rattled as the wind blew through the doors that wouldn't close.

'You remember that day before you left,' he said to Gerald, 'I took you to Fairyhouse with what's-her-face.'

'Belinda,' I said.

'Yes,' he said.

'Fool's gold,' I said.

And the drugs must have worked their magic because he repeated it, and seemed to understand.

'Did we win that day?'

'Twice,' I told him. 'Widow's Peak and Mountain View.'

'That rings a bell,' said Gerald.

'Yes,' I said. 'You gave your wife's brothers a tip. Widow's Peak to win and each way on Mountain View.'

'I didn't. Know nothing about horses.'

'Okay then. Since we're all coming clean. I did.'

And we pushed him through the turnstile and past the winners' enclosure where the smell of horse sweat and dung seemed to revive him even more. Down to the track where he used to do his bookie's thing with the hieroglyphic fingers and the chalked board.

Gerald placed a bet for him that lost, and I tried my luck and lost as well. 'I'm getting cold,' he said as the horses trailed off their thundering into a lazy canter, so we turned his wheelchair back towards the turnstiles. 'Who's he?' he asked Gerald of me, when I pushed him through. And when Gerald said, 'Kevin,' he said, 'No, you're Kevin.' 'He's my brother,' I said, and 'There was never any brother,' he said, 'you were an only child.'

The conversation was irrational, but there was a certain comfort in that. We both lifted him into the Hiace van and I told him about the circus lady and the grieving lioness and he said, 'The circus, did I ever take you there?' and I said, 'No, not that I remember.'

'Always hated circuses,' he said, 'preferred horses on the open, the hurdle, or the flat.' And as the van rattled its way back to the profusion of Portakabins they called a hospital he responded to one voice, then another, as if both voices had a single source.

'An only child,' he said softly. 'You were both only children.'


WE WERE BOTH there, when he went. And in the pale green light of the heart monitors, there was the same, somehow appropriate confusion. 'Kevin,' he said to Gerald, 'there was a horse called Out of this World. Didn't like soft ground. But when the ground was hard, nothing could beat it.'

I took out swimming things, for his funeral. I saw her lime-green swimsuit still crumpled in the drawer. Two pairs of togs that were mine from all those years ago, two towels, and I folded them inside neatly, like chocolate and marzipan inside one of those old Swiss rolls. 'You can see the beach from the graveyard,' I told him, 'by the Hole in the Wall.'

There was a single car behind the hearse as we drove out to the flattened graveyard. We wore identical suits. The day was calm and sunlit, and the bay glittered like a spoon of mercury underneath Howth Head. We were the only ones to watch, as the undertakers edged the coffin down.

'Is that it?' he asked.

'Yes, that's it,' I said.

'Shouldn't you say something?'

'Like what?'

'He was your father.'

'Not strictly speaking. And the thing is,' I said, 'he's with her. She's talking to him now.'

'We just walk away then?'

'Yes, we just walk away.'

A warm breeze blew down from the Summit, bringing a flock of crows with it.

'You're cold,' he said.

'No, I'm too warm, actually.'

'I mean, you're a cold one.'

'Maybe. You fancy a swim?'

And he told me he had never been a swimmer, but I said to him it could prolong his life and he said, 'I'm not sure that would be advisable,' and I laughed, but in a sad kind of way because I knew that he meant it.

So I drove him down to the Sutton House Hotel which had always been the marker for me for the beach we called the Hole in the Wall. But there was no hotel there, everything had changed; there was a new apartment complex with access to the beach available only to the owners.

I turned the car back towards Sutton Cross and swung in right across the railway track, over the small bump of a bridge and the small tarmac road that led to the houses that backed onto the beach. We parked, got out with the towels and things, and walked and found a small sandy track, which seemed to promise a sandy beach.

'Why the Hole in the Wall?' he asked.

'Because there's a wall with a hole in it that leads to a beach,' I said. 'You would have known that if we'd done it back when.'

There was no wall, no hole in no wall, but there was a bit of broken breeze block which might have been a wall once and a glimpse of sea beyond and a spit of beach.

We trudged over the scutch grass and found our spot, a vacant parcel of sand among the families there, and we sat down in our funeral clothes. There were three voluminous women behind us with a gaggle of kids and the women screamed at the kids when the kids displeased them. 'Come back here, you simple cunt,' the largest of them shouted, looking like a circus lady, and a naked girl ran back, was told to call her brother from the water and ran off again. 'Hamlet,' the water baby screamed at the sea, and Gerry wondered idly what kind of mother would call her son after the melancholy prince. 'Hamlet,' she screamed again, 'you're fucking dead, you are.'

He took off his pin-striped funeral suit and put on the togs I had brought him and walked to the water, his back to the city, facing the hump of Ireland's Eye. The sea had a layer of brown scum on it and young Hamlet was splashing through it, his off-white underpants clinging to his thin groin.

And I took off my suit and followed him and walked out beyond the brown scum to where the water at least seemed clean, and said, 'Come on, you'll get your depth out here,' and he followed and he dove in once and came back to the surface, swimming, and his thin junkie frame looked like a boy's with the water clinging to it, and I imagined that, from Hamlet's perspective, we would have looked identical again, two skinny bodies covered in the questionable waters of Dublin Bay.

# ENNISCRONE

T HEN I DROVE you down to Courtown, Emily, to see if we could find your real grandmother, but of course when we got there the circus had upped and gone. It sounds funny saying it like that, as if one was using a metaphor or one of his objective correlatives, but no, it was real, there was a sagging chicken wire fence around an empty field of squashed, deadened grass.

'We could chase them,' you said, 'we could make an adventure out of it, drive round a series of God-awful seaside resorts until we run them to ground in somewhere like Enniscrone.'

'Why Enniscrone?' I asked.

'I saw a circus there,' you said, 'when I was a kid. My other grandmother—what do I call her now—' and you twitched your nose—'my fake grandmother, my ersatz grandmother? Anyway, she had a house near there. And there was a sandy car park, near the beach, where they would pitch their tent. We could take a seaweed bath and look for two old acrobatic ladies in leopard-skin tights twirling round a big top.'

'I don't imagine she twirls much now,' I said.

'Twins,' you said.

'Yes,' I said. 'The Hassett twins. They were well-known in their day.'

We walked round the sagging wire fence and I could see sand dunes up ahead, the grasses above them blowing like thinning hair. I could hear the distant roar of an ocean. And we were both drawn to it, without saying a word. You walked with one hand to your back, as if the weight of the baby was already slowing your movement.

'I could never tell anyone how much I missed him.'

'Him?' I asked, and you said, 'Your brother, my father.'

And we had reached the top of the dunes now and the wind brushed the grasses off your feet and the sea boiled beneath us, brown coloured, like the shingled sand.

'My own brother never really knew him. But I did. There was a scent inside me, a hand holding mine, a shadow walking along with me. Even when he had left, for good—and as kids they never tell you things, do they, at least they didn't then, but he had gone and I knew it, and I knew I would never lose this sense inside me. And then it came back.'

'When?' I asked.

'I think you know,' you said. 'It must be nearly a year.'

WE STOOD ON the dunes, watching the brown, boiling ocean. It seemed not to want us to come near.

'I got the feeling,' you said, 'that someone was following me. It was just a whiff of something I remembered, someone's eyes on me, turning round the corners of those central city streets. An odour, a memory, a shiver. Sometimes I would turn and see a figure in a windy doorway, a coat flapping. It was him, I knew, he wanted re-acquaintance, and I waited for him to make his move, to make the first step. I saw him across the rails of the Dart station then, where

Blackrock Baths used to be. He looked—not quite like a ghost, that would have been too dramatic, but like a black-and-white version of himself, of the one I remembered. Two trains came then and we both were gone. And one day I was in one of those Bewley's cafés, Westmoreland Street or Grafton Street, I can't remember which, and I was waiting for the waitress and he sat down. It was a day or two after the event in the Killiney house that I told you about, the hairless chest and the unmentionable etcetera, and I was wondering what to think about things like that, about the sea blowing outside and the rattling windows and the crumpled lace doily on the floor. Anyway, he sat down and his face was thinner than I remembered it, but there was an immediate and very odd sense of comfort about his presence there. I must have been pregnant already. Would that account for the sudden feeling of weightlessness I had, the sudden feeling of a return home—to what home I wasn't sure—to that square maybe where I was running with my dog around the tennis court, while the girls in white played their desultory game of tennis? He loved me, I was always sure of that, and now here he was, a witness to that fact. He ordered something he called a Mary cake, after the first few words between us which I don't remember and are utterly unimportant. Because what I remember was the smell. Of the material of his coat, of that roll-up Golden Virginia tobacco he kept in his pocket, of that musty, half-bathed sweaty musk I remember as a girl and which always said to me, father. And then the tiny cakes arrived, and he said, "Your mother liked these." They were yellow and chocolate brown with a marzipan twirl on top like a tiny Chinaman's hat, and I bit into my one. There was yellow gooey stuff inside and soft chocolate and although I never had a sweet tooth, I let the tastes fill my mouth as if they were someone else's memories, memories I had never had. And I wondered if our meetings carried on, once or twice a week maybe, on those grey Dublin afternoons, in this dusty café over these Mary cakes, would I acquire my own set of memories to fill up the gaps where he should have been. But those memories were not to be because by the end of the week he was dead and I met you at his funeral.'

# NOWHERE

Y OU WERE WRONG about the coat. It wasn't his. It was his father's.

And you can't have remembered the smell of roll-up tobacco. Golden Virginia. He smoked tipped cigarettes, as I remember. The roll-ups came with the poverty, the junk, the AA meetings.

I mention these details, not because they are important, but because I have found a brother, late in life, and I need to be exact about my memories of him. It was odd to realize a brother was what I had always wanted. It was odd to realize you don't have to be alone. How different it all could have been . . . but there is no point in wondering, regretting; what happened happened and what's now is now. He wasn't well, I knew that, and I imagine he knew it too, but what was important was to make the most of what we had left.

I tried to fix his life, it was well broken and maybe I was the one who had broken it, maybe we both had broken it. I gave him money so he could stop the daily cycle down East Wall to the railway depot. I offered to buy him a typewriter, a desk, all of the writing accessories, but he told me the urge had gone. The thing about endings, he told me, is that they are a necessary part of life, they are implicit in beginnings, if the beginnings are any good. I presumed he was talking about fiction and so I bought them anyway, set up the desk and an old-fashioned typewriter in that room with the clocks.

We would wake in the morning, always at the same time, as if the same clock motivated the two of us. I would make him tea and squeeze some fruit juices. I tried to introduce some health into his diet and would wait for that moment when he went to the room upstairs, when I would hear the *tip-tap* of that typewriter, but it never came. Give my brother some time, I would think, then watch him pull on my father's gabardine raincoat, with the flaps and the belt, the kind he always wore at the racetrack, and go and wander the city.

I would go up to the room myself then, and imagine him walking the streets, hope he had a school copybook wrapped in one of his pockets, was wandering from café to café, beginning his scribbling. Let this one not be, I hoped, about some imagined past but about the past and the story we shared together. I would stare at that typewriter and hit a key or two and see the letters planted on the page by the ribbon and wonder why I hadn't bought him a computer and a printer, that's the way it is done now after all.

He would come back before dark and I would ask him where he had been. 'Just out,' he would say, and I would think of Darragh and her wanderings. He had to see his daughter, he told me; he had glimpsed her once or twice, and once on opposing platforms of a Dart station they had both looked each other in the eye. He had run towards the crossbridge as the trains arrived, but when he had reached the opposite side, he had found her gone. But he felt that a meeting was imminent. And maybe that's what made me think it was safe to return to Berlin, Babelsberg, for a day or two. I had a business to run, after all.

I left him money to tide him over, and perhaps money was the worst thing I could have given him because I came back from Babelsberg on a Friday and found him on the floor among all of the dying clocks. The greatest danger for addicts, the doctors told me, is a relapse, because the toxins they withstood through addiction become lethal after abstinence. And maybe the ending he had been talking about was his own all along.

So I took him in an ambulance to Beaumont and there, back in that waste of Portakabins, he was put in a room and fixed to a drip. Whatever was in that drip, he asked me to increase the dosage, to turn the little plastic spigot below the plastic bag. I said I wouldn't of course, and we argued through the night with the green light of the heart monitors on our faces. What was he looking for, I remember asking him, death or oblivion? 'Neither,' I think he said, and maybe the drip was working its magic by then, 'what I'm looking for is bliss.' And we both fell asleep with the green light on our faces. But only one of us woke up.

ONE OF US died then, Emily. I can never be sure which one. I am left here, but it seems like death some days, and I think it was me who died. And other days it seems like life and I think it was him. I went to a funeral and saw his family there, so it must have been him. But it could as well have been me. I am the writer, after all, who now types on that old-fashioned thing I bought him, who resuscitates memories— the swans on the Tolka river, the tulips in Fairview Park, the vampire, all of that. But memories are unreliable, and strangely pleasurable, one can wallow in them, invent a detail. Sometimes an afternoon goes by and I look at two typed pages and wonder, whose life was that?

# ABOUT THE AUTHOR

Neil Jordan was born in 1950 in Sligo. He is the author of several critically acclaimed novels, including *The Past*, *The Dream of a Beast*, *Sunrise with Sea Monster*, *Shade*, and *Night in Tunisia*, a collection of short stories which won the *Guardian* Fiction Prize. He has written, directed, and produced a large number of award-winning films, including *The Crying Game*, *Michael Collins*, *The End of the Affair*, and, most recently, *Ondine*. He lives in Dublin.